The Usborne Book of

TRUE ADVENTURES

First published in 2003 by Usborne Publishing Ltd,
Usborne House, 83-85 Saffron Hill, London
EC1N 8RT, England.
www.usborne.com

A catalogue record for this title is available
from the British Library

UK ISBN 07460 5842 X

First published in America 2004
American ISBN 07945 0612 7

Printed in Great Britain

Designed by Glen Bird and Brian Voakes
Illustrated by John Woodcock and Glen Bird
Cover designed by Neil Francis
Cover image © Getty Images
Series editors: Jane Chisholm, Rosie Dickins and Jenny Tyler
Series designer: Mary Cartwright

TRUE
POLAR
ADVENTURES

Paul Dowswell

CONTENTS

The top and bottom of the world

If you have a globe, spin it around. The two places where your globe is anchored to its frame are the North and South Poles – the top and bottom of the world – once thought to be as unreachable as distant planets. What an explorer would actually find at these two spots provoked feverish speculation right up until the early 20th century. Would they provide an entrance into new worlds inside our planet? What strange creatures might live in such inhospitable surroundings? Perhaps the North or South Pole might be the location of the Garden of Eden?

But the Poles are only the creation of human mathematics – just positions on a map marked by a reading of 90° degrees north or 90° degrees south, based on a system of map coordinates known as latitude and longitude.★ As actual places, they are

★Latitude gives the location of a place north or south of the equator, with 0° being the equator, and 90° north or south being the furthest point away from the equator. Longitude gives the location of places east and west of a central 0° line, which runs through Greenwich in London. For greater accuracy, these degrees are also divided further into measurements of 60 "minutes", with each minute being divided into 60 "seconds". By giving map references in degrees, minutes and seconds, it is possible to locate any spot on earth with great precision.

remarkably unremarkable. Explorer Robert Falcon Scott noted with some disappointment, when he got to the South Pole in 1912, that there was "very little that is different from the awful monotony of past days".

These days, explorers carry GPS (Global Positioning System) navigation tools. These extraordinary little electronic devices use a network of 24 satellites to take an exact reading of their position anywhere on earth. Before the invention of these devices in the 1990s, navigators used compasses to determine which direction they were facing, and sextants to establish their latitude or longitude. (An essential seafarer's tool, a sextant looks like a big wooden triangle; it works by comparing the position of the sun or a particular star with the horizon, at a set time.)

The Arctic (see map opposite) is a huge frozen ocean around the North Pole, surrounded by an intricate mosaic of bleak islands – especially off its Canadian shore. In the days before whole continents and oceans could be captured in a single satellite photograph, it proved fatally difficult to chart and explore. Although the Arctic has been visited by European traders and settlers for more than 1,000 years, it wasn't until the last century that a detailed map of its icy core was completed.

The first serious attempts to explore the Arctic were prompted by the need to discover a sea route

Map of the North Pole

from Europe to China and other Far Eastern countries. There were two basic ways around: northeast above the coast of Russia, or northwest through the Canadaian Arctic. Here, Europeans came into contact with the *Inuit*, the inhabitants of the Arctic (also sometimes referred to as Eskimos). In

9

their arrogance, many early explorers dismissed the Inuit as Stone Age savages, but their ability to survive in such a barren, inhospitable region showed great ingenuity.

The initial exploration of the regions north of Russia and continental Canada was tortuously slow and exceptionally dangerous. In 1553, English seafarer Sir Hugh Willoughby led an expedition of three ships off the Siberian coast, in search of the northeast passage. Willoughby died and two of his ships were lost.

In 1594, Dutchman Willem Barents made another epic voyage from Russia into the Arctic Ocean. He reached Novaya Zemlya – a pair of islands the length of the United Kingdom, which point from the coast of Siberia deep into the Arctic Ocean. Trapped there when ice destroyed their ship, his crew built a house from the remains of the ship to keep them alive in the cruel Arctic winter. The following spring, they sailed two small boats back to the Russian mainland. Barents died during the voyage, but the sea northwest of Novaya Zemlya was named after him.

In 1610, Henry Hudson set out to North America to explore the northwest passage. A mutiny left him stranded, and he died in a small boat in the polar wastes with his 16-year-old son and eight loyal members of his crew. The mutineers sailed the ship back to England, where they were treated with surprising leniency. Sailors with such vital knowledge of unknown lands were too valuable to string up on the yardarm of a ship.

From 1733 to 1743, the Russian Admiralty mounted a "Great Northern Expedition" to chart the Arctic coasts of Siberia. Facing extreme hardship, seven parties, numbering 977 men in all, succeeded in charting the entire Arctic coast of Russia, from the Atlantic to the Pacific.

At that time, however, the Arctic coast of Canada west of the Hudson Bay was virtually unknown. This was to change in the first half of the 19th century, when British explorers made repeated efforts to open up the northwest passage. These efforts culminated in Sir John Franklin's expedition of 1845-1848. The journey was a disaster; his ships were lost and all his crew died. But, over the next 10 years, 40 expeditions were launched to find him. In the course of their travels they surveyed their surroundings, which contributed greatly to the mapping of this fiendishly complex region.

The discovery and exploration of Antarctica, the continent where the South Pole is located (see map on next page), was simpler, as it is not surrounded by such a complicated maze of islands. Nonetheless, it was only sighted for the first time in 1820 – although explorers had guessed there was an "uninhabited land" to the far south for a couple of hundred years before this. Antarctica is a vast continent, twice the size of Australia. In places, land lies beneath a layer of ice 4km (2½ miles) deep.

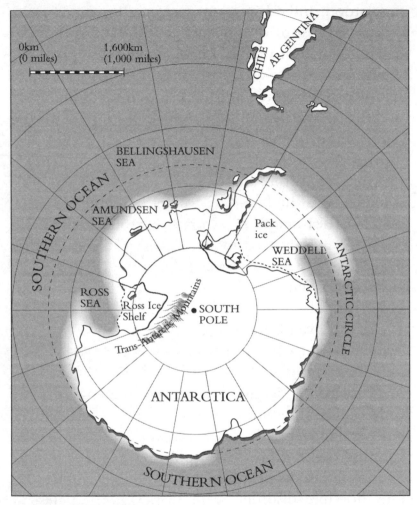

Map of the South Pole

The great age of polar exploration occurred in the decades before the First World War. In the Arctic, by this time, the complexities of the northeast and northwest passage were much more clearly understood, and adventurers were advancing steadily towards the top of the world. In the Antarctic, seafarers felt more confident they could build ships strong enough to withstand the crushing ice fields that surround the continent – although their confidence was sometimes misplaced. It is still less than a century since both poles were first visited by humans. In those days, radio and aircraft were such new inventions that their use was barely considered. Instead, it was the fate of the polar explorer to spend months at sea before reaching these unknown lands. Once there, they ventured into them in the certain knowledge that, if anything went wrong, they would be beyond rescue.

So many things could go wrong, it was astounding that anyone went at all. The cold was incessant, and pierced men to the bone. Even the strongest ships could be caught in pack ice and crushed to matchsticks. At the top and bottom of the world, midsummer and midwinter are marked by days of constant light or dark. In the polar winter, the endless darkness drove men insane. Lack of a proper diet, especially food containing vitamin C, led to scurvy. This horrible disorder, known among all seafarers until the 20th century, takes its name from an old English word for "gnawing". An exhausted sailor battling with the disease feels he is being eaten away from the inside by its hideous symptoms. His gums turn black and recede until his teeth drop out. His arms and legs swell up, and his joints ache, so that every movement is a trial. His skin is covered with livid rashes and ulcers, which ooze blood and pus. Scurvy attacks the body's weakest points. Fresh wounds never heal. Old wounds, long since healed, open up again, to add to the torments inflicted by the condition. Early in the 20th century, scurvy still occurred, and was still fairly misunderstood. Captain Scott's famous expedition, for example, was fatally hindered by the disease.

Along with scurvy, men also suffered from frostbite. Here, body tissues in the most exposed parts of the body, such as the hands, toes, noses and ears, freeze, preventing blood from reaching them. Deprived of its normal blood supply, the skin and flesh of these parts dies. When the affected area thaws, the victim suffers extreme pain. Left untreated, frostbite can turn to gangrene, where the flesh rots, poisoning the whole body. Frostbite remains one of the greatest threats to explorers of both poles. It affected such modern-day explorers as Børge Ousland, in 2001, just as surely as it blighted Sir Hugh Willoughby's expedition in 1553.

Today, if you have the time and the money, you can book a vacation which will take you to the North or South Pole. Here, you can stand on the exact spot before hopping aboard a warm plane or icebreaker which will take you back to civilization in a matter of hours. One travel company even drops clients off at 89° north or south, and they ski the final degree, to be met by a plane for the return journey. In 2002, one pilot made an emergency landing on an Arctic icefloe off the coast of Greenland. Not only did he use his mobile phone to summon help, but he even managed to transmit to his rescuers images of his surroundings, taken with a digital camera, to give them a clearer idea of where he could be found.

But these comfortable tales of hi-tech adventure are not typical of the experience of most polar explorers. Almost a century ago, British explorer Apsley Cherry-Garrard famously said: "Polar exploration is at once the cleanest, most isolated way of having a bad time which has ever been devised" – as you'll find out in the stories in this book...

The *Polaris* mystery

How Charles Hall's wife must have regretted the day he ever picked up a book about Sir John Franklin and his lost expedition. The story was to spark an interest in the Arctic that would frequently take her husband away on long expeditions, and eventually leave her an almost penniless widow, with a 10-year-old son who had barely met his father.

Hall's interest in Franklin was further stoked when he went to hear Lady Franklin speak about her ill-fated explorer husband, in the Halls' home town of Cincinnati, in 1849. Eleven years later, in 1860, Hall had managed to raise enough money to embark on a two-year exploration of the southeast coast of Baffin Island. Here, he searched unsuccessfully for any clue to Franklin's demise.

Hall was not an adventurer by profession. He made his living as a newspaper publisher. The only known photograph of him shows an intense, heavily built, dark-haired man, with a huge, bushy beard. He had a deeply-held Christian faith, and the Arctic sent him into a state of religious ecstasy. On observing the Northern Lights, also known as the *Aurora Borealis*, he recorded: "*It seemeth to me as if the very doors of heaven have been opened tonight, so mighty and beauteous and marvellous were the waves of golden light.*"

While on his exploratory trip to Baffin Island, he met an Inuit couple named Tookolito and Ebierbing, who had been taken to London in the 1850s by a British whaling captain. Here, they had learned to speak English, and had adopted the manners and fashions of polite English society. They were a sensation in both Britain and the United States. Eventually, when people tired of this novelty, the pair were returned to Baffin Island. But they would feature heavily in Hall's unfortunate future, as would Sidney Budington, the captain of the ship that first took him north.

Two years after his Baffin Island trip, Hall set off on another epic expedition in search of Franklin. This time, he was away for five years, and returned with a few relics left behind by a previous British expedition – mainly sacks of coal. But what Hall really wanted to do was travel to the North Pole. Over the years, this ambition grew into an obsession. He was, he declared, "born to discover the North Pole. Once I have set my right foot on the Pole I shall be perfectly willing to die." (Mrs. Hall and their son obviously inspired no great feeling of responsibility.)

Like all explorers, of course, he needed money to get there. It was now several years since Tookolito and Ebierbing had visited the United States. So, to raise funds, he brought the Inuit couple over for a lecture tour. While Hall talked about the mysterious Arctic, they were exhibited alongside seal-skin clothing and boats known as kayaks. He even leased them to P.T.

17

Barnum's infamous circus of freaks and curiosities.

Eventually, though, his fund-raising efforts proved unnecessary. In 1870, Hall managed to persuade the US government to back him. He was given a Navy tug, the *Periwinkle*, which he promptly renamed the *Polaris* – another name for the North Star, which lies almost directly above the North Pole. $50,000 was spent strengthening the tug's bow, which transformed it into a formidable Arctic vessel, strong enough to withstand the ice and storms it would have to face.

No polar explorer could have hoped for a better ship. But in choosing its crew, Hall seriously hindered his chances of success. The extreme conditions and dangers of polar exploration in the 19th century called for men with a special kind of spirit – team players with a combination of boundless optimism and common decency. Alas, these were qualities that most of Hall's companions lacked to an alarming extent.

First of all, Hall picked his old Arctic companion Sidney Budington. But this once-respected whaling captain was now a secret drinker. Furthermore, he had no great respect for Hall, and no interest at all in reaching the Pole. Still, he must have thought, a job is a job. Hall, who was mainly used to working on his own, had no experience of commanding an expedition. As if to compensate for this, he hired two other former sea captains as senior officers on the ship: Hubbard Chester was taken on as first mate, and George Tyson was to be assistant navigator. Tyson, as it turned out, would be the hero of the sorry story that followed.

In order to secure US government help, Hall had agreed to bring several scientists along, to keep records and collect rock, plant and animal specimens. Chief among the scientists was a respected but forbidding German academic and surgeon, Dr. Emil Bessels. Another German, Frederick Meyer, was the expedition meteorologist. Hall resented having the scientists on board, fearing that their work would interfere with his own ambition to reach the Pole. The crew included Tookolito, Ebierbing and their young son, and a large number of German sailors. And, when the *Polaris* stopped off in Greenland, they were joined by another Inuit couple with their three children.

The *Polaris* sailed from New York in July 1871. Just before departure, Hall declared their future would be "glorious". George Tyson's own view of the expedition, recorded in his journal a week after the voyage began, was to be much more prophetic: "*I see there is not perfect harmony between Captain Hall and the Scientific Corp, nor with some others either. I am afraid things will not work well.*"

Hall's inexperience as a leader of men showed at every turn. Almost immediately he fell out with the scientists, and with Budington, who would raid the storeroom for medicinal alcohol to feed his addiction. (This alcohol was intended for use as an antiseptic, and also as a preservative for animal specimens.) Budington, Chester and Tyson, all experienced sea captains, saw each other as rivals. The Germans, Americans and Inuit formed their own cliques, rarely mixing with each other.

Yet, despite the sometimes heated arguments and open animosity, the voyage of the *Polaris* was quite a success. Good weather ensured remarkable progress. By August 29, the ship had passed through Smith Sound into the narrow channel that separates the north west coast of Greenland from Ellesmere Island. Here, existing navigation charts came to an end, and they began to map out virgin territory. In early September, the *Polaris* reached 82°. Ahead lay a clear sea, and the promise of more fine weather. But Budington had gone as far north as he was prepared to go. His years of experience told him that the further they went, the more difficult it would be to get back.

Autumn was approaching. The crew settled in a bay in the newly named territory of Hall Land, in northern Greenland, to wait out the winter. Hall called their berth "Thank God Harbor". When they were settled, and ice had frozen around their ship, Hall gave his men a grateful pep talk. He eloquently summed up the sacrifices they had made and the quest they had undertaken: "You have left your homes, friends, and country; indeed, you have bid a long farewell for a time to the whole civilized world, for the purpose of aiding me in discovering the mysterious, hidden parts of the earth." When the spring came, he told them, they would head north again.

So far, Hall had been lucky. His fractious and divided crew had worked well together so long as there had been good weather, they were reasonably warm and well fed, and there was plenty to keep them occupied. The coming months, when they would be stuck in bleak, monotonous surroundings, with dark winter nights, blizzards and gales, would test them all to the limit.

Sure enough, before the year was out, disaster struck. Hall had never been a particularly healthy man, and previous Arctic expeditions had taken their toll. The first clear sign of his demise came in October. On an exploratory sled trip with a team of dogs, Hall forgot to pack several vital pieces of equipment. A companion had to be sent back to the *Polaris* to fetch warm winter clothing, a stove and a chronometer (which they would need to find their way back to the ship). Hall's mind was obviously failing him fast.

When Hall returned two weeks later, he complained about his inability to keep up with the dogs, meaning he had often had to ride on the sled. Physical as well as mental weakness was overtaking him. Then, as soon as he came aboard and drank a warming cup of coffee, he was violently sick. His decline thereafter was steady and certain. Confined

21

to his bed, he became delirious and began to accuse his companions of poisoning him.

In early November, Hall seemed to make a startling recovery, and raised himself from his bed to work on his journal. But all was clearly not well. He was distracted, and would lose track of what he was saying. Paralysis set in, and his eyes took on a doomed, glassy appearance. He slipped into unconsciousness, and died on November 8, 1871. He was buried close to the ship in the cold, pebble ground of Thank God Harbor.

His death is a mystery to this day. He could have suffered a stroke, or a heart attack – both ailments present symptoms similar to those described by Hall's companions. But he could also have been poisoned. Arsenic produces similar effects to both these illnesses. In the 1960s, a biographer of Hall's asked for permission to visit the grave and examine the body. Hall was duly exhumed and found to be fairly well preserved (as bodies generally are in such a cold environment). Samples of hair and fingernails were removed and sent to a forensic laboratory in Montreal, which specialized in the examination of long-dead bodies. Tests showed conclusively that Hall had ingested a large quantity of arsenic. But had he been murdered?

There are several arguments for and against this. Given the acrimonious relations between Hall, his captain and the scientists, it is possible that one of them decided to kill him. Bessels, as a doctor, was a prime suspect. Perhaps he thought they would be free to carry out their work more efficiently with Hall out of the way. Budington, too, might have poisoned Hall, because he did not wish to take the ship any further north.

But arsenic, in small doses, was a common medicine in the late 19th century. It was a standard ingredient in remedies for indigestion, from which Hall regularly suffered. Perhaps Hall suffered a heart attack or massive stroke, and trusting no one, tried to treat himself from his own medicine supply, accidentally giving himself an overdose of arsenic. Perhaps he was poisoned deliberately. We shall never know.

With Hall gone, control of the expedition passed to Captain Budington, who had already made it clear to everyone that he thought the whole trip was a waste of time. Taking command did not change his view. The morale of the already divided crew sank dramatically.

Before he died, Hall had made some successful efforts at uniting his crew. For example, a regular Sunday service had been established, but this was now abandoned. As well as providing an opportunity for all the crew to come together, the service had been a weekly ritual that marked the passage of time. Now the crew's winter existence became formless, and the days and weeks slipped into an unmarked void. Budington made other, seemingly bizarre, decisions. The whole crew was issued with firearms, the idea being that if any animal came by – a stray bird or a lone seal – it could be shot whenever the chance arose. But the prospect of a fractious, divided crew, all carrying weapons, was alarming.

The atmosphere on the *Polaris* plummeted further when some of the crew broke into the scientists' supply of alcohol. Officers and men would terrorize the ship in drunken rampages. It was difficult enough getting by in the endless polar winter, but now everyone's nerves were in tatters. The ship's carpenter, Nathaniel Coffin, went insane. Convinced the rest of the crew was trying to murder him in the most gruesome ways, he would never sleep in the same spot. Instead, he wandered around the decks and passageways of the *Polaris*, muttering and raving according to his mood.

Winter passed, but spring brought no thaw in the ice surrounding the ship, although wildlife was now more plentiful and there was no danger of starvation. By midsummer, there was still no sign that the ice would crack and allow them to escape.

Then, on August 12, 1872, two events occurred to brighten their dreary existence. One of the Inuit women, who had come aboard at Greenland, gave birth to a baby. This was a total surprise to everyone except her and her husband, as her swollen belly had been concealed by her bulky, seal-skin clothing. The baby was named Charles Polaris, after the dead commander and his ship. On that same day, the ice broke up, and the *Polaris* set out to sea after nearly a year at Thank God Harbor. But their luck did not last. Within three days they were stuck fast in pack ice once again, but at least this ice was slowly drifting south.

As the nights grew longer and the supply of wildlife to hunt grew sparser, the crew had to accept that they were in for another Arctic winter. By now, the *Polaris* was leaking badly, and tons of precious coal were being used to keep the ship's pumps working to clear the hold of seawater. An argument between Budington and members of his crew, over whether they should pump water by hand to save coal, ended with a cabin door being slammed in his face. And these tensions were to grow worse. Much worse.

On October 15, during a terrible storm, the ice around the *Polaris* was hit by a huge iceberg, dramatically increasing the pressure on the hull. The ship's engineer ran up onto the deck, shouting that water was pouring into the hold. In the panic that followed, Budington ordered two lifeboats and some crates of supplies to be lowered overboard onto the ice. But, after four hours, the *Polaris* seemed to be no lower in the water than she had been before the iceberg had struck. It had been a false alarm.

George Tyson was on the ice, helping to supervise the unloading of the ship. He and Captain Budington had a heated shouting match from ship to ice, about whether to load the boats and supplies back onto the *Polaris*. Budington, strangely, ordered the men on the ice to move these items even further away from the ship. While Tyson pondered this peculiar order, the ice surrounding the ship began to crack. As the snow whirled around their heads, and the wind tossed the sea into a swirling inferno, the men on the ice watched the *Polaris* drift beyond their reach and vanish into the dark night.

Morning came and the storm passed. The 19 members of the *Polaris* stranded on the ice now had the chance to examine their new home. In other circumstances they might have been charmed by their surroundings. The floe was like a miniature island. There were lakes of fresh water, formed by melted snow, and little hillocks. Altogether, the ice measured about 6km (4 miles) in circumference.

Tyson, as the most senior officer, was supposedly in command. He faced an impossible task. His fellow castaways, already a divided bunch, would be driven even further apart by their desperate circumstances. Aboard the *Polaris*, when it had lurched away from the ice, had been Budington, Bessels and 12 of the crew. Here on the floe, Tyson had Frederick Meyer, most of the Germans, the two Inuit couples and their five children, including baby Charles. The Germans seemed to regard Meyer as their leader, but his authority was fragile. To make matters worse, he had little respect for Tyson.

That first day, a large chunk of ice broke off, carrying one of the boats, several bags of biscuits and their only compass – although in an amazing stroke of good fortune, the chunk of ice floated back to them a week later. The castaways set up two separate camps. The Germans put up tents in their own little community. The Inuit built igloos, and Tyson and the other crewmen joined them.

In circumstances such as these, people stand a much better chance of survival if they work together, helping the weakest and conserving supplies. But despite his best efforts, Tyson could not get the German sailors to cooperate. They would raid his food supply, often bingeing until they were sick. They burned one of the boats to keep warm. They even stole some of his clothing. Worst of all, when their food supplies grew dangerously low and no animals could be caught, they suggested eating the Inuit children. Tyson was horrified. But, when the *Polaris* had broken away from the ice, the German sailors had been carrying their guns, and he had not. There was nothing he could do to enforce his control.

Fortunately, one group among the castaways was prepared to help them all. Starvation that winter was prevented thanks mainly to the Inuit's hunting skills. By some extraordinary miracle, no one died and no one killed anyone else. But, just as the worst seemed to be over and the survivors could begin to look forward to spring, the floe began to break up.

By the middle of March, their little world had shrunk to a mere fraction of what it had been, and it was getting smaller by the day. Then, towering icebergs surrounded them, threatening to smash the shrinking floe into ice splinters. There was nothing left to do but take to the remaining boat. Cramming 19 people into a rowing boat meant for eight wasn't easy. Having already threatened to eat the Inuit children, some of the Germans loudly suggested that the children should be thrown overboard to make more room.

The nightmare journey that followed would haunt them all for the rest of their lives. In heaving seas of ice and mountainous waves, the tiny, overloaded boat battled against the freezing wind to reach land. By night, they would stop on a floe and try to sleep. By day, they would cower in their tiny boat, weakening by the hour through lack of food and fresh water.

On April 8, when a crack unexpectedly opened on the edge of a floe they were resting on, Meyer fell into the freezing sea. Ebierbing, and another Inuit named Hans, ran out through wobbling chunks of ice to pull him out. The shock of falling into sub-zero water almost killed Meyer. He stopped breathing and would have died, had not the Inuit pummelled his body until he regained consciousness. The fall crushed his spirit, and left him frost-bitten and feverish. Recalling his appearance in the days after, Tyson wrote: *"he is very tall and thin. If [an artist] had wanted a model to stand for Famine, he might have drawn Meyer… He was the most wretched-looking object I ever saw."* Tyson feared that Meyer's decline would bring him further trouble. Meyer had had some authority over his fellow Germans. As he grew weaker, it all but evaporated.

In their darkest hour, the men seemed to rediscover their humanity. On the evening of April 19, the castaways made camp on a floe, but then a fierce storm broke around nine o'clock, and torrents of water swamped their icy refuge. The men bundled the Inuit women and children into the boat, and then held onto their slippery perch as best they could. After each wave washed over them, they would haul the boat back into the middle and wait for the next onslaught.

In the early morning light, they could see the floe was melting into the sea, and the boat was launched. Aside from the sound of crying children, a strange silence fell over the usually mutinous crew. Stunned by their narrow escape and the horror of their circumstances, they finally looked to Tyson for leadership, and readily obeyed his every command as he attempted to steer the overcrowded boat.

In the days that followed, the weather grew worse. Of the wind and the sea, Tyson wrote in his journal: *"They played with us and our boat as if we were shuttlecocks."* Reviewing their situation, he concluded: *"Half-drowned we are, and cold enough in our wet clothes, without shelter, and not sun enough to dry us* even on the outside. We have nothing to eat; everything is finished and gone. The prospect looks bad."

However the situation was not as bad as Tyson imagined. By now, they had drifted far enough south to have reached the usual limits of the whale and seal ships that roamed the Arctic. They sighted their first ship on the afternoon of April 28. This must have been the moment when everyone on board allowed themselves to hope that they might survive their journey after all. But fate had not finished with them yet. The first two ships they sighted did not see their frantic signals. It was only on the morning of April 30 that they were finally rescued, by a Newfoundland sealer called the *Tigress*.

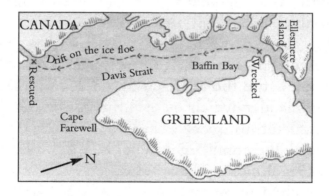

This map shows the castaways' journey to safety.

Safely back home in the United States, Tyson learned of the fate of the *Polaris*. The men on board had fared little better than those stranded on the ice floe. As the ship floated away, it had sprung a serious leak, and Budington had been forced to land on the west coast of Smith Sound. Having previously abandoned the ship's lifeboats on the ice, the crew had had to dismantle their vessel to build smaller boats. These they used to travel down the coast until they reached the whale and seal hunting grounds, and were rescued by a Scottish whaler.

When news of Hall's disastrous expedition broke, it caused a sensation and a scandal. It read, after all, like a cross between a boy's adventure story and a psychological murder mystery. The ordeal of the Inuit women and children provoked particular sympathy among American newspaper readers, and the Inuit families were inundated with gifts of bundles of clothing.

But there were also serious questions to be answered. The United States government launched an inquiry into the loss of the ship and the death of its commander. Much of the story came out, but it was difficult to piece together any clear picture among all the conflicting accounts. If any dirty deeds had been done, neither the officers nor the crew were willing to admit them. The Board of Inquiry decided that Hall had died of a stroke. Despite the discovery of arsenic traces when his body was exhumed in the 1960s, there is still no solid evidence to suggest he was murdered, and no obvious prime suspect.

Interlude

From 1873-1908

Charles Hall's disastrous failure to reach the North Pole, and the terrible hardships that befell his crew, merely whetted the appetite of other explorers to do better. In 1879, an American expedition, under the leadership of Lieutenant Commander George Washington De Long, set sail through the Bering Strait, off the coast of eastern Siberia, in the ship *Jeanette*. De Long intended to sail as far north as possible, and then use sleds to reach the Pole itself. But the ship became caught in ice and drifted for 22 months, before sinking off the coast of eastern Siberia.

When wreckage from the *Jeanette* drifted over to Greenland, Norwegian explorer Fridtjof Nansen hit on the idea of reaching the North Pole by drifting there in a strong ship. Accordingly, he set out in a ship specially designed to resist crushing by ice. The ship was called the *Fram* (which means "forward"). During the three-year journey that followed, between 1893 and 1896, Nansen and his crew gained vast amounts of knowledge about the Arctic, establishing once and for all that the North Pole was just part of a huge icy sea, rather than solid land. At one point on the journey, Nansen and a colleague left the *Fram* intending to sled and ski their way to the North Pole. They failed, and were forced to spend the winter on Franz Josef Island, until they were rescued by a British explorer.

At the turn of the century, American, German, Swedish and Italian teams all crept closer to the Pole, and it seemed only a matter of time before someone would stand at that elusive point where their navigational instruments would read 90° North.

Over in the Antarctic, an international team aboard the Belgian ship *Belgica* was trapped in ice in the Bellinghausen Sea. Between 1898 and 1899, they became the first people to winter south of the Antarctic Circle. A year later, a British expedition under Carsten E. Borchgrevink spent the winter on the continent itself, at Cape Adare.

It was the British who made the greatest progress exploring the Antarctic. In two expeditions, from 1901–1904, and again from 1907–1909, Captain Robert Falcon Scott and Sir Ernest Shackleton both led sled parties deep into the heart of Antarctica. Scott and Shackleton became rivals, and it seemed certain that one of them would be the first explorer to reach the South Pole.

"Won at last by the Stars and Stripes"

More often than not, success is not half as interesting as failure. When the North Pole was finally conquered, the story of the first team to reach this anonymous spot on the map was notably lacking in drama – aside from the murder of one of the party by his Inuit companion. It was what happened afterwards that proved to be far more interesting.

The man popularly credited as being the first to the North Pole was US Navy engineer Robert Peary. At the start of the century, he was already the most eminent Arctic explorer of his age. He was a tall, wiry man, with a huge walrus moustache. In almost all his photographs he stares out at the world with haughty disdain. A lifetime dedicated to reaching the North Pole had turned Robert Peary into a rather objectionable human being. Yet, from such arrogance and self-belief, heroes are often made.

Despite his disagreeable personality, there were some qualities, at least, to admire in Peary. He was a person of great contradictions. As a white man, he regarded himself as superior to other races. (This prejudice was commonplace at the time.) Yet he had a black servant, Matthew Henson, who was both his right hand man and loyal companion. Peary repaid this loyalty by taking Henson with him on the first trip to the Pole. (Although his detractors say this was because he did not want to share the glory of being first with another white man.)

The Inuit, then known as Eskimos, he also saw as an inferior race. But he admired their ability to survive in their barren, frozen environment, and learned a great deal from them. This was not true of all explorers. For example, many British explorers were highly sceptical that they could learn anything from a people they regarded as savages, and suffered as a consequence. For his time, Peary had a commendable respect for the Inuit. When asked whether attempts should be made to convert them to Christianity, Peary was certain they should be left to their own religious beliefs. After all, he remarked, "the cardinal graces of faith, hope and charity they seem to have already. They are healthy and pure-blooded; they have no vices, no intoxicants and no bad habits, not even gambling."

Peary's accounts of his trips make much of the hardship of polar exploration. One passage describes his feet feeling "*hot, aching, and throbbing, till the pain reached to my knees*". His own courage could not be doubted. During an Arctic expedition in 1898, he lost nine toes to gangrene brought on by frostbite. Thereafter, he walked with a curious sliding gait. But even this didn't put him off further Arctic travel.

The adversity and deprivation he suffered for his

Arctic ambitions were all too obvious. Like many explorers throughout history, he was away from his family a great deal, and once had a letter from his daughter begging him not to go on any more expeditions. *"I have been looking at your pictures and it seems ten years and I am sick of looking at them,"* she wrote. *"I want to see my father. I don't want people to think me an orphan."*

Peary's wife, a formidable woman named Josephine, remained one of his greatest champions throughout his life. She supported him tirelessly, and raised funds for his expeditions. But, like many explorer's wives, she suffered greatly for her husband's ambitions. During one of Peary's lengthy absences, she gave birth to a daughter. Peary never saw the child, for she died aged only seven months. As well as bearing this tragedy alone, Josephine suffered the strain of not knowing, from one month to the next, whether her husband was still alive. In the days before radio, this was a normal part of the life of any explorer's next of kin. And, in addition to this awful uncertainty, she also had to endure the torment of knowing Peary had an Eskimo mistress, with whom he had had two sons.

The journey that Peary claimed took him to the Pole began in 1908. He had been to the Arctic six times before. His last trip, in 1906, had taken him to latitude 87° 06', less than 3° from the Pole. Peary had learned a lot from these journeys. He designed his own sleds, stoves and clothing, all based closely on tried and trusted designs. He made a habit of sleeping in the open, as many Inuit did. Shunning tents, he only built an igloo when the temperature dropped to extreme levels of cold. He even ate some of his food cold, gnawing on frozen "pemmican" – dried meat and fat pounded into a paste. After all, eating uncooked food saved on fuel.

Ever practical, he chose the members of his team not only for their character, but also for their size. He preferred small, wiry men. They needed less food than big, tall men, and took up less space in an igloo. His ship, the *Roosevelt*, was built on much the same principals. It was short, to make it easier to steer, and its heavy greenwood flanks were strong enough to survive the crushing Arctic ice – the sides were an impressive 76cm (30 inches) thick. It was the only vessel in North America built especially for the northernmost reaches of the Arctic Ocean.

When he set off, aged 52, Peary had already spent much of his life exploring the region. His age was against him, his health was shaky, and his backers were impatient for a success after so many previous failures. He must have known this was going to be his last chance. After a grand send-off from New York, on July 6, 1908, the *Roosevelt* headed for Cape Sheridan on Ellesmere Island's northern coast. Supplies were unloaded and the expedition made their winter headquarters at Cape Colombia. Before the winter came, sled parties were sent off to lay down supplies on the route north.

Then, on February 28, 1909, 24 men set out, with 19 sleds and 133 dogs. Each sled carried 230kg (500lb) of supplies. Peary's plan was for them all to head north, and then return sled by sled, as their food and fuel supplies were used up.

Right from the off, the going across the ice was exceptionally good. It was very cold that season, and the ice had frozen hard – ideal conditions for sleds pulled by dogs. The only problems they encountered were when huge "leads" (cracks in the ice which left gaps of water) opened up in the trail before them. Sometimes they had to wait several days for a lead to close before they could continue going north.

For Peary, everything went brilliantly well. But, for others on his party, the story was not so rosy. One of his colleagues, an American named Ross Marvin, was returning to their base camp, as part of the planned reduction in the number of accompanying sleds. During the journey, Marvin was said to have fallen into a hole in the ice and drowned. The truth, when it came out, was much messier. Accompanied by two Inuit, Marvin had driven his companions on relentlessly. One of the Inuit had repeatedly asked him for permission to rest on the sled, but Marvin had kept refusing. Finally, this man had killed the American and, helped by his companion, he had then dumped the body under the ice.

As Peary's men neared their destination, fewer

and fewer sleds remained. Within 246km (154 miles) of the Pole, Peary sent the *Roosevelt's* Captain, Bob Bartlett, back south. Bartlett had been brought on this trip with an explicit promise that he would be taken to the Pole if circumstances permitted. He was furious to be asked to return south, and never forgave Peary for this decision. (A decade or so later, Bartlet was interviewed about the trip in a restaurant and, when he spoke about Peary, his language became so heated that the head waiter had to ask him to leave.)

Finally, all that remained of the original party was Peary, Henson his servant, who was also a capable translator, four Inuit, five sleds and 40 dogs. Peary claimed to have reached the Pole on April 6, 1909, at around one o'clock in the afternoon, and stayed there some 30 hours.

It was an historic occasion, remembered with a typical lack of modesty by Peary, who summed it up like this: "The discovery of the North Pole stands for the inevitable victory of courage, persistence, endurance, over all obstacles... The discovery of [this]... splendid, frozen jewel of the north, for which through centuries men of every nation have struggled, and suffered and died, is won at last, and is won forever, by the Stars and Stripes!"

It was undoubtedly a significant moment: "The closing of the book on 400 years of history," according to Peary, further blowing his own trumpet.

Peary and his companions raced back to Cape

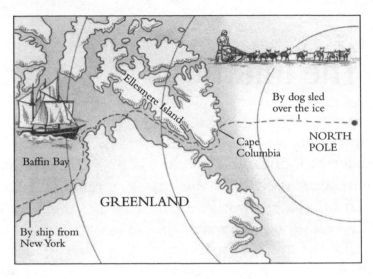

This map shows Peary's claimed route to the North Pole.

Columbia. The journey to the Pole had taken them 40 days. The return took a mere 16. The *Roosevelt* sailed for home, navigating through a sea of fractured ice. By September 6, they had reached Indian Harbor, Labrador, on the very furthest reaches of the international cable network. Here, Peary sent four messages – to his wife Josephine, to *The New York Times*, to the Associated Press news agency, and to the Peary Arctic Club, the organization he had set up to fund his polar ambitions.

But, here at Indian Harbor, Peary also discovered something that was to sour his sense of triumph. Four days earlier, his rival Frederick Cook had announced to the world that he had been to the Pole too – and that he had got there a whole year earlier.

The infamous Dr. Cook

Peary's rival was a likeable doctor of medicine named Frederick Cook, who worked in Brooklyn. The two men knew each other well, and had sailed for the Arctic together over 1891-1892. Quietly ambitious for polar fame himself, Cook had sensed a clear rivalry. For this reason he first turned his attention to the Antarctic. But when circumstances changed it was inevitable that the two would become adversaries. Lacking Peary's prestigious and wealthy backers, Cook set out to raise funds for a polar trek by bringing an Inuit couple to the United States and taking them on a lecture tour. This was exactly the same tactic that had been employed by Charles Hall, and it worked. Public interest in the polar regions was high – they were, after all, among the last places on earth still to be visited by human beings. Audiences flocked to see Cook and his Inuit, and were fascinated by the ingenious construction of Inuit sleds, fur and animal-skin clothing, and kayaks made entirely of seal bone and skin.

Cook's next money-making venture had a tragicomic edge to it. He hired a 1,100-ton steamer named the *Miranda*, and offered places on a summer cruise to the Arctic for $500 a berth. The *Miranda* set out on July 7, 1894, with 50 passengers, most of them academics or big-game hunters. Several collisions followed, the crew mutinied and went on a drunken rampage after breaking into the wine store, and the *Miranda* struck an iceberg while en route to Greenland. She sank shortly after her passengers had been transferred to a fishing schooner. Amazingly, rather than suing Cook for the shirt off his back, the passengers seemed to revel in their misadventure. Aboard the boat chartered to bring them home, they formed "The Arctic Club", soon to become one of New York's most prestigious societies for explorers. (Honorary members included Shackleton, Scott and Amundsen, all coming up in the next three chapters of this book.)

But before Cook set out on his own expedition, he got the chance to join another one. In 1897, the Belgian government sent the sailing ship *Belgica* to explore Antarctica with an international crew. Cook was taken on board as the ship's surgeon. Few polar vessels had ever ventured this far south. The *Belgica* became trapped in the pack ice and was stranded for the entire Antarctic winter. Men went insane in the endless dark and relentless cold. Cook, however, excelled himself. By all accounts, he was a much valued and useful member of this very difficult expedition. The Norwegian polar explorer Roald Amundsen was among the crew, and wrote of Cook: "*[He was] a man of unfaltering courage, unfailing hope, endless cheerfulness, and unwearied kindness.*" Amundsen even went so far as to attribute the survival of the Belgica's crew to Cook's "*skill, energy and persistence*".

Such reports did much for Cook's burgeoning reputation as an explorer. Further fame followed in 1903, when Cook announced he had climbed Mount McKinley, the highest peak in North America. He wrote a best selling book about it, *To the Top of the Continent*, and was elected president of the American Explorer's Club. Unlike the imperious Peary, whose haughty character was all too obvious, Cook appeared to be a genial, good-natured man. Photographs invariably show him with a smile and a twinkle in his eye, as if he is about to make an amiable quip.

But all this was to change. Such was the "leprous blanket of infamy" that would be heaped on Cook in the years to come, he once, rather pitifully, described himself as "the most shamefully abused man in the history of exploration". Maybe he was, but there was something in his character which led him astray, and which would eventually destroy his reputation as a great explorer.

The first steps to Cook's downfall began in 1907, when he set off from New York to try to reach the North Pole. This change of polar destination was prompted by a meeting with John R. Bradley, a wealthy American gambling-club owner and big-game hunter, who had offered to finance the trip. Bradley suggested they keep the voyage secret so that, if Cook should fail, they could pass off the trip as a hunting expedition. Cook sailed to the Arctic Circle aboard a ship named the *John R. Bradley*, after his backer. Bradley came along too, intending to add some seals, walruses and polar bears to his collection of stuffed animals. By a strange coincidence, the captain of their ship was one Moses Bartlett, cousin of the *Roosevelt's* captain, Bob Bartlett.

Bradley couldn't help boasting about his voyage, and news of Cook's attempt on the Pole reached Peary while his ship, the *Roosevelt*, was holed up in dry dock, undergoing repairs on damage sustained during his last polar attempt. Peary, frustrated by his inability to prevent Cook's voyage, and fearful that he would be beaten to the Pole, huffed and puffed that such a move was "one of which no man with a high or even average sense of honor would be guilty..." Peary had put so much effort into trying to reach the Pole, he felt he was entitled to do so without anyone else trying to get there before him.

Cook, and the ship's cook Rudolph Francke, were dropped off by the *John R. Bradley* in the Inuit village of Anoatok, near Etah, Greenland. After spending the winter there, the two of them, together with nine Inuit, set off for the Pole. At first they went west, via Cape Sabine, then crossed Ellesmere Island, and reached Cape Thomas Hubbard at the tip of Axel Heiberg Island. Here, they left a large supply dump. On March 18, they headed north across the frozen Arctic Ocean on a 1,600km (1,000 mile) round trip to the North Pole. For this daring leap into the unknown, Cook took only two other people. Francke, stricken with scurvy, had given up, as had seven of the Inuit. Accompanying the two sleds and 26 dogs were the Inuit Ahwelah and Etukishook. According to Cook's account, they covered the 800km (500 miles) to the top of the world in 34 days, and claimed to have reached the Pole on April 21, 1908, almost a whole year before Peary.

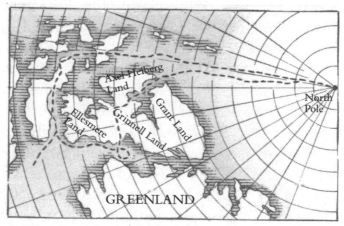

This map shows Cook's claimed route to the Pole. It is based on a drawing by Cook himself. Nowadays, Ellesmere Land, Grinnell Land and Grant Land are known as Ellesmere Island.

The return journey was harrowing. The sleds held only two months' supply of food, but Cook's small party was gone for 14 months. They shot what food they could find, mainly polar bears and seals. But, at several points on the journey, they were so starved that they resorted to eating their candles, and even the leather straps of their sleds.

Cook's party eventually arrived back at the fringes of human habitation in Greenland. From here, he took a boat to Scandinavia via the Shetland Islands, where he sent a telegram announcing his triumph to the world on September 2, 1909. Then he headed for the Danish capital, Copenhagen, where he was greeted by a phalanx of journalists. The Danes hailed him as a great hero, and awards were heaped upon him – he was presented with a gold medal from the Danish Royal Geographical Society, and an honorary degree by the University of Copenhagen. But Cook was not allowed to enjoy his fame for long.

During a banquet to celebrate his triumph, a telegraph arrived with news of Peary's own claim to have been the first to the Pole. This had been announced on September 6, only four days after Cook's own message to the world. An extraordinary photograph was taken mere moments after the telegraph was read out at the banquet. The diners, all dressed in stiff, white shirts and formal dinner jackets, look stunned. Some stare accusingly at Cook. One man is puffing out his cheeks in astonishment. Cook stands in the middle, a garland of flowers draped incongruously around his dinner jacket. He wears an almost comical expression of disappointment and surprise, rather like a pantomime villain about to say, "Curses! Foiled again!"

With hindsight, the battle for credibility was heavily weighted towards Peary right from the start. He was funded by the American Museum of Natural

History, and some of the richest and most respected men in America. He had the blessing of the illustrious National Geographic Society, and had even lunched with President Roosevelt (after whom he had named his ship) on his way out to the Pole. The prestigious *New York Times*, with whom he had a contract to tell his story, also supported him unquestioningly.

Cook, on the other hand, was backed by a raffish big-game hunter who had made his fortune from gambling, which was considered even more disreputable then than it is now. He had returned with no written account of his journey at all, claiming he had left his navigation records and journal in the Arctic. Furthermore, as the controversy raged around him, his two Inuit companions, Ahwelah and Etukishook, later confessed that, in all their time away with him, they had never been out of sight of land. They also claimed that a photograph supposedly showing them at the Pole had been taken with them all perched on top of an igloo, two days' march from land. Then, as a further blow to his reputation, it was revealed that his earlier claim that he had climbed Mount McKinley was a fraud. Photos produced to prove he had reached the summit had been cropped from ones taken on a much lower peak.

Amazingly, all was not lost. Cook was backed by the *New York Times's* major rival, the *New York Herald*.

He stuck to his story about his records, claiming he would have them returned to America as soon as possible. He dismissed Ahwelah and Etukishook's allegations by playing on racist perceptions common among Americans and Europeans at the time. His ignorant Inuit companions had been frightened of straying away from land, explained Cook. To soothe their fears, he had frequently pointed to low-lying clouds on the horizon, telling them that this was land. This was quite plausible – it was not uncommon for seafarers to mistake banks of low clouds for distant land, which would, of course, vanish when they pointed their boats towards them.

The New York Times and *Herald* slugged it out on behalf of their respective champions. The whole western world was riveted by this unseemly and rather comical dispute. The British satirical magazine *Punch*, for example, printed a cartoon showing the Cook and Peary waxworks at Madame Tussaud's punching each other, while British explorer Ernest Shackleton looks on in amazement. To begin with, public opinion was behind Cook. Despite his extremely flimsy evidence, opinion polls at the time generally indicated that eight out of ten people thought Cook had been first to the Pole. The main reason for his success was Peary's unpopularity. Peary's haughty attacks on Cook always lost him support, rather than gaining it. In terms of public appeal, the amiable Cook won hands down against the imperious Peary.

But, over the next few months, Cook's case crumbled – especially when his records failed to appear. His awards were ignominiously withdrawn. Sensing total defeat, he vanished, being reported variously in London, Santiago and his home ground of Brooklyn.

Peary had won. The National Geographic Society pronounced him the first man to the Pole. The United States government awarded him the rank of rear admiral, and he retired with a handsome pension. But his fame and acclaim never bought him any great happiness. His own records, exposed to a glaringly bright light during the controversy with Cook, offered far from conclusive proof that he had actually reached the Pole himself. Recognition came with a slight sense of doubt. Britain's Royal Geographical Society, for example, while hailing him as a great explorer, always hedged their bets when it came to recognizing him as the first man to reach the Pole. Anaemia, first diagnosed by none other than Frederick Cook after an earlier expedition, came back to claim him. Peary died on February 20, 1920. He was 64.

Cook's fate was altogether more tragic. Seeking to make a living in the world of property and land speculation, Cook had sold land to one customer with the assurance that it contained oil. When no oil was found, Cook was charged with fraud, placed on trial in 1923, and found guilty.

The judge at the trial was merciless. "This is one of those times when your peculiar and persuasive personality fails you, doesn't it?" he taunted. "Oh God, Cook, haven't you any sense of decency at all?"

The sentence was harsh: Cook was fined $14,000, and sent to Leavenworth Penitentiary for 14 years and 9 months.

Cook's disgrace was complete. His old friend, the esteemed polar explorer Roald Amundsen, loyally paid him a visit at Leavenworth, while visiting America on a lecture tour. The National Geographical Society immediately cancelled a speaking engagement they had made with him in disgust.

But Cook did not stay in Leavenworth forever. He was still a winning character, and he managed the formidable task of being popular with both the guards and the inmates. He was paroled in 1930, and then given a presidential pardon in 1940. It turned out the land he had sold did contain oil after all – millions of gallons, in fact.

Cook died soon after his presidential pardon, leaving a final taped message to the world: "I have been humiliated and seriously hurt. But that doesn't matter any more. I'm getting old, and what does matter to me is that I want you to believe that I told the truth. I state emphatically that I, Frederick A. Cook, discovered the North Pole."

Nearly a century later, the argument is still to be won conclusively, and modern polar historians have come to ask whether either of them reached the Pole. Cook's own case was pretty much destroyed in the year after he presented it. But Peary's extraordinary speed across the ice on his return journey also seems too good to be true. He kept careless navigational records, with no measurement of longitude, and made no allowances either for the constant drifting of the ice he crossed, or for compass variations caused by the earth's fluctuating magnetic field, for which adjustments are usually made at these latitudes. His lack of "reliable" witnesses (*i.e.* white men who would be able to verify his own sightings) also undermined his case in the eyes of his contemporaries.

When all is said and done – and millions of words have been written on what one writer called "the dispute of the century" – it's unlikely either of them reached the Pole. But Peary probably got considerably closer than Cook.

Amundsen's hollow victory

American sports coach "Red" Saunders once said: "Winning isn't everything. It's the only thing." Saunders had obviously never heard of Roald Amundsen. This tremendously capable Norwegian explorer became the first man to lead a team to the South Pole, beating a rival British team, led by Robert Falcon Scott, by a month or more. Confounding the expectations, and sometimes open scorn, of fellow explorers, Amundsen showed that careful planning and good sense could take five men to the most remote spot on earth with relative ease. Scott's expedition, by contrast, ended in tragedy, his poor planning and misjudgment leading to his own death, and that of four other men with him. Yet although Amundsen won the race to the Pole and brought his team home alive, it was Scott who would be celebrated as a hero — a twist of fate that would have puzzled Saunders.

As a boy, Amundsen had read about the exploits of Sir John Franklin, and was determined to follow in his footsteps. His great hero was fellow Norwegian Fridtjof Nansen, the world-famous Arctic pioneer. Amundsen made his first polar trip in 1898. Aged 25, he had been aboard the *Belgica*, on the Belgian-led international expedition to Antarctica, which had also included Dr. Frederick Cook. The expedition ship was trapped in the pack ice and forced to wait out the long polar winter. And, while some men went insane in the endless dark, and the crew fell to squabbling and scurvy, Amundsen thrived on the hardship. One officer recalled he "was the biggest, the strongest, the bravest, and generally the best-dressed man for sudden emergencies".

Amundsen's lifelong ambition had been to be the first man to reach the North Pole. To this end, in 1910, he had borrowed the Norwegian vessel, the *Fram*, which had been used by Nansen on his intrepid voyage. Amundsen hired a crew, and was all set to sail north when word reached him that Cook and Peary were both claiming they had reached the Arctic Pole. Others would have been crushed by disappointment, but within minutes of hearing the news Amundsen just changed his destination. He would sail south for the Antarctic instead.

In his quest for fame, Amundsen was canny enough to know he had to be sly. The funds to finance his expedition (from both the Norwegian government and private backers) had been for an Arctic trip. Perhaps his backers would withdraw if they knew they were paying for an Antarctic expedition? The British had also made it plain to other nations that they wished to be the first to reach the South Pole. At the time, Britain had an empire which covered a quarter of the world, and the Norwegian government had no wish to upset such a powerful country. But, in particular, Amundsen knew that the British explorer Robert Falcon Scott was preparing for an assault on the South Pole at that very moment. Anything that delayed Amundsen would rob him of the chance of beating Scott to the Pole.

So Amundsen told no one of his change of plan, not even his crew. But some of them must have been puzzled when components for a base hut were brought on board, as were teams of dogs – huts were only put up on land, and there was no land at the North Pole, only frozen sea. And, for Arctic expeditions, dogs were usually acquired nearer the destination.

The *Fram* slipped away from Norway on August 9, 1910, with a crew of 19 men. Only when they reached Madeira, off the coast of Morocco, were the men told of their true destination. Here, Amundsen also notified the Norwegian government, figuring that revealing his plans when he was already well into his journey would prevent them from stopping him continuing on his way.

Amundsen's knowledge of polar travel had led him to believe the best way to travel was with skis and sleds pulled by dogs. This method, perfected by the Arctic inhabitants, seemed so transparently better than any other that he couldn't understand why everyone didn't use it. It was known his rival, Scott, intended to use Manchurian ponies as well as dogs, and to have his men haul sleds to the Pole. (This is known as manhauling.) But one thing about Scott's party did bother Amundsen. The British were also taking three motorized sleds. If these were a success – and so far they were an unknown factor – then there was every chance Scott would reach the Pole before the Norwegians.

The *Fram* sailed to Antarctica through the Ross Sea, taking only a single week to negotiate the pack ice. The crew unloaded their equipment and hut in the Bay of Whales, and named their camp Framheim (meaning "*Fram*'s home"). Then immediately they set about preparing for the trek south and making themselves comfortable for the coming winter. The plan was to lay down supply dumps at intervals along the route, and then wait until the Antarctic spring in September or October, when they would dash for the Pole.

Probably because they came from a country well-used to snow and cold and long, dark nights, the Norwegians adapted very easily to Polar conditions. They worked through blizzards, laying down three hefty supply dumps on the way south to the Pole. When the winter weather forced a stop to the preparation of the route, they retired to the hut. It was uncomfortably crowded, so they built a warren of underground corridors and chambers next to it, hewn from the snow and ice that soon built up around them. Here, there were workshops, a place to cook, a room for the cook's slops, a lavatory, and even a stove-powered sauna. In their underground warren they prepared for the trip, shaving the wood on their sleds to remove any unnecessary weight, until all the sleds were one third lighter.

Amundsen's men passed the winter amiably enough, although they couldn't help noticing that Hjalmar Johansen was keeping an icy distance. Johansen was a friend of Nansen's whom Amundsen had taken on the expedition as a concession to his hero. Johansen had a serious lack of respect for his new leader. This erupted into full-scale contempt after Amundsen began an early – and disastrous – dash for the Pole.

Fearing the British would beat them, the Norwegians began their southward trek in early September – the very beginning of the Antarctic spring. Johansen had cautioned against this. The weather proved too harsh, and Amundsen and his men were forced to return, suffering from frostbite and exhaustion. A bitter argument blew up between Amundsen and Johansen. They quarrelled so fiercely that Amundsen removed Johansen from his South Pole team, and instead sent him and two other members of the expedition to explore an unknown coast to the east.

The source of friction removed, Amundsen's men waited patiently for the season to turn. By October

20, conditions were judged to be right, and the Norwegians set off for the Pole. Along with Amundsen were Olav Bjaarland, Helmer Hanssen, Sverre Hassel and Oskar Wisting, and 52 dogs pulling four sleds. Their supplies had been meticulously packed in the sleds over the winter. The men did not ride the sleds, as this would have created unnecessary additional weight for the dogs to pull. Instead, they ran or skied alongside them. Every sled was pulled by a team of dogs in a fan formation, each dog having its own leash and harness, so that if it fell into a crevasse it wouldn't drag any of its fellows with it.

Amundsen planned a daily rate of 24km (15 miles). He could have gone faster, but didn't want to exhaust the dogs. Right from this second start, luck was with them. They made very good progress and, by November 4, they had reached the last of the dumps laid down the previous autumn. It was 82° south. From here, they managed to advance a further 1° every four days: a distance of roughly 112 km (69 miles). Amundsen decided to set up a new dump at every 1° on the way to the Pole. This way, they would have less to carry with them on their return journey. These dumps were clearly marked by a flag on a stick, and by a series of smaller penants, placed either side of the dump. These markers would direct them back to the dump if their navigation was faulty, or if they became lost in a blizzard.

Each night, when they stopped to make camp, the men would set up their tents and sleep comfortably in sleeping bags made of three layers of fur. At the top of the Axel Heiberg Glacier, half the dogs were shot. With supplies left behind in a trail of dumps, they were simply not needed to pull the sleds anymore. Their bodies were fed to both the other dogs (who had no problem at all about eating their own kind) and the explorers. There were now 18 dogs left, to pull three sleds in teams of six a piece.

But it wasn't all plain sailing. As they neared the Pole, the sleds had to cross a terrifying stretch of ice the men named the Devil's Glacier. Here, crevasses stretched in every direction, often hidden by snow, and all promising a swift demise to anyone unwary enough to plunge into their hidden depths. Hassel and Amundsen, roped together, probed gingerly forward, painstakingly charting a safe route through. Immediately after this obstacle there was a vast plain of thin ice, which the men named the Devil's Ballroom. Here, the surface was often too weak to support the weight of a man, and it was all too easy to plunge down through the ice into a deep crack.

Taking regular sightings with a sextant, they edged towards their goal. Finally, at three o'clock in the afternoon, on December 14, 1911, Amundsen came forward to be the first to stand on a spot they took to be the very bottom of the world. The Norwegians set up a tent over this spot, which they also marked with their national flag. Inside the tent, Amundsen left a letter for the Norwegian monarch, King Haakon VII.

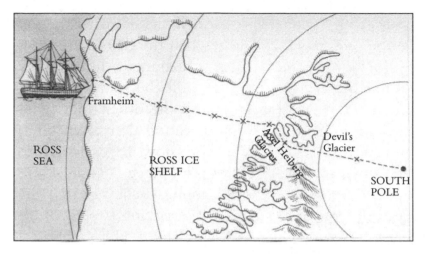

This map shows Amundsen's route to the
South Pole (the crosses mark depots).

With it was a note for Scott, asking him to deliver it.
Ever practical, Amundsen feared his party might not
survive their return journey, and he wanted the
world to know he had made it to the Pole first.

The men set up camp, and celebrated their victory
with a feast of seal meat, and tobacco saved especially
for the occasion. Then, after spending two days taking
readings to ensure they were exactly where they
thought they were, the party set off for home. The
weather on the way back was not as good as it had
been on the way out, but they still made good
progress.

Back at the Framheim base, the men waiting for
them had hardly even begun to wonder when they
might be returning. Quite unexpectedly, they were
roused by a knock on the window. It was four

o'clock in the morning of January 26, 1912. Amundsen and his team had made 2,993km (1,860 miles) in 99 days. Coffee was swiftly brewed. Strangely enough, it was a full hour before anyone got around to asking whether Amundsen had made it to the Pole.

The *Fram* sailed soon after, arriving at Hobart, Tasmania, on March 7. Here, news of Amundsen's success was telegraphed across the world. But Norway's polar heroes were soon to have their extraordinary achievement eclipsed by a glorious failure.

The noble art of dying like a gentleman

From the earliest days of Antarctic exploration, the British behaved as if it was their right to reach the South Pole first. After all, so much of the world was theirs anyway. The president of the Royal Geographical Society, Sir Clements Markham, appointed a Royal Navy officer named Robert Falcon Scott to lead a team to claim the Pole.

Scott, fated to become one of the most famous polar explorers ever, was a complex and not entirely likeable man. Aloof, given to black moods, and steeped in the social snobbery of his era, he was driven by a strong sense of duty and patriotism. A whiff of his haughty character can be gained from this diary entry, where he is describing his expedition deputy Teddy Evans: *"a thoroughly well-meaning little man but rather a duffer in anything but his own peculiar work."* Scott was something of an enigma, though. Despite his starchy character, he married a free-spirited sculptress named Kathleen Bruce.

Scott had first been to Antarctica in 1901. He had set out to explore the interior, but scurvy had undermined his expedition. With him on that trip was Ernest Shackleton (see page 33). Both strong characters, the two men had fallen out, and thereafter became rivals. Another passenger was a young doctor named Edward Wilson, who was a keen ornithologist and a talented artist. Wilson had recently suffered from a bout of tuberculosis, but this didn't stop him from wanting to explore the most hostile region on earth. He and Scott forged a friendship that would endure until their deaths.

Heavily influenced by his mentor, Sir Clements, Scott had a romantic vision of polar exploration, which involved heroically determined men hauling heavy sleds through ice and snow, and triumphing against daunting odds. This approach was exhausting, but other, more practical alternatives were not fully taken up, for reasons which we would now consider questionable. Scott was a product of his age, and carried the usual prejudices of a man of his class and background. Skis, for example, were looked down on as a foreign invention. They were used, for sure, but few of the British party ever really mastered them. Arctic inhabitants had used dogs to pull their sleds. Other polar explorers, such as Peary and Amundsen, had copied this idea with great success. But the British were well-known as a nation of animal lovers. Men like Scott saw dogs as loyal and much-loved companions of the hearth or hunting field. The thought of using them as beasts of burden, driving them to exhaustion and then killing them for food when they were no longer needed, was immensely distasteful to him. This did not stop Scott from using dogs altogether, but he never employed them with the same ruthlessness as his rivals.

By 1910, the South Pole had still to be reached. This was not for want of trying. Scott and Shackleton had both led expeditions, in 1901 and 1907 respectively. The Germans, Swedes and French had also explored the continent. Scott began to plan and recruit for his trip as the decade drew to a close. A meeting with the great Fridjof Nansen convinced him to review some of his prejudices: they would take skis with them after all, and they would also use animals. The sleds would be towed by Manchurian ponies, and they would also take a small team of dogs. Scott still preferred ponies over dogs, despite the fact that Shackleton had used ponies on his 1907 expedition and found them unsuited to polar conditions.

Over 8,000 men volunteered to go on the expedition – most of them from the Royal Navy. By the summer of 1910, Scott had funds, a ship named the *Terra Nova*, and a crew of 67. Among them were his friend, Dr. Wilson, and another veteran from the 1901 expedition, Edgar "Taff" Evans. Scott greatly admired this energetic Welshman, whose resourcefulness and good nature made him an ideal companion. Also among the crew were two men who had made their careers in the British colony of India. No doubt both felt the Antarctic would make a refreshing change from the sultry heat of Asia.

Captain Lawrence "Titus" Oates was a cavalry officer, whose job was to look after the expedition ponies. He seemed to have little idea of what he was letting himself in for, and described the Antarctic climate in a letter to his mother as *"healthy but inclined to be cold"*. Lieutenant Henry "Birdy" Bowers was an officer in the Royal Indian Marine. He too had never been to the Antarctic, but he had read a great deal about it.

The *Terra Nova* sailed from Cardiff on June 15, 1910. The Welsh capital was their last port in Britain, as Welsh coal merchants had offered to provide free fuel for the trip. Alongside the 67 crew were 19 ponies, 33 dogs and three motor sleds. Scott hoped that these expensive vehicles, which were then at the cutting edge of transportation technology, would make the business of setting up camps on the way to the Pole much easier. Heavily loaded with provisions for Scott's large crew, the *Terra Nova* took an age to reach its destination. During the voyage, Scott worried constantly about the welfare of his ponies, writing sentimentally about their *"sad, patient eyes"*, as they endured the long voyage in cramped stables.

The ship reached Melbourne, Australia, on October 13. Here, Scott discovered that Amundsen was also on the way to the Pole. From this moment on, Scott knew he was in a race. When Dr. Wilson learned of Amundsen's parallel attempt, he wrote in his diary: *"he will probably reach the Pole this year, earlier than we can, for not only will he travel much faster with dogs and expert ski runners than we shall with ponies, but he will be able to start earlier than we can, as we don't want to expose the ponies to any October temperatures."*

They sailed for Antarctica via New Zealand, where Taff Evans disgraced himself. Despite all his great qualities, Evans liked a drink – especially when his ship was in port. On their final stopover before the Pole, he got so drunk that he fell off the ship. Much to the relief of many of Scott's officers, who viewed such failings with distaste, Evans was fired. But he managed to talk Scott into letting him back on board, little suspecting what fate had in store for him.

It took the *Terra Nova* three weeks to make it through the pack ice. (The *Fram* managed it in a week.) The ship reached McMurdo Sound on January 2, 1911, and unloaded its cargo at Cape Evans. Almost at once, disaster struck. No sooner had one of the three motor sleds been taken off the ship than it broke though the ice and sank like a stone.

While Scott prepared for his attempt on the Pole, Amundsen was doing the same over in the Bay of Whales, 650km (400 miles) to the east. Both his and Scott's parties laid down food and fuel depots in a line heading south away from their base camps.

As the polar summer turned to autumn, Scott's team discovered that their ponies had not been a wise choice. On one exploratory trip south, seven out of eight ponies died. The ponies also needed a great deal of looking after, and had to eat hay rather than meat, unlike dogs, who would even eat each other if necessary. The dogs Scott had brought were much faster, and adapted to the freezing conditions with much greater ease. But Scott and his men were never able to train their dogs, nor master their skis, as well as their Norwegian rivals.

The winter brought an end to the laying of depots. Scott's schedule here was not entirely successful. He had intended to set down fuel and food at latitude 80°, in a spot they called One Ton Depot. But the ponies found it such a struggle that the men had to settle for a spot 50 km (30 miles) further north. As the expedition drew to its tragic end, this distance would prove to be vital. Perhaps the ponies would have done better if the men had remembered to bring special pony snowshoes called *trugers*. As it was, only one set was available, the rest having been left at the camp. By the time the stores had been laid, there were only 11 ponies left alive out of the original 19.

During the winter, the men settled into their wooden hut. It was divided down the middle, in the navy tradition, by a row of packing cases. On one side slept the officers, and on the other, the "other ranks".

The Antarctic winter passed and spring came. On October 24, 1911, Scott began his bid for the Pole. Over in the Bay of Whales, Amundsen had left four days earlier – and he had also chosen a starting point noticeably closer to the Pole.

Scott's team had problems right from the start. The motor sleds, on which Scott had spent so much of his expedition budget, set out first. They were supposed to lay down supplies along the route, but lasted a mere five days. Their engines could not cope with the extreme cold of the Antarctic. Scott himself set off with his main party on November 1. Once again the ponies proved to be a disappointment. They sank into the snow and suffered terribly in the cold. By December 9, all of them had had to be shot. The dogs were a greater success, but Scott, still uncomfortable with the idea of using them, sent them back to his base camp on December 11.

Scott's exploration and mapping of the route was far more thorough than Amundsen's, which made his progress slower. As Amundsen neared the Pole, Scott's team were still manhauling heavy sleds up the Beardmore Glacier. When they reached the top, four men returned to Cape Evans, leaving another eight men to press on, in two teams of four. The plan was that, as they neared the Pole, Scott would choose a team of just four men to make the final journey. This reduction in numbers as they grew nearer their destination was designed to ensure that they had the manpower to take sufficient supplies, but also that these supplies would only be needed by a small party on the return journey.

In 1911, radio technology was still very new, and the idea of carrying a radio set out to the Pole to keep in touch with events was unthinkable – so they could not follow Amundsen's progress. Unknown to them, or anyone else at the time, Amundsen reached the Pole on December 14. While Scott was making his final decision on who would accompany him to the Pole, Amundsen was already on his way back to the Norwegian base camp.

The decision as to who would make up the final team was eagerly awaited by the eight men on the British expedition. Scott announced that his own team would accompany him – Evans, Oates and Wilson – and that one man from the other team, "Birdy" Bowers, so-called because he had a big, beaky nose, would also come. Such were the men's intense ambitions to reach the Pole that one of the men not selected, a tough Irish sailor named Thomas Crean, wept when he was told he had not been chosen.

With hindsight, Scott's decision to take an extra man was one of his greatest mistakes, although he had good reasons. Hauling the sleds was exhausting work, which would be done more easily by five men rather than four. Bowers also had a reputation as a skilled navigator. At the time, food supplies looked plentiful. And there was a good mixture of men in the polar party – navy, army, marines, a civilian doctor and, in Evans, one of the "other ranks".

Where Scott's logic was especially faulty was that everything on the trip had been made for four people. The tents were for four, and the sleds carried rations for four. The supply dumps on the way back had also been made assuming there would be four men in the party returning from the Pole. And there was another, unforeseen, problem. One of Scott's chosen team, Taff Evans, had cut his hand, and the wound was festering rather than healing. Evans chose to conceal this injury from Scott – whether from sheer pluck and determination, or from the fear that such a disability would deprive him of a place in the final party, we shall never know. Oates too, was suffering from a wound he had sustained in the Boer War, although this was common knowledge among his companions.

Amundsen was blessed with great good luck on his polar trek, but not Scott. As his five-man team trudged on to the Pole, the fates began to conspire against them, weaving a cruel trap of misfortune and delusion from which they would never escape.

On January 16, a few miles short of their goal, they spotted a black flag in the snow. It was one of Amundsen's food store markers. This evidence of a human presence so near the Pole could only mean one thing – the Norwegians had arrived before them. They reached the Pole the next day, to be confronted by the Norwegians' silk tent. Hopeful that Amundsen might have calculated its position wrongly, they made a thorough check. With mounting disappointment, it gradually dawned on them all that Amundsen had found the exact spot.

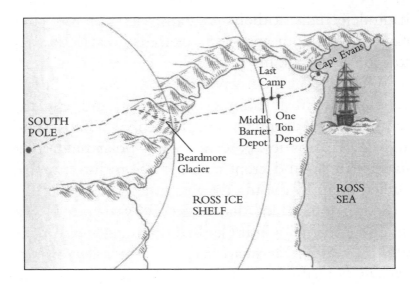

This map shows Scott's route to the South Pole.

The proud Scott was greatly offended by the note from Amundsen asking him to deliver a letter to the Norwegian monarch, King Haakon. It probably didn't occur to Scott that the Norwegians feared for their own return. Then the five men prepared for a ritual team photograph.

These shots taken at the Pole are among the most poignant images from this great era of exploration. Scott and his men pose as if for a school sports photo. Evans and Oates sit cross-legged at the front, with Bowers, Scott and Wilson standing behind them. Scott, ever mindful of his own position, is in the middle of the picture. The men's disappointment is pitifully apparent. Their bodies slump, their hands hang dejectedly at their sides, and they stare into the camera with dour and glum faces, like resentful boys forced out on a rainy picnic.

What photos such as these never convey is the cold. Adding misfortune to their disappointment, the temperature dropped considerably when they arrived. As the men posed for their polar pictures, a sharp, damp wind crept through their clothing and chilled them to the marrow.

Scott's journal of that day conveys some of his disappointment. "*Great God! This is an awful place,*" he wrote, "*and terrible enough for us to have laboured to it without the reward of priority.*" But not only was he distressed at not having got there first, more ominously he also began to worry if they would get back alive. "*I wonder if we can do it,*" he wrote.

Scott was right to worry. He was already suffering from frostbite. The weather was much colder than they had expected. They were one man more than their dwindling food and fuel supplies were intended for. Scurvy was beginning to weaken them. As a final twist, fuel containers they had left at supply depots were now showing a worrying tendency to let fuel evaporate through their frozen leather seals.

Scott's progress had been slow, but this did not stop him from permitting his party to spend half a day collecting rock samples on the Beardmore Glacier on the way back. Time they lost here would prove immensely precious later in the journey. Still, the samples they gathered were of great scientific interest, providing the first clues that Antarctica had once been covered with green forests. Fossilized ferns found among the 16kg (35lbs) of rocks they collected were very similar to ferns found in South Africa, South America, India and Australia, offering proof that Antarctica had once been part of a "supercontinent" made up of all the southern hemisphere land masses.

Much of Antarctica's icy surface is riddled with crevasses. On February 3, Evans and Scott both fell into one. As they were roped to their heavy sled, they did not fall far, and suffered no more than a nasty shock — or so it seemed at the time. Later that day, Evans' actions became particularly odd, or "*rather stupid and incapable*", as Scott recorded sternly in his diary. Given the evidence of his symptoms, it seems Evans's fall left him with serious concussion. Over the next few days, his health deteriorated terribly.

By February 16, Evans was giddy and sick. Pathetically, his ski boots kept falling off his feet, and he was forever lagging behind the rest of the men. This once indefatigable tower of strength had been slowly worn to a frazzle by his festering hand-wound and concussion. It is also likely that Evans, being by far the biggest of the men, most keenly felt the greatly reduced diet now forced upon them. On that February day, as they trudged through the snow, he collapsed. When his companions went back to collect him, they found him kneeling down, his clothing muddled, his speech slurred, and his eyes wild with fear and confusion. As they picked him up to carry him forward, he fell into a coma. He died soon after midnight the next day. The party was back to four.

All of them were now suffering from severe frostbite, but Oates was affected worst of all. His feet were so badly swollen that he had to slit his snow boots to get them on, which did nothing for the boots' ability to keep out the cold and damp. Before the trek had begun, Oates had had a rather macabre conversation with his fellow officers about the responsibility of a man in a sled party who was too weak to keep up with the rest. In the comfort of their winter quarters, Oates had said quite plainly that it was the injured man's duty to kill himself.

Now he was faced with exactly such a situation. He suggested several times that his friends should leave him behind, as he was obviously holding them up. But their own code of loyalty would not let them abandon him. Instead, one morning, after they had made camp at their Middle Barrier Depot, Oates stood up and announced: "I am just going outside and may be some time." No one stopped him as he stumbled into the blizzard outside the tent. Then there were three.

At Middle Barrier Depot, Scott made some alarming calculations. They were 90km (55 miles) from One Ton Depot, where there was enough food and fuel to ensure they would survive their journey. For now, they had supplies for another seven days. In their crippled condition they could cover no more than 10km (six miles) a day. At this rate, at the end of seven days they would have covered 70km (42 miles). They would still be 20km (13 miles) short. The sum added up to almost certain death, as Scott was all too aware. *"I doubt if we can possibly do it,"* he wrote at the time. But, he reasoned, with Oates no longer holding them up, they might still have a chance. Maybe they would have had, if the weather hadn't got worse.

On March 21, two months after the crushing disappointment of finding Amundsen had beaten them to the Pole, Scott and his two remaining companions set up their last camp. They had managed to get to a point 17.5km (11 miles) from One Ton Depot. By now, Scott's frostbite had turned to gangrene. *"Amputation is the least I can hope for,"* he wrote in his diary. And the men's luck, which had so thoroughly deserted them, was not about to turn. There was talk of Bowers, still the strongest of the three, making a go of reaching One Ton Depot to bring back food and fuel. But the blizzard that raged outside their tent blew full and furious for the next ten days. It was the final straw.

To modern eyes, Scott is not a greatly appealing character. He kept a strict distance from men who were beneath him in rank, and he was a disciplinarian whose Royal Navy training led him to insist on unbending routine and etiquette, often to the annoyance and irritation of the men he led. But in his final days, when the prospect of death was utterly certain, his dignified acceptance of his fate was deeply moving. Stuck in their tent, Scott, Bowers and Wilson knew they were going to die as surely as a condemned man knows he is to be executed. But unlike a condemned man, who usually knows when the end is coming, they could only wait for nature to take its course.

Here in the tent, the 43-year-old Scott composed twelve eloquent letters. He wrote to his family, colleagues and friends, and penned comforting words to the wives and mothers of his companions.

To the expedition backers, he wrote: "*we have been to the Pole and we shall die like gentlemen.*"

To his own wife, he wrote: "*I had looked forward to helping you bring [our son] up... Make the boy interested in natural history if you can. It is better than games.*" (She succeeded. Their son, Peter Scott, became a famous wildlife artist and conservationist.) He added, "*You know I cherish no sentimental rubbish about remarriage. When the right man comes to help you in life, you ought to be your happy self again...*" Then he wrote, with painful regret, "*What lots and lots I could tell you of this journey. What tales you would have had for the boy, but oh, what a price to pay.*"

Finally, fully aware of the great interest his demise would spark in the world, he wrote a measured explanation of his actions and their consequences in a final "*Message To The Public*". It concluded, "*Had we lived, I should have had a tale to tell of the hardihood, endurance, and courage of my companions which would have stirred the heart of every Englishman. These rough notes and our dead bodies must tell the tale…"*

He finished his journal with the words: *"It seems a pity but I do not think I can write more — R. Scott"*. The handwriting looks calm, almost unhurried, as if he were writing a leisurely postcard.

There is one final entry underneath, another sentence, this one scrawled in a noticeably more agitated hand, with little attention to punctuation or even capital letters: *"Last Entry For Gods Sake look after our people"*.

It is all too easy to imagine Scott lying starving and shivering to death in his sleeping bag, tormented by his gangrenous foot and by his failure, full of remorse for the men who were dying with him and the family he would leave behind. Perhaps, days later, he roused himself, slowly and agonizingly, to add that final message to the world with clumsy, freezing fingers.

Over the weeks that followed, the tent was half-covered by successive snow storms. Its tip was eventually spotted eight months later, on November 12, by a search team from the *Terra Nova*. Edward Atkinson, the expedition surgeon, was the first to enter. Preserved by the extreme cold, Bowers and Wilson looked as if they were sleeping peacefully. Scott, his face contorted, was twisted half-out of his sleeping bag. His had evidently not been an easy end.

His diary lay beneath his shoulders. Something everyone noted about the interior was how tidy it was. Clearly Scott's regime of ship-shape neatness had been kept up to the end.

The tent had an outer and inner layer. The search team removed the outer layer and took it with them, along with the men's journals, letters, photographic plates and rock samples. The inner layer they let fall over the three dead men, and a cairn of stones, topped by a cross made of skis, was built over the spot. Then the search team journeyed on to Middle Barrier Depot. Of Oates there was no sign, although they did find his sleeping bag.

The expedition was expected back in New Zealand in April 1913. Like the rest of the world, Kathleen Scott was ignorant of her husband's fate, and set out from England in January of that year to meet him. The *Terra Nova* carried no radio, so the crew was only able to pass on the news when they returned to New Zealand. So Kathleen Scott was aboard a ship in the Pacific when a telegraph informing her of Scott's death reached her, on February 19.

In Britain, the news was greeted with widespread disappointment and led to huge public displays of grief. The outer layer of Scott's tent was erected at the Earl's Court Exhibition Centre in London, and thousands filed silently past this canvas shrine. Reports that his expedition was £30,000 in debt led to a massive outpouring of donations, which eventually raised £75,500. Such was the surplus that, after the expenses had been paid, wages settled and funds provided for relatives, there was enough left over to form the Scott Polar Research Institute in Cambridge. There is a small public museum there now, containing, among other items, Oates's sleeping bag.

The tragedy robbed Amundsen of his victory. Eclipsed by the stoic heroism of the beaten Scott, the Norwegian was often ridiculed. When Amundsen was present at a dinner given by Britain's Royal Geographical Society, then the most prestigious scientific and exploratory organization in the world, a toast was proposed, not to Amundsen, but to the dogs who had pulled him to the Pole. The British, in their pride, could not forgive the Norwegians for reaching the Pole first, and with dogs. It seemed to them to be, in a phrase popular at the time, "unsporting".

Amundsen was to die on yet another polar escapade, this time on a flight to the Arctic to rescue the Italian airship designer Umberto Nobile (see pages 100–111) in 1928. The rest of the men with him at the Pole died in obscurity. Scott and his four companions were immortalized, despite their failure, perhaps proving the old saying that: "It's not the winning that counts, but the taking part". In their case, it had proved to be all too true.

"What the ice gets, the ice keeps"

Frank Worsley lay on his hotel bed, sleeping the unsettled slumber of a deep-water sailor away from the sea. He was in London on shore leave. It was the summer of 1914 and, all around, there was talk of war. Worsley, a born adventurer from New Zealand, who had been at sea since he was 16, sensed interesting times ahead.

As he drifted through the night, a strange dream disturbed his restless sleep. He was at the wheel of a sailing ship, but the boat was not at sea. It was slowly edging down Burlington Street, off London's famous Regent Street. All around were huge, glacial ice-blocks, and Worsley needed all his skill as a steersman to avoid them.

He woke the next morning, threw on his clothes, and hurried down to Burlington Street. There, a sign on a door reading "Imperial Trans-Antarctic Expedition" caught his eye. Worsley was immediately drawn inside, and the first person he saw was Sir Ernest Shackleton, an adventurer and polar explorer of some renown. Shackleton had been to the Antarctic twice before, with Robert Falcon Scott in 1901, and as leader of his own expedition over 1907–

1909. With both Poles now "conquered", he was planning one last, epic trip – the crossing of the entire Antarctic continent. It was a venture Shackleton described as "the largest and most striking of all journeys". An explorer by profession, he was sure it would bring him both lasting fame and financial security.

The two men struck up an instant rapport, and Worsley recalled, "The moment I set eyes on him, I knew that he was a man with whom I should be proud to work." Shackleton, who hired his crews on gut instinct, knew at once that Worsley was his sort of fellow. Worsley was taken on as captain of the expedition vessel, the *Endurance*.

Fifteen months later, the two men and their crew were stranded on an ice floe, and the *Endurance* was about to sink through the ice into the freezing waters of the Weddell Sea. They were hundreds of miles from any other humans, totally without hope of rescue in the cruellest environment on earth.

Shackleton turned to Worsley and said wistfully, "Perhaps it's a pity, skipper, that you dreamed a dream that sent you to Burlington Street that morning we met."

Worsley replied, with no hesitation, "No, I've never regretted it, and never shall, even if we don't get through."

Shackleton had that effect on his colleagues – he inspired a deep, fierce loyalty. In the terrible circumstances they now faced, he would need every ounce of his ability and charisma to hold his team together.

The Imperial Trans-Antarctic Expedition had set sail from London in August 1914 – the very month the First World War broke out. On hearing the news, Shackleton immediately offered to make his ship and crew available for the war, but received a one word reply from the British Admiralty: "Proceed". And so the *Endurance* sailed away from England, leaving a sedate, elegant world of blooming prosperity, straw boaters, brass bands and seaside promenades, which the coming war would change forever.

Aboard the ship were 29 men – a hand-picked selection of officers, seamen, scientists and craftsmen, as well as a photographer and artist. The ship's carpenter, an irascible Scot named "Chippy" McNeish, also brought his cat, known to everyone as Mrs. Chippy.

Shackleton's plan was a bold one. There had been much to learn from recent polar successes and failures, and the Imperial Trans-Antarctic Expedition intended to cross the South Pole using a team of nearly 70 sled dogs. These would haul a six-man party over the Pole. The team would set out from the Weddell Sea and head for the Ross Ice Shelf and Ross Sea. Here, another ship, the *Aurora*, would be waiting to ferry them home. As they set out from the west, a team from the *Aurora* was to lay down a series of depots on the route back to the Ross Sea – places for the sled team to replenish their supplies and rest on the way back to safety.

Shackleton fitted his chosen role of adventurer and seafarer perfectly. He exuded great determination and sense of purpose. The Shackleton family motto was "By endurance we conquer", and he did everything to live up to it. Of medium build, but solid, he had a handsome, brooding face, with a square, forceful jaw. A manly character through and through, when first shown his new-born son, Raymond, he remarked that the baby had "good fists for fighting". But formidable and forbidding though he could be, he had a generous nature and a wry wit. When presented with stowaway Pierce Blackboro, who had sneaked aboard the *Endurance* in Buenos Aires, he growled: "If we run out of food and anyone has to be eaten, you'll be the first."

Exploring was his livelihood and passion. "You cannot imagine what it is like to walk in places where no man has walked before," he once confided to his sister. But he also said, "Sometimes I think I'm no good at anything, except being away in the wilds." It was a reckless way of life that would cost him and his family dear.

By the time the *Endurance* reached the Antarctic island of South Georgia, it was November. Here, the ramshackle whaling station at Grytviken, where the bodies of whales were stripped of their oil and blubber, provided a last, superficial glimpse of civilization. The news there was that the Weddell Sea was heavy with ice, and a route through to Antarctica would not be easy. Shackleton hesitated. This was not a good omen. But, if he turned back, he might never have the chance to go again. He had already failed to reach his objective on previous polar expeditions. He was now 40 years old, and his health was not improving. He had staked everything he had on this trip. Driven by the conviction that this would be his last chance for polar glory, he set out from Grytviken on December 5, at the height of the polar summer. If the ice was bad now, it was not going to get any better.

As the *Endurance* sailed south, the crew were treated to a fantastic display of the Antarctic at its most benign and brilliant. As the ship forged a route through the half-frozen sea, they passed huge, gleaming icebergs, cut by the wind and waves into fantastic, towering sculptures. The perpetual daylight of the polar summer often cast a beautiful pink glow over these bergs and ice floes. The sea bubbled and teamed with life. Huge whales, some twice the length of the ship, would pass by, their blow holes spouting fountains of steam. As albatross and petrels circled above, lazy seals basking on the ice floes would raise a sleepy head to watch them pass. When the seals were not to be seen, penguins (the seals' main prey) would slither and waddle across the ice, croaking out to the ship as it passed. Best of all was the strange phenomenon of the ice shower, when moisture in the air would freeze into ice crystals and float slowly down in a sparkling, magical haze.

But, as Christmas approached, it became obvious that the *Endurance* was making very slow progress. On January 18, 1915, only 50km (30 miles) from the coast, ice closed in around the ship. In a single night the temperature dropped by 40°C (72°F). The crew was about to see a very different side of the Antarctic. They attacked the ice that surrounded the ship with picks, shovels and saws. But, after an entire 48 hours of digging and sawing, there was no doubt that the *Endurance* was stuck solid – "like an almond in the middle of a chocolate bar", as one member of the crew put it.

The days were changing, too. Night fell for brief but lengthening periods, and the once plentiful seals and birds that surrounded the ship were now infrequent visitors. Their animal instincts were telling them this frozen world would soon be uninhabitable, and they were heading north to warmer waters. The *Endurance*'s crew could only stay and prepare for whatever the polar winter could throw at them.

They were so close to land that the coast could sometimes even be seen from the ship. In clear water, it would have taken less than a day to reach. But Shackleton never made his frustrations known. His job was to lead his men, and he did this by projecting an apparently effortless optimism. He knew that the coming winter was going to be very difficult, but he had prepared for it well. Ever mindful of the fate of the crew of the *Belgica* (see page 42), he was determined to keep his men in good spirits. There was a generous library on the *Endurance* and, during the day, men were busied with a well-ordered routine keeping the ship in good condition. Football matches and dog sled races were also played out on the ice. The men began to forge close working relationships with their dogs, and many built elaborate ice kennels for them. Puppies were born, much to everyone's delight. In the evening there were gramophone concerts, or the men would all sing along as meteorologist Leonard Hussey played the banjo.

Shackleton had seen how Scott had bred resentment among some of his men with his authoritarian style of leadership. In contrast, Shackleton worked side-by-side with his crew, and left no one in any doubt that their lives, rather than the aims of his expedition, were his most important concern.

On the darkest day of the polar winter, June 22, there was not a fleck of light in the sky. Shackleton declared it a day of celebration. The ship's mess was decorated with flags and bunting. An improvised stage was constructed and many of the crew came forward to do a turn. Appearing dressed up as a penniless vagabond, a Methodist minister, a crazy professor, and a female flamenco dancer, the men drank and sang their way through the polar night.

Officer Lionel Greenstreet recorded in his diary: "*We laughed until the tears ran down our cheeks.*" These, clearly, were men determined not to let their fearful circumstances get them down.

The ship's crew may have been in good spirits, but the *Endurance* itself was ailing badly. The ship had been built of greenheart – an especially tough wood – but even this was not strong enough to withstand the crushing pressure of thousands of tons of pack ice pressing around the hull. This was now building up so much that the ship was being squeezed to destruction. Some polar ships had been built with hulls designed to rise above crushing pack ice. Not so with the *Endurance*. Deck planks or hull timbers would split with sudden, ferocious cracks like gunshots. Once again, the men tried to dig the ice away from the hull to ease the pressure on their ship, but it was an endless and pointless task.

In the midst of an interminable July blizzard, Shackleton confided in Captain Worsley, "The ship can't live like this, skipper. It's only a matter of time. What the ice gets, the ice keeps."

By the end of October, the *Endurance* had ceased to be a safe place to live. It had seen them through the winter, but now the order was given to abandon ship. Supplies, sleds, three of the ship's large lifeboats, the dogs, puppies and ship's cat, all were bundled overboard. Tents were set up on the ice, near to the ship. In another stroke of canny leadership,

Shackleton announced that they would draw lots to divide up the sleeping bags. The *Endurance* carried both wool and fur sleeping bags, but the fur ones were much warmer. The draw was fixed. All the officers got wool sleeping bags – almost all the men got fur.

But there were difficult decisions to be made. In their perilous circumstances, there was little room for sentimentality. Shackleton decided that the puppies and the cat would have to be shot. His decision to kill the animals was a considerable blow to the crew's shaky morale. His men were, in the main, hardened sea dogs, few of whom were married or had children. In the robust, all-male world of the *Endurance*, the puppies and cat had provided an opportunity for the crew to show a softer side. On the journey over, the cat had fallen overboard, and the ship had turned around to rescue her from the Atlantic. This time, Mrs. Chippy was not so lucky.

With the ship creaking and groaning behind him, like a huge, beleaguered animal in its death throes, Shackleton called his men together. With no trace of drama or regret, he told them plainly that the *Endurance* could no longer carry them, so now they, and their dogs and sleds, were going home. Put so plainly, it sounded like a reasonable, logical course of action. But the reality was very different. Hauling the heavy sleds was hot, sweaty, exhausting work. They made such slow progress across the ice fields that, even after three days, they could still see their ship.

Shackleton had a talent for constantly revising his objectives. Heading for safety across the frozen sea with the sleds and dogs was clearly not going to work. They returned to the ship – now a frozen, eerie hulk, its once-cozy interior covered with a veneer of ice – and rescued many of the supplies that had been left behind. Expedition photographer Frank Hurley had left many beautiful photographic plates in the ship. (Known as glass-plate negatives, these heavy, pane-of-glass sized images produced much better photographs than the recently invented photographic film.) When Hurley entered the *Endurance*'s frozen interior, he found the storage area where he'd left the plates under 1.2m (4ft) of mushy ice and water. There was nothing else to do but strip down to his underwear and dive in to get them.

On November 21, the broken, waterlogged hulk finally sank. Surrounded by the wreckage of fallen masts and rigging, the bow went down into the icy water, which could be briefly glimpsed, and the stern rose high in the air. At this point, the heavy, steel bolts which anchored the *Endurance*'s powerful steam-engine in place were wrenched out. With a terrifying sound of splintering wood, the iron engine dropped through deck partitions into the now-vertical bow, dragging the ship down to the black bottom of the Weddell Sea. It was a heart-breaking moment. Shackleton wrote in his journal: "*At 5:00pm she went down. I cannot write about it.*" For a brief while there was a small hole in the ice, but it soon closed. The *Endurance* was gone.

The crew settled uneasily into their new home on the ice. The frozen crust was 1.5m (5ft) thick, and might have given the impression they were on solid ground. But seeing the ship go down was a graphic reminder that, below them, there was a vast sea of freezing water. Still, Shackleton made every effort to keep his men cheerful, despite his own failing health. (Soon after the *Endurance* sank, a bout of sciatica forced him to spend two weeks in his tent.)

Another attempt to march north seemed to be the only thing left to do. But the ship's lifeboats each weighed at least a ton. They had to be hauled along by teams of men in harness, which was terribly difficult to do over rough ice. And, as they tried to start their long journey home yet again, Shackleton was faced with open mutiny. Chippy McNeish, still bitter about the death of his cat, refused to haul the boats. He told Shackleton his duty to him relinquished now that the ship had sunk. Shackleton knew that the only hope they had of getting back alive was to work together as a team. If McNeish was allowed to become the focus for other resentful crew members, the party would split into warring factions, and they would all be doomed. Forceful action was required. McNeish was bluntly told he would be shot if he did not obey orders.

Shackleton then called his men together. He

reassured them that they would still be paid until they reached a safe port, and explained that it was essential for everyone to work together. Finally, he announced that the hauling would stop. It was too exhausting. They would simply have to drift north with the ice, as they had been doing when the *Endurance* was still afloat, and then take to the boats when the pack began to break up.

Shackleton may have seemed forceful and in command but, that night, he was so shaken by McNeish's rebellion that he could not sleep. There were difficult decisions to make, too. With the idea of sledding north abandoned, there was no sense in continuing to feed their teams of dogs. They had enough problems keeping themselves alive on the limited supply of seals and penguins they managed to catch. Shooting the dogs was heart-wrenching, but kinder than letting them loose to starve to death in the ice. Frank Wild, the expedition second-in-command, was the executioner. He wrote in his journal: "*I have known many men I would rather shoot than the worst of the dogs. It was the worst job I have ever had in my life.*"

For four months, the men drifted on the ice. At night, they curled up in their sleeping bags and tried to gain enough warmth to sleep. They ate a monotonous diet of seal meat, supplemented by their dwindling food supplies, and prayed that they would soon reach the open sea. In early April, just as the polar summer was drawing to an end, the ice they stood on began to move with the swell of the ocean. Men began to feel seasick, but this could only mean they were nearing open water. On April 9, the boats were readied and set out to sea. They had been stranded on the ice for 14 months. Now, they were finally free – but free to do what?

The journey that followed was seven days of freezing, wet torment. 240km (150 miles) to the north lay Snow Hill Island. Although the island was uninhabited, they knew supplies had been left there to help any shipwrecked mariners. It was here they set their sights. By day, they pushed on through towering seas, while men not rowing bailed furiously to keep their open boats afloat. By night, they clambered aboard passing ice floes, to shiver in their tents. But one night there was a loud crack, and the ice split through the middle of a tent. Ernest Holness, one of the *Endurance's* stokers, fell through. He floundered in the freezing sea, trapped in his soaking sleeping bag, stunned almost to paralysis by the shock of the icy water. Shackleton ran over, thrust a hand into the gap, and pulled Holness out, bag and all. An instant later, the split closed up with a crash. From then on, the men slept in the boats.

Perhaps it was the thought that they were actually doing something, rather than just passively drifting, that kept the crew going. Their hands were so cold that they had to be chipped off the oars at the end of a shift. Dysentery swept through the boats, and everyone suffered from a raging thirst and hunger. Now, at night, the three boats were roped together to prevent them from drifting apart. But as men tried to sleep they would be disturbed by killer whales, which blew air through their blow holes "like suddenly escaping steam". The whales brushed against the boats, threatening to sever the ropes that held them together. Occasionally they would peer out of the water, presenting the crew with a huge, dark maw and sharp, white, gleaming teeth. Men wept in despair, and the threat of death hung in the air. His boats swamped and his men nearly finished, Shackleton changed his plans again. If they kept on to Snow Hill Island, they would not all reach there alive. Instead, the boats altered course for Elephant Island, which was nearer, but had no supplies.

On their seventh day at sea, the brooding cliffs of Elephant Island loomed before them. This barren slab of rock, ice and snow would have to serve as their new home. The boats forged ashore through swirling reefs and treacherous currents, and the men staggered onto the shingle beach, some delirious with joy. It was the first time any of them had stood on solid land for 497 days. They had had yet another close escape. One of Shackleton's men estimated that some of them would have died within a day if they had not landed on the island.

It had been impossible to cook at sea but, once ashore, hot drinks and food were prepared. Tents were quickly set up, and each man could feel his strength returning. But Elephant Island was not a place where anyone would wish to stay, and the men soon grew to loathe it. Aside from elephant seals (from which the island took its name) and penguins, there was almost nothing there to eat. Constant sleet, snow and rain hammered down. And the rock was not on any known shipping route, so there was still no chance of rescue. So Shackleton did the only thing he could do. He prepared to set out to an inhabited island.

There were several options open to him, all of which were terribly dangerous. The nearest inhabited land was near Cape Horn, on the tip of South America. But the wind blew constantly east on the route to the Cape, making it impossible to reach in a small boat coming from the opposite direction. An alternative destination was the island of South Georgia. It was from here that they had set off for the South Pole, in the faraway days of December, 1914. This, at least, was in the path of the wind – but it was 1,300km (800 miles) away, across one of the most dangerous oceans on earth.

Not all of them would go, of course. Shackleton decided six men would make the journey. Frank Worsley would come, and second officer Thomas Crean, who had been with Scott on his final, fatal expedition. Shackleton also took a couple of men who were known troublemakers, including the quarrelsome carpenter, Chippy McNeish. But, for all his faults, McNeish was proving to be indispensable.

He had a genius for improvisation. Such was his skill and confidence with wood that, while she was stranded, he had offered to build a smaller ship from the remains of the *Endurance*. Now he set to work on the biggest lifeboat, the *James Caird*, to make it as seaworthy as possible for the journey ahead. The gunnels (sides) were raised with wood from packing cases, and bits and pieces from the other two boats were taken to strengthen the hull. Oil paint and seal blood was used to make the new seams watertight.

Leaving the rest of the men behind with the expedition second-in-command, Frank Wild, the *James Caird* put to sea on April 24, 1916. Shackleton and his small crew watched the 21 men left behind wave them off until they were out of sight. Perhaps it was lucky they could not see that many of the men had tears streaming down their faces. Most of those on the shore were convinced they would never see the crew of the *James Caird* again.

The journey was every bit as dreadful as everyone expected. They set out in calm weather, but it soon turned stormy. Huge waves dwarfed the tiny boat, and freezing rain constantly hammered down on them. The six men took turns to row and steer and bail and sleep – four hours on, and four hours off – but there was not a single moment when they were not soaking and freezing. How they did not succumb to hypothermia or frostbite remains a mystery. Most extraordinary of all, navigator Frank Worsley was only able to take four sightings with his sextant in over two weeks at sea. For the rest of the time he steered by "dead reckoning", a sailor's term meaning guesswork and instinct.

On the 14th day of the journey, seaweed floated past the boat – a sure sign that land was near. But, as the cliffs of South Georgia began to peer over the horizon and the men could sense their troubles were nearly over, a ferocious storm blew up. Again, Frank Worsley was the hero of the hour. With extraordinary skill, he managed to steer the *James Caird* away from reefs and rocks that would have dashed the men to death. Elsewhere off South Georgia, the same storm claimed a 500-ton steamer.

On the evening of May 10, after 17 days at sea, they landed at King Haakon Bay on South Georgia. It was the wrong side of the island, 35km (22 miles) from Stromness, the nearest inhabited settlement, but it would have to do. After four days recovering from the trip, Shackleton, Worsley and Crean felt strong enough to set out for help. The boat, and the other men, were no longer in any state to take to sea, so the three of them would have to go on foot.

Between them and rescue lay a series of steep mountain peaks and glaciers – an uncharted island interior no one had ever crossed. But Shackleton was not a man to let such details bother him. After McNeish had fitted screws from the *James Caird* to their boots, to act as crude crampons, Shackleton,

Worsley and Crean set off under a luminous full moon.

The journey they made would not be repeated until 1955, and only then by experienced and fully-equipped mountain climbers. The three men waded through snow, dodging glaciers and precipices, knowing that to stop would be to risk death from exposure. High on a ridge and tiring fast in an icy wind, Shackleton took a huge, devil-may-care risk. Knowing that they would freeze to death if they stayed there much longer, he coiled his rope to make an improvised toboggan. All three sat on it, and shot down a steep snow slope to the valley below. They could have been dashed to pieces on sharp rocks, or fallen into a crevasse or over a cliff. But they didn't. Their luck held.

By daybreak, they were looking down on Fortuna Bay, near to Stromness and rescue. At seven o'clock that morning, they heard the steam whistle that signalled the start of the morning shift at the whaling station. It was their first indication of other human life since December 1914.

At three o'clock on the afternoon of May 20, 1916, three bedraggled, hairy men staggered into Stromness. They were black from the soot of their blubber stoves, stinking abominably, their clothes in tatters. They were such a terrifying sight that children ran screaming away from them. Factory manager

This map shows the progress of Shackleton's expedition
to the Antarctic, starting from Buenos Aires.

Thoralf Sörlle, who knew Shackleton well, was
summoned to meet them.

"Who on earth are you?" he demanded, when
confronted with the bizarre strangers.

One came forward and said, plainly, "My name is
Ernest Shackleton."

97

Sörlle burst into tears. These men had come back from the dead.

The wait at Elephant Island was an unimaginable ordeal. After the first month, each man would awake thinking today was the day they would be rescued. But days, weeks and months went by, and still no one came. By August, Frank Wild had reluctantly come to the conclusion that the *James Caird* had been lost. He began to plan another voyage away from their island prison. The truth, however, was more mundane. It took Shackleton three months and four attempts to get through the storms and ice, and onto Elephant Island. Eventually, he had to travel to Punta Arenas, in Chile, to obtain a boat equipped to make the journey.

On August 30, the men were preparing a meal of boiled seal backbone when a cry went up: "A ship!" Only then could anyone believe they would ever see their homes and families again. Shackleton was there on the rescue ship to greet them, barely able to speak. *"Not a man lost, and we have been through Hell,"* he wrote to his wife soon afterwards. His ambitious journey had failed. No one, in fact, would cross the Antarctic until 1958. But his other ambition – to get every single member of his crew back to safety – had been achieved against extraordinary odds.

At Stromness, Shackleton had asked Sörlle when the war had ended.

"The war is not over," he had answered, "Millions are being killed. Europe is crazy. The world is crazy."

So the crew of the *Endurance* sailed back to a dreary, war-torn country, which was indifferent to their ordeal. Heroes were dying everyday on the Western Front. Amid the barbed wire, tanks and poison gas of the trenches, adventurers like Shackleton were men out of time.

Flying and floating to the Pole

The first powered flight was made at the very beginning of the 20th century, by the Wright Brothers of Kittihawk, Ohio. Then, the outbreak of the First World War in 1914 transformed the science of aeronautics. Before the war, crude, single-engine, canvas-and-wire flying machines could barely limp across the English Channel. Yet, in 1919, only a year after the war ended, a four-engine British bomber flew across the Atlantic Ocean in an astounding 16 hours. This emerging new technology aroused great interest among polar explorers.

Reaching the Poles by air was not an entirely new idea. A Swede, Salomon Andrée, had attempted to go to the North Pole by balloon many years before. He and two companions, Knut Fraenkel and Nils Strindberg, had set off from the small island of Danskøya, off Spitsbergen, on July 11, 1897. After two years without news, it was assumed the men had perished. Only in 1930 did their fate become known, when their remains, some photographs and their diaries, were found by a Norwegian seal ship. Three days into the flight, when they had covered 830km (520 miles), the balloon crashed. Lacking any means of summoning help, the men walked south. After a gruelling three months, they reached the island of Kvitøya, where they all died.

Twenty years on from Andrée's flight, Roald Amundsen was determined to do better. The distinguished polar explorer had entered into a partnership with Lincoln Ellsworth, a wealthy American. Ellsworth, the son of a Chicago millionaire, was keen to investigate how the North Pole could be reached by air.

Their initial venture ended in near tragedy. They acquired two Dornier-Wal seaplanes to fly to the Pole. En route, the planes landed on the ice, where one of them was damaged beyond repair. The explorers, and their four crew mates, had to make an improvised runway. The remaining plane, now loaded with six people instead of three, took off, clearing the runway and an iceberg in their path by a whisker. When they returned, after 26 days away, they were greeted like men back from the dead. The narrow escape merely whetted their appetite for another attempt. This time, they thought, they would try with an airship.

In the 1920s, airships had become the most exciting prospect in aeronautics. Developed as bombers during the First World War, these flying machines were raised high into the air by bags of lighter-than-air gas, such as hydrogen, and pushed through the sky by propellers. After the war, airships began to make transoceanic flights, and were increasingly thought of as passenger liners in the sky.

At the time, the finest airships in the world were built in Italy. So Amundsen and Ellsworth approached a well-known Italian airship designer named Umberto Nobile. Rather than designing a new ship, Nobile talked them into using one he had already built, which they bought second-hand for $75,000. They also decided to take Nobile along on the flight, reasoning that the designer of the airship would be the best possible person to have around if anything went wrong. The airship was given the Norwegian registration number N-1. Amundsen and Ellsworth thought something more romantic was required for their expedition, so the craft was named *Norge*, meaning Norway.

Nobile was a small, self-important and excitable man, and he attempted to dominate the expedition. This led to much ill feeling between him and Ellsworth and Amundsen, who regarded him as a hired hand. But, as it happened, Nobile had a very useful ally in his quest for personal fame. Benito Mussolini, the fascist dictator of Italy, realized that an Italian at the Pole, in an Italian-designed flying machine, would bring his country much prestige. Nobile's flight with Amundsen and Ellsworth would be a classic opportunity for propaganda. As far as the rest of the world was concerned, the flight was known as the Amundsen-Ellsworth Expedition, but in Italy it was reported as the Amundsen-Ellsworth-

Nobile Expedition.

Amundsen and Ellsworth had another rival in their quest to reach the Pole by air: US Navy pilot Richard Byrd. In May 1926, as they prepared to set off from the Bay of Kings, in Spitsbergen, Byrd arrived with his co-pilot, Floyd Bennet. Byrd and Bennet took off shortly after midnight on May 10, returning just after four o' clock that afternoon. The Pole, they reported, had been reached. News flashed around the world, and the two men were hailed as heroes. Only after Byrd's death in 1957 did the truth about the flight come out. Byrd's records of the flight had been long disputed. Aeronautical scientists had already suspected, at best, faulty readings, at worst, fraud. After Byrd's death, Bennet confessed that his leader had just told him to fly around out of sight of land long enough for the plane to have flown to the Pole and back.

Still, said Amundsen and Ellsworth, if they could not be the first to fly to the Pole, they would be the first to get there in an airship. They took off with Nobile and their crew the very next day, May 12, just after midnight. Their intention was to fly over the Pole and then on to Alaska. By half past one in the morning, the *Norge* was indeed circling the Pole. A landing was not attempted, but the craft flew low and Norwegian, American and Italian national flags on poles, weighted to land upright and stick in the snow, were dropped from the cabin.

The occasion was marred by an unseemly dispute over the size of the flags. Nobile had specifically told Amundsen and Ellsworth that they could only bring small, bath-towel sized flags, as the weight the airship carried had to be kept to a minimum. (He had already forbidden them warm flying clothes for this reason, although he and fellow Italian crew members wore heavy fur outfits.) But, when the time came, Nobile appeared with a heavy wooden case containing a huge Italian flag, the size of a bedsheet, which dwarfed the others.

The journey away from the Pole was fraught. Ice formed on the *Norge*, including on the radio antenna, which prevented transmissions. More alarmingly, chunks of ice were flung from the propellers into the body of the airship. It seemed only a matter of time before one of the hydrogen bags that lifted the craft into the air would be pierced.

But their luck held. The *Norge* reached Alaska on May 14, where the local Inuit were amazed by the airship, which they called a flying whale. The expedition was hailed as a huge success. Amundsen, Ellsworth, Nobile and their crew had covered 4,956km (3,180 miles) in just over 70 hours.

On their return to the USA, Mussolini promoted Nobile to the rank of general, and instructed him to go on a lecture tour of the "Italian colonies" there. This was a typical piece of fascist bluster. What Mussolini meant by "colonies" were those areas of the United States where there were large numbers of

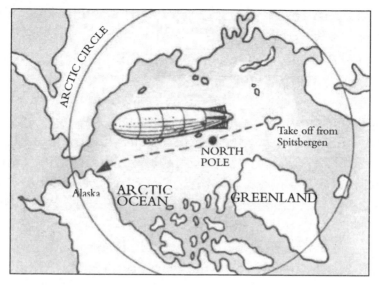

This map shows the flight of the airship *Norge*.

Italian immigrants.

Amundsen and Ellsworth greeted the American press wearing shabby, dirty clothing. Nobile had insisted that, to save weight, they should not bring any spare clothes. Again, he outraged his colleagues by appearing in a full ceremonial uniform that he had sneaked aboard. Because he was so smartly dressed, many people assumed Nobile was in charge of the expedition, and he did everything he could to claim credit for both the planning and leadership of the trip. Nobile might have built the machine that took them to the Pole and back, but Amundsen and Ellsworth must have regretted the day they ever set eyes on him.

The dispute over who was to gain the greatest

credit for the 1926 flight bothered Nobile so much that he was determined to mount his own Italian-only flight to the Pole. Another airship was procured, this one named *Italia*. In mid-May 1928, he made several successful Arctic flights around the Russian Arctic islands, with a mainly Italian crew.

Then, on May 23, Nobile and 16 comrades set off for the Pole, along with Nobile's dog, Titina, who went everywhere with him. Accompanying them as far as it was able was a support ship named the *Città di Milano*. There was little interest in this attempt, even in Italy. After all, it had already been done two years earlier. But, like the flight of Apollo 13 some four decades later, the mundane was transformed into the sensational by a hair-raising accident.

After a couple of days, the weight of ice forming on the *Italia's* huge body brought the airship down low. Around half past ten in the morning, on May 25, the control cabin struck the icy surface of the Arctic Ocean and was ripped from the rest of the airship. Freed of the extra weight, the *Italia* rose into the air, carrying off six men inside the hull to their deaths.

The remains of the craft were never recovered, but one can imagine the frantic efforts of the six on board, fumbling with increasingly freezing fingers as the craft rose higher in the sky, in an attempt to release the hydrogen and get them back to the ice pack. Perhaps the airship crashed and its gas ignited because, somewhere away from the wreck of the control cabin, a column of smoke was seen rising into the sky.

Back on the ground, the men who had been in the cabin when it was torn off were in a desperate situation. One man had been killed, Nobile had broken an arm and a leg, and another man, Natal Cecioni, also had a broken leg. All the *Italia's* crew members were aeronauts, rather than explorers, and none of them had any experience of polar conditions. Their radio was broken, and there was little hope of rescue.

The men fell into acrimonious argument. Three of them, two Italians named Mariano and Zappi, and a Swedish scientist named Finn Malmgren, decided they would walk south through the ice, to try to reach help. The rest stayed with the shattered cabin, hoping their food supplies would last.

Soon after the three men set off south, the *Italia's* radio operator succeeded in fixing his set. An SOS was repeatedly transmitted to the *Città di Milano*. The message was picked up, but when the radio operator reported it to a senior officer, he was told to ignore it. Having lost both sight and radio contact with the *Italia*, the officer was convinced no one had survived and that the message must be referring to something else. But the *Italia* crew was not totally without luck. In Archangelsk, on the northern tip of Russia's western border, the message was picked up by a radio ham (an amateur radio enthusiast).

The radio ham alerted the Russian government in

Moscow, who, in turn, got in touch with the Italian government. Six nations took part in the search to rescue the crew of the *Italia*, and 18 ships, 22 planes and 1,500 men were sent out to comb the area where the crew reported they had crashed.

On June 18, 23 days after the crash, the cabin and a red tent erected by the men were spotted by a plane. The plane was not equipped to land on ice, so it flew low over the spot, to assure the survivors they had been seen. Five days later, after a lull caused by poor weather, a small plane landed on the ice next to them.

There was only room on the plane for one other person, and Nobile suggested they take Cecioni, who was the most badly injured. But this noble gesture went awry. The Swedish pilot argued with Nobile, suggesting it would be much better for him to come himself, so he could coordinate the rescue operation. Nobile was persuaded, and hopped aboard, together with his dog, Titina. This turned out to be a public relations disaster. The newspapers wasted no time in portraying Nobile as a coward who abandoned his men to escape with his dog. Mussolini, watching the whole debacle with mounting rage, demoted Nobile from his recently acquired rank of general. The trip had turned into a national humiliation.

While all this was going on, Nobile's old companion and now resentful enemy, Amundsen, had resolved to help with the rescue too. It's not clear whether his motive was to humiliate Nobile, or whether he was prompted by genuine concern for the stranded men. But his offer to help was certainly strange in the light of hostile comments he had made about Nobile in the autobiography he had recently published.

Mussolini, sensing further humiliation, told the Norwegian government in the strongest terms that Amundsen's help was not required. But, having offered his help, Amundsen felt obliged to go. So when the French provided him with a Latham 47 seaplane, together with a pilot and crew of three, he came aboard, bringing a friend with him. As the heavily loaded plane struggled north to the Arctic town of Tromsø, it became obvious that it was not up to the journey. But French and Norwegian national pride drove the men to continue. On June 18, the day the *Italia* survivors were spotted by a Swedish plane, the Latham took off from the northern coast of Norway, and was never seen again. Amundsen and the others vanished with it.

For the survivors of the *Italia*, freezing, starving, and thoroughly miserable, there was more torment to come. The day after the first plane landed and took Nobile away, it returned with only one pilot, intent on taking the men off two at a time. But, when the plane came down to land, it flipped over on the snow, and the pilot joined the wretched men waiting for rescue. Then, over the next few days, thick fog came down, making further flying impossible. But, as more flights were being planned, a magnificent Russian icebreaker, the *Krassin*, came to the rescue. Sent toward the spot found by the aircraft, the ship reached their camp on July 12, and picked up the hapless men.

Soon after Nobile's men had been rescued by the *Krassin*, a lookout plane from the icebreaker spotted the men who had set out on foot after the *Italia* had crashed. But there were no longer three of them, only two. When they were picked up, they revealed that Malmgren was dead. Bit by bit, a squalid story emerged. Malmgren had become too weak to walk, and had asked the others to carry on without him. This they had readily agreed to do, but they had also taken his food and some of his clothing. Gossip soon spread that the two Italians had murdered the Swede so they could eat him. This too did nothing for Italian national prestige.

Further tragedy followed. An Italian seaplane sent to help in the rescue crashed on the journey home, killing its crew of three. Finally, on August 31, some remains of the French seaplane carrying Amundsen were found in the sea. A float and a fuel tank had been lashed together to construct a makeshift raft. Whoever had survived the crash into the sea had made one desperate attempt to get back south alive. The cold had defeated them. Their raft was still afloat but, perhaps one by one, too numb to hold on to their precarious platform, they had fallen off and slipped under the icy sea.

Nobile, his disgrace complete, went to live in Russia. Then he moved to the United States, and later to Spain. He eventually died in 1978, at the age of 93.

Interlude

From 1928-1992

Once almost impossibly remote, the Arctic and Antarctic are now easily accessible. The North Pole can be reached by powerful icebreakers, by submarines and by ski planes. Weather stations drift across its frozen surface. At the South Pole, there is a permanent settlement, the Scott-Amundsen Base, where huge C-130 transport planes land and take off when weather permits. The continent has 42 coastal and inland research stations.

But, despite the everyday evidence of human habitation, the Poles have remained a challenge for adventurers. As the 20th century came to an end, explorers competed to reach or cross the Poles in the most dangerous, hair-raising fashions. Where once whole teams of men would work together to reach a Pole, now they set out in ones or twos. At first, these attempts were "supported", with supplies being dropped by plane, or left along the route by others. Once this had been achieved, it became necessary to set new challenges, and some polar enthusiasts attempted to reach the Poles "unsupported".

It seems extraordinary, but less than a century after the epic journeys of Amundsen, Peary, Shackleton and Scott, one man, with a sled full of supplies, can now cross the Arctic or Antarctic entirely unaided.

Hard times at the bottom of the world

Ranulph Fiennes and Mike Stroud's 2,170km (1,350 mile) trek across the Antarctic had barely begun when Stroud fell into a crevasse. The two British adventurers were using parachute-like sails to haul them and their sledloads of equipment across the Filchner Ice Shelf, on the opening stage of their journey.

It was Fiennes who first saw the dark blue maw of the crevasse loom before them. He immediately threw himself to the ground, sliding to a bruising halt just before he reached its lip. Stroud was not so quick. As he fumbled with his sail-release cord, he heard Fiennes shout an anguished, "*Noooooooooo...*", before the ground dropped away beneath him.

In a continent devoid of man-eating wildlife, crevasses offer the single greatest threat of violent death to an unwary explorer. They are often concealed by a thin coating of snow, like a trap door, and anyone who stumbles over one can find themselves plummeting into a dark and deep ice cavern.

Fiennes's thoughts turned to what he would say to Stroud's wife and children. But fortunately Stroud had not fallen far. He had swung against the crevasse's hard ice wall and banged his head, then grabbed an icy nub before his sled caught up with him, dragging him down. He had glimpsed the terrifying depth of the crevasse as he veered over the top, and was convinced he was now falling to his death. Luckily, though, he landed on a narrow platform of hardened snow, about 6m (20ft) down, right next to his sled. On either side of him, vertical blue walls plunged down into deepening shades of darkness. The bottom of the crevasse was too far below to be seen.

As Fiennes peered over the edge, Stroud managed to cry, feebly, "I'm OK." Getting him out would not be too difficult, but the 220kg (485lb) sled was too heavy to haul up. It carried essential supplies, so they had to retrieve it or their adventure would come to a premature end.

Every time Stroud moved, snow fell away from his precarious perch. When he tried to stand up, his foot went straight through the snow. Unbalanced, he fell forward. He stretched out an arm to stop his fall, but that too broke through the snow platform. By now, the shock of the fall was beginning to wear off, and Stroud felt sick with fear. Fiennes called down, reminding Stroud that he had their long rope on his sled, and needed to throw it up to the surface. But this entailed finding it first. As he leaned over to unzip the cover on the sled, it lurched away from him, and more snow and ice fell away. Fortunately, the rope was right at the front, and Stroud managed to get hold of it and throw it up to the top. As Fiennes caught it, more pieces of ice dislodged themselves, piercing the snow platform as they fell into the depths.

Stroud's basic instinct was to get out as quickly as possible, but the only way to get the sled up to the surface was to throw up the food and equipment it held, until it was light enough to haul to the top. Feeling more confident now he was attached to a rope anchored above him, Stroud began to lob up fuel bottles, food packages and other equipment, until the sled was empty and light enough to pull up. Only then could he climb up the side of the crevasse. Once on top, he lay panting in the snow, elated but haunted by his narrow brush with death.

Sir Ranulph Twisleton-Wykeham-Fiennes ("Ran" to his friends) and Dr. Mike Stroud were attempting the first unsupported crossing of the Antarctic. It was late November 1992. In the hundred or so days ahead of them, they hoped to walk, ski and sail to the South Pole, and then carry on down the Beardmore Glacier and Ross Ice Shelf to the Scott Base on the shores of the Ross Sea. Their motives for making such an epic journey were many. Stroud, aged 37, was a medical researcher specializing in nutrition, and a survival consultant for the Ministry of Defence. He planned to take careful records of the slow deterioration of their bodies as they battled against the appalling hardships to come. Fiennes, a former Eton schoolboy and SAS army officer, was an old-fashioned professional adventurer. At 48, he was beginning to wonder if he was too old for such punishing expeditions – but, as he said at the time, "[This] is my job. It's the way I make my income." Fiennes was following in the footsteps of Peary and Shackleton. A veteran of many a hair-raising trek to the world's most dangerous locations, including several previous polar expeditions, Fiennes made a living by writing books and giving talks about his exploits. On this particular trip, the two men also hoped to raise funds for research into multiple sclerosis – every mile they walked would make huge sums of money from sponsors.

Fiennes and Stroud had been on polar expeditions together five times before. Experience told them that, as they grew frailer and more exhausted, their resolve to continue would ebb away. It was almost inevitable in conditions of such extreme hardship. On one Arctic trip, Stroud – who had been finding it hard to keep up with Fiennes – became so desperate to stop that he fantasized about killing his partner. He imagined shooting Fiennes with the gun he carried in case they were attacked by a polar bear. In the cold light of day, such murderous grudges could be seen as useful insights into the irrational thought processes of exhausted men. Such was their trust and friendship that, after the journey was over, both men could talk freely about it without animosity. But now, as they slogged through the

Antarctic, their friendship was once again about to be tested to the limit.

Part of the success of their partnership lay in the confidence each man had in the other's strengths and abilities. The two men were roughly physically equal. True, Fiennes was much taller, and also stronger, than Stroud, but he was 11 years older, and perhaps less resilient. Fiennes was a skilled navigator, with a wealth of experience and an iron determination. Stroud had an expert knowledge of the human body under stress. Both men admired the other's drive and resilience. But, as Fiennes pointed out in his account of the trip: "*If two saintly monks were to manhaul heavy loads, whilst increasingly deprived of food and subjected to mounting discomforts, they might maintain at least an outward show of mutual tolerance. If so, they would be the exception to the rule.*"

Early on, two decisions were made that would cause them dreadful hardship later in the journey. In an effort to save weight, when progress was good and the weather was mild, the two discarded rations and extra layers of warm clothing. But all too soon the wear and tear on their bodies – caused by an unholy combination of pulling heavy weights, trudging through sludgy snow, enduring the fierce ultraviolet rays of the Antarctic sun, and suffering from intense cold and fierce winds – caught up with them.

Their feet were especially vulnerable. Frostbite in their toes and fingers brought acute agony. Rubbing sores on their heels turned into blisters, which turned into festering ulcers. Halfway to the Pole, Stroud had to perform an exquisitely painful operation on his own foot, taking a scalpel to an infected abscess and draining it. They carried antibiotics to help treat such problems, but these often gave the men acute digestive trouble. In a howling gale, both would suffer the agony of churning guts for hours, until they could stand it no longer and have to unbutton their padded overalls, and squat down in the snow. Doing this, in the open, chilled their bodies to the core and carried a further risk of frostbite.

The thermos flask they used to carry their lunchtime soup soon became contaminated, inflicting additional torment on their tortured intestines. As well as being deeply unpleasant to cope with, this also meant their bodies were not digesting their limited rations properly. As the journey progressed, both men lost a third of their weight. First, their ravenous bodies used up any excess fat, which otherwise acted as insulation against the fierce cold. Then, their digestive systems began to eat into their muscles. By the time the men reached the South Pole, Stroud calculated that, on the days they walked, they were burning up 8,000 calories, but only eating 5,500.

Fiennes and Stroud were not the only people wanting to attempt an unsupporting crossing. They had a self-declared rival. At the same time as the two

British explorers were making their trip, a Norwegian named Erling Kagge had announced his intention to make the first unsupported journey alone to the Pole. The newspapers had turned this into a race. Fiennes and Stroud argued crabbily over whether or not they should reveal their own position to Kagge. To do so would be useful to the Norwegian, but not to do so would acknowledge that they felt a competitive rivalry with Kagge, which they were both uneasy about. Fiennes told Stroud that, "as expedition leader", he did not wish Kagge to know where they were. Stroud deeply resented this rank pulling – it did, after all, seem rather pompous on a two-man expedition. His festering anger turned into a blazing argument the next day, when Fiennes lagged behind him considerably as they trudged through the snow.

"I'm going as fast as I can," said Fiennes, "and I don't expect some little runt to tell me it's too slow."

Most of the journey was being made on foot, as it was often too windy, bumpy or dangerous because of crevasses to use the para-sails. Walking further drained Fiennes and Stroud's waning physical strength, and added greatly to their foot blisters and ulcers, although it did at least keep them warm. When they were able to make use of the sails, it was much quicker and used less of their energy. But because they did not have to work so hard, it was uncomfortably cold, and the sail harnesses also chafed, causing injuries to their shoulders and backs.

Christmas Day, which fell a few days before they reached the Pole, was a low point. As the two drank glutinous, luke-warm soup – which they never managed to keep hot enough to make its energy-giving high-fat content palatable – they both reflected glumly on what their own families would be eating. Fiennes presented Stroud with a huge chocolate bar as a present. Stroud, both touched and surprised by this generous gesture, wolfed it down, but also felt guilty that he had not thought to bring anything to give Fiennes.

At this stage of the journey the two men began to realize they had underestimated how much food they would need to consume. Their daily rations weren't giving them enough energy for the demands of the trip. Perpetually hungry, their bodies were breaking down their reserves of fat, and this process was producing chemicals called ketones, which make people feel both ill and depressed.

Stroud, especially, began to fantasize about faking an illness, such as a stroke, which would be serious enough to make Fiennes call off the expedition. Fiennes was despondent too, but his circumstances were different from Stroud's. As leader of the expedition, he was liable for the cost of any air rescue. He was also in serious financial trouble. Unwise investments had left him with massive debts, and, understandably, he had every reason both for wanting to finish the expedition and for avoiding additional costs.

54 days into the trip, Stroud had another bout of serious digestive trouble. Too weak to continue, he told Fiennes he had to stop to rest for a few hours. He was surprised and hurt to discover that Fiennes was actually angry with him. The two men put up their tent in strained silence. Then Stroud took some medicine and slept for several hours. He woke feeling much better, but was astonished to hear Fiennes tell him that he had decided to continue the journey alone once they'd reached the Pole.

"This is the second time we've had to stop for you," Fiennes said. "If you can't take it, I'm not going to wait for you."

Fiennes went on to say they were close enough now to be certain of reaching the Pole and, when they got there, Stroud could take a plane out with minimal expense.

Stroud was astounded, and very angry. His response seemed to shake Fiennes out of his plan. Fiennes looked ashamed, and apologized. After weeks of feeling weak, he explained, he had suddenly had a second wind. He had been unreasonably frustrated at being held back by Stroud's stomach problems.

Later, Stroud sat fuming in the tent, writing his journal. Fiennes turned to him and said, in a rare display of affection, "Mike, you're a real brick."

Just at that moment, Stroud was writing: "*Ran is a real ★★★★★*" in his journal. The journey was not halfway over, and they were in danger of seriously falling out. Yet despite their occasional arguments, both men were well aware of how their physical deterioration was contributing to their bad tempers. This enabled them to keep on good terms for most of the time.

68 days into the trip, they reached the South Pole. Here, at the Pole itself – marked, in a rather tongue-in-cheek fashion, by a large, silver bauble placed on a striped barber's pole – they met a party of American women who had walked to the Pole. It was a great joy for Fiennes and Stroud to meet and talk to other people. They set up their tent and offered tea to their new friends. Seeing their filthy, porridge-encrusted cups, the women declined, but they sat together happily, swapping stories.

Close to the Pole lay piles of packaging and spent fuel containers. There were also research and accommodation buildings, complete with all the trappings of a comfortable life: showers, hot food, books and company – all the things they longed for. But the South Pole base has a policy of not supporting independent adventurers (such expeditions, they feel, are dangerous and should not be encouraged, although they are always prepared to assist and rescue in an emergency). Besides, this was an "unsupported" attempt, and that meant no help in any way from anyone. Stroud, especially, felt quite tearful as they packed up their tent and walked away from this oasis of human habitation.

Soon after their brief stop at the Pole, they encountered a strange and unsettling phenomenon. Walking over an area of thin, flat ice, they would often plunge 15cm (6 inches) down to another layer beneath. It was unsettling, because it felt like the start of a fall into a crevasse. Sometimes, triggered by their footsteps, the ice in a large area around them would break up and drop down to the layer below. When this happened, it made a colossal noise, like a jet plane approaching.

Fiennes and Stroud plodded on through a stretch of their journey that seemed to be permanently uphill. They were demoralized to hear that, when news of their reaching the Pole had been announced, they had been mocked by a couple of British newspapers. Articles had put forward the idea that, with modern clothing, equipment and communications, polar exploration was now all too easy, belittling the suffering they had been through. Both men felt indignant about this. It was true that their sleds were made of a combination of metal and plastics, making them lighter and stronger than Scott and Shackleton's wooden ones, but the men were probably just as hungry and exhausted as their predecessors. Their synthetic-fabric clothing might have been lighter than the furs and natural fabrics worn earlier in the century, but these modern clothes were not necessarily warmer.

Their one indisputable advantage was that they carried the latest hi-tech navigation aids. Although their satellite locator device would frequently bleep and whirr for several minutes before declaring "ERROR", and have to be reset, when it did work, it gave them their exact position. Both men, though, were wounded by the common misconception that, if disaster struck, they could be rescued in a flash. True, they could summon help. But, if the weather was bad, they might have to wait a week or more before a plane could fly out to look for them. Besides, as Mike Stroud had already discovered, a crevasse could claim him just as easily as it could a Scott, Wilson or Oates.

The second half of the journey was possibly even worse than the first. As January passed, the coming Antarctic winter began to take a hold. As colder, stormier weather became more frequent, their chances of a prompt emergency air rescue also became more unlikely. Fiennes's foot grew worse, but he gritted his teeth and tried to forget this nagging pain. Stroud lost both his ski sticks, so Fiennes generously gave him one of his.

Then, 81 days into the journey, Stroud, already weakened, fell and fractured his ankle, adding greatly to the pain he felt in his feet. This additional handicap led to arguments with Fiennes. It might seem heartless to berate a man with a damaged ankle for not keeping up, especially as Stroud had led the way for much of the journey. Yet Fiennes's frustration was understandable. Stopping for up to 10 minutes to allow Stroud to catch up, Fiennes would be literally freezing to death by the time he could begin walking again and start to feel warmer.

By now, both men were bags of bones. Stroud noted: "*My bed is getting bonier every night*".When they rested, sleep was difficult to find. Frost-bitten hands and feet, frozen numb during the day, would thaw and ache, painfully and insistently. Stroud's hands were so raw that he could not bear the thought of taking his gloves on and off. Fiennes had such a badly frost-bitten left foot that his toes had merged into one grotesque, black, fluid-filled bag, from which oozed a repulsive, stinking liquid. Afterwards he wrote that, when his feet were like that, he would rather have been tortured by the Gestapo (the Nazi secret police) than have to put on his boots.

Nonetheless, they battled on through the Beardmore Glacier. Now starvation began to take hold, and both men fantasized wildly about food. Each night in the tent, each would eye the other warily, to make sure neither got a mouthful more than the other – a situation that could easily have led to more arguments. But, in a commendable display of manners and courtesy, they took turns in strict rotation, to lick the spoon and mug of every last scrap of food.

On day 91, shortly after Fiennes had fallen up to his chest through a snow-covered crevasse, they eventually reached the Ross Ice Shelf. Now they could claim to have crossed the Antarctic continent.

But the ocean itself, beyond this stretch of sea ice, was still 580km (360 miles) further north. They pressed on, intending to complete their route to the Scott Base. But then Stroud began to suffer from delirium, the effect of severe hypothermia, and Fiennes's rotting, frost-bitten feet were causing him constant agony. It was time to call it a day. They were 96 days into their trip, and only 400km (250 miles) short of their final intended destination.

Fiennes set up their tent and called up a rescue plane on his radio. They were lucky with the weather and were told to expect to be picked within a few hours. Now their supplies no longer needed to last, they ate like there was no tomorrow. Waiting for their plane, Stroud ate 12 chocolate bars in three hours.

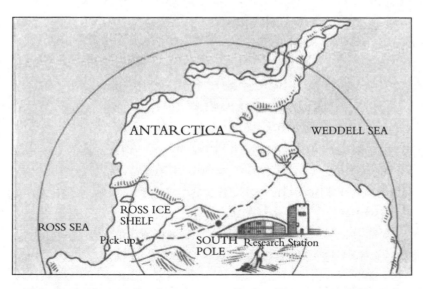

This map shows the journey made by Fiennes and Stroud.

Afterwards, Fiennes reckoned that, had they continued, they would both have died somewhere on the Ross Ice Shelf. In the days that followed, their bodies succumbed to extreme exhaustion. Their limbs swelled to grotesque proportions, and they had to be helped on and off planes. When they didn't sleep, they ate. Back in England, in the weeks after his return, Fiennes would have muesli, sugar puffs, toast and eggs for breakfast, and then eat five doughnuts with coffee an hour later.

Both Fiennes and Stroud wrote books about their extraordinary adventure. Neither made any secret of their animosities and arguments. These accounts leave readers in no doubt that both men felt considerable anger towards the other at certain times during the journey, though there is also a deep sense of regret at the way they behaved with each other. But explorers have argued their way across both frozen Poles. Even that most amiable and likeable explorer, Sir Ernest Shackleton, threatened Captain Robert Scott with violence, and once hit a crewmate until he did as he was told. Stroud and Fiennes were immensely courageous in their determination to carry on through extreme suffering. Perhaps it's surprising they didn't quarrel more.

Stroud and Fiennes both finish their books on a conciliatory note. Stroud writes that some of Fiennes's conduct *"made me spit"*. But he also said that he would gladly go with him on another expedition.

Fiennes might have compared Stroud to "*a crotchety old woman*", but he also spoke openly of his admiration for his colleague, and quoted Captain Oates: "*when a man is having a hard time he says hard things about other people which he would regret afterwards.*" Today, the two men are still good friends and, since their Antarctic expedition, have made another trip together in the Canadian Rockies.

Been there,
done that...

At the dawn of the 21st century, the polar regions had little left to offer the world's elite band of professional adventurers. Interviewed in the literary magazine *January*, in October, 2001, Sir Ranulph Fiennes was asked if he would visit the Poles again. He sighed and said regretfully, "I'm not planning polar expeditions because they've all been done; every single one of them has been done... the only [challenges] left are gimmicky: you have to go by camel or motorbike or something to be first. So the genuine firsts – supported and unsupported – are all now done."

The taker of many of these records is an ex-Norwegian Army commando and deep-sea diver named Børge Ousland. Now a professional guide who takes tourists on planes to the North Pole, he managed to accomplish with ease polar feats which would leave his early 20th-century predecessors open-mouthed with astonishment. But it was not all plain sailing. To do what Ousland did still required a character every bit as courageous and determined as those who came before him.

Ousland's first serious bid for polar fame occurred

in 1990, when he set off with Geir Randby and Erling Kagge from Ward Hunt Island, on the north coast of Ellesmere Island, on an unsupported trip to the North Pole. Nine days into the journey, Randby injured his back and a plane was called to fetch him. Despite successfully reaching the Pole, Ousland and Kagge found their achievement was not accepted by many fellow adventurers, as they had had some help – the airlift of their injured colleague.

Ousland settled the matter spectacularly when he set off on his own from Cape Arktichesky, Severnaya Zemlya, on March 2, 1994. Starting each day before dawn, his heavy sled tied behind him, he would head through the fractured ice of the Arctic Ocean. Alone in a vast white canvas, the only sound he would usually hear would be the squeaking of his sled on the ice, his own muffled breathing, or the howl of the polar wind. In the first days of his journey, he was particularly struck by the beauty of his surroundings. The clear, frosty air and sunshine on the ice, snow and water create a special kind of light unique to the North Pole.

As the journey progressed, Ousland established a rhythm: one and a half hours walking, then a rest for food and water. Despite the extreme cold, which caused icicles to form in his beard and pearls of frost to line his eyelashes, he felt warm enough in his bright red waterproof overalls. Sometimes, his path was impeded by enormous leads (gaps in the ice), and his journey became like a foray through a giant maze,

131

with endless detours to find a safe way through. But Ousland's strength and luck held. By April 22, he had reached the Pole – the first successful, unsupported solo attempt.

Over in the Antarctic, the final challenges were also falling fast. In 1993, Ousland's Arctic colleague Erling Kagge had made the first unsupported solo journey to the South Pole (see also page 120). With time and opportunity running out, Ousland decided to try for an unsupported solo crossing. His first attempt, in 1995, ended in frostbite and failure, but he was back within a year. On his 1996 journey, he faced stiff competition from two other polar adventurers – Ranulph Fiennes and a Polish explorer, Marek Kaminski. Both were intending to do the same thing – although in the end they proved to be no competition at all. Fiennes fell victim to kidney stones and had to be evacuated, and Kaminski injured himself in an accident and stopped once he had reached the Pole.

Ousland set out on skis from Berkner Island on the Weddell Sea on November 15, with a 180kg (400lb) sled and a parachute-like sail. The sail was a phenomenal success. With a smooth surface and a good wind, he once covered 226km (140 miles) in a single day. But Ousland had to keep his senses about him. Temperatures dropped as low as -55°C (-67°F) and, when the weather was bad, the sky seemed to be enveloped in a sheet of white. There was no horizon and forward visibility was severely limited. Ahead lay crevasses and fragile snow bridges, which Ousland called "potential trap-doors into the abyss". It would be all too easy to fall in and vanish forever.

But on good days the sun shone, bringing a frosty glow to the strangely stark landscape. Much of Ousland's success lay in his positive attitude. He decided from the start that he would try to seek as much beauty as he could from his surroundings. "*I had two alternatives,*" he wrote. "*I could look about me and say that it was white, deserted, exhausting and wretchedly dull. Or I could invert it into something new and positive; seek out the beauty in nature, the changes in light, shapes and colours.*" As he trudged along, he listened to music. His personal stereo played a selection of songs by Jimi Hendrix, ZZ Top and Tom Petty: driving, strutting rock, or "something that will keep you going", as Ousland described it. Good days like this filled him with euphoria.

He reached the South Pole on December 19. Here were the white domes and buildings of the Amundsen-Scott Station. He knew, of course, that the station was famous for giving a frosty reception to adventurers like himself. This suited him down to the ground. He was desperate for human company, warmth, a shower and other ordinary 20th-century creature comforts. His diet of freeze-dried meat, porridge and other basic foods was boring him intensely. But he knew if any hospitality was offered to him, he might decide then and there to end his journey. He would also no longer be able to claim he had made an unsupported trip.

From the Pole, he followed Amundsen's route down the Axel Heiberg Glacier. During this section of his journey, Christmas Day fell. The weather had closed in around him, with storms and gales shaking his tent. But he was determined to make Christmas special. Well-prepared, he had brought a traditional Norwegian Christmas dinner: smoked and salted lamb, and a small almond cake. He had even brought presents and cards with him, carefully stashed in his sled.

Then, he crossed over the Ross Ice Shelf and headed for the Scott Base at McMurdo Sound. As he approached the end of his journey, the sun shone benignly, and a gentle breeze blew towards him. Around 20km (12 miles) from the end, he realized he could smell the sea. Then, he saw a speck on the horizon – a plane was taking off from the airbase there. The nearer he got, the more he became aware of human activity: there was a whiff of exhaust, and the hum of generators, and then buildings came into view.

Ousland wondered what sort of reception he would get from the people on the base. As he walked across the airfield, he came upon a mechanic working on a fire engine. The man looked up, then just ignored him. After all the isolation of his journey, Ousland felt crushed.

"You are the first person I have seen since the South Pole," he told him.

Now the mechanic looked astounded. It was January 17, 1997. Ousland's astonishing 2,840km (1,775 mile) journey had taken him only 64 days.

Other Arctic records came and went. In February 2000, two Norwegians, Rune Gjeldnes and Toré Larsen, made a complete, unsupported crossing of the Arctic Ocean via the North Pole. There was only one more record left to break — unsupported and solo — and it was Børge Ousland who was determined to do it. Starting off again at Cape Arktichesky on March 3, 2001, he stood on its barren, wind-battered cliffs, staring at the forbidding Arctic Ocean. Right by the coast, huge chunks of ice crashed into each other, tossed by titanic currents and winds. In areas where ice had packed together, the ocean would open and close into huge leads, almost as if it had a life of its own.

Ousland set out, retracing the steps he'd taken seven years previously. For this journey, he took an inflatable drysuit, to allow him to cross open leads in the ice. Especially designed for lethally cold water, the watertight suit kept a layer of air between the wearer and the water, both protecting him from the cold and allowing him to float easily, dragging his supplies behind him. As ever, Ousland's equipment was carefully chosen. His sled contained 166kg (365lb) of food and fuel. He carried a mobile phone, a Global Positioning System (GPS) satellite navigation device, and a sail. On a good day, he could sail through the ice for maybe ten hours. But the sail also spelled potential disaster. At speed, a fall could mean a broken arm or leg and an abrupt end to his journey.

Right from the start, Ousland knew he was facing a terrible ordeal. He described his skiing, walking and swimming journey as "a triathlon from hell". Before him lay 1,996km (1,240 miles) of broken ice and water. The Arctic, he recalled, was so much more forbidding than the Antarctic, because you were never on solid ground. On ice, he could never be entirely certain of his surroundings, and knew that he could fall through into freezing water at any point.

Almost at once, he encountered a problem that was so basic he felt embarrassed about it. That night, as he made camp and began to prepare an evening meal, he realized there was no fresh water to drink or cook with. He was surrounded by frozen water, but it was *seawater*, so all of it was salty. Ousland had expected to find snow, which when melted becomes fresh water, but none had fallen for several days. He retired to his tent that night with a raging thirst, knowing he had to find drinking water the next morning.

During the dead of night, he was woken by the terrifying sound of moving sea ice. All around him, the ice piled high in layers around his camp site, grinding and cracking as floe piled upon floe.

Expecting to be crushed at any moment, Ousland piled all his essentials, his emergency beacon and cooking equipment into his sleeping bag. As the ice edged closer, he thought he would have to pick up his belongings and run. But, as day began to break, the moving ice subsided, and an eerie calm descended on the camp site.

With darkness fading, Ousland could see that his entire surroundings had changed. Only a space around his camp site, about 10 x 15m (30 x 50ft), remained untouched. His luck held, for in the bright morning light he could see ice crystals glistening on the surrounding ice blocks. He tasted them, and was delighted to discover they were pure water. He spent an hour gingerly collecting the frozen morning dew, until he had enough to fill a cooking pot.

For the next week, Ousland battled through compacted walls of iron-hard ice. It was heavy going and exhausting work. Battered by the rough terrain, his sled cracked. He tried to repair it, drilling 262 holes in the side and sewing the cracks together, but his best efforts failed. There was nothing to do but call for assistance. A new sled arrived by helicopter. Watching the helicopter prepare to take off was one of the worst moments of the trip. Ousland desperately wanted to join the crew and return to warmth and human company. It was several days before his resolve and morale returned to normal.

But, amid all the struggle, there was still time to

admire his harsh environment. As evening fell, the sky turned from deep blue to black. In the clear polar air, the stars came out to twinkle with an unaccustomed brightness. As night fell, a frosty mist rose from surrounding leads of dark water. When the Northern Lights played in the night sky, the whole scene had an unreal, hallucinogenic magic about it.

Ousland battled on through fierce winds and fractured ice, finally arriving at the Pole on April 23. After six weeks alone, he was confronted by the sight of a party of tourists flown in for the day, including an Arab man dressed, rather incongruously, in full national costume. The tour leaders, two esteemed polar explorers named Mikhail Malakhov and Richard Weber, offered him a warming meal of chilli con carne, which Ousland was delighted to accept.

Reaching the Pole meant Ousland was more than halfway through his journey, for it lies approximately three-fifths of the way between Severnaya Zemlya and his destination, Ellesmere Island. The rest of the journey went smoothly enough. Ousland reached Ward Hunt Island, just off the north coast of Ellesmere Island, on May 23. He had covered 1,996km (1,250 miles) in just 82 days. Waiting to greet him with a bottle of champagne were his girlfriend and his mother, forewarned by mobile phone. Ousland was fit and well, but he had lost around 23kg (50lb) in weight. He might have had a little help along the way, but he had succeeded in completing a remarkable solo journey.

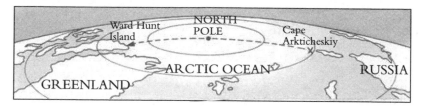

This map shows Ousland's trans-Arctic crossing of 2001, from Cape Arkticheskiy to Ward Hunt Island.

Today, it really does seem that there are no more genuine "firsts" left for the Poles – and, until someone walks there backwards with their eyes shut, or stark naked and carrying a giant panda, it is difficult to imagine the world's media taking much of an interest in any further polar adventures.

Fantastic leaps in technology over the last century mean that it is no longer remarkable for human beings to explore these once forbidding, bleak and beautiful places. Dependable air travel can now place people at either Pole, and radio communication can keep them in touch with the outside world. At the South Pole, buildings made of strong, lightweight materials enable researchers to live in a reasonable degree of comfort and security. But, despite this, the Poles are still the same unforgiving, lethally hostile environments they always were. All of which makes the courage and determination of the explorers and adventurers who have risked their lives to go there all the more extraordinary.

Glossary

This glossary explains some of the specialized words used in this book. Words which appear in *italics* are defined elsewhere in the glossary.

Antarctica *Also known as the* **Antarctic**. Huge frozen continent at the bottom of the world.

Antarctic circle An imaginary circle around the earth on a map, at *latitude* 66° south.

Arctic Huge frozen ocean at the top of the world.

Arctic circle An imaginary circle around the earth on a map, at *latitude* 66° north.

Aurora australis *Also known as the* **Southern Lights**. Bands of green, red or yellow light seen in the sky in the *Antarctic*.

Aurora borealis *Also known as the* **Northern Lights**. Bands of green, red or yellow light seen in the sky in the *Arctic*.

Blizzard An extreme snowstorm.

Chronometer A timepiece designed to be extremely accurate, and used as a navigation instrument at sea.

Crevasse A deep crack or hole in thick ice, especially in a glacier.

Eskimo An old-fashioned word for the people who live in the *Arctic*.

Frostbite A dangerous medical condition where parts of the body become frozen and can be irreparably damaged.

Glacier A large river of ice, usually flowing down from a mountain.

Iceberg A large chunk of ice floating in the sea, which has broken away from a glacier or iceshelf.

Ice cap A huge layer of very thick ice, which covers a vast landmass, such as Greenland or *Antarctica*.

Ice floe A free-floating block of flat ice in the sea.

Ice shelf A layer of thick ice attached to a large bay.

Inuit Modern name for people who live in the Northern Polar region, especially the native people of Canada and Greenland. Inuit is used for the plural, and Inuk for the singular.

Kayak A small *Inuit* canoe made from animal bones and skin.

Latitude Horizontal lines on a map which divide the world. The *North Pole* is at latitude 90° north and the *South Pole* is at latitude 90° south.

Longitude Vertical lines on a map which divide the world. All lines of longitude meet up at the *North* and *South Poles*.

Manhauling Pulling sleds without the aid of animals or windpower.

North Pole The northernmost point on earth.

Northeast passage A route from Europe to China and Japan, via the north coast of Russia.

Northern Lights *See Aurora Borealis.*

Northwest passage A route from Europe to China and Japan, via the north coast of North America.

Pemmican Dried meat or fish mixed with fat, vegetables and cereals to make a highly nutritious, hard, cake-like bar.

Scurvy A disease caused by lack of Vitamin C, with symptoms including extreme fatigue, bleeding and ulcers.

South Pole The southernmost point on earth.

Southern Lights *See Aurora Australis.*

Specimen An item collected for the purpose of medical or scientific study.

Supported crossing In the sense used in this book, a journey across either Pole, undertaken with assistance, for example, food being left en route by plane.

Unsupported crossing In the sense used in this book, a journey across either Pole, undertaken without any assistance.

TRUE
DESERT
ADVENTURES

Gill Harvey

CONTENTS

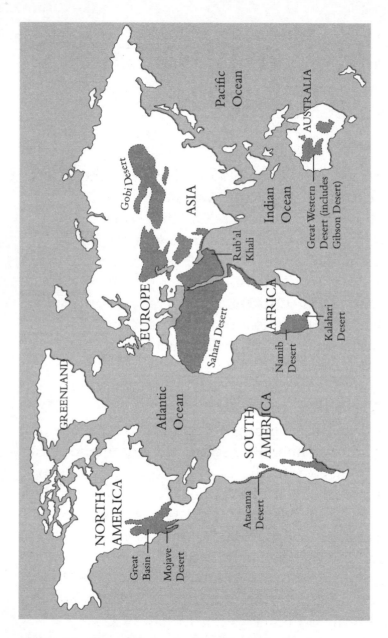

This map shows the main deserts of the world (marked by the dark shaded areas).

Life and death in the desert

Deserts are dangerous places. Wild and inhospitable, their extreme temperatures push human endurance to its limits, while their endless sand dunes and rocky plains make it incredibly difficult to navigate. But the greatest danger they pose is this: they are the driest places on earth. They suck water out of everything like a dry, hungry sponge. A desert is an area where less than 10cm (4 inches) of rain falls each year. That's very little indeed – so little that only the toughest, most specialized plants and animals can survive. So for humans, not only is there nothing to drink, but there's very little to eat, too.

It's true some groups of people have made the deserts their home, and have developed the necessary skills to survive. In the Sahara and Arabian Deserts, tribes of nomads lead a footloose lifestyle with their flocks of hardy sheep and goats, constantly on the move to find enough to live on. They know all the oases and wells, and can find their way even when the wind shifts the patterns of the dunes. But they've been doing this for thousands of years. Everyone else would really do much better to stay away...

Deserts take up a fifth of the world's land surface. The biggest of them all, the Sahara, covers a third of

Africa – an area roughly the size of the United States. It is also one of the hottest places on earth, with temperatures soaring as high as 58°C (136°F). The record for the driest place, though, goes to the Atacama Desert, in Chile, which can go for years without getting any rain at all.

Deserts are more varied than you might think; they're not all sandy and they're not all scorchingly hot. The Gobi Desert in Asia, for example, is classified as a 'cold desert'. Although it's hot in summer, in winter temperatures drop dramatically to well below freezing, bringing icy winds and even snow.

Despite the dangers, deserts still hold a romantic fascination, and people have ventured into them time and time again, often relatively unprepared. Deserts may be stunningly beautiful, but the attraction is more than that. Until recently, they were among the last great challenges for the adventurer, the last places on earth to be explored and mapped.

The stories in this book are about people who, for a variety of reasons, risked their lives in the world's driest places. For them, the desert may have been a challenge, a place that holds hidden secrets, or simply an obstacle to be crossed. Their adventures began when they stepped out of their own world, into the unknown. Their tales are of hardship, thirst and desperation, mixed with wonder and discovery. But, above all, they show that the perils of the desert have to be taken seriously. A harsh fate awaits anyone who dares to think otherwise...

Two men
and a dog

The world, it seemed, was going crazy. It was 1940, just after the outbreak of the Second World War, and the German army was marching across Europe. Far away in Africa, two Germans, Henno Martin and Hermann Korn, listened to the news on their radio with growing horror. The war's long tentacles could be felt even in Windhoek, the capital of Namibia, where they lived. Germans were being rounded up, in case they were Nazis, and were being locked away in internment camps. Their turn would come soon…

They sat on their porch one evening, thinking hard. They were geologists, and wanted nothing to do with a bloody, senseless war. They didn't like the idea of being locked up just because they were German, either.

"You know what we could do," said Hermann in a low voice.

"What?" asked Henno curiously.

"We always said that if a war came, we'd hide in the desert."

Henno stared at him. It was true – they had said that once, as a joke. But could they really do it? They had no idea how long the war would last. It might go on for years.

"What about Otto?" asked Henno.

"Otto?" Hermann looked at their dog, who was gazing at them, as always, with wagging tail and shining eyes. "We'll take him with us, of course."

On all their trips into the desert, Otto had been their faithful companion. There was no reason to change that now. Quickly, they made up their minds. They would load up their truck – and go. The Namib Desert offered plenty of places to hide. They would trust their luck to the wilds, until the war was over.

In four days, they had gathered together everything they needed. They could take basic foodstuffs with them – dried and canned food, tea, coffee, sugar and jam. To these they added a few luxuries such as chocolate and brandy. They took some kitchen equipment – sharp knives and a frying pan. They needed sleeping bags, a tarpaulin, and a few clothes; they added sewing equipment and a first aid kit. For the truck, they needed plenty of fuel, spare parts and tools. What else?

"My violin," said Hermann firmly. "I'm not leaving that behind."

Most important of all, however, was their radio and their guns. The radio would give them essential news of the outside world, and the progress of the war. It would run on the truck's battery, and let them know when it was safe to emerge from the desert. The guns were their lifeline. Their stores of food would have to be carefully rationed, and wouldn't be enough to live on. If they were going to survive, they would have to hunt. Rifles would have been best for hunting, but all rifles had been confiscated at the beginning of the war. They had only a shotgun and a pistol – not ideal, but these would have to do.

With the truck loaded, they set off along a route they knew would be difficult to trace. Not many white people knew the desert as well as they did. They set course for a secret canyon in the heart of the Namib Desert.

The Namib Desert stretches down the western edge of Namibia, a long strip of land that borders on the sea. The northern section of this coast is known as the Skeleton Coast. It is named after the victims of shipwrecks in the past – those who were lucky enough to reach the shore found no water or food to keep them alive; they would simply die in the merciless desert.

Part of the desert consists of some of the most spectacular sand dunes in the world, which rise and fall in shades of deep rust and orange. These offered little shelter or life for the two runaways, but there are other areas where the desert is rocky and rutted with deep canyons. Here, there are waterholes – and where there is water, there is life.

Taking a treacherous route with their truck, Henno and Hermann made their way to the top of the Kuisib canyon. Here, they stopped and surveyed the view – a wild, desolate landscape of jutting rocks and deep gorges, sheer cliffs and, far below, the sandy bed of the canyon.

"They won't find us here," Hermann remarked.

It was a relief to realize this, but also slightly frightening. This was a total wilderness, where even the hardiest animals struggled to survive. How could they be sure they would manage it?

It was too late to turn back. Leaving the truck at the top of the cliffs, the men followed a zebra track into the canyon, looking for water and a place to live. The riverbed was dry – there had been no rain that year. But there were still enough waterholes. To their delight, one of them contained fish – fat, healthy carp. They drove one into the corner of the muddy pool, where Hermann managed to grab it with his bare hands. Their first catch! They immediately lit a fire, and cooked and ate it.

They continued through the canyon until they came to a kind of cave, an overhanging rock that provided ample shelter. They decided that this would be their home. Over the next two days, they moved supplies from their truck, and made the cave as comfortable as they could. Then they hid the truck under an overhanging cliff so that it wouldn't be visible from the air.

They were feeling desperately hungry. They had eaten some of their pasta supplies, but they dared not eat more. They allowed themselves a cup of flour each day for breakfast, mixed with water, along with a spoonful of jam. There was nothing else to do: they had to find more food.

The obvious solution was to catch more fish, but this was easier said than done. The luck of their first day wasn't repeated. They made fishing hooks with wire, but all they caught were frogs. With their stomachs rumbling, they decided to go hunting. The fight for survival had begun.

On their way into the canyon, they had spotted the tracks of some wild cattle – a bull, a cow and a calf. To their delight, they soon stumbled upon the bull, grazing on the floor of the canyon. But how could they get close enough to shoot?

"I'll go back this way with Otto and the shotgun," said Henno. "You go ahead with the pistol. My scent will drive him in your direction."

It was a good idea. Henno set off carefully, not wanting to disturb the massive creature. He crept closer, and closer… and then the bull looked up. He saw Henno, and charged. Henno fired the shotgun straight at the bull's face. It still kept coming. At the last minute, Henno leapt up onto a rocky ledge, out of its way. The bull glared at him. The small shotgun pellets (generally used only for small game such as birds) had barely scratched him.

But now Hermann ran up and fired his pistol. The bullet hit the bull behind the ear, and the huge animal dropped to the ground like a stone.

"Is he dead?" gasped Hermann.

Henno threw a stone at its head, just to be sure. Immediately, the bull got back to his feet – very much alive! Now Otto, wildly excited, threw himself at the bull and grasped his nose. Hermann stepped closer, and shot the bull in the forehead. It had no effect. The bull simply tossed his head, throwing Otto into the air as he did so.

Otto got to his feet again, but now he was whimpering. Hunting wasn't as much fun as he'd expected. Hermann shot the bull once more behind the ear. As before, this stunned him and he dropped to the ground again – only to get up when he'd recovered.

He was definitely weaker now, only able to glare at the men balefully. They felt slightly sick. They were out of pistol bullets, because they had not expected this to be such a gruesome, long-winded battle.

"We'll have to go and get more bullets," said Hermann. "And work out how to finish him off."

Henno nodded. "We should bring our sleeping bags, too, and anything else we'll need. He's too big to carry up to the cave. We'll have to stay here until we've eaten him."

So they scrambled back to their home, bringing back knives, ropes, a frying pan and other essentials. The bull was now lying down, but scrambled to his feet and charged again as they approached. Two more bullets still didn't kill him. They knew they should aim for his heart. "*But where exactly was the heart in that enormous body?"* wrote Henno later. *"Neither Hermann nor I had ever slaughtered an ox and we had no idea… By this time Hermann and I were both quite shaken. It was a shocking business and our inability to end it made us feel ashamed."*

Eventually, they had the idea of slinging a rope around the bull's horns and tying the rope to a tree, so that he couldn't move. Then, with great relief, they slit his throat.

They gorged themselves on meat that night. But now came the task of preserving the rest of the carcass. It would quickly go bad in the hot sun. So they carved it up, discovering as they did so that none of their bullets had actually gone through the creature's tough skull. They cut part of the flesh into thin strips to dry, making *biltong*, as it is called throughout southern Africa. The rest had to be smoked over a slow-burning fire. It was a tricky technique to master; the men had to make several attempts before they got it right. And then it was wild bull for breakfast, lunch and dinner for many, many days to come.

Killing the bull was their first major encounter with the difficulties of hunting. They quickly learned that it was a cruel, desperate way to live. With their own limited resources, they had to think first of their own needs, and could not afford any kindness. Frequently, their bullets only wounded an animal, and they would have to trail it for hours to finish it off. Often it got away altogether. When it was injured badly enough, they would simply have to wait for it to weaken and lie down. They could not waste their precious bullets on giving it a quick, clean death.

The constant diet of meat rapidly became tiresome, and they worked on new ways of catching the carp in the waterhole. Eventually they hit upon the ingenious idea of making a net with tamarisk branches and pairs of underpants, which they then trawled through the water between them. It worked – and for a while, they had plenty of fish suppers.

But the waterhole was gradually drying up. This source of food would clearly not last forever. What was more, they realized that someone was sharing it with them. The carp were being attacked in the night. Footprints revealed the culprit – a hyena.

A hyena

Henno was furious. "I'm not letting him get away with this!" he announced. "I'm going to lie in wait for him and shoot him."

"Don't be silly," said Hermann. "If you're anywhere near, he'll smell you. And anyway, you won't be able to shoot him in the dark."

But Henno was determined. He took his sleeping bag to the waterhole and settled down to wait.

On the first night, nothing happened. Henno returned to the cave empty-handed in the morning, and Hermann greeted him with an amused smile and a cup of coffee. He clearly didn't think that his friend would try again. But Henno, annoyed at his attitude, took up guard again the next night.

He was just dozing off when he heard the bloodcurdling howl of the hyena, close at hand. He reached for the shotgun as the hyena continued to screech and cackle. It was terrible; no other animal in the desert makes a sound anything like it. But it was just what Henno needed. Even though he couldn't see the beast, he simply aimed in the general direction of the noise. To his glee, the howling stopped and an injured yelping took its place.

"Got it!" he thought and, curling over in his sleeping bag, he slept soundly until morning.

By daylight, he got up and surveyed the scene. There was strange-looking trail, which suggested that the hyena could no longer use its hind legs. Henno wondered how far it could get by dragging itself along. He followed the trail until he eventually found

157

the brute cowering under an acacia tree.

He didn't want to waste another bullet. Instead, he began to pound the back of its head with stones. It was another long, gruesome battle before the hyena finally collapsed. Exhausted, but feeling he had somehow triumphed, Henno skinned the animal and took its pelt back to the cave. Hermann didn't laugh at him this time.

The days passed, blending into one another. Henno and Hermann watched the changing seasons, and had to make their own adjustments. Their carp pond dried up, and they began to get headaches from the lack of vitamins in their diet. They realized that, to correct this, they would need to drink more blood and eat raw meat. Ever inventive, they made sausages from the blood of a gemsbok, using its intestines as the skin.

A gemsbok

They also began to run out of salt, and water – two of the essentials for survival. Just like the animals around them, they had to move to find both. Nothing was going to come to them in their cave. So they marched through the parched canyons, staving off thirst and hunger, until they found salt deposits and fresh waterholes.

On one of these marches, they sheltered for a while under a rock face to cool off. The ground where they sat was infested with sand ticks, as many animals had used this shady spot before them.

"I think a tick just got me," said Hermann suddenly, shaking his hand. The tick had bitten him on the palm – not surprising, in the circumstances. But within a few seconds, he began to keel over.

"Hermann!" said Henno, alarmed, as Hermann slumped to the ground. "Are you all right?"

"My head…" groaned Hermann. Henno stared at him. He had come out in a strange rash, all over his body. Quickly, Henno hunted for the tick that had bitten him.

"Look at this!" he exclaimed, when he found it. The tick was full of old, black blood. Hermann clearly had acute blood poisoning from its bite – and wasn't capable of looking at anything. He vomited violently.

"I can't see," he muttered. "My eyesight's going."

Panicking, Henno slashed open the tick bite and crammed some permanganate of potash (a kind of antiseptic) into the wound. There was nothing else he could do. Hermann could barely stand, and was now half-blind, but Henno got him into a small cave nearby. They spent the rest of the day and the night there, waiting for the poisoning to subside.

It was not until the next afternoon that Hermann felt well enough to move again. It was a frightening incident, showing them just how fragile their lives were in the wilderness.

As the seasons wore on, their fortunes changed. There were droughts, and they were forced to abandon their first home in search of water; they lived in several places, setting up camp wherever there was enough water to keep them alive. There were also times of plenty after the occasional rains, which brought the desert dramatically to life. Henno later described the tremendous power of a flash flood, and the beautiful sight of four thousand springbok grazing together after the rains.

A springbok

Throughout it all, Otto stayed with them. He never tired of hunting, even though he was twice impaled on a gemsbok's horns. He learned survival methods just as the men did, and they marvelled at how all animals, even domesticated ones, adapt to their changing surroundings.

But overall, they were getting weaker, and they were constantly hungry. As a second dry season took its toll, they found that they were almost too weak to hunt.

They grew desperate. One day, a big lizard scuttled past, and Henno lunged at it. He caught it by the tail just as it got halfway into some rocks. "*That lizard provided us with two good meals,*" he wrote. "*The flesh was firm and white and tasted like a cross between chicken and salmon.*"

And then Hermann began to get seriously ill. He suffered from pains in his back, which gradually spread to his legs, and eventually to his neck and head. Henno did his best to take care of him, shooting fresh game, which they ate raw. But nothing seemed to help.

Hermann obviously needed to see a doctor. He could no longer hunt, and could barely even crawl around. There was only one thing to do. They would have to leave the desert, after all they had been through. With a heavy heart, Henno prepared the truck and drove the treacherous way back to Windhoek.

Afterwards

Henno didn't give himself up immediately. He dropped Hermann off and went back into the desert with Otto. But friends persuaded Hermann to tell them where he was hiding, and the police soon found him.

As they had expected, the two men were interned in prison; but not for long. They were transferred to a hospital, where Hermann began to recover. He had been suffering from a deficiency of vitamin B.

Then they had to stand trial. There were many charges against them, large and small, including failure to pay their dog licence. But they were lucky. Their adventure had been so extraordinary that they got off with a few small fines.

Tragically, after making a full recovery, Hermann Korn was killed in a car accident in 1946. Otto lived on for a few years, then mysteriously disappeared. Henno Martin continued to live in Namibia, and wrote a book about their two and a half years in the Namib. It is called *The Sheltering Desert*, and this story is based upon his account.

The real
Indiana Jones

As the long line of camels set off in the shadow of
the Great Wall of China, the men leading them began
a strange, eerie chant, a prayer for safety from evil
spirits. The heavily laden camels were bound for the
vast expanses of the Gobi Desert in Mongolia, and in
spite of their chant, the men all carried rifles. They
knew they would have more than spirits to worry
about before their journey was over.

A tall, athletic man watched the 75 camels pace
away from him. When he was sure that they were
safely on their way, he turned and walked briskly
across to his car. He had a lot to do. The camels were
only part of a vast expedition that he had organized.
His name was Roy Chapman Andrews, and he was
one of America's most famous 20th-century
explorers.

Roy Chapman Andrews was 38 years old, and he
had already established a reputation as a fearless,
daring adventurer. He had explored many parts of
the Far East and South-East Asia, and had spent two
weeks stranded on a desert island. He had killed a
20-foot python, hunted man-eating tigers, and seen

the opium dens of Japan; he had narrowly escaped death by poisoned bamboo stake, by typhoon at sea and by shark attack. To add to his fame, he had been an American spy in the Far East during the First World War, and was not merely an adventurer, but a zoologist, with a skill for stuffing animals and a unique understanding of whales. Now, in March 1922, he was about to begin the biggest adventure of his entire career.

Andrews was based at the American Museum of Natural History in New York. Its director, Henry Osborn, believed that the earliest humans had come not from Africa, but from the heart of Asia. But there was no proof of this. So Andrews made a daring proposal. Why not send a major expedition to the Gobi Desert, to test the truth of Osborn's theory? It could take place over five summers, with Andrews at the head of a varied, experienced team of scientists. Osborn was delighted with the idea – and Andrews was the ideal man to carry it out.

When the American press found out, there was a frenzy of excitement. *"Scientists to seek Ape-man's bones,"* announced *The New York Times.* " *'Missing Link': Expedition to seek remains of near-man in Gobi wilds,"* claimed *The Washington Post.* Donations from the wealthiest people in New York began to flood in, quickly amassing the $250,000 needed – an enormous sum at the time, more than $5 million in today's money. And about ten thousand people wrote to Andrews, begging to join the expeditions.

Even so, as he watched his camel train begin its slow, dignified procession out into the desert, it seemed incredible to Andrews that his idea was becoming a reality... The Central Asiatic Expeditions, as they came to be known, were actually happening.

The camels carried the supplies for Andrews and the other scientists, who followed in five Dodge cars several weeks later. They set off on April 17, 1922, from their base in Kalgan, China, into what Andrews liked to call the 'Great Unknown'. He was well aware that they were taking an enormous risk – the fact was that hardly any fossils had ever been found in Mongolia. But the pressure was on for Andrews to discover some now.

The Gobi Desert was full of dangers, especially then. Wild, inhospitable and immensely varied, it was full of pitfalls for the Dodge vehicles, which often sank up to their axles in soft ground or sand. There were vast gravel plains, craggy buttes and rocky outcrops, and areas of sweeping sand dunes. The climate was also wildly changeable; temperatures could drop to well below freezing, and storms of all kinds were a constant threat. Sandstorms in particular could arise unexpectedly, howling viciously and wrecking everything in their path.

The Dodge vehicles depended heavily on the camel train, which carried fuel, oil and spare parts; but even for the camels, surviving in the desert wasn't easy. There was often little that they could eat, and with no food they quickly weakened under their heavy loads.

But, above all, both camels and Dodge vehicles had to deal with the threat of bandits. The political situation in both China and Mongolia was unstable. With unrest and civil war breaking out constantly, there were increasing numbers of marauding bandits, who sometimes joined together in wild, ruthless gangs of up to a thousand men. They raided anything of value that passed through the Gobi, killing without mercy. Andrews' men had to be constantly on their guard; they all carried shotguns and pistols.

But as this first season got underway, the scientists soon forgot the dangers. There were so many species of animals in the desert to record. The team watched wild asses, which roamed freely in great herds. Scientists had known of their existence, but had never before had the opportunity to observe them close up. Andrews shot several as exhibits, and took detailed notes of how they behaved. More importantly, though, the scientists began to find fossils. Fossils of ancient creatures: fish, toads, insects, rodents and other small mammals, long extinct.

But what about early man? Nothing. No human-like fossils were found at all. Instead, there was something else – something unexpected. *Dinosaurs.* And not just any old dinosaurs. These were new species, never seen before. One of the first to emerge from the eroded rock formations was a strange creature from the Cretaceous period (between 135 and 65 million years ago), with a beak like a parrot. They named it *Psittacosaurus mongoliensis*, which means 'parrot lizard from Mongolia'.

The team was very excited. They didn't have to worry any longer about returning from the desert empty-handed. They worked feverishly, desperate to make the most of their finds. But, towards September, the temperatures began to drop and the Gobi became ever more threatening. They would have to leave, and return in the spring. The first season was at an end – or so they thought...

While hunting for the northbound road to Mongolia's capital, Urga, the team got lost in a vast area of desert. It seemed never-ending. For three days they hunted for some signs of life, or clues as to where to go. Eventually, they spotted a small group of Mongol nomads' huts, known as *yurts*. Andrews drove over to see if they could help, leaving the others to await news. While he waited, the photographer, Shackelford, got out of his Dodge to stretch his legs. There was a strange outcropping of rock nearby, and he wandered over for a closer look.

What he found was astonishing. Before him lay a huge basin of dramatic sandstone cliffs, carved into fantastic shapes by years of erosion. *"There appear to be medieval castles with spires and turrets, brick-red in the evening light, colossal gateways, walls and ramparts..."* wrote Andrews.

It was stunning. But more importantly, lying casually on the surface of the rocks, lay fossils. Hundreds of them. Very excited, the team pitched their tents immediately, and began to explore. It was, as Andrews put it, 'a paradise for palaeontologists'. They named the spot the 'Flaming Cliffs'.

Hurriedly, the scientists gathered what they could. Among their finds was a piece of fossilized eggshell – perhaps left by some ancient bird? But it was a race against time. Soon, they would have to tear themselves away and, with the guidance of the local people, continue on to the capital. Freezing winds and even blasts of snow were beginning to assault the Gobi. They had to get out before the desert engulfed them.

But now they knew that the Flaming Cliffs awaited them on their return.

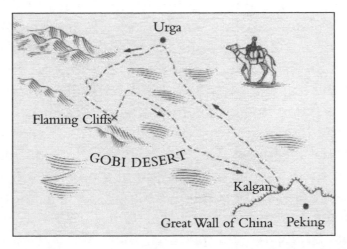

This map shows the expedition's route to the Flaming Cliffs.

The American Museum and the New York press were waiting for news of the expedition with great excitement. Andrews was never shy, and loved publicizing his exploits. As soon as he reached Urga he sent a long cable. "*Scientific results surpassed our greatest hopes,*" he announced.

Osborn was completely delighted at the news. He wrote back, "*You have written a new chapter in the history of life upon the earth.*" Andrews had done it again. His reputation soared. By the time the winter was over and it was time to begin the second expedition, he had become a household name in America.

In April 1923, Andrews and his team were back in Kalgan, China. They soon discovered that the dangers had not diminished since their last trip. If anything, the threat of bandits had grown worse. Some Russian traders had recently been robbed and brutally murdered, and the Kalgan soldiers did a poor job of keeping things under control. The scientists knew they had to keep their eyes open, and keep plenty of guns on show, to ward off the bandits.

They didn't have to wait long for the danger to surface. As Andrews was driving along near the spot where the Russians had been ambushed, he suddenly spotted the glint of sunlight on a gun barrel. It came from the top of a hill nearby. A bandit! As he drove closer, Andrews could see a man on horseback. Hurriedly, he drew his pistol and fired. The horseman disappeared. But as the car rounded a corner, Andrews saw that there was now not one horseman, but three.

Andrews thought quickly. There wasn't time to turn the car around, and if he did he would be fired upon anyway. *"Knowing that a Mongol pony would never stand against the charge of a motor car, I instantly decided to attack,"* he wrote later.

He was right. He drove at full speed at the horses, the car engine roaring. The bandits' horses panicked, and began to buck and rear in terror. The bandits, unable to reach their guns, began to panic, too. There was only one thing they could do – they turned and galloped away as fast as they could.

The team had survived. For now, there were no more bandit attacks – just the long, gruelling trek through the desert to the Flaming Cliffs, where the scientists were eager to continue searching for fossils. As soon as they had set up camp, the hunt began.

The previous season had given the team great hopes, and they were not disappointed. The fossilized bones lying around were quickly discovered to be whole skeletons and well-preserved skulls. Many of them were of a strange Cretaceous creature that had walked on all fours, and had a bizarre bony head, ending in a curved, parrot-like beak. The scientists named it *Protoceratops andrewsi*, after their intrepid leader. Roughly, it means 'Andrews' first horned-face dinosaur'.

But a more revolutionary discovery was yet to come. On July 13, 1923, one of the scientists, George Olsen, made an announcement as everyone sat down for lunch.

"I found some fossilized eggs this morning," he said casually.

Everyone stared at him. It didn't seem possible – they had now established that the fossil bed was from the Cretaceous period, which was too early for large birds. And as far as anyone knew at the time, dinosaurs didn't lay eggs. *"We did not take his story very seriously,"* wrote Andrews. But after lunch, they all went to see what he had found. The chief palaeontologist, Walter Granger, couldn't believe his eyes. There was no doubt that the fossils lying before them were eggs – but not birds' eggs.

"They're reptiles' eggs!" he exclaimed. "And that means… they have to be dinosaur eggs."

The discovery was groundbreaking. *"It was evident that dinosaurs did lay eggs and that we had discovered the first specimens known to science,"* wrote Andrews. It was wildly exciting.

And there was more. As the nest of eggs was uncovered, another skeleton was found – not of a Protoceratops, but of an odd, birdlike creature. It seemed to have died in the very act of raiding the nest of eggs. The men named it *Oviraptor philoceratops*, which means 'egg thief that loves horned-face dinosaurs'. The Central Asiatic Expeditions were truly surpassing all expectations.

But amid all the excitement, Andrews was feeling worried. While the Dodge cars had arrived at the Flaming Cliffs safely, the supply camels were late. The camp was running out of food. This didn't make life too difficult at the time, as there were plenty of antelopes to shoot – but things would get serious if the team was stranded in the desert over winter. And, in any case, what had happened to the caravan? Had the camels died on the way? Or had the whole caravan been attacked by bandits?

Andrews sent out some of his Mongol helpers to search for the camels. But this almost ended in disaster. One of them was attacked, and nearly killed. He made it back to the Flaming Cliffs barely alive. Things were not looking good. By now, Andrews was even prepared to listen to the words of an old wise man who was passing, and who claimed to be an expert astrologist.

"The caravan is still far away," the old man said. "The camels are dying. But you will receive news within three days."

Strangely, the old man was not far wrong. Four days later, one of the searchers found the caravan. The camel drivers had been unable to find food for the camels in the parched desert. They had gone out of their way to find grazing, but even so, many of the camels had died. When the caravan finally arrived at the Flaming Cliffs, only 39 of the 75 camels were still alive. It was a grim reminder of the dangers they all faced.

However, with enough fuel in camp, the team members now knew they could get back to civilization. The vast numbers of fossils were carefully loaded onto the backs of the remaining camels. The news of dinosaur eggs was about to hit the world.

Back in America, Andrews received a hero's welcome. Everyone had dinosaur fever. And Andrews' ambition was growing. The Central Asiatic Expeditions should continue for ten years, not five! He began a whirlwind fundraising tour that included 'auctioning' one of the egg fossils. It fetched $5,000, an enormous sum at the time.

But all the publicity had a negative effect, too. The Mongolian officials suddenly became aware that Andrews was taking many things of value from the Gobi Desert, and that they were getting little in return. Getting permission for his expeditions would gradually prove more and more difficult.

Nevertheless, in early 1925 Andrews was back. He battled with the Mongolian officials for permission, and eventually they gave in. But, from now on, he was under increasing pressure to leave his discoveries in Mongolia, and not to ship them to America. Andrews was fiercely patriotic and the Mongolians' attitude infuriated him.

Mongolian officials were not his only problem that season. Sandstorms raged, and the camel caravan lost many camels. Moving on from the Flaming Cliffs, the terrain of sand dunes, canyons and rocks was often impossible to cross with the trucks.

And then, near the end of the season, when the nights were getting colder, the camp had some very unwelcome visitors. Andrews was the first to spot the danger. Snakes! There were three venomous pit vipers slithering towards the tents, attracted by the warmth inside. He raised the alarm – none too soon. There were vipers everywhere: around people's bedposts, in their shoes…

The men attacked the snakes viciously, using tools, guns, hatchets or whatever came to hand. Incredibly, no one was bitten. In total, they killed 47 vipers between them. But the problem didn't go away. The scientists were forced to break camp, and move on. The desert winter was once more forcing them back to civilization.

Yet despite the problems, Andrews was proving that the Gobi Desert was indeed, as he himself had put it, 'a paradise for palaeontologists'. But now that he was not the only one to realize this, his dream of ten years of excavations began to fade. Neither the Chinese nor the Mongolians were happy about his activities. Moreover, the political situation in both China and Mongolia remained explosive. Civil war broke out in China, and Andrews witnessed many terrible atrocities in Peking and elsewhere. He himself narrowly avoided being shot by some ruthless Chinese soldiers. The 1926 season had to be abandoned.

Determined not to give in, Andrews managed to get another expedition going in 1927. Everything seemed to conspire against it: the Chinese civil war, the authorities (such as they were), increasing numbers of bandits, and wild, wild weather in the Gobi Desert that smashed equipment and ripped up tents. Work on finding fossils in these conditions was almost impossible.

And then Andrews accidentally shot himself. He was hunting antelopes, and had his revolver slung over his hip. Somehow, he pressed the trigger and the revolver exploded into his left leg. The bullet ripped through his thigh and came out underneath his knee. Fortunately, the team doctor did an excellent job of treating the wound, but Andrews had to recover under terrible conditions. The sandstorms raged constantly, causing everyone intense discomfort. *"Often I had to bury my head in the blankets to keep from screaming,"* he wrote.

Faced with such immense difficulties, there were no more trips for three years. Then, in 1930, Andrews led one more Central Asiatic Expedition into the desert. Again, in spite of all the dangers, there were incredible discoveries. One was of a creature like a huge elephant, with enormous, flat, shovel-like teeth at the end of its trunk. The scientists named it *Platybelodon* (which means 'shovel-tusked elephant') and were delighted to find a mother and baby, lying close together.

But it was becoming clear that the Expeditions' days were at an end. The resistance from the Chinese authorities grew too great. Andrews was forced to leave China for the last time in 1932. He returned to America, where his glowing reputation ensured a glittering career as a public speaker, writer and, eventually, director of the American Museum of Natural History.

Afterwards

The expeditions never did find the 'Missing Link'. Osborn's theory was false – or still remains to be proved. But the discoveries of dinosaurs were some of the greatest ever made.

Later discoveries showed that the dinosaur eggs were not those of Protoceratops, as Andrews and his team had thought. They belonged to *Oviraptor philoceratops*, the dinosaur they had found 'raiding' the nest. So Oviraptor was not in the act of thieving the eggs, but sitting on them.

It was also not quite true that these were the first dinosaur eggs ever found. In 1859, a clutch of eggs had been discovered in the French Pyrenees. A paper had been written about them, but it had been largely ignored at the time.

Thanks to movies like *Jurassic Park*, most people now know about some of the dinosaurs discovered by Andrews. The best known is the *Velociraptor* (which means 'quick thief'), the vicious carnivore that is featured in the movie, with its razor-sharp teeth and lethal hunter's instinct.

And what about Indiana Jones? Many have compared Roy Chapman Andrews to this fictional action film hero, and suggested that he was the original model. The creator of *Indiana Jones*, George Lucas, has always denied it. But there is no doubt that Andrews captured the imagination of a whole generation of Americans as the fearless, intrepid explorer who would let nothing stand in his way. There was no one quite like him, before or after; so it is easy to see how he might have influenced a writer, perhaps unconsciously.

Roy Chapman Andrews died on March 11, 1960, at the age of 76.

A desert disguise

"I am only an eccentric, a dreamer anxious to live a free and nomadic life, far away from the civilized world…" wrote Isabelle Eberhardt in June 1901, making her life sound very simple and romantic. It was far from being either. She led a strange, difficult existence, seeking answers to life's questions in the harsh sun of the Sahara Desert. She broke all the rules that women of her time were supposed to follow; she deeply shocked some people and inspired thousands of others. After her death, she became known as 'the Amazon of the Sahara' or, to some, 'the good nomad'.

Isabelle was born in Switzerland in February 1877. Her mother was a Russian exile, who had left her husband, a Russian general, in 1871. She never admitted who Isabelle's father was. She gave her new daughter her maiden name – Eberhardt.

Her father was probably the family tutor, Alexander Trophimowsky, a strange, intense man who had a big influence on Isabelle's childhood. They lived in a rambling villa outside Geneva, where there were few home comforts. Trophimowsky refused to send Isabelle or her sister and three brothers to school, or allow them beyond the grounds of the villa, so they were isolated from the outside world. They all spoke French and Russian, and Trophimowsky also taught Isabelle German, Latin, Italian and a little English, as well as Arabic.

In this strange environment, Isabelle became a dreamer, wandering around the grounds of the villa on her own. She read many, many books, and became interested in the Muslim religion, Islam, when she was quite young. She lived in a fantasy world, and got used to inventing new identities for herself. Trophimowsky encouraged her to dress as a boy, with her hair cropped short. Who was she? Who was her father? She was never really sure...

Through it all, she developed a longing to escape; and the place she longed to see was North Africa, and the Sahara Desert. Eventually she persuaded her mother to make a trip with her. They set off in May 1897 for Bône (now Annaba), in northern Algeria.

It was here that Isabelle began to create her 'desert' identity. She dressed as a young man, calling herself Si Mahmoud Saadi, and claimed to be a Tunisian scholar of the Koran (the holy book of Islam). In this disguise, she could mingle freely with the people of Bône, and quickly picked up the Algerian Arabic that was spoken on the streets. She felt perfectly safe, and very much at home.

But the dream couldn't last. Isabelle's mother died in Bône, and Isabelle was forced to return to Geneva. Within a year, her old tutor Trophimowsky had died, too, leaving her a small amount of money. Isabelle could now do as she pleased. When her grief had subsided, she realized she was free to go back to her beloved North Africa.

She set off in June 1899 for Tunis. There, she became Si Mahmoud Saadi once again, and made plans to fulfil her lifelong dream – to go to the desert.

In Tunisia and Algeria at the end of the 19th century, there were no easy roads connecting the desert towns. The only way for Isabelle to reach her destination, Ouargla in Algeria, was on horseback, accompanied by guides on donkeys.

It was an eventful journey. There was little water to be found along the route, and Isabelle suffered constantly from thirst and a high fever. Even where there were wells, they were not always easy to find, especially if the party arrived at night. On one occasion, they hunted for a well in total darkness, with matches as the only light to guide them. She and her guides slept under the stars, wrapped in their *burnous*, the cloaks worn by people of the region.

It took them eight days to reach the town of Touggourt – a journey of 220km (135 miles). Isabelle was welcomed there, and she made inquiries about heading further south to Ouargla. But the further she went, the more dangerous her trip would become, and the French authorities were keeping a closer eye on her than she imagined. The nomadic people of the desert, the Tuareg, had already killed a number of Europeans who had naively believed they would be welcomed; so it was perhaps not surprising that the French authorities refused to give Isabelle permission to go further south.

Instead, she made the journey to the Souf, part of the Great Eastern Erg, which comprises a number of oases set amongst undulating white sand dunes and salt pans. The principal town in the Souf is El Oued, and this was Isabelle's destination. It was another difficult desert crossing — it took five days to complete the 100km (60-mile) journey.

But, once she was there, the oasis enchanted her. To this day, El Oued is one of the most beautiful towns in Algeria, known also as the 'City of a Thousand Domes' because of its architecture. Its domed houses are painted white, its palm groves are green and lush, and the Sahara is just at hand, its beautiful sands stretching out in every direction. For Isabelle, it felt like home.

Isabelle completed her round trip in a few weeks: an extraordinary journey for a European woman at that time. What was even more amazing was that she was openly welcomed by the local people she met — especially the religious leaders. Was it because of her disguise, perhaps? In a way... but Isabelle was different from many Europeans, in that she genuinely wanted to be part of North African life. She was not like the French invaders who had taken over the country; she believed in Islam passionately, and could talk intelligently about the Koran and Islamic beliefs.

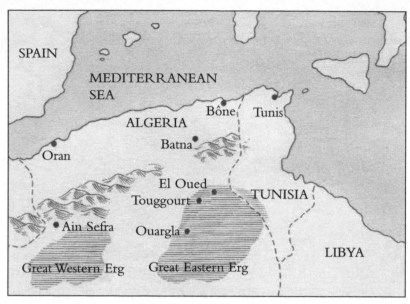

This map shows the parts of the desert Isabelle visited.

The religious leaders probably knew that they were talking to a woman, but they forgave her because she clearly believed everything she said.

She headed back to Europe, but it was not long before the desert drew her back again. This time, she decided that she would not just make a trip. She would return to the desert to live.

El Oued had captured her heart. There, she thought, she could lead a life of tranquillity; she could concentrate on being a writer and developing her Muslim faith. She would be surrounded by the sights and sounds that she loved.

"*Oh Sahara, menacing Sahara, hiding your dark and beautiful soul in bleak, desolate emptiness!*" she wrote. "*Oh yes, I love this country of sand and stone, this country of camels and primitive men and vast, treacherous salt-flats."*

So, after another long, tiring journey, she arrived in El Oued and rented a house. She exulted in her arrival. *"I am far away from all people, far from civilization and its hypocritical shams. I am alone, on the soil of Islam, out in the desert, free..."* she wrote happily.

She settled into a simple life, mingling with the people and meeting the local holy men. She bought a horse and named him Souf, after the region, and wandered the white sand dunes at night on horseback. She wrote of the beauty of the dunes and of the sunsets over the desert: *"To the west... the sun was a veritable ball of blood sinking in a blaze of gold and crimson. The slopes of the dunes seemed to be on fire below the ridges, in hues that deepened from one moment to the next."*

She was often accompanied into the dunes by an Algerian soldier named Slimène, who later became her husband – although this friendship was one of the many reasons why some people thought badly of her. On the whole, Europeans thought of themselves as superior to North Africans, and kept themselves apart from them. Most found the idea of a European actually marrying an Algerian totally shocking. But with Slimène, and living in El Oued, Isabelle was happier than she had ever been in her life.

At this time, she took her Muslim faith a step further. She got to know the leaders of the oldest Sufi sect in the world – the Qadrya brotherhood. Sufism is a mystical form of Islam, and only selected people can become members of its sects. The two leaders of the Qadrya, Sidi el Hussein and Sidi el Hachemi, warmed to Isabelle, although it's almost certain that they saw through her disguise. Before long, they initiated her into the sect – something completely unheard of for a European, let alone a woman.

But Isabelle's dream of a tranquil life was not to last. She was, in fact, rather naïve to think that she could just disappear into the desert. The French authorities knew about her even before she arrived and, without her knowing it, she was kept under careful surveillance all the time that she lived in El Oued. Why were they so suspicious of her? She was doing no one any harm.

The problem was that the French rulers in Algeria were afraid of the people around them. They feared that the Algerians might rise against them, and fight for their freedom. Isabelle, although a European, was a Muslim and loved the local people. Some thought that she might encourage them to rebel against the French. And in any case, the way she lived was shocking – dressing as a man, wandering around on her own… and despite what she thought, Isabelle's relationship with Slimène was no secret, either. There were mutterings that Isabelle represented a threat on many levels, not only to the authorities, but to people's ideas of decency, too.

In the meantime, Isabelle's 'idyllic' life was growing harsher. The weather in the Sahara could be ferocious – winds whipped up the sand, blasting the houses and making life very uncomfortable. In winter, it was also surprisingly cold. And Isabelle had run out of money. She had always intended to establish herself as a writer and earn money that way, but it wasn't easy. Now, she was in debt. She was often ill, and rarely ate enough.

Then came some bad news. The army was sending Slimène away from El Oued, to the town of Batna, further north. Isabelle didn't know it, but the authorities hoped that, by sending him away, they could get rid of her. They were sure that she would follow Slimène – and they were right.

But before she left, a terrible and extraordinary event took place. She went to visit some of her Sufi friends, and stopped off in a village called Béhima. There, she was welcomed into the house of a local wealthy man, and sat in his courtyard surrounded by members of the Qadrya. As she sat quietly among them, helping a young man translate a letter, she suddenly felt a violent blow to her head.

Before she had time to think or react, there were two more blows, this time to her left arm. She looked up and saw a man wildly waving a weapon over her head, as her Qadrya friends leaped to defend her. Shocked and dazed, Isabelle herself jumped up and ran to the wall, where a sword was hanging. Her friends had already wrestled the man's weapon from him, but he himself escaped, and ran off.

"I shall bring back a gun to finish her off!" he was heard to cry as he disappeared.

The Qadryas returned to Isabelle, who was bleeding heavily from her wounds.

"This is what the cur wounded you with!" cried one of them, showing her a sword that was dripping with blood.

There was no doubt who the attacker was. Several of the people present had recognized him, although Isabelle herself did not. His name was Abdallah Mohammed ben Lakhdar, and he came from the village of Béhima itself. He belonged to another Sufi sect called the Tidjanya brotherhood, the greatest rival sect to the Qadryas. The leader of the Tidjanyas was quickly summoned, and was told to hunt the man out. At first he refused.

"If you don't find him, we will say you are an accomplice to the crime," he was told. Reluctantly, he sent people to find Abdallah – not a difficult task in a village so small. Abdallah was caught, and brought to the wealthy man's house where Isabelle still lay injured.

A bizarre scene followed. Abdallah was brought into the room where Isabelle lay bleeding on a mattress. She had still received no treatment for her wounds, which were quite serious. Instead, Abdallah was interrogated in front of her, and she joined in herself with more questions.

"Why have you done such a terrible thing?" he was asked.

At first, Abdallah pretended to be mad. But none of the local people believed him, because they knew him well. So he dropped the sham, and simply stated that God had sent him to kill Isabelle.

"But you don't know me," said Isabelle. "And I don't know you."

"No," agreed Abdallah. "I have never seen you before. But I must kill you, nevertheless. If these people set me free, I would try to do so again."

"Why?" asked Isabelle. "What do you have against me?"

"Nothing. You have done me no wrong. I don't know you, but I must kill you."

His responses made no sense at all.

"Do you know she is a Muslim?" asked one of the other men.

"Yes," said Abdallah.

It was all very mysterious. Several hours later, a doctor arrived from El Oued, and Isabelle was treated. She had been very lucky – a laundry line had deflected the blow to her head, which might easily have killed her otherwise. The worst injury was to her left elbow, which had been slashed through to the bone.

The delay in treating her meant that Isabelle had lost a lot of blood. She was very weak. The next day she was transferred to the military hospital in El

Oued, where she spent almost a month recovering. It was the end of her desert idyll. When she was well enough, she made her way north, to join Slimène in Batna.

In spite of what had happened, the French authorities were still determined to get rid of her. She was banished from Algeria, and only allowed to return for the trial of Abdallah, which took place four months later.

The trial did little to clear up the mystery. By this time, Abdallah seemed sorry for the attack, and begged Isabelle's forgiveness. But he still didn't explain why he had done it. Isabelle herself believed that he had been a paid assassin, employed either by the French authorities or by the Tidjanya Sufis. There was talk that he had been able to pay off his debts and buy a palm grove. But even if the gossip was true, he ended up paying a much higher price himself. The court convicted him of attempted murder, and he was sentenced to a lifetime of hard manual work.

Isabelle was appalled. It was a terrible sentence, especially as he had a wife and children. Believing that he was not the true criminal, she pleaded with the authorities to be more lenient. They responded by reducing Abdallah's sentence to ten years in jail.

After the trial, Isabelle was once more banished to France, where she lived with her brother in Marseilles. Slimène joined her there, and they were married. The marriage gave Isabelle the right to return to Algeria – but little did she know that it would be for the last time…

Isabelle found it difficult to stay in one place for long. Even in Algeria, the northern coastal towns didn't fully satisfy her yearnings. The desert, further south, always called her. When the opportunity arose to work with the French army south of the Atlas mountains, she jumped at the chance.

Isabelle's job was to travel around listening to the nomads and helping to smooth relations between them and the French colonials. It was strange work for her to take on, because she was not really a supporter of French rule. *"Whatever their unenlightened way of life, the lowliest of Bedouins are far superior to those idiotic Europeans making a nuisance of themselves,"* she wrote. But the section of the army she was working with wanted to proceed by persuasion and mutual understanding rather than force; perhaps she felt it was the better of two evils.

And, of course, the work allowed her to return to the desert. She moved from town to town, and lived for a while in a monastery, as she had the right to do as a Qadrya initiate.

But her health was suffering. As always when in the desert, she suffered from fevers, mostly caused by malaria, and they were getting worse. She was admitted to the military hospital in the town of Aïn Sefra, just where the Atlas mountains meet the Sahara Desert. She spent almost three weeks there in

October 1904, before discharging herself.

Her husband Slimène, whose work had kept him in northern Algeria, came to be with her when she left hospital on October 20. Their reunion was a short one, because on October 21 a flash flood hit the town of Aïn Sefra.

The desert is a place of extremes. Most of the time it is terribly dry, terribly hot in the daytime and sometimes terribly cold at night. But when rains occur anywhere nearby, especially if there are mountains, the results can be devastating.

There had been no rains in Aïn Sefra in recent weeks. The *wadi*, the riverbed that ran through the town, was completely dry. But somewhere in the Atlas mountains there must have been rain, for suddenly, on the morning of October 21, there was a great roar and a ferocious torrent surged down the mountain, engulfing everything in its path. The yellow, turbulent waters picked up debris, tree trunks and bushes, crashing into houses and sweeping people away.

There was little time to react, and the flash flood subsided almost as quickly as it had appeared. Only then could the real damage be assessed. More than 20 people had died – and among them was Isabelle, found buried under rubble inside her house. Considering how much she had packed into her life, it is astonishing that she was only 27 years old when she died.

Afterwards

After her death, a friend gathered together all Isabelle's writings for publication. She became a romanticized heroine in Parisian circles – much was written about her, including two plays, and people still ponder her controversial life to this day.

What made her stand out among the 'desert adventurers' of her time, however, was her genuine desire to belong to the local people. She was not alone in adopting a disguise; the most famous example was the explorer Richard Burton, who disguised himself as a Muslim to enter the holy city of Mecca. But he was a Christian who merely wanted to enter a place that was otherwise forbidden to him. Isabelle was different. Although her identity as Si Mahmoud Saadi helped her to fit in, it was also an identity she felt comfortable with. She wasn't a man, and she wasn't Tunisian, but she *was* the Koranic scholar she claimed to be – and that was why the people of North Africa loved her.

Lawrence
of Arabia

The London audiences sat spellbound, hanging on every word.

"The wild sons of Ishmael regarded their quiet, fair-headed leader as a sort of supernatural being who had been sent from heaven to deliver them from their oppressors," the journalist told them. "He dressed in the garb of an Oriental ruler, and at his belt he carried the curved gold sword worn only by the direct descendants of the prophet Mohammed."

The people of London held their breaths. Who was this amazing, romantic British hero? Where was he now?

"The young man is at present flying from one part of London to another, trying to escape the fairer sex," the journalist assured them.

It was September 1919. The First World War was at an end, but at what a terrible cost. In Europe, millions of Britons, Frenchmen and Germans had died in a gruesome, drawn-out stalemate in muddy trenches. Britain and France had defeated Germany, but there seemed little to celebrate; the tales of trench warfare were just too horrible to think about.

But here was something different − a different

kind of war, with a different kind of hero: Lawrence of Arabia – who, if the journalist was to be believed, had led the Arabs single-handedly in a revolt against the Turks, riding majestically to victory across the desert, robes flying behind him as he charged ahead on his camel.

Far from running around London 'trying to escape the fairer sex', the real Lawrence – Thomas Edward Lawrence, to be precise – was sitting in Oxford, deeply depressed at what he saw as his failure to give the Arab people what they deserved. And, in the next few years, he tried his best to avoid the publicity caused by this well-meaning American journalist, whose name was Lowell Thomas.

First of all, he entered the Royal Air Force at a very low rank, under the assumed name of John Hume Ross. When the press found out his real identity, he changed his name again, this time to Thomas Edward Shaw, and joined the Tank Corps in the army. He returned to the Air Force under this name, still in the lower ranks, and spent the next 12 years in obscurity. His fellow servicemen never guessed who he was.

So what was the truth? Was 'Lawrence of Arabia' just a myth, created by a journalist who knew how badly the British needed a boost of morale? Or was there really something extraordinary about the quiet man who spent the rest of his life hiding from the press?

The truth lies somewhere in between. T. E. Lawrence began his career with an Oxford degree in history, and it was at this time that he developed an interest in the Middle East. He wrote a thesis on the Crusader castles of Palestine and Syria, journeying there for research, and began to learn Arabic. In 1910, after finishing his thesis, he returned to Syria to work on an archaeological dig at the ancient city of Carchemish. There, until the beginning of the First World War in 1914, he expanded his knowledge of the region and grew to love the people around him.

At that time, most of the Middle East was ruled by the Turks. Their empire (called the Ottoman empire) stretched from Turkey to modern-day Iraq. They were officially in control of Egypt, too. But the real power in Egypt was Britain, which kept a close eye on the Suez Canal – a vital route for its shipping.

This map shows the extent of the Ottoman empire at the time of the First World War.

When the First World War broke out, Turkey joined Austria and Germany against Russia, France and Britain. In the Arabian city of Mecca, the deposed *sherif* (Islamic leader), Sherif Hussein, now considered his options. He could back his Turkish rulers; or he could approach the British in the hope that they would help him gain independence for all the Arabic peoples, from the Arabian peninsula to Iraq and Syria.

The British liked the idea of having the Arabs on their side – it would help them in their battle against the Turks. They agreed with Hussein that if there was a successful Arab revolt, they would guarantee Arab independence after the war. So, on June 10, 1916, Hussein symbolically fired his rifle at the Turkish barracks in Mecca. The Arab Revolt had begun.

It was obvious that Sherif Hussein couldn't beat the Turks on his own. They had vast armies, and the sherif had only badly organized tribesmen. The British would have to launch a major offensive themselves, and give whatever help they could to the Arabs. So the British army sent representatives to Mecca, to see what was needed – and one of these was T. E. Lawrence.

At the start of the war, Lawrence had been posted to the British Intelligence department in Cairo, and he quickly became interested in the Arab Revolt. He decided that what the Revolt lacked was a leader. The sherif himself was a cantankerous old man, so

Lawrence visited the sherif's four sons to see what they were made of. Lawrence decided that the sherif's third son, the Emir Feisal, was the one with the necessary qualities. The two men got along well, and Lawrence was soon involved in helping him plan the desert campaign.

The Arab Revolt wouldn't stand a chance if it fought the conventional way, as a disciplined army. The Arab Bedouin were fierce warriors, but they belonged to many different tribes who tended to end up fighting each other. Wanting to understand them and learn about desert customs, Lawrence watched Feisal. He was impressed with Feisal's handling of tribal issues, which took a huge amount of patience. Gradually, he began to understand how to make the most of the Arabs' limited resources.

Before long, Lawrence had helped the Revolt to develop a strategy. They would use guerrilla warfare to attack the Hejaz railway, which ran through the desert, from Damascus in Syria right down to the holy city of Medina. There were vast stretches of desert track that the Turks could not possibly guard; and by disrupting their system of transport, the Arabs would hinder the Turkish war effort while losing very few men themselves. Other British officers agreed with the strategy, and supplied Lawrence with explosives and other artillery.

Very quickly, Lawrence became personally involved in the attacks against the railway. He understood how to use the explosives and, unlike many other British officers, seemed ideally suited to the desert war. He now spoke fluent Arabic, so he was able to communicate; he learned how to ride a camel and prided himself on enduring the harsh physical demands of life in the desert. It was Feisal who suggested to Lawrence that he wear Arab clothes. He gave him a beautiful set of robes made of pure white silk, which became part of the Lawrence 'image'; these helped him to mingle more effectively with the tribesmen.

On his trips, Lawrence was often accompanied by Arabs from different tribes, or even different countries. As a British officer in their midst, he had to act as mediator, resolving tribal issues along the way. On one of the early expeditions, a Moroccan killed a Bedouin tribesman. Knowing that this could spark a blood feud, in which tribal members were obliged to start killing in revenge, Lawrence realized that the only solution was for him to execute the Moroccan himself. Sick with fever and boils and weak from the hardships of the desert, he could hardly shoot straight, and took three shots to kill the man. It was a foretaste of things to come.

Meanwhile, Russia, France and Britain were secretly discussing what would happen if they won the war. Who would rule what, and where? France wanted to share out the former Ottoman empire with Britain. Despite the agreement with Sherif

Hussein, Britain felt obliged to agree. The result was the Sykes-Picot agreement of May 1916. According to this, France would rule Lebanon, Syria and part of Turkey, while Britain would rule Iraq and what is now Jordan. In other words, all the wealthy, highly populated areas would go to Britain and France, while the Arabs would get only the Arabian peninsula, which consisted mainly of desert.

One of the controversies surrounding Lawrence is whether he knew the terms of this agreement. He later denied that he did, but this denial was slightly unconvincing. He certainly had more than an inkling of its contents; in any case, it became public knowledge after the Russian Revolution of 1917, when the Russians published all their former agreements. His position seems to have rested on the hope that, once the war was over, the British would act justly to protect Arab interests. Lawrence was deeply loyal to Britain, and believed in British fair-mindedness. He didn't see why France should get a share of the Middle East when they hadn't done any of the fighting. If it was the Arabs themselves who defeated the Turks and entered Damascus, the British couldn't possibly allow the French to take their lands – could they?

So the Arab Revolt continued. Lawrence worked on plans for the Arab army to move north up the Arabian peninsula to Akaba, on the Red Sea – an important strategic port held by the Turks. It was well guarded from the sea, so the only hope of taking it was from inland, via the desert, and to use the weapon of surprise.

Lawrence found the help he needed in the form of a tribal leader named Auda abu Tayi, a hardened desert warrior. Lawrence suggested that they approach Akaba via an inland route. This way, they could recruit tribal support along the way, and they would never be spotted by the Turks. Auda agreed that it was feasible, and a small party set out from the town of Wedj on May 9, 1917.

The journey was tiring and difficult. There were long stretches of desert riding with little water. Lawrence himself fell ill again with boils and high fever, but struggled on. They crossed the Hejaz railway, blowing part of it up as they went. Then they spent a morning crossing the desolate mud flats of Biseita, a vast plain in the desert. Suddenly, they realized that one of the party was missing. His camel was still with the group – its rider had obviously dozed off in the searing heat and simply fallen off.

The missing man, Gasim, was part of Lawrence's own team. He realized with a sinking heart that he would have to go back and look for him personally, or lose the respect of the others. So he turned his camel, and forced it back across the mud flats.

Gasim was almost delirious from the desert heat when Lawrence found him. They caught up with the others, but were both near total exhaustion. What was worse, one of the tribal leaders beat Lawrence's servants for letting him go back alone. *"Think tonight was worst of my experience,"* wrote Lawrence in his diary.

After the hardships of trekking through the desert, Lawrence had the task of persuading other Arab tribes to join the Revolt. Fearing that the British might uphold the Sykes-Picot agreement, he felt terrible. *"We are calling them to fight for us on a lie, and I can't stand it,"* he wrote to one of his fellow-officers. But it was too late to change the plan. Fired by the idea of the Revolt, the Arab tribes were putting their weight behind it. By early July, they were close to Akaba.

The first encounter took place just north of Akaba, at Abu el Lissan. Taken by surprise, the Turks didn't know how to deal with the Arab snipers, who were hidden in the hills. When the Arabs eventually charged on their camels, the Turks simply panicked. A few days later, Akaba had fallen. It was now in Arab hands.

The British were very impressed. It made them realize that the Arabs really were strong enough to help them defeat the Turks. After this, the Arab Revolt worked much more closely with British forces, pushing northwards under the direction of the British Commander-in-Chief, General Edmund Allenby. The British army advanced north through Palestine, and Jerusalem was captured in December 1917. The Arabs played a vital role throughout, by constantly disrupting the railway further east, so distracting the Turks from the main British offensive, and confusing them about their enemy's strength.

By now, Lawrence had two main roles. He was liaising constantly with Allenby and other British officers, demanding supplies and discussing strategies, but he was also deeply committed to guerrilla fighting with the Arabs. He loved the desert, especially areas such as Wadi Rumm, where the desert rock formations are some of the most awe-inspiring in the world. Later, he wrote evocative descriptions of this harsh but beautiful landscape.

But the reality of the war had little romance to it. Lawrence was undergoing physical hardships that stretched him to the limit. There were occasional camel charges, but Lawrence was only one of many British soldiers involved. And, although he was a famous leader, he was not always in the front line. In fact, the famous charge into Akaba happened without him – in the confusion, Lawrence shot his own camel in the head, and it crumpled, throwing him off.

As the campaign wore on, Lawrence himself began to feel weary and sickened. After one raid on a Turkish train, in which 70 Turks were killed, he wrote to a friend, "*This killing and killing of Turks is horrible... you charge in at the finish and find them all over the place in bits.*"

Moreover, the Turks had proved to be brutal, cruel fighters – and barbaric in their treatment of wounded enemies, sometimes burning them alive. As a result,

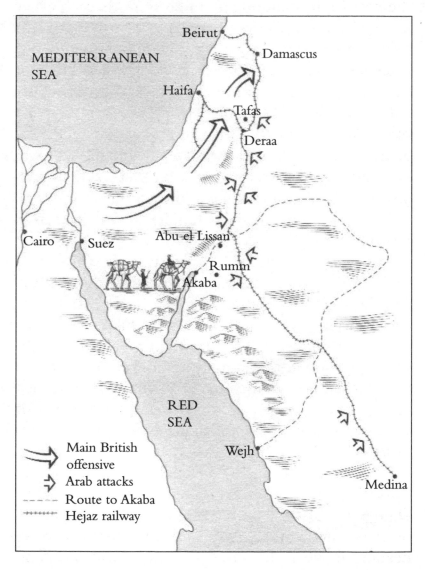

This map shows the Arabs' desert campaign and the route they took to Akaba.

the Arabs agreed among themselves to kill each other if they were too badly wounded to be carried away.

In April 1918, Lawrence himself had to put this rule into practice. On a reconnaissance mission behind enemy lines, one of his faithful servants, Farraj, was terribly wounded. As Lawrence and some other Arabs tried to carry him away, the alert was given – a group of Turks was approaching. There was nothing that could be done. Lawrence reached for his pistol, and pointed it at his friend's head.

"God will give you peace," muttered Farraj, as Lawrence pulled the trigger.

As 1918 wore on, at last it seemed that the British–Arab plan was working. After the successes of Akaba and Jerusalem, it had sometimes looked as though the campaign was stuck. But in September the Arabs succeeded in destroying the railway north and south of Deraa, one of the main lines of Turkish communication; and, in the same month, the British offensive wiped out the 7th and 8th Turkish armies in Palestine.

It was now just a case of trapping the remaining Turkish armies before they could retreat to Damascus. On September 26, 1918, Lawrence received news that two Turkish divisions were heading north in his direction, one of six thousand and the other of two thousand men. He and his fellow leaders decided they had enough men to tackle the smaller division.

They met the Turks just north of the village of Tafas, near Deraa, forcing them to turn back, and following them through the village of Tafas itself. What they saw appalled them. The Turks had massacred all the women and children; Lawrence himself noticed a pregnant woman who had been impaled on a bayonet.

The sheikh of the village, a warrior named Talal, was fighting alongside Lawrence. When he saw what had happened to his villagers, he gave a howl of grief and charged the retreating Turks on his own, only to be brought down in a shower of machine-gun bullets. But the whole Arab army was now enraged. Lawrence and the other leaders were so sickened that they gave the order to "take no prisoners" – which meant to kill all the Turks, whether they surrendered or not.

The Arabs swooped upon the Turks in fury at what they had done, and as a result soon captured Deraa. Then they went wild, looting and slaughtering Turks in vengeance for the massacre of Tafas. Lawrence later described it as "one of the nights in which mankind went crazy".

Meanwhile, the rest of the Arab army had taken on the larger Turkish divisions. In a few days, about five thousand Turks were killed, and eight thousand taken prisoner. Damascus was, at last, there for the taking.

The British allowed the Arab armies to march into Damascus ahead of them, in acknowledgement of their rights to the region. Lawrence went in with them, and witnessed the ecstatic welcome they were given by the people. Sherif Hussein was proclaimed King of the Arabs, and Feisal entered the city in triumph as his representative. For a short while it looked as though the Sykes-Picot agreement would be forgotten.

After hastily helping the Arab chiefs to establish order in Damascus, Lawrence left as soon as he could. Already, he seemed depressed. He knew that the Arabs' position was precarious, and that, in one sense, Feisal's struggle had only just begun. Exhausted, he headed home for London only four days later.

Sure enough, French demands quickly wiped out Feisal's dreams. By the end of 1920, the peace settlements had handed Lebanon and Syria over to France. To pacify the Arabs, Britain made Feisal king of Iraq under their indirect control; they gave an area known as Trans-Jordan (modern Jordan) to his brother Abdullah, under a similar arrangement. The only area ruled directly by Arabs remained Arabia itself, where Hussein was quickly toppled from power by a local rival, Ibn Saud, whose family gave its name to Saudi Arabia.

Afterwards

Lawrence played an important part in the post-war negotiations, fighting for the Arab right to independence. Although the eventual outcome was better than he feared, it was very different from the vision that had fired the Arab Revolt. It is clear that he felt the British had betrayed the Arabs; he was offered many distinctions and medals for his military service, including the Distinguished Service Order, but he turned them all down. Much to many people's disappointment, he began to retreat from the limelight.

But the legend of 'Lawrence of Arabia' began to grow, largely thanks to the journalist and public speaker Lovell Thomas, who went on a series of morale-raising tours. Lawrence himself regarded it as absurd that he had been singled out. Many other British officers had been involved in the Revolt, and he himself had certainly never been the leader of the Arabs. He claimed that Lovell Thomas was telling "red-hot lies".

Nevertheless, Lawrence began to write his own account of the Revolt, *Seven Pillars of Wisdom*. This made its own contribution to the legend, and some historians have claimed that it twists and exaggerates the facts. It contains many romantic descriptions of the desert, an idealized view of the Emir Feisal, and dramatic accounts of the battles. It also plays down the role of the British in defeating the Turks. As a result, the debate about Lawrence has gone on and on, and he still remains an enigmatic figure.

It has recently come to light that, in 1934, Lawrence was approached by the famous film director Alexander Korda, who wanted to make a film called *Lawrence of Arabia*. Lawrence was furious. *"Presumably he means me, and I have strong views as to the undesirability of any such film. So I have sent him word that perhaps he ought to discuss his intentions with me before he opens his silly mouth again,"* he wrote.

But the idea persisted. In 1962, 27 years after Lawrence's death, another film director, David Lean, did make a film called *Lawrence of Arabia*, starring Peter O'Toole as Lawrence. It quickly became a film classic, and ensured that the romantic image of war in the desert, with its heroism, flowing silk robes and charging camels, lived on to capture the imagination of millions.

T. E. Lawrence stayed in the RAF until 1935, when he was 46 years old. Only three months after leaving the service, he was killed in a motorcycle accident near his home in Dorset.

The legend of Zerzura

Somewhere, hidden away in the endless sands of the Libyan Desert, it was said that there was a beautiful lost oasis, where the palm trees were tall and lush, and where birds sang in their branches. There, in the white-walled ruins of an ancient city, a king and queen lay in an enchanted sleep from which one day, they would awake...

The name of this oasis was Zerzura, 'The Oasis of the Little Birds'. An Englishman and a Hungarian sat discussing it one day.

"You don't really believe in it, do you?" queried Dr. Richard Bermann, with an amused smile.

The Hungarian, Count Ladislaus Almasy, squinted against the sun, and shook his head impatiently. "The ancient city? Of course not. It's an old Arab myth from the *Kitab el Kanuz* – 'The Book of Hidden Treasures'. But people have talked about Zerzura for hundreds of years. It's mentioned as far back as the 13th century. Even so, I'd think it was all nonsense if it wasn't for Wilkinson."

"Wilkinson?" Dr. Bermann looked at his friend curiously.

"Sir Gardiner Wilkinson. He was the chap who

first discovered Dakhla oasis," explained Almasy. "The locals told him about three oases out towards Kufra. They've since been found. They also told him about three other wadis [dry riverbeds], on the road to Farafra. Claimed there were palms, springs, ruins, just as the legends described. Zerzura..." Almasy's eyes grew pensive as he gazed into the distance. "Now if the people of Dakhla were right about the Kufra oases, why shouldn't they be right about Zerzura?"

Dr. Bermann nodded. It was difficult to disagree with Almasy when he was convinced of something. He was passionate about everything he did, but above all he was passionate about the desert – and the legend of Zerzura had fascinated him for years.

This map shows the region explored by Almasy.

Almasy was not alone in his love of the Libyan Desert (also known as the Western Desert), the vast expanse of the Sahara that stretches from eastern Libya to the river Nile in Egypt. Many others had been drawn to it before him. In 1879, German explorer Gerhard Rohlfs had crossed it from the east. He had reached the Kufra oasis in Libya, but had nearly lost his life along the way. Both he and his camels had been close to dying of thirst when a freak shower of rain fell, saving them. He named the spot Regenfeld (Rainfield), and ever after this it was a tradition for voyagers to stop and place a bottle there, containing details of their journeys.

Then, in the 1920s, a whole succession of explorers began to zigzag their way across the desert. One was a wealthy Egyptian, Sir Ahmed Hassanein Bey. He found two lost oases, Arkenu and Uweinat – but not Zerzura. Another Egyptian, Prince Kemal el Din, pioneered exploration in caterpillar vehicles, while an Englishman, Major R. A. Bagnold, hunted for Zerzura by car. But none of them found it. The oasis remained elusive.

Now, it was the early 1930s, and Almasy was one of the most single-minded explorers in the region. In 1932, he organized an expedition to find the oasis once and for all. He was joined by three Englishmen – Sir Robert Clayton-East-Clayton, Wing Commander H. Penderel and a cartographer (map maker) named Patrick Clayton – and six Egyptians.

They decided that they would hunt for the oasis by car, and make additional surveys from a Gypsy Moth plane named *Rupert*.

The main party set off from the Kharga oasis in Egypt on April 12, 1932 and headed for the Gilf Kebir, a vast mountain plateau in the south-east corner of the country. It was here, Almasy was sure, that they would find the lost oasis.

In the 1930s, desert exploration had come a long way, but it still had its fair share of dangers and excitements. Desert explorers had to keep their wits about them and look after each other; this was not the place to develop petty disagreements. The four Europeans worked together and, if they disliked each other, they did their best not to show it, at least at the time.

Taking turns flying *Rupert*, the Gypsy Moth, they weathered sandstorms and thirst to reach the Gilf Kebir, where the real exploration would begin. As they drew nearer, they realized they were running out of water. There was a fairly easy solution to this; they were within striking distance of Kufra, an oasis in Libya.

"We should go to Kufra for water before we carry on," said Almasy. "It won't take long."

"Kufra's in Italian territory," objected Patrick Clayton. "We can't go there. They'll arrest us."

"Don't be absurd," retorted Almasy. "Why on earth would they do that?"

"Because they don't like the British stamping on their territory, that's why!" snapped Clayton, who was well known for his dislike of the Italians.

"I'm not British," pointed out Almasy.

"No. You're not," said Clayton, in a strained tone of voice. The two men stared at each other. It was a strange moment. Perhaps it was a sign that the carefree days of desert exploration were coming to an end. The desert was no longer free of boundaries; no longer a hiding-place for legends... With the possibility of war looming, explorers were beginning to think about loyalties. Exploration meant information – as all the men knew only too well.

"What do you think, Penderel?" asked Almasy eventually.

The Wing Commander shrugged. "You're probably right," he said to Almasy. "They'll welcome you readily enough. But I'm a British soldier. If you want to go, you'd better go alone."

So Almasy headed west, leaving the rest of the team to make the first forays into the Gilf itself. The Italians gave him a warm welcome. He quickly stocked up on water and headed into the desert once more – but not before taking a number of interesting photographs.

In his absence, Sir Robert and Penderel flew the Gypsy Moth over the Gilf Kebir. To their great excitement, they spotted a long wadi in which many acacia trees were growing. Could this be the first of the three wadis spoken of by Wilkinson? When Almasy got back to camp and heard the news, he was just as excited. He was convinced that they had found Zerzura. Now the task remained of reaching the wadi by car.

But although the men flew over the enticing wadi several times, they were unable to find a way around to its entrance in their cars – the mountainous desert terrain of the Gilf Kebir blocked their way. They did find another wadi, but it was small and insignificant compared to the one they had seen from the air. And they were running out of time. Frustrated, they had to turn back.

The expedition party reached Cairo again in May 1932. In September that same year, tragedy struck. Sir Robert Clayton-East-Clayton contracted an acute viral infection. Within days, he was dead. He was only 24 when he died.

His wife, Lady Dorothy, was an intrepid woman who was determined to complete the exploration that her husband had begun. She discussed her options with Patrick Clayton in Cairo. The obvious thing to do would be to join up with her husband's former companions, including Almasy; but suddenly, Clayton's personal dislike of Almasy seemed to get the better of him. He knew how much Almasy wanted to continue the hunt for Zerzura, but he was out of the country at the time.

"Almasy won't be coming back to Cairo," Clayton

lied. "But I'm going on another expedition myself. I would be more than pleased for you to join me."

Lady Dorothy was delighted. "I shall certainly come with you," she told him. "I wouldn't want to travel in Almasy's company, anyway. Horrid man."

Lady Dorothy didn't like Almasy either, because she thought he was untrustworthy. More than once, she had refused to shake his hand on social occasions in Cairo. When Almasy returned to Egypt – as Clayton knew he would – he met her, and she treated him very coldly. He learned of her plans to follow up the Zerzura expedition with Clayton. He was furious, and hurriedly made plans of his own.

So it was that two expeditions, fired partly by rivalry, set out in 1933 to hunt for the missing wadis of Zerzura. This time, Almasy's expedition included his old friend Dr. Richard Bermann, a journalist who was very interested in the old legends, having discussed them with Almasy many times. They set out from Cairo on March 14, 1933, in four cars.

Their first stop was at a place called Abu Ballas, which means 'Father of Jars'. Here, hidden in the sand, were about three hundred water pots. They had been found by the people of Dakhla in the 19th century, when chasing off a gang of desert robbers. The pots obviously belonged to these robbers, who used them as a water supply point in their raids across the desert.

Excitedly, Almasy laid out a map.

"See here, Bermann," he said to his friend. "These jars are situated about two-thirds of the way between Kufra and Dakhla. That suggests that anyone trekking across the desert would have needed to stop for water somewhere else, as well – about one-third of the way between the two oases."

Almasy's finger traced the old caravan route with his finger. He let it hover over the Gilf Kebir.

"The Gilf Kebir… Zerzura?" asked Bermann, with a smile.

"Why not?" responded Almasy.

They left Abu Ballas and headed for the east side of the Gilf Kebir, hoping to find an entrance to the wadi they had seen the previous year. They drew a blank – but not before making another very useful discovery. Everyone had always thought there was no way through the Gilf Kebir. But they'd been wrong. The vast plateau was actually divided in two – there was a gap in the middle running from east to west. This was not a wadi, but an enormous rift in the rocks, through which their cars could pass easily.

"Very interesting," muttered Almasy. "Very useful, indeed."

Using this new discovery, they drove west to Kufra to stock up on supplies. There, they heard news of the other expedition. Patrick Clayton and Lady Dorothy had discovered the entrance to the wadi in the Gilf Kebir and, now satisfied, had headed back to Cairo.

"We'll follow their tracks into the wadi,"

announced Almasy immediately. "Then we'll go one better – once we're there, there might be clues about the other two wadis. But before we go, I'm going to talk to the locals."

Almasy was sure that the people of Kufra must know about the wadis hidden in the Gilf. Getting them to admit to it was another matter. The desert people did not like to give up their secrets to strangers. Eventually, he found an old caravan guide named Ibrahim who was willing to talk.

"This wadi you are talking about is called Wadi Abd el Melik," he told Almasy in strange, strongly accented Arabic. "There is another nearby. We call it Wadi Talh."

After a little persuasion, Ibrahim described how to reach the second wadi. But he refused to say whether there was a third. Satisfied for the time being, the expedition party set off once more.

"Wadi Abd el Melik and Wadi Talh," mused Almasy, as they drove along. "Only two. Is old Ibrahim telling the truth, do you think?"

They wound their way through the Gilf and, following the tracks of the Clayton expedition, eventually made their way into the Wadi Abd el Melik. It was long, and studded with acacia trees, but there was little else to say about it. All the other vegetation was dry and withered; there were two small rock springs, but they were almost dry. It was hardly a vision of paradise.

But Almasy was still determined to find Wadi Talh. With one of the Arab men, he drove the treacherous route to the top of the Gilf plateau and followed old Ibrahim's directions. Soon, sure enough, he came upon another wadi filled with acacia trees.

Jubilant, he returned to camp. Only one wadi remained to be found. Feeling pleased with themselves, the party headed for the oasis of Uweinat – where, once again, they bumped into Ibrahim. This time, the old man unbent a little further. When he heard of their discoveries, he admitted that there was indeed a third wadi, called Wadi Hamra – the Red Wadi. All three wadis were used by local herdsmen for grazing after the occasional rains. When it didn't rain for a long time, the vegetation disappeared.

So… Zerzura, or not? These poor wadis were hardly the stuff of legends – even the irrepressible Almasy had to admit that. The legend of Zerzura seemed like a mirage that was disappearing before their eyes. But it didn't matter too much; they had mapped out the area and had made some important navigational discoveries. And in those times of change, what was more important – a legend, or some well-drawn maps?

The party rested at Uweinat, and explored their surroundings. Almasy, who always tended to go further than everyone else, soon found something extraordinary. High up in the cliffs was a series of small caves containing prehistoric rock paintings in beautiful hues. They showed domesticated animals, especially cattle, and warriors carrying bows.

These were not the first paintings to be found in the area. In the 1920s, when Sir Ahmed Hassanein Bey had discovered Uweinat, he was told by a local nomad that djinns (spirits) had once lived in Uweinat, and had left their drawings on the rocks. Hassanein immediately sought out the pictures, and found they showed lions, giraffes, ostriches, different kinds of gazelles, and perhaps cows. He had pondered the fact that this region must have been much more fertile in ancient times and populated by many people, who had led a life of relative plenty.

Patrick Clayton had also discovered caves near the Gilf Kebir, which contained pictures of many giraffes, and also some lions. But it was Almasy's determined foraging that brought yet more of these caves to light. He and his team made photographic records, and Almasy himself made some sketches.

But the season had once more come to an end. The expedition packed up and headed back to Cairo. There, they heard that Patrick Clayton's party had made no further discoveries; but it had driven back from the Gilf right through the middle of the Great Sand Sea – the vast area of dunes that had almost killed Gerhard Rohlfs half a century before – which was a great achievement in itself.

When the summer heat was over, Almasy returned to Uweinat once again. On this occasion, he discovered the now-famous Cave of the Swimmers, in a rugged valley leading from Uweinat towards the Gilf Kebir. There, more paintings were found, which clearly showed people swimming. It offered final proof of how fertile this region had been in the old days. There must even have been a lake. Perhaps this, and not the three wadis, had given rise to the ancient legends of Zerzura – but who could really say?

Zerzura had once again eluded discovery and, as Europe drew closer to war, explorers had to turn their minds to other things. They could no longer be neutral. Their knowledge was too valuable, and the maps they made took on a new significance.

For most, there was no question as to whose side they were on. National loyalties ran very deep. But as a Hungarian, Almasy presented a mystery. Whose side was he on? The Hungarian government was sympathetic to Hitler and fascism, but it didn't follow that Almasy was himself a Nazi. He had acted inconsistently during his desert expeditions. In 1932, on the first Zerzura trip, he had taken photographs of the Italian military headquarters in Kufra oasis, and handed them to his British colleagues. Then, in 1933, he had revealed to the Italians in Kufra the east-west route through the Gilf Kebir.

A strange division of loyalties? Perhaps. But he had to come down on one side or the other – and eventually did so in style. He joined the German airforce, the Luftwaffe, as a desert adviser. By 1941,

German counter-intelligence, the Abwehr, was becoming very frustrated, because it couldn't seem to get any spies behind British lines and into Cairo. Almasy, spotting an opportunity to use his knowledge, stepped into the breach.

"I can get two German agents into Cairo for you," he told the Abwehr. "I will take them through Libya, via Kufra, and through the Gilf Kebir to Kharga, and from there to Assyut on the Nile."

At first, the Abwehr scoffed. But so far, all their other attempts had failed; and if anyone could get behind British lines, it was Almasy. They gave him the go-ahead, and the daring *Operation Salaam*, as it was called, was launched.

Almasy's first priority was his vehicles. In Tripoli, Libya's capital, two captured British Fords were given a thorough overhaul, and prepared for their long drive through the desert. Three trucks were to go with them, carrying supplies. Then Almasy met the German spies, agents Eppler and Sanstedte. In early 1942, *Operation Salaam* was ready, and the men set off.

It was Almasy's knowledge of the Gilf Kebir that made the mission a success. The trucks had no problems traversing the east-west gap that he had discovered nine years before. Eppler and Sandstedte were delivered safely to Assyut on May 24, 1942, after an incredible 3,200km (2,000-mile) drive.

Almasy's trip was one of the most daring

intelligence exploits of the Germans' desert campaign; although as it happens, they made little use of it. Shortly after the spies' arrival in Cairo, the British managed to catch the wireless operators who would have deciphered their messages. And, foolishly, the agents themselves squandered money in Cairo and threw lavish parties. It was not exactly difficult for the British to keep an eye on them.

Almasy himself disappeared back into the desert, and successfully made his way behind the Italian-German lines. The British had little chance of catching him; his long-time quest for Zerzura had made him as elusive as the legendary oasis itself...

Afterwards

Almasy survived the war, and wrote a number of books about his adventures in the desert. He died in Salzburg in 1951. Upon his grave is the Arabic epitaph *Abu Raml*, or 'Father of the Sands'.

If you have read Michael Ondaatje's novel *The English Patient*, or seen the film, some of this story may seem familiar to you. The novelist did use this extraordinary adventurer's life as material, although he changed many of the details. Katherine Clifton, Almasy's lover in Ondaatje's story, has no equivalent in reality. Some people have suggested that she was based on Lady Dorothy Clayton-East-Clayton, Sir

Robert's widow; but Lady Dorothy's dislike of Almasy seems to have been very real, and he was in any case alleged to be homosexual. Like her husband, Lady Dorothy met with a tragic end – in 1933, she was killed in a plane crash.

The oasis of Zerzura remains to be found.

Naming a desert

The landscape was desolate as far as the eye could see. To the west, there were never-ending red sandhills, rolling away into the distance. To the north-west, the land was flatter, but just as monotonous. There was nothing of interest to be seen to the south. Sweeping the scene with his binoculars, the only notable feature that the explorer could see lay to the north-east. There, in the far distance, through the shimmering haze, Ernest Giles saw a mountain.

He studied it carefully. "There are ridges running all the way down it," he informed his companion, lowering his binoculars. "That suggests water. I estimate it's about 50 miles [80km] away. That's where we're heading next."

William Tietkens, the man at his side, nodded in agreement. He didn't have much choice – Ernest Giles was the undisputed leader of the expedition. Along with just two other men, he had joined Giles in his dogged attempts to cross western Australia.

It was January 1874. Australia presented a great challenge to British explorers, who wanted to stake their claim to this vast 'uncivilized' land. Most had little respect for the people already living there, the Aboriginal people who knew the land intimately.

Instead, they saw it as their duty to reach the furthest corners of their new territory as quickly as possible, simply fighting off the Aboriginals along the way. As they went, they named each feature of the landscape – as though no one had ever seen it before.

In 1862, John McDouall Stuart had been the first white man to cross the continent from north to south. By 1872, a massive telegraph line had been built along his route. Now, the challenge was to cross Australia from the telegraph line to the west coast. Much of this land was desert.

The race was on. Ernest Giles made his first attempt in 1872. He got as far as the MacDonnell mountains, but then ran out of water and was forced to turn back. He decided to try again the next year. But by this time, two other explorers were in the race as well. Their names were Peter Warburton and William Gosse. Determined to beat them both, Ernest Giles set off on August 4, 1873.

By January 1874, Giles had reached mountains that he named the Rawlinson Range. He explored the area, and set up a base camp named Fort McKellar. To his disappointment, the mountains petered out. Beyond them, to the west, it seemed that there was nothing but more desert.

This was when he spied the mountain to the north-east with his companion William Tietkens. The two men returned to their camp and told the others – a young man named Jemmy Andrews, who was barely 20, and Alfred Gibson, who was slightly older. On February 1, 1874, the four men and over 20 horses set off for the tantalizing mountain.

It was a big mistake. Giles' estimation of the distance was not far wrong, but his other guess – that they would find water – was sadly mistaken. The horses were tired, and there was no water for them on the way. On top of this, it was the middle of summer, and the heat was blistering.

As soon as they found that the mountain was dry, Giles realized they had to get back to the Rawlinson Range as fast as they could. They walked by night, when it was cooler. But, even so, the trek proved too much for some of the horses. By the time they got back to Fort McKellar, four had died of thirst and exhaustion.

"Mount Destruction – that's the best name for this place," he announced in frustration.

So what could he do now? There seemed to be nothing but desert to the west. Knowing that others might already be ahead of him in the race, Giles desperately didn't want to admit defeat. While the horses recovered their strength, he considered his options.

Eventually, he decided to make a quick dash into the desert – just as far as they could go in a few days, to see what lay over the horizon. Perhaps the desert didn't stretch too far; he might find another source of water. This time, he wouldn't risk all the men and horses – he'd take just four horses and one other man. But which of the three should go with him?

The obvious choice was William or 'Mr.' Tietkens. He was very capable, and Giles referred to him by the title 'Mr.' because he was of the same social class as Giles himself. Taking Jemmy Andrews was out of the question. He was hard-working and willing, but young, uneducated and not very intelligent.

But the third man, Alfred Gibson, declared very strongly that he wanted to go with Giles. Like Andrews, Gibson was uneducated, but he was a little older, with a disagreeable, moody character. Giles didn't like him, and didn't really want to travel with him alone. He never washed, smelled very badly and he was always boasting. And although he had shown that he was quite good at taking on some responsibility, he could be careless. But Gibson insisted and, in the end, Giles gave in.

On April 20, they packed all they needed onto four horses. Two of the horses, a big bay cob and another horse named Darkie, were to carry enough supplies of dried horseflesh and water to last a week. Giles rode his best horse, the Fair Maid of Perth, while Gibson rode Badger, a steady horse with plenty of stamina. Off they set for the Circus, the last place in the Rawlinson Range that was known to have water. They spent the night there, and set off into the unknown early the next morning.

Gibson was in a cheerful mood that day. He chatted freely, much to Giles's surprise, for he was often sullen and sulky.

"How is it," he asked Giles, "that so many people on these sorts of expeditions go off and die?"

Giles considered his response. "Well, Gibson," he said thoughtfully, "there are many dangers involved in exploring – other than the risk of accidents, of course. But I would say that most people die through lack of judgement, or knowledge, or courage. Then again, of course, we all have to die, sooner or later."

"Well, I wouldn't like to die in this part of the country," said Gibson.

"Nor I!" agreed Giles.

They rode along in silence after this, through a landscape of sandhills covered in spinifex, the most common plant of the western deserts. After a few hours they stopped and allowed the horses to rest.

The men were very hungry by this stage, so Giles unpacked some of the horseflesh from Darkie's back. What he found appalled him.

"Gibson!" he called. "I thought I told you to pack enough horseflesh for a week."

Gibson looked at him sullenly. "I did," he said defiantly.

"There is barely enough to feed one man here," said Giles angrily. "And certainly not two."

He had given the job of packing the meat to Gibson, and hadn't checked it since. Gibson was silent, and Giles sighed. There was no point in arguing over the issue; they would have to make do with what they had. They rested in the shade for a

227

while, then set off again in the scorching afternoon heat. By nightfall, they had covered a good distance.

"40 miles [65km] in one day," said Giles, as they set up camp. "Not bad at all."

Giles slept badly. He had a horror of ants – which were everywhere – and found it amazing that his companions could sleep with them crawling all over them. This night was no exception. Gibson slept soundly.

At daybreak they set off again, and plodded for another 30km (20 miles) through a landscape that gradually changed – but only from one sort of desert to another. The sandhills gave way to gravel, then to larger stones. It was hard going on the horses' feet. Then, when they stopped to rest, Giles discovered that one of the water bags had leaked. They had not only less horseflesh to eat, but less water to drink, too.

"We had better get rid of the packhorses," said Giles. "We'll send them back. Then we shall have the remaining water for ourselves and the other horses."

Giles hoped that the horses would instinctively follow the tracks they had made on the way out, and slowly make their way to where there had last been water.

"Well, I'd rather ride the cob than Badger," said Gibson. "I'll send Badger and Darkie back."

Giles looked doubtful. "Gibson, I chose Badger for you because I know he can stay the course. He has stamina."

Gibson shook his head stubbornly. "I prefer the cob," he insisted. "He's fresh enough now."

"Yes," said Giles patiently. "But we haven't tested him to the limit. He might not be up to it. We only know what Badger and the Fair Maid of Perth are made of."

Gibson shrugged sullenly. "I want to ride the cob," he repeated.

Giles sighed in exasperation. Gibson really was impossible sometimes. "Very well," he said. They needed to make up their minds, and send the horses on their way. "You shall ride the cob."

It was a fateful decision. Giles might well have remembered his own words at this point – that people met their deaths in the desert through lack of judgement, knowledge, or courage… a serious error of judgement had just been made.

At this spot, they left some kegs of water, which would be much needed on their return. They rested until the heat began to die down, then set off again and managed another 30km (20 miles). There was still no sign of an end to the desert. It stretched in all directions, to the horizon and beyond.

That night they tried to sleep, but their two remaining horses gave them little rest. The desperate creatures nosed around for the waterbags, craving a drink. Giles had hung their last few pints in a tree, and smelling it, the Fair Maid of Perth marched up to the bag and grasped it between her teeth. As she

229

pulled at it, the stopper flew out, and a jet of water shot into the air and splattered on the ground. Giles and Gibson stared at it in disbelief, their throats dry and choking. They now had only about a pint of water left between them.

The cob was even more desperate than the mare. He nosed around the camp frantically, looking for water. Gibson stared at the wretched animal with resentment.

"I wish I'd stuck to Badger," he announced. "The cob's been getting slower all afternoon. Funny. He was always game before."

Giles said nothing. What could he say, after all?

They started out again before daybreak, and trudged another 15km (10 miles). There, they saw some ridges up ahead – a change in the landscape, at last! A little further on, things were definitely looking hopeful. There was a range of mountains in the distance, about a day's journey away. Giles gazed at them longingly, but they had come 160km (98 miles) from the last water. And things were not going well.

"Giles!" called Gibson, who was riding behind him. "I think the cob is dying."

Giles looked back and stared at the sorry creature in dismay. The cob's head was hanging low, and he could barely put one foot in front of another. There was no doubt about it – they had to turn back. Immediately.

"I name those mountains the Alfred and Marie

range," said Giles, with one final, regretful glance in their direction. "After the Duke and Duchess of Edinburgh. I hope, please God, I shall one day set foot there."

But the plight of the cob was terrible. He had not gone far when he stopped in his tracks.

"I'll get off," said Gibson. "We'll have to drive him forward instead."

The cob dragged himself a little further, but then his legs collapsed beneath him. He lay down, his eyes dull and glassy. It was clear that he was never going to rise again.

The men were now in a dreadful situation. Two men and one horse – all exhausted and with barely

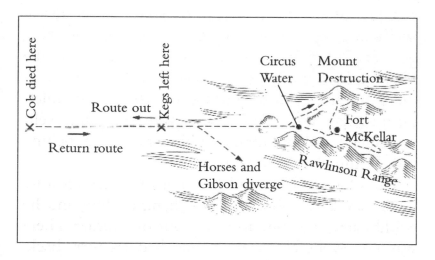

This map shows the trip to Mount Destruction, and Giles and Gibson's route into the desert.

any water. Giles dismounted, and allowed Gibson to ride the Fair Maid of Perth while he walked. It was tough going. After an hour or two they stopped, and gulped down the last of their water. Giles had been thinking hard.

"Gibson," he said, "we can't carry on like this. One of us must go ahead on the horse. I shall stay behind. Now, listen to me. Get to the kegs of water that we left, and give the mare a drink or she will die. Leave as much water as you can for me, then carry on. Stick to the tracks we've made, and don't leave them. When you reach camp, send Mr. Tietkens with water and fresh horses. I will follow, and get as far as I can on foot."

"Very well," said Gibson. "But I'd be better off if I had a compass."

Giles hesitated. Gibson didn't really know how to read a compass, he was sure. Besides, he had only one. Reluctantly, he handed it over, and Gibson pocketed it. He turned the horse, and set off.

"Remember – stick to the tracks!" called Giles after him.

"Alright," called Gibson back to him.

And then he was gone.

With Gibson gone, Giles plodded on through the desert, growing more and more thirsty. He knew the water kegs were 50km (30 miles) away. "If I keep going, I'll reach them tomorrow afternoon," he said to himself.

With sheer effort and determination, he reached the kegs the next day. Gibson had been and gone, leaving him two and a half gallons of water, and a few sticks of smoked horseflesh. Giles was ravenous, and choking with thirst, but he knew he had to ration himself carefully. He sat down and thought the situation through. He was 100km (60 miles) from the Circus, and 130km (80 miles) from camp. It would take at least six days for anyone to get back to him. Should he just sit and wait, or keep on going? Walking further would mean carrying the water keg, which was very heavy and cumbersome. It was a terrible dilemma.

"After I had thoroughly digested all points of my situation, I concluded that if I did not help myself Providence wouldn't help me either," wrote Giles later. Shouldering the heavy water keg, he staggered forward, following the tracks – as he had told Gibson to do.

The next few days passed in a blur. Giles could only walk very slowly, because of the heat and the weight of the keg. 25km (15 miles) beyond the kegs, he stopped.

"That's funny," he muttered to himself.

The main line of horse tracks carried on in front of him, but the tracks of the two horses they had set free now wandered off to the south. And, as he studied these tracks carefully, Giles' heart sank. Instead of following the main line of tracks, it was clear that Gibson had followed the loose horses.

"Perhaps they will all return to the main line soon," thought Giles. He staggered on, looking anxiously all the time for Gibson's tracks, in the hope that he had realized his mistake and come back. But there was never any sign of him.

Giles plodded doggedly on, growing weaker and weaker. Whenever he sat down to rest, his head would swim when he tried to rise again. He fell over many times, but forced himself to keep on going. When he finished the last of his water, he was still 30km (20 miles) from the Circus. But, now that he could dump the heavy keg, he made one last enormous effort. He reached the Circus at daybreak, after a long night's walking. It was a whole week since Gibson had left him.

Giles sat down at the waterhole, and drank and drank. There were now only 30 km (20 miles) between himself and camp, where at last he would find some food. But he was so desperate that he resorted to other means of feeding himself.

"*Just as I left the Circus,*" he wrote, "*I picked up a small dying wallaby, whose mother had thrown it from her pouch. It weighed about two ounces [60g], and was scarcely furnished yet with fur. The instant I saw it, like an eagle I pounced upon it and ate it raw, dying as it was, fur, skin, and all. The delicious taste of that creature I shall never forget.*"

Now out of serious danger, Giles made the final 30km (20 miles) and arrived at Fort McKellar at daybreak about two days later. He woke Mr. Tietkens, who stared at him as though he was a ghost.

"Give me – food," Giles croaked hoarsely.

Tietkens hurriedly did so. "Where's Gibson?" he asked, as soon as Giles could speak properly.

Giles shook his head, and they realized in horror that he must surely be dead by now. There had been no sign of him, either at the Circus waters or at the camp. Giles told Tietkens about his tracks, and how they had left the main line.

"We must go back and look for him," said Giles, although he could barely move. When he was strong enough, they loaded up the horses and launched a search. But, despite all their efforts, they found nothing at all.

Afterwards

With Gibson assumed dead, Giles was forced to end the expedition. He named the desert the Gibson Desert, in memory of his companion.

Sadly, the group retreated, and reached Charlotte Waters on July 13, 1874. There, Giles received bitterly disappointing news. Although his rival Gosse had been forced to turn back, Warburton had taken a more northerly route across what became known as the Great Sandy Desert. With camels instead of horses, he had succeeded where Giles had failed.

What was worse, another explorer named John

Forest had started out from Perth in the hope of crossing the desert from the west. He, too, had succeeded.

But Giles' exploring days were far from over. In 1875, he took a more southerly route, and reached the west coast via the Great Victoria Desert. Then, in 1876, he crossed back again, this time through the ill-fated Gibson Desert. He hoped to find some trace of his old companion; but, to this day, Gibson has never been found.

The Abode
of Emptiness

In the southern half of Saudi Arabia lies a vast area of desert, so barren that even its name suggests a desolate place where nothing can survive. This name, in Arabic, is the *Rub'al Khali*, which translates as 'the Empty Quarter' – or, more poetically, 'the Abode of Emptiness'. Right up until the 1930s, no white man had ever ventured any distance into this wilderness of rock and sand; and certainly no one had ever crossed it.

But, as more and more of the world's areas of wilderness were reached by explorers, it seemed that there was little else to be conquered. The Rub'al Khali was one of the last great challenges – and there were two men who were determined to be the first to cross it.

Both of them were English. One was Harry St. John Philby, a close supporter of the Saudi king, Ibn Saud. He lived in Mecca, the holy city of Islam, and had become a Muslim, taking on the religion of his chosen country.

The other man, Bertram Sidney Thomas, had none of Philby's contacts in the Saudi royal court. He had the friendship of the Sultan of Muscat in Oman, but that wouldn't really help when it came to his desert adventure. If he was going to succeed, he would have to take care of himself.

For Philby, crossing the Rub'al Khali was an obsession that had consumed him for years. In 1924, he had been on the verge of making the expedition, but a revolution in Saudi Arabia had prevented him from setting off. He had then suffered a very bad bout of dysentery, and was forced to give up his plans. By 1930, with Ibn Saud safely on the throne, Philby was desperate to try again, and constantly pestered the king for permission and support.

Meanwhile, Thomas was going about things very differently. Between 1927 and 1930, he made a number of preparatory journeys by camel, in the area just south of the Rub'al Khali itself. He knew that he would have to win the trust of the local Bedouin tribes to make the crossing, because he had no intention of asking for the king's permission.

"*I knew the mind of authority,*" he wrote, "*and so avoided the pitfall of seeking permission for my designs… So my plans were conceived in darkness, my journeys heralded only by my disappearances.*" He immersed himself in Bedouin customs, dressing like them, speaking their language, and making sure he did nothing to offend them.

It was a shrewd policy. While Philby sat impatiently in Mecca waiting for the king to make his mind up, Thomas was putting together his final plans. In October 1930, he sailed from Muscat to the region of Dhufar, on the south coast of Saudi Arabia, where he had arranged for guides and camels from the Rashid, a Bedouin tribe, to meet him.

Philby heard of Thomas's arrival in Dhufar, and grew desperately impatient. The king knew how badly he wanted to go, so he consulted a local governor.

"Is such a trip wise, at this time?" he asked.

The governor said that the political situation was still unstable. "Wait another year," he advised.

There was nothing Philby could do. He was absolutely furious.

But for Thomas, things were not going smoothly either. On arrival in Dhufar, his camels and guides were nowhere to be found. It appeared that the Rashid tribesman he had negotiated with had simply pocketed the money that Thomas had given him, and disappeared back into the desert. Frustrated, Thomas sent out messengers to find him; meanwhile, he just had to wait.

Six weeks later, there was still no sign of his guides and camels. Thomas was on the verge of despair: the ship that had brought him from Muscat was now scheduled to return. Thomas thought he would have to give up his plans, board the ship and return unsatisfied to Muscat. Perhaps Philby would get his chance to beat him in the end.

But then, at the eleventh hour, about 40 Rashid

men appeared with the same number of camels. He could set off after all!

Thomas's route ran from the south of the Rub'al Khali, more or less in a straight line north-east. The main problem he faced was crossing the different tribal areas. The Rashid tribesmen of the south would not enter the feared Murra territory to the north. But, thanks to a great deal of patient negotiation, Thomas found a solution. He would travel in relays. When he reached Murra territory, a new set of camels and Murra tribesmen would meet him, and he would leave the Rashid tribesmen behind.

With this all arranged, Thomas set off. The going was very slow. Whenever there was good grazing – as there was in the early stages of the trip – his guides insisted on allowing the camels to feed, in case they did not come across any later.

This was one of the many desert practices that Thomas had to learn. Another was the Bedouin rule of hospitality. If strangers appear in a desert camp in need of food, they must never be turned away hungry. The knowledge that a rich foreigner was crossing the sands caused a number of such 'strangers' to appear. How on earth were his supplies going to last, Thomas wondered in frustration.

But the days of patient trekking passed by without any major problems. Thomas got along well with the tribesmen. At night, around the campfire, they told him their stories and legends, and he wrote them all down. Many were about an ancient tribe known as the Bani Hillal, and their hero, Abu Zaid. It was said that no spear or sword could kill him, because his mother was descended from a *djinn* (a spirit). Abu Zaid was also famous for his generosity – he had killed all his camels to feed to strangers...

Thomas listened, fascinated, immersed in this world of softly padding camels and never-ending landscapes. But by the time the group reached the waterhole of Shanna, where Murra guides were to take over, one of the camels was very sick. Its fate was brutal and swift. It was dragged into a shallow in the sand, and the men cut its throat, relishing the idea of meat instead of camel milk and oatmeal. Despite his hunger, Thomas was not quite so delighted. He found the meat tough and stringy, and could barely force it down. He watched in astonishment as the tribesmen enjoyed another desert delicacy – they slit open the camel's bladder, and drank her urine. Delicious! Or so they said – much better than the salty, bitter water of the waterholes.

Thomas set off again on January 10, 1931, with a smaller group of men and camels. This second leg of the journey was disrupted by sandstorms, which made life very miserable and wrecked some of Thomas's instruments. Added to this, it was bitterly cold, especially at night. "*Sand filled my eyes, and my notebooks,*" Thomas wrote; "*sand was everywhere; note-taking with numbed fingers was impossible, and all that could be done was to sit idly in the swirl of sand and cold discomfort..."*

But none of this was life-threatening. Thomas's troubles were minor, considering what could easily have happened. The warlike tribesmen remained peaceful, there was an ample supply of camels' milk, and Thomas remained in good health – as did everyone else, including the camels. In early February 1931, Thomas reached his destination of Doha, in present-day Qatar, on the Persian Gulf coast.

Thomas had done it! The news soon reached Mecca, and Philby took it very badly. He was so disappointed that he shut himself away for a week.

When he appeared in public again, he was full of fury about Thomas's achievement – fury mixed with scorn. "What's the point in marching in a straight line?" he stormed. "Thomas's journey was useless. He hasn't *explored* the Rub'al Khali. I'll show him how it's done."

But he was still waiting for the king's permission to set out. Months passed. Philby sat in Jeddah, depressed, disillusioned with the king and Saudi Arabia in general. Then, in December 1931, out of the blue, came the news he was longing for – he had permission at last, and the king's support. Philby was jubilant.

As soon as possible, he headed for his starting point: Hufuf, an inland town not far from Thomas's finishing point, Doha. Everything he needed was waiting for him: 32 camels, 14 men and provisions for three months. His journey could begin at last. Philby set off on January 7, 1932.

Heading in the opposite direction from Thomas, Philby was determined from the outset to cover more ground and make more discoveries. First of all, he wanted to find the ruins of a mythical city that a guide had once told him about. It was called Wabar, and was said to have been the home of a sinful king, Ad Ibn Kinad. To punish the king for his sinfulness, God had destroyed Wabar by fire.

Philby followed the guide's instructions and found the site quite easily. What he discovered, however, were not ancient ruins, but the craters left by a large shower of meteors. Fragments of iron and silica lay around the area, and Philby was careful to collect specimens. The mystery solved, he moved on.

But his journey soon took on a different character from Thomas's. Philby had not developed any personal trust with the Bedouin. They didn't understand why he insisted on taking a more difficult route than he needed to, or why he constantly made detours to fill in his maps. They also wanted to spend time hunting a desert antelope called the oryx, but Philby wouldn't let them. Unwillingly, they got as far as the waterhole of Shanna.

At Shanna, the disputes reached a new level. Philby wanted to take a completely new route to the west, while his guides wanted to follow the route taken by

Thomas. They couldn't see the point of heading into a wilderness with no known waterholes. Philby had to bribe them to continue by paying them in advance.

With tempers still simmering, the group set off again. But things didn't improve. After five days, when they were 230km (140 miles) into the desert, the disputes brought the group to a halt. The camels were at the point of collapse, and all the men were desperate with hunger; they had eaten nothing but dates since leaving Shanna. But Philby still refused to let them slow the expedition down by going off to hunt oryx. To make matters worse, he insisted on walking in the daytime, when it was hot, so that he could make all his observations.

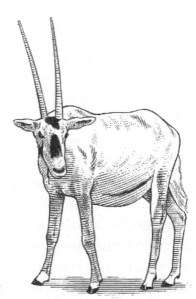

A desert oryx

The men had had enough. Philby was forced to give way, and allow the group to turn back. He described this day as *"the worst of the whole journey from beginning to end, and perhaps the most terrible of all my experience"*. But turn back they did, towards the waterhole of Naifa, north of Shanna.

Now encouraged at the thought of water, the guides kept up a fast pace, and Philby had little choice in the matter. They stopped only to allow one of the camels to give birth — and the baby camel was killed immediately for food. The men made a small fire and tried to roast it, but they were so desperate they couldn't wait for it to cook. As they ate ravenously, it was still quite raw. *"I could have eaten anything, cooked or raw,"* wrote Philby later.

After four days of relentless marching, the men reached Naifa and drank its bitter water with relish. They slaughtered another camel for some much-needed meat, and rested. But now Philby had to decide what to do next. He was still determined to cross the desert to the west, as he had planned; but it was now clear that the baggage camels simply couldn't take the pace, and were slowing everything down. The only way to succeed would be to travel light, and fast. He decided to split the group up and send the heavy baggage back to Hufuf.

Now the men could choose whether or not to come with him on the tough journey that lay ahead — 560km (350 miles), with no certainty of water.

When they had rested, a surprising number said they would come. In the end, he sent only seven men back to Hufuf.

This part of the journey was particularly gruelling. Philby squabbled with the men over his rations. When they tried to shame him for not sharing his camel's milk, he refused to drink any more milk for the entire journey.

Choking with thirst, Philby stared out across a bleak gravel plain that contained nothing else whatsoever – not even thorny desert vegetation. Philby's guides, taking the matter into their own hands, decided that the best way to cross it was just to keep going. It was a fantastic feat of endurance – 110km (70 miles) of non-stop travel, with 18 out of 21 hours in the saddle.

But once they were over the plain, the guides began to recognize landmarks. They were nearing their destination, the oasis of Suleiyil on the north-west fringes of the Rub'al Khali. The hungry, thirsty men and their camels walked into the oasis on March 14, 1932.

Afterwards

So whose achievement was greater? Both Philby and Thomas wrote detailed accounts of their journeys, including maps, long lists of wildlife and

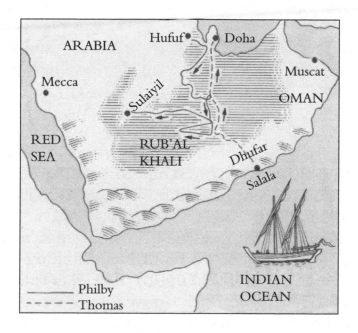

This map shows the routes taken by Philby and Thomas through the Rub'al Khali.

flora and geological features. It's difficult to say who contributed more knowledge of the region. Thomas indisputably made the first crossing, but Philby's route was the more difficult one.

Perhaps Thomas cheated by avoiding the issue of permission. Philby would certainly have won the race otherwise. But neither of the men could set out without the help and guidance of the Bedouin tribes, for whom the whole idea of a 'first crossing' was probably very strange. Thomas won their support through patient dealings, and kept their good will throughout – a great personal achievement in itself.

Philby, on the other hand, made his trip with the

king's protection. As it turned out, he'd needed it. Many years later, he discovered that his disgruntled guides had planned to kill him at Shanna, but fear of the king had stopped them. So he was lucky to survive at all.

Harry St. John Philby continued to explore Saudi Arabia for many years, and was acknowledged as an expert on both Arabian geography and politics. However, in his later years he became critical of the Saudi government and accused it of being corrupt. The government was offended and banished him from the country in 1955. He went to live in Beirut until the Saudis relented and let him back in. He returned, but didn't settle in Arabia again. He died in Beirut in September 1960.

Bertram Sidney Thomas also lived in the Middle East for much of his life. He held a number of important posts in Bahrain, Palestine and Lebanon. He died in Cairo in December 1950.

The vanished airman

If a human body is left in the sands of the Sahara, it doesn't rot away. Instead – as the ancient Egyptians knew very well – the intense, dry heat quickly sucks away all the moisture, and the skin turns to brittle leather. The body becomes a mummy.

In 1962, a French army patrol was driving through one of the most remote parts of the Sahara, south of the town of Reggan in Algeria. It is so remote that even the desert nomads rarely enter it, and call it Tanezrouft – 'the land of thirst'. So it was particularly surprising when someone suddenly spotted the glint of sunlight on metal, up ahead.

"What's that?" the men called to one another. They drove closer.

"Looks like a plane!"

It was indeed a plane, lying upside down in the sand, a total wreck. And underneath one of its wings, his body parched and mummified, lay the pilot. His name was Captain Bill Lancaster, and he had lain there undiscovered for a total of 29 years.

Carefully, the French patrol inspected the wrecked plane. It was an Avro Avian, a single-seater biplane of the kind used by aviation enthusiasts in the 1930s. Tied to a wing strut were the plane's documents, the logbook, Lancaster's passport and a wallet, all carefully wrapped in fabric to protect them. Lying nearby was a Shell fuel card with a final message:

"*So the beginning of the eighth day has dawned. It is still cool. I have no water... I am waiting patiently. Come soon please. Fever wracked me last night...*"

On opening the fragile logbook, the patrol found 41 pages detailing the pilot's last flight, his crash, and the terrible eight days that he spent hoping to be rescued, but instead dying slowing of thirst. His bravery in the face of death was astonishing – and said a great deal about a man who, only 12 months before, had been accused of murder...

Captain Bill Lancaster had led an eventful life. He was born in England in 1898, but emigrated to Australia during his teens. During the First World War he trained as a pilot, and joined the British Royal Air Force after the war. In 1927, the RAF no longer needed him, and he wondered what to do. He didn't want to give up flying; so when he had the idea of becoming the first man to fly from England to Australia, it seemed like the perfect way to make a name for himself as a pilot.

Things soon fell into place. He was offered an Avro Avian plane at a special price, and Shell offered to pay for his fuel. When he met an Australian woman who wanted to become the first woman to make the journey – and offered to find half the funds – the idea suddenly became a reality. The woman's name was Jessie Miller, 'Chubbie' to her friends.

The pair set off on October 14, 1927, from Croydon Airport near London. The flight turned into an adventure that lasted five months, as they struggled with bad weather conditions, mechanical failure and a crash-landing in Sumatra, Indonesia. When they finally arrived in Australia, hundreds of people were there to greet them. But only Chubbie had achieved her goal. She was the first woman to make the flight, but Bill just missed being the first man. Their flight had taken so long that another pilot, Bert Hinkler, had overtaken them on the way.

During their adventure, Bill Lancaster and Chubbie Miller fell in love, although both were already married. It was a love affair that would have devastating results.

Chubbie built on her fame by getting her own pilot's licence and entering flying competitions. She and Bill went to America, where she became well known in aviation circles. Then she had the idea of writing a book about her adventures, and she looked for a writer to help her. She found Haden Clarke, a handsome young man, who came to live with her and Bill in their house in Miami to work with Chubbie on the book.

For Bill, things were not working out quite so well. He consistently had problems finding work. In

1932, he was given the job of piloting a plane in Mexico. Unable to pick and choose, he set off, leaving Chubbie and Haden alone in the Miami house.

Chubbie was left alone with very little money, and she soon grew frustrated and bored. Stuck in the house with Haden, the charming writer soon captured her heart, and she even agreed to marry him. The pair both wrote to Bill to tell him the news, and he flew home from Mexico at once. He was distraught. He adored Chubbie, and couldn't believe that she had betrayed him so easily,

With the three of them staying in the house in Miami, it is hardly surprising that things reached a dramatic climax. On the night of April 20, 1932, Haden Clarke was shot in the head, and died soon afterwards in hospital. There were two suicide notes, but it didn't take the police long to decide that they were forgeries – and that Bill had written them. A week after Clarke's death, Bill Lancaster was arrested for his murder.

The trial was a big sensation. Everyone was sure that Lancaster must be guilty. Haden Clarke had been his rival – Lancaster had had an obvious reason and every opportunity to kill him. But Lancaster denied it. He insisted he was innocent. And, as the trial wore on, it began to seem that he might be telling the truth. It was clear that he was an honest, decent man, whereas evidence about Haden Clarke showed him to be unstable and a heavy drinker. He had even threatened suicide before.

The day of the verdict was desperately nerve-wracking for Lancaster. His whole life hinged on this moment… As the foreman of the jury intoned "Not guilty", the whole court rang out with applause from the people listening.

But, in fact, Lancaster's life was in ruins anyway. Finding work had been hard enough, but no one wanted to have anything to do with him after the trial, despite the verdict. What could he do? He and Chubbie headed to England, away from the glare of bad publicity. There, Lancaster pondered his future. He had no money. His flying career was in tatters. His only idea was to set another flying record, which might restore his reputation in aviation circles.

Lancaster's father, seeing that his son was desperate, agreed to fund the trip. Lancaster decided to go for the England-Cape Town record, which had recently been broken by the British pilot Amy Johnson. She had set a time of four days, six hours and 54 minutes. It was a tough challenge, and from the start, Lancaster didn't really think it through properly.

He chose for his plane another Avro Avian, this time a single-seater called the Avian Mk.V Southern Cross Minor. He was particularly fond of flying Avians, having flown to Australia in one; but it was still a rather foolish choice. Amy Johnson had made her flight in a De Havilland Puss Moth, which had a cruising speed of 37kph (20mph) faster than the Avian. To beat her record, Lancaster would have to make the flight almost non–stop – a physical feat of endurance that would test the strongest man.

But Lancaster was no longer strong. Both mentally and physically, he was exhausted from the ordeal of the previous year. Everything he said before the flight suggested that he was in no fit state to do it.

"I want to make it clear that I am attempting this at my own risk," he told a reporter. "I don't expect any efforts to be made to find me if I'm reported missing." They were hardly optimistic words – perhaps even fateful…

On the morning of April 11, 1933, Chubbie and Lancaster's parents came to see him off from Lympne Aerodrome, near the South Kent coast.

"Goodbye, darling," said his mother, handing him some chicken sandwiches and a bar of chocolate.

Lancaster embraced them all tightly, then climbed into the cockpit. He started the engine. It was 5:38am.

His first stop was supposed to be at Oran, in Algeria – a big hop from England of 1,770 km (1,100 miles). But from the word go, he had terrible luck. The winds were against him, and he had to land in Barcelona in Spain to refuel. He battled on to Oran, his nerves becoming frayed. He was already behind schedule. The officials at Oran looked concerned when they saw him. He was jittery and bad–

tempered, and certainly in no condition to make the treacherous desert crossing.

"Monsieur, we really think you should reconsider," said one official. "You need to rest."

"Rest!" exploded Lancaster. "I'm already late. I can't rest. And you fellows are only slowing me down."

"It's in your own interest, monsieur," said the official patiently. "Crossing the desert is exhausting at the best of times. And I might remind you that we require a £100 deposit against our search costs, should we need to come and look for you."

"I've already paid my deposit!" exclaimed Lancaster – which was true. He had paid the sum in London.

"I'm afraid we have no record of that," said the official. "You will have to pay it again."

Lancaster was furious. "Well, I don't have £100!" he argued. "I'll take my chances, and I don't expect you to look for me."

With these words, he climbed back into his cockpit and taxied down the runway. The officials shook their heads. It was three o'clock in the morning. Lancaster had been on the go for nearly 24 hours.

The next leg of the journey took Lancaster over the Atlas Mountains and across the first stretch of desert. He flew on through the night, checking his compass by flashlight.

As dawn broke, he looked down from his cockpit anxiously, straining to catch sight of the trans-Sahara track that led down to the town of Reggan, his next scheduled stopping point. To his relief, there it was, stretching southwards across the arid wastes. He decided to stop at Adrar, 160km (100 miles) north of Reggan, then skip Reggan altogether and get the desert over with in one mammoth flight.

But Lancaster's exhaustion was getting the better of him. He took off from Adrar at about half past nine in the morning, and immediately lost his way. Below him, a sandstorm was raging, which obscured the track heading south. Instead, he headed east. This was disastrous. He flew on for over an hour and a half before realizing what he had done. He then landed at a small place called Aoulef to check exactly where he was. Eventually, he headed south to Reggan – but he had lost hours of valuable time and was running out of fuel. He would have to land at Reggan after all.

Did Lancaster know that this stop would be his last contact with the world? It almost seems as though he had a death wish. He landed at Reggan and clambered out of the cockpit. He had not eaten or slept for 30 hours, and his condition alarmed officials.

"Look at him! He can hardly walk," commented one, as Lancaster staggered towards them.

"We can't let him carry on," agreed another. "He's a danger to himself."

The officials, like those at Oran, did everything in

their power to stop him from continuing. But Lancaster was as determined as ever. Passing a hand over his face in exhaustion, he was very clear about his intentions.

"I'm carrying on," he told them. "This is my only chance. My only chance, do you hear me? I am not going to fail. I cannot fail."

Impressed with his courage, one official tried to reason with him more gently. "But you are already 10 hours behind schedule," he said. "You are exhausted. It would not be in any way disgraceful to give up now. Better to fail than to die in the desert."

But the look in Lancaster's eyes revealed that failure was his biggest fear of all.

The man sighed, and relented. "I can't stop you from going," he admitted. "And of course, we can't ignore you if you don't arrive. If we don't hear anything by six o'clock tomorrow, I will send a search car down the track to Gao. If you can burn something to light a beacon, we should see you."

So, at eight o'clock that evening, Lancaster once more climbed slowly into the cockpit. The officials watched him with heavy hearts as the plane weaved and wobbled down the runway. It was clear that Lancaster could barely concentrate on the controls. The plane lurched into the sky.

But as they watched, the Avian swung around smoothly enough, and began to fly south. Lancaster was on his way again — but his chances of survival were looking slim…

Up above the Sahara, Lancaster knew he had 800km (500 miles) of desert ahead of him. If he could just stay awake, and keep to the trans-Saharan track, all would be well... He was staring intently at his cockpit controls when the engine gave a cough. Lancaster's heart started pounding. He checked all his controls, but could find nothing wrong. Then the engine coughed again – and again...

The plane started to drop. Lancaster fought with the controls, but there was nothing he could do. He was coming down. It was dark, and he couldn't judge his distance from the ground. He tried to guess, but it was hopeless.

There was a sickening crunch as the plane crashed into the desert sands and turned over. Lancaster knew no more. Everything went black...

This map shows Lancaster's flight path and the site of the crash.

When he came around, Lancaster could see nothing. He wondered where he was, and what had happened to him. Had he gone blind? He seemed to be upside down, and the air was heavy with fumes. He put a hand to his eyes, and realized they were clogged with congealed blood. He rubbed them until they opened.

Now, he could assess his situation. He was indeed upside down in the tiny cockpit, which was spattered with blood. He felt his face carefully. There were deep cuts on his forehead and nose, but at least they had stopped bleeding now. How long had he been unconscious? He had no idea, but he could tell he had lost a lot of blood. He felt weak and faint. He scrabbled around and managed to heave himself out of the cockpit.

"*I have just escaped a most unpleasant death,*" he wrote in his logbook. It did not seem to occur to him that an even more unpleasant one lay ahead. He checked his supplies. They were pitiful. He had two gallons of water and the lunch that his mother had given him. But Lancaster was determined to be optimistic. He worked out that the water could last him seven days. In that time, he was sure he would be rescued.

The long wait began. Every day, Lancaster drank his ration of water, and wrote his thoughts in the logbook. On the first night, he made flares from the fabric of the plane, soaking strips in fuel and setting them alight. He continued all night, lighting one flare every twenty minutes or so. But even though they burned brightly, no one saw them.

In the next few days, he wondered whether to set out on foot to find help, but knew that he would probably die all the more quickly this way. From the air, a man walking in the desert is almost invisible; at least, if rescuers flew overhead, they would see the plane. "*I must stick to the ship*," he wrote.

It was a terrible place to have crashed, right in the heart of the Sahara. The dunes spread out in all directions. The daytime heat was scorching, and Lancaster wore only his underwear as he tried to conserve his energy in the shade. But the nights were bitterly cold, and he wore everything he had to stay warm enough. "*Truly am I atoning for any wrong done on this earth. I do not want to die. I want desperately to live*," he wrote.

There were few signs of any life at all. Once, he spotted a vulture circling above him, no doubt hoping for a meal. He also saw a small brown bird nearby, and wondered if it was far to an oasis. But he kept his resolve, and stayed under the wing of the plane.

By the end of the fourth day, however, his hopes of rescue were beginning to fade. "*Do not grieve,*" he wrote to his parents and Chubbie. "*I have only myself to blame for everything.*" But after writing this, his heart suddenly gave a leap of hope. There, in the darkness, was an aircraft flare! Trembling with excitement,

Lancaster lit a flare himself. "*I assume I am located,*" he wrote in the log. "*I trust so.*"

In his relief and jubilation, Lancaster drank two rations of water. He would not die after all! The next day, he watched the horizon hopefully. Not long now, he thought to himself. Not long now...

But still no one came. His hopes faded again, and he felt tortured by thirst. "*I wish I had not drunk that extra flask of water,*" he wrote regretfully. "*Oh for water, water.*" His thirst was terrible. It was driving him crazy. But, in spite of everything, he kept his dignity. In his desperate state, he began to think about death. "*Please God I pass out like a gentleman,*" he wrote. And it certainly seems as though he managed to do so.

On the seventh day, he realized he had only a few more hours to live. With the last of his strength, he wrote messages to each member of his family, assuring them of his love. "*The chin is right up to the last I hope. Am now tying this log book up in fabric...*"

With all his documents tied to the plane, Bill awaited the end. It must have taken slightly longer than he had imagined, for he found the energy to write one last message on the Shell fuel card: "*No one to blame... Goodbye, Father old man... And goodbye my darlings. Bill.*"

While Bill lay dying, the search for him was still going on. The French officials at Reggan had sent out a search car, as they had promised; but, as the plane had crashed 60km (37 miles) from the road, there was little chance of it being spotted. The airborne searches took place much further south; no one imagined that he would crash quite so soon after taking off, even in his weary condition. Eventually, the search was called off.

Those left behind had to face an agonizing question. Had Bill wanted to die? His life had certainly pushed him to the edge. As the years passed, they had to accept that they would probably never know. 29 years is a very long time to wait.

Afterwards

Chubbie Miller resigned herself to Bill's death and married a British pilot in 1936. She was still alive when the French patrol finally found the Avro Avian in 1962. They handed Bill's logbook and other documents to her.

Bill Lancaster's mummified body was buried in Reggan by the French patrol.

In 1975, an Australian team set out to rescue the remains of the Avian. They took the plane back to Australia, where it can now be seen in the Queensland Air Museum.

Into the Valley of Death

Something glistened in the waters of the river. Something small, like a pebble. But this was no ordinary pebble. James Marshall bent forward and picked it up. He examined it carefully, turning it over in the palm of his hand.

"Looks like…" he muttered under his breath, his heart thumping. "Can it be? Surely not. Can it really be gold?"

He stared around him in the waters of the river. Soon, he found another. Suppressing his excitement, he pocketed the strange pebbles to show to his boss later. It was January 24, 1848 – the most fateful day in the history of California.

Marshall and his employer, John Sutter, tested the 'pebbles' and found that they had indeed struck gold. They tried to keep it quiet. Sutter had settled in California to run a farm, not dig for gold. He didn't want to be overrun with treasure-hunters. But it was no good. Somehow, over the next year, the word trickled out – gold! Gold! There was gold to be found in the American river.

In 1849, the 'Gold Rush' began. People from all

over America began to head west to California, seeking their fortune. But getting there was a problem. Some people risked the terrible sea voyage that took them all the way around the tip of South America and up the west coast. Thousands and thousands of others packed up their wagons and headed west on foot, risking the desert and its treacherous mountains instead. Either way, the journey took months, and the suffering along the way was dreadful.

By the summer of 1849, there was a well-established trail over the Rocky Mountains to the gold fields, which became known as the Oregon Trail. Its final stretches were the most difficult – the mountains of the Sierra Nevada formed a monstrous barrier, even greater than the huge expanses of desert. With winter snows on the way, these mountains would soon become impassable.

Despite the coming winter, the flood of people over the Rockies continued. Many stopped at the Mormon town of Salt Lake City, in Utah, where there was plenty of grazing for their livestock. The Mormons advised against taking the mountain route in winter – people had been trapped in the snows the winter before. People wondered what to do, and some just settled down to wait until the spring.

But there was another option. There was a route that led south, skirting around the Sierra Nevada. It was longer than the Oregon Trail, but it was said to be easier, with no major mountains to cross. A Mormon named Captain Hunt came forward and said he could lead the way for $10 a wagon. "I'll get you to California in nine weeks," he claimed.

About 150 people took up his offer. One group was a band of 36 young men from Galesburg, Illinois, who called themselves the Jayhawkers. There were also many families with women and children – the Bennetts, the Arcanes, the Briers and the Wades, to name a few. And there were individuals, loosely grouped together or on their own. Two of these men were to play a very important role in the weeks to come. Their names were William Lewis Manly and John Rogers.

The wagon train set off, heading south. Everyone was in a great mood. The weather was beautiful and they were on the move again towards their exciting new life. But, after about ten days, Captain Hunt began to get into difficulties. He didn't seem to know the way very well after all, and the land was getting dryer. Soon it would be difficult to find water.

Discontent began to spread. There were stories of another route that went directly west. Some people remembered seeing a map of it, in Salt Lake City. They came to the conclusion that Captain Hunt didn't know what he was talking about. Why not leave him, and cut a way through west? The Jayhawkers were the most excited by this idea, and gradually others began to agree with them.

When they reached the place where the 'short-cut' was supposed to begin, Captain Hunt lost his control of the group. The Jayhawkers had too many followers. About a hundred wagons followed them, leaving Captain Hunt with only seven.

"I think the route is unsafe," Captain Hunt told them. But he wished them well, all the same. "Goodbye and good luck," he shouted, as he waved them off.

Still in good spirits, the split-off group headed west. But, after only three days, there seemed to be no easy trail for the wagons. This alarmed many people. They were running out of food, and what kind of a short-cut came to a dead end after only three days? After much discussion, more than seventy of the wagons turned back, to chase after Captain Hunt. The Jayhawkers and a straggling selection of other people stayed on, determined to forge a way west.

The remaining group was soon in serious trouble. The land grew more and more arid, and the grazing petered out. They had now reached the desert, and everyone was thirsty. As the oxen grew weaker, they couldn't pull the heavy wagons, and people began to throw their belongings away to make the loads lighter. Tools, books, furniture – they didn't matter any more. All that mattered was getting across the desert.

They were now completely, utterly lost. They had no idea how far it was to California. The desert seemed to go on forever – a terrible land, covered in the white salts and alkalis that came up from the ground. The cattle began to collapse with exhaustion, one by one. When they did so, the people killed and ate them, because they were now very short of food. The situation was looking desperate. The group began to splinter into fragments. The Jayhawkers – mainly young, fit men – forged on ahead, leaving the families behind. The Bennetts and Arcanes stuck together, joined by a few others, making a group of about 20 people. William Lewis Manly and John Rogers stayed with them, helping to scout ahead and bring whatever water they could find.

After many days of parched walking, the Jayhawkers wandered into a deep, desolate valley. Nothing grew there; it was barren, covered only in the salts that made any water foul and bitter to drink. Gradually, the other groups converged there, too, and wandered around trying to find a way out. The Bennett-Arcane group stopped at a spring where the water was drinkable. It was almost Christmas – but what a terrible, cheerless Christmas they faced. There seemed to be no way out of this desert abyss. The sheer wall of a mountain rose to the west.

The Jayhawkers made up their minds. They decided to abandon their cumbersome wagons and pack everything they could onto their oxen, and try to find a way through the mountains. A few others followed them, including the Brier family. Mrs. Brier had to leave behind her best silver tableware, because the truth was staring them in the face. They had to abandon everything – or die.

But not everyone wanted to take this risk. The Bennett–Arcane group decided it was hopeless to continue without knowing what lay ahead. Both the Bennetts and Arcanes had a young child in the family, and Mrs. Arcane was five months pregnant. What if they got stuck in the mountains without any water? They decided instead to stay by the spring, while two went on ahead to find a way through and come back with provisions. The two men chosen were William Lewis Manly and John Rogers.

"We will wait for 18 days," said Mr. Bennett. "If you're not back after that, we will assume you have died in the mountains, or that Indians have killed you."

Another ox had died, so the men packed away some dried meat for their journey. Everyone pooled their money, a total of $60, and gave it to them for provisions. Then the whole camp gathered to wish them goodbye. In their hearts, many doubted that the two men would ever return. The atmosphere was heavy, and the women stood weeping.

"God save you," muttered the men. "Good luck to you."

Manly and Rogers shook hands with everyone, solemnly. Then they turned and made their way up the canyon.

When they had gone, a desolate air settled over the camp. Everyone knew that they might be facing death in the valley. They had some meat, for now.

But, other than that, their supplies of food were very low. They put the rest of their flour aside, to feed the children.

The hours crawled by. The children cried constantly in hunger and misery. There was nothing for them to do. The valley was one of the bleakest places on earth – just bare rock and salt. It would be a terrible place to die.

Meanwhile, Manly and Rogers struggled up the mountains. Once they had reached higher ground, they tried to assess how far they would have to walk. What they found was very depressing. There was not just one mountain range to cross, but three – with long, parched desert valleys in between.

"We will never be able to return in 18 days," said Manly grimly.

As they plodded on, they came upon something lying in a ravine, roughly covered with sage brushwood. "What's that?" exclaimed Rogers. They crept closer.

"It's a body," said Manly.

It was a man's body, lying where he had finally collapsed. Manly and Rogers recognized him. His name was Mr. Fish. He had been part of a small group who had followed the Jayhawkers. The parched mountains had been too much for him, and here he was – lying deserted on the rocks.

Their hearts heavy, Manly and Rogers continued. The going was treacherous and difficult, even for strong men such as themselves. They drank the last of their water, but soon their mouths became so dry that they could not eat their ox-meat. On one day, they were lucky enough to find a piece of ice. They melted it, gulped down the water thirstily, and ate some of their meat. Refreshed, they pressed on – but they knew they would need to find more water soon, or meet the same fate as the unfortunate Mr. Fish.

As they walked, Manly suddenly stopped. "Rogers! Look," he said, pointing.

Rogers stared. "Smoke," he exclaimed. A thin plume was rising from a valley nearby. "That means people... and water."

The two men looked at each other. The fire might belong to Native Americans, who might well kill them. Could they take the risk of finding out? Their thirst decided the issue for them. Even if it meant fighting, it was worth going to see.

To their delight, they had stumbled across the Jayhawkers, who welcomed them warmly. Sitting around the fire, the weary men heard how everyone else was doing. Some people had abandoned all their cattle and gone on ahead. The Brier family were struggling on behind. But another man had died.

"His name was Isham," said the Jayhawkers. "He couldn't keep up. When we stopped to camp, we went back and took him some water. But he was too far gone, and he soon died."

Manly and Rogers were very grateful for the company, and for all the information. They thanked the Jayhawkers, and went their own way again. Time was passing, and the families would be wondering what had become of them.

Back at the camp, the passing days grew only more miserable. The group was terrified of being attacked by Native Americans, and many did not really believe that Rogers and Manly would come back for them. "No one but a fool would come back to this place to save us," they said.

Some of the individuals soon decided to try their chances on their own. "It's everyone for themselves," they said. "We're eating our cattle, but soon there won't be any food left. It's crazy to sit around waiting."

The Bennett and Arcane families watched them go, feeling desolate. It was all very well for these people, who had no children to look after; even if they were right, there was little the families could do. It was too much of a risk to take the children over the mountains. They would just have to wait.

"Are you going, too?" they asked an older man named Captain Culverwell. He hesitated, his face troubled. He didn't like to leave the families on their own, without a way to defend themselves. But there was something in what the others had said – it really was everyone for himself. There was no point in dying in the desert. He waited for a few more days, trying to make up his mind. Then he, too, said his farewells, and trudged off on his own.

18 days came and went, and still there was no sign of the rescuers. The families grew more depressed with each passing day. "They're lost," said Mrs. Bennett sadly. "I'm sure of it. They would have returned by now."

But Manly and Rogers were not lost. After almost two weeks of trekking, they had reached a ranch, and then a whole settlement. California, at last! Hurriedly, they bought provisions with the money entrusted to them, and three horses and a mule to carry everything. Then off they set once more, back across the desert.

It was easier now that they knew the way, but the horses and mule posed a new problem. How could they manage the treacherous mountain passes, which the men had only just managed to scramble through themselves?

They reached one particularly difficult canyon, and the horses stopped. They would go no further. A precipice rose in front of them, and there was no way around. Desperately frustrated, the men realized they would have to let the horses go. They removed the baggage from their backs, and released them. "They'll die here," said Manly bitterly. "There's nothing for them to eat or drink."

Having lost the horses, they were determined to save the mule. He had proved himself to be strong and brave, even though he had only one eye. They pushed and shoved and shouted until at last the mule leaped upwards, onto a precarious ledge. Another leap, and the worst was over. The two men almost cried in relief.

But a sad sight awaited them further on. Rogers, who was walking ahead, suddenly stopped and stared.

"What is it?" called Manly.

"It's Captain Culverwell," replied Rogers. "He's dead."

The two men stared down at the old man. He was lying on his back, with his empty water container beside him. The desert had claimed another victim.

It was almost a month since Manly and Rogers had set out when, finally, they walked back into the little camp. The Bennetts and Arcanes were so moved and relieved to see them that they could barely speak. They stood silently, tears streaming down their faces. Then Mrs. Bennett ran to Manly and fell down at his feet, clasping her arms around his knees. "We didn't think you'd come back," she said in a trembling voice. But once they had overcome their disbelief, the camp came alive with eagerness and chatter. Manly warned them that the road ahead was not an easy one. California was much further than they had thought. The families listened, then bravely made their preparations. They had survived this long – they would not be defeated now.

The group set off with eight oxen and the faithful little mule. After a couple of days, they had climbed up into the Panamint Mountains and could look

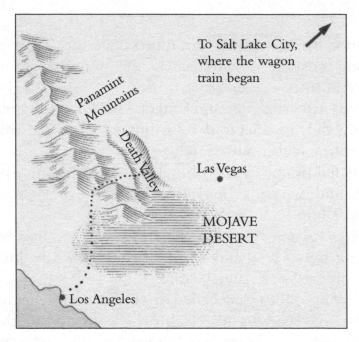

This map shows the route taken by Manly and Rogers.

down upon the barren valley where they had almost died. It stretched out behind them, desolate and empty. Mr. Bennett shook his head, and turned away.

"Goodbye, Death Valley," he said.

The valley has been known by this name ever since.

Afterwards

Like most of the 25,000 people who headed west in the 1849 Gold Rush, few of the Death Valley survivors made their fortune in the gold fields. Many

274

did not even work in the mines; but the flood of people created a whole new community, where many businesses were able to flourish. John Rogers worked as a carpenter and a mechanic; William Lewis Manly did a variety of jobs, including some time working in the mines. He kept in touch with many of his fellow survivors, who always viewed him as a hero, and wrote a book about their experiences, called *Death Valley in '49*.

Mrs. Arcane had her baby four months after leaving the desert, and named her Julia. Sadly, Julia died only 19 days later.

Captain Hunt succeeded in bringing the main group of wagons to California. Most of the Jayhawkers also survived, and went on to start panning for gold. A few of them had some success for a while, but they found it very hard work and the rewards were not as great as they had expected. Most of them gave up and turned to other trades, or became farmers. Some even left California and returned home.

Mrs. Brier was one of the few people to recover her possessions from Death Valley. When the gold in California began to dry up, stories began to spread of gold and silver in the desert. Prospectors began to hunt, and some of them went to Death Valley. There, Mrs Brier's silver tableware was found, untouched; and the prospectors returned it to her.

The road
to Timbuktu

"The greatest traveller in the world!" At least, that's how Abu'Abdallah Ibn Battuta has been described by some historians. In the 14th century, not many men would relish the idea of crossing the Sahara Desert – let alone at the age of 49. But for Ibn Battuta, this was his final challenge before settling down to everyday life in his homeland of Morocco.

Ibn Battuta was born in Tangiers, on the north coast of Morocco, in 1304. When he was only 21, he set off on a pilgrimage to the holy city of Mecca, in Arabia. This journey is called the *hajj*, and all Muslims are expected to go on it at least once in their lifetime, if they can afford it. Little did Ibn Battuta know where his journey would take him: along the North African coast to Egypt, Palestine and Syria, before he even got to Mecca... then, before returning home, to Iraq, Persia, the east coast of Africa, Oman and the Persian Gulf, Asia Minor (modern-day Turkey), the Black Sea and Constantinople, and eventually India, via Afghanistan. From there, he journeyed to the Maldive Islands, and headed further east to China and Indonesia. When he at last returned home to Morocco, he had been exploring for 24 years.

Even by modern standards, you'd think that would be enough for anyone. But there was one place that Ibn Battuta still wanted to visit, and that was Mali, to the south of the great Sahara Desert. He had heard that it was a country of fabulous riches, one of the world's greatest sources of gold. He couldn't resist going on one last trip; so, in the autumn of 1351, he set off from the city of Fez, and headed south.

It has never been easy to cross the vast expanses of the Sahara. In the 14th century, though, there were many established trade routes across the desert, which meant that it was relatively busy. The big caravans preferred to travel in the early months of the year when the desert was not unbearably hot; so, after crossing the Atlas Mountains, Ibn Battuta settled down to wait in a town called Sijilmasa. This was on the fringes of the desert – the ideal place to buy some camels and get ready for the big journey ahead.

Despite being such an adventurer, Ibn Battuta had no plans for a heroic journey on his own. When he eventually set out across the desert, he had plenty of company. As well as his own camels, there was a whole caravan of merchants of Sijilmasa. They were all guided by a nomadic Berber tribesman, who knew the desert very well.

The caravan plodded along slowly, walking in the early morning, and resting in the heat of the day; then setting off again as the afternoon wore on. It took 25 days to reach the first settlement, a strange

277

and desolate place called Taghaza. Nothing grew there – it existed only because of its salt mine. Ibn Battuta hated it. "*This is a village with nothing good about it,*" he wrote. "*It is the most fly-ridden of places.*" The people of Taghaza had a miserable life, hauling huge blocks of salt from the mines to be carried south by camel. They relied on merchants to bring them food, because the land was so barren. But it was an interesting place, nevertheless. There was so much salt that the people built houses with it. Ibn Battuta stayed in a house with walls of salt, and a roof made of camel hide, and he worshipped in a mosque made the same way. He also noticed that there was plenty of money around. Large amounts of gold were changing hands in exchange for the salt.

Much as he was relieved to leave, he knew that the toughest part of the journey lay ahead – 800km (500 miles) of sand, with only one waterhole. But Ibn Battuta was lucky. There had been rain in the desert that winter, and the caravan found pools of water along the way, trapped in the rocks. It made the treacherous journey a lot easier. Even so, they lost one of their companions. After an argument with another member of the caravan, a man named Ibn Ziri lagged behind. He never caught up – and no one ever saw him again.

Ibn Battuta himself reached the waterhole safely, but he was worried about the rest of the trip. They were only halfway across the sands, and the desert, as far as he was concerned, was full of horrible dangers.

He worried that their guide would lose his way and that they would run out of water or get caught by the 'demons' that lived in the barren wastes. He wasn't enjoying himself much. But he needn't have worried. After a trek of about ten days, the caravan entered Walata – now in modern-day Mauritania, but at the time a provincial town of the sultanate of Mali. Ibn Battuta had safely completed yet another journey.

Ibn Battuta may have been getting grumpy after his lifetime of travel, because he complained about many of his experiences in Mali. He certainly didn't have the wonderful riches of Mali lavished upon him as he had perhaps hoped. He was very sick for two months of his stay – he ate some poorly cooked yams and nearly died – which can't have helped his impressions much. And he was thoroughly disgusted by the welcome he received. As such a seasoned explorer, he saw himself as an important diplomatic figure, and expected kings to welcome him with extravagant gifts. The Sultan of Mali gave him only a meal of bread, meat and yogurt.

Ibn Battuta was very offended. "What shall I say of you to other sultans?" he asked.

After that, the sultan was more generous, and gave him a house and later, when he left, a gift of gold.

Ibn Battuta was interested in the customs of Mali, but shocked by many of them. Mali was a Muslim country, but its customs didn't fit in with his idea of how Muslims should behave. In Walata, he was horrified to discover that men and women were often friends, and could quite openly meet up with each other to chat and enjoy themselves. Ibn Battuta was used to the sexes being kept strictly apart. Later, in the capital of Mali, he was disgusted that slave girls were allowed to wander around without any clothes, and he didn't like the royal poets, either, in their flamboyant feathery costumes and masks.

But it wasn't all bad. He was fascinated to watch the sultan's lavish festivals, and he was impressed with how strictly children were taught the Koran, Islam's holy book. He explored much of the country and visited the famous city of Timbuktu before it was famous. In the 14th century, it was still a fairly small provincial town. There was little to indicate that it would become a wealthy trading post and a place where Islamic studies would flourish over the next two centuries.

From Timbuktu, he went east to Kawkaw, now known as Gao. It was the easternmost of Mali's important towns, and here Ibn Battuta decided he'd seen enough. He began to think about going home. Gao was a long way east from Walata, and he didn't want to retrace his footsteps. Instead, he planned to head north across the Sahara by a different route – north-east from Gao as far as the oasis of Takedda, then north-west back to Sijilmasa. This route would take him through some of the most inhospitable desert in the world, and this time he wouldn't have the advantage of the cool winter months. It was the

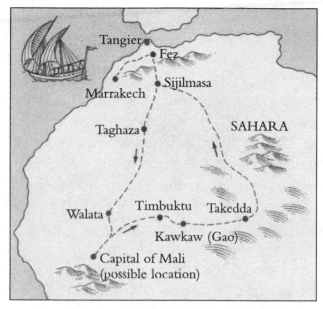

Map showing Ibn Battuta's last great trip

height of summer. Ibn Battuta clearly relied heavily on the caravans he joined, because he bought only two camels for this exhausting trek north: a male camel to ride, and a she-camel to carry his goods. It was not the best kind of planning for a summer's march across the Sahara.

The journey went badly right from the start. The poor she-camel couldn't take the heat and all her baggage, and she soon collapsed. Now the intrepid voyager was in real trouble. Fortunately, other people with the caravan offered to help him carry his provisions, sharing them out between them – or most of them did. Tempers were evidently frayed in the heat, for one man refused to help, and even refused to give water to Ibn Battuta's servant.

They now passed though the lands of some Tuareg people, desert nomads who still live in northern Mali and Mauritania. They survived partly by extorting 'protection money': caravans were obliged to take them on as guides, or risk being attacked. Despite this, Ibn Battuta was fascinated – especially by their women, who fattened themselves up with cow's milk and pounded millet. At that time, thin women were not considered beautiful (modern Tuaregs still have the same opinion), and Ibn Battuta admired these women very much. But his pleasures on the journey to Takedda were few. He became sick in the searing heat, and was greatly relieved to reach the oasis.

Takedda was a big trading post and, like Taghaza, made a great deal of its wealth from a local mine – this time a copper mine. It was not as barren as Taghaza, and the people were able to grow a little wheat. Here, Ibn Battuta found a community of fellow Moroccans to stay with and settled down for a rest. He didn't seem at all interested in continuing his exhausting journey.

But then, unexpectedly, he received orders from the Sultan of Fez to return immediately. It's not clear why, and it seems odd that the sultan should have kept such a close eye on where he was, even in the desert. But Ibn Battuta set off soon afterwards, joining a huge slave caravan of 600 black women slaves, bound for Sijilmasa. It must have been a terrible journey for them, and they had little to look forward to – they would be sold in Morocco as servants or prostitutes. But Ibn Battuta didn't give the issue a second thought; this was all perfectly normal in North Africa at the time.

On the way to Sijilmasa, the caravan encountered more nomads – this time a Berber group, who wore veils across their faces. They extorted a payment of cloth before allowing the group to continue, which annoyed Ibn Battuta very much. "There is no good in them," he complained. But this was the only major problem he encountered, apart from the constant discomfort of desert travel. After this, they passed through the Berber country in peace.

He arrived in Sijilmasa in the winter, and made a treacherous journey across the Atlas mountains in the snow. Despite his great treks across the desert, he declared that this final leg of the journey to Fez had been the most difficult of all.

Afterwards

Once back in Fez, Ibn Battuta was home for good. We don't know much about what happened to him after this – we can only assume that he settled down to a luxurious life in the sultan's court, where he would have had many tales to tell. He certainly lived long enough to write an account of his travels, known as the *Rihla* – a fascinating insight into many of the world's Muslim countries in the 14th century.

Glossary

Arabian camels *Also known as* dromedaries. One-humped camels. Originally from Arabia, but now seen across the Sahara.

Bactrian camels Two-humped camels from the Far East.

Bedouin *Also called* Beduin *or* Bedu. General name for nomadic tribes of the Middle East and part of the Sahara. There are many different tribes, each with their own name and customs.

Caravan Group of people, usually traders, making a journey together across the desert, often with a large number of camels.

Date palms Trees commonly found in the Middle East and the Sahara. A valuable source of food.

Dehydration Literally, 'losing water'. In dry conditions, especially hot deserts, people lose water very quickly by sweating, and this can be fatal.

Desert An area of land which receives less than 10cm (4 inches) of rain each year.

Desertification Process by which land that was once fertile turns into desert.

Dune A mound of windswept sand. The highest dunes in the world are in the Namib Desert (Namibia).

Erg An area of shifting sand dunes, particularly in the Sahara.

Two of the biggest ergs are in Algeria – the Great Eastern Erg and the Great Western Erg.

Flash flood Sudden flood in the desert caused by rain.

Islam Main religion of people of the Sahara and Arabia. Founded in the 7th century by the prophet Mohammed, in the Arabian city of Mecca.

Mirage The illusion that you can see something up ahead when it is actually far away. Mirages are often experienced in deserts because they are caused by hot air, which refracts (bends) the light.

Mud flat Flat area of mud or clay that was once covered in water but has now dried out.

Muslim A follower of Islam.

Nomad Someone who doesn't live in one place, but moves around constantly. Most desert people are nomads because they need to travel to find water and food.

Oasis Area of naturally occurring water in a desert, usually from underground springs.

Salt flat Flat area of salt left behind by water as it evaporated.

Tuareg Nomadic tribes of the western Sahara.

Wadi Dried-up desert riverbed, which only flows if there is rain.

TRUE
EVEREST
ADVENTURES

Paul Dowswell

CONTENTS

Into the death zone

Everest, the highest mountain in the world, towers 8,850m (29,035ft) above sea level – that's over 20 times taller than a skyscraper. Half in China, half in Nepal, it forms part of the Himalayas, a colossal mountain range stretching between India and China.

This map shows the location of Everest.

Many climbers have attempted to reach the top of Everest, but this is a goal fraught with peril. Everest climbers have to face treacherous mountain slopes, extreme weather and avalanches, only to reach altitudes which are dangerous in themselves. Climbers refer to heights above 5,800m (19,000ft) as "the death zone". Human beings were never designed to live at such an altitude, where there is only one third the usual amount of oxygen in the air. Yet despite these dangers, Everest has been climbed by at least 15 different routes.

The route that originally led mountaineers two-thirds of the way through the Earth's atmosphere, and onto the roof of the world, leads up the South East Ridge. This was the route taken by the first men to reach the summit, Edmund Hillary and Tenzing Norgay, in 1953. In the years since, over a thousand climbers have stood puffing and panting on top of the world's tallest mountain, on a summit said to be little bigger than a billiard table. This seems like a lot of people until you realize that over 170 climbers have died on Everest. For every four or so climbers who got to the summit, someone died on the mountain – frightening odds that still make getting to the top an extraordinary achievement.

Because the South East Ridge is by far the most popular route, the world's elite climbers tend to be a bit snooty about it. They refer to it dismissively as "The Yak Route", after the famously hairy cattle found in Tibet. But such talk is mountaineer bravado.

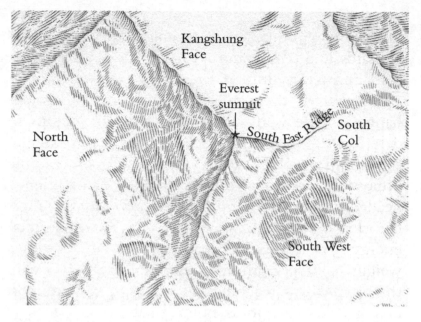

This aerial view of Everest shows all the faces of the mountain at once.

Any route up Everest is an endurance test and life gamble unimaginable to most ordinary people.

Even on the way up to the South East Ridge, a climber has to pass through a fractured glacier of tottering, cathedral-size blocks of ice, that could come crashing down on them without warning. Then they must reach a flat, dreary plain, around the size of a large sports stadium, called the South Col, which huddles between the twin peaks of Everest and its smaller companion Lhotse.

The South Col has been called the most desolate campsite in the world. Here, at 7,860m (26,200ft), the wind howls so constantly and loudly it is often likened to a jumbo jet at takeoff. The wind brings blizzards, and temperatures can drop as low as -40°C (-40°F). At this altitude, even the healthiest climber can feel as if they are suffering from a ferocious hangover. The body almost immediately begins to deteriorate – the lungs become clogged with mucus, the brain swells, eating and drinking become impossibly weary chores, and climbers become light-headed and easily confused. Because of this, most climbers on the mountain carry oxygen. The extra energy oxygen provides makes up for the additional weight of the breathing equipment. But even with this artificial aid, reaching the summit is still the most taxing, exhausting journey imaginable.

Bodies on Everest are a frequent sight – especially this high up. Although some are brought down the mountain for burial, this can be an extremely dangerous procedure, so most are left where they died. After all, why risk another life for someone who is dead already? During the 1990s, one of the most pitiable sights on the South Col was the body of an Indian climber from an expedition in 1985. He could be seen crouched on his knees, leaning forward as if to open the zipper flap entrance on his tent, his face set in a grimace of utter misery.

Returning from a summit attempt, he had reached the safety of his tent only to find his frozen hands lacked the strength and dexterity to unzip the entrance. Perhaps he was too tired to call for help, but if he had done, his cries would have been carried away by the wind. Besides, his colleagues might well have been too weak to come to his aid – a climb up the South East Ridge can leave even the most experienced mountaineer so exhausted they can hardly speak. So, with his warm sleeping bag and the prospect of a stove and a hot drink a mere zip away, the climber died. In time, the fierce winds blew his tent to tatters, but his body remained, like a strange, frozen statue, reaching out to a safe spot that would be forever beyond his grasp.

The final route to the top, up the knife edge of snow, ice and rock that make up the South East Ridge, is a seven or eight hour slog, or more. Climbers usually set off before daybreak, or even the night before, to ensure they reach the top in good time to return in daylight.

Getting to the top is only half the battle – on the way back, darkness and exhaustion can be a lethal combination, making coming down even more dangerous than going up. One wrong step can send a climber tumbling down the rock and scree of the South West Face, or plunging down the icy Eastern "Kangshung" Face – both falls of thousands of feet. One Everest expedition leader once remarked: "With enough determination, any b***** idiot can get up this hill – the trick is to get down alive."

The distance from the South Col to the summit is little more than a mile (1.6km). But it is also 1,200m (4,000ft) upwards, and by the time climbers are halfway there, they probably need to stop every two or three steps to get their breath back. Some determined climbers even drag themselves to the top on all fours. On Everest, even the best and most experienced climbers will take foolhardy risks to stand among the tattered flags, keepsakes and discarded equipment that now litter the summit.

If they succeed in reaching the summit and the weather is good, the view is astounding. Depending on the time of day, the shadow of Everest can stretch hundreds of miles over the dusty, brown plateau of Tibet, or it can hang magically in the atmosphere. Even the curvature of the Earth can be seen, along with Himalayan peaks over 160km (100 miles) away. Above, the sky is virtually black, and a climber can feel as if he or she is on the very edge of space.

Read on, and discover why it took 30 years of intense effort just to climb to the top of this forbidding peak, and marvel at the extraordinary adventures of the men and women who are driven by bravery, tenaciousness, determination and folly to stand on top of the world.

First steps to the Third Pole

The expedition of 1921

One cheerless January morning in 1921, British newspaper readers were treated to exciting news about the tallest mountain in the world. Typical of the reports was this, from *The London Daily Mail*:

> The decision to attempt the climbing of Mount Everest – the last and perhaps hardest of the great adventures to be achieved by man in the terrestrial world – was taken by the Royal Geographical Society at its meeting in London last night. The North and South Poles have both been conquered in this generation, but Everest, the mightiest mountain in the world, and a name of magic to all, still lifts its snowy peak unscaled to a level, according to the latest survey, of 29,140ft [8,740m], in the romantic recesses of the Himalayas between Nepal and Tibet.

As they read on, the public was left in no doubt as to the danger and difficulty of such an enterprise.

TOP OF THE WORLD – WILL HUMAN BODY STAND THE PRESSURE?

screamed a headline in *The Glasgow Citizen*. Only in

296

the previous two years had advances in aircraft design seen planes flying to heights as great as Everest. There was much interest in the practicalities of survival at such a high altitude. As *The Glasgow Citizen* reminded its readers: "At such heights it is very difficult to work. There is less oxygen in the air… the chief effect of the rarefied air is a feeling of lassitude [fatigue]."

It was exciting stuff. In the years before the First World War of 1914–18, the newspapers had been full of stories of Polar exploration. People had been thrilled by the exploits of men such as Scott, Amundsen and Shackleton, who had become household names. Here again, in the dreary years that followed the war, was another great adventure to grip people's imaginations.

Curiously, Everest's frozen inaccessibility had led to it being commonly referred to as the "Third Pole". Now, this trip to the roof of the world – a spot so remote and dangerous that no one in the entire span of human history had even stood on its lower slopes, let alone its summit – was about to be played out before an eager public.

Not everyone welcomed the idea of an expedition. With almost every area of the globe explored and mapped, a few sceptics wondered whether there should be some small parts of the Earth left alone by man. Even those who prepared to offer financial backing to such a trip wondered why they were doing it. There was "no more use in climbing Everest than kicking a football about, or dancing", said one eminent geographer. Still, he felt, such an extraordinary human achievement would "elevate the human spirit".

In Britain in the early 1920s, the world of mountaineering was a rather select one. It was presided over by two distinguished organizations: the Royal Geographical Society and the Alpine Club. Between them, they set up an association known as the Everest Committee, to direct the climbing of the mountain.

At the time, climbing was a pastime only the rich could afford. Such men had been cut down in their thousands leading soldiers into battle in the First World War. Accordingly, the ranks of those suitable for an attempt on Everest had been thinned quite drastically.

So it was that the first expedition sent to explore Mount Everest was made up mainly of men in middle age. Those among them who had fought in the war had generally been too old or distinguished for the most dangerous front line service. The team leader, Lt. Col. Charles Howard–Bury, was a landowner in his late thirties. He had an impressive estate in Ireland and he bred race horses. A rather forbidding person, he was described by one of his team members as having "a very highly developed sense of hate and contempt for other sorts of people than his own". The head of the climbing team, a Scotsman named Harold Raeburn, was 56. Another colleague, a fellow Scot named Alexander Kellas, was 53 years old, and an expert on the effects of high altitude on the human body.

Also on the team were two younger men, Guy Bullock and George Mallory, who were 34 and 35 respectively. Both were gifted mountaineers, and they knew each other well. It was expected that they would do most of the serious climbing, and here Mallory established himself as the star of the team. A former school teacher who had served as an artillery officer during the war, he was tall, handsome and intelligent, and had a charisma unmatched by any other mountaineer before or since. "His limbs and all his movements were free and full of grace," said a friend, "and he had a strikingly beautiful face…"

Looking at Mallory as he peers from the grainy, mottled black and white photographs taken to record that first expedition, it is easy to see why he stood out. Among a forest of beards he is clean shaven, aside from a dashing moustache (which came and went). While his companions look distracted, crotchety and exhausted, Mallory stares into the camera, exuding strength and determination. The challenge of climbing Everest must have seemed a noble goal, well-suited to someone of such obviously heroic qualities. But there was another side to Mallory. While he was just the man with the guts and resolve to climb to the top of a previously unconquered mountain, he was also hopelessly impractical and forgetful – a shortcoming which would forever rule him out of leading an expedition.

In May 1921, the team arrived in India, which was then part of the British empire. They assembled in Darjeeling, a city near the Himalayan mountains, where they recruited a team of porters to carry their equipment. Among this team were men and women from Nepal, known as Sherpas. Over the centuries, the Sherpas had supported themselves by trading, taking yaks laden with hides, grain, butter and textiles along steep mountain paths to other parts of Nepal, as well as India and Tibet, which had made them experts at transporting heavy loads at high altitudes. Right from the start, the Sherpas became an essential part of any expedition to the Himalayas.

Almost immediately Howard-Bury's party

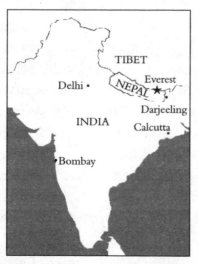

Map showing the countries around Everest at the time of the first expedition

was hit by ill-fortune. The trip to Everest was a long and difficult one, which required them to travel a dreary, dusty route through Tibet. Alexander Kellas, exhausted by the strain of the journey, and suffering from dysentery, died of a heart attack. Harold Raeburn was tormented by dire stomach pains caused by the poor food the team had brought along to eat. He had also fallen from his horse and been badly kicked, so was forced temporarily to abandon the expedition. Most of his colleagues were secretly pleased, for Raeburn had been an incompetent and irascible companion.

As Howard-Bury and his men were drawn towards Everest, they entered territory no westerner had ever visited before. They had literally "walked off the map", as Mallory described it. He wrote regularly to his wife Ruth, and their three young children, and in one memorable account he described his first proper view of Everest. Gazing at the distant peak through binoculars, the mountain was at first shrouded by mist. Then, "a whole group of mountains began to appear in gigantic fragments... like the wildest creation of a dream. A preposterous triangular lump rose out of the depths; its edge came leaping up at an angle of about 70 degrees and ended nowhere. Gradually, very gradually, we saw the great mountainsides and glaciers... until far higher in the sky than imagination had dared to suggest the white summit of Everest appeared."

Tibet is the highest country in the world, being,

on average, 4,900m (16,000ft) above sea level. As the men journeyed on, the high altitude began to take its toll. They all found themselves tiring quickly, as the thin air sapped their strength and stamina. "It is only possible to keep oneself going by remembering to puff like a steam-engine", Mallory wrote to his wife. Despite the exhausting work, the men's appetites seemed to have deserted them – this too was an effect of high altitude on the human body.

As they surveyed the territory around Everest, they could see that the mountain presented many possible routes to the top, but almost all of them looked dangerous and difficult. A massive three-sided pyramid, it was surrounded entirely by glaciers, as all great mountains are. Its three awesome faces were bisected by three great ridges of rock and ice – one to the South East, one to the North East and one to the West. The expedition decided that the North East Ridge reached via the North Col – a small snow-covered dip between the two peaks of Everest and nearby Changtse – looked like the surest way to the top.

The highest the expedition got up Everest was the edge of the North Col, which stood 6,700m (22,000ft) above the East Rongbuk Glacier. But getting there completely exhausted most of Howard-Bury's men, who were constantly tormented by

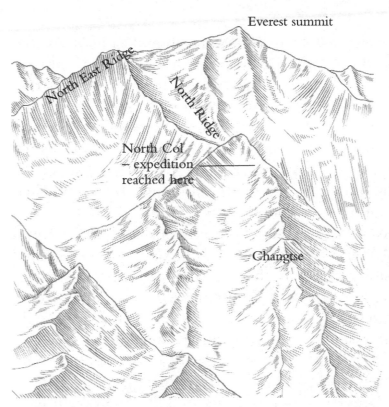

Everest showing the North Ridge and the North East Ridge

strong winds which prevented them from getting a proper night's sleep. Only Mallory wanted to press on to the top. But by then it was September and the Himalayan autumn was closing in fast. Howard-Bury wisely decided the expedition had done its job. They had taken a first close look at the mighty Everest from all sides, and now it was time to retreat and try again another year.

They had learned many useful lessons. Climbing Everest, it seemed, was a job more suited to younger men – it required the kind of stamina and toughness that older men usually lacked. The climate around the mountain was fearsome, but the weather was best in May and early June, just before the arrival of the Monsoon, the formidable wind which brings rain and snow to Asia. Most of all, Howard-Bury's men established that high-altitude climbing was just as exhausting as they had expected. But, with the optimism of a nation whose empire controlled one quarter of the world, they were convinced that, with a little grit and determination, the summit was there for the taking.

Three more shots with "Bruiser" Bruce

The expedition of 1922

Such was the interest and excitement generated by Howard-Bury's trip that a second expedition was being planned even before the 1921 expedition had left India to return to Britain. Mallory, especially, seemed the focus of attention for the newspapers that followed the progress of the explorers. A lecture tour he undertook on his return also made his face better known to the public.

But despite its successes, Howard-Bury's team had been fractious and divided, largely because of the leader himself, who had taken a dislike to Mallory. So, behind the scenes at the National Geographic Society and Alpine Club, significant changes were planned for the 1922 expedition. A new leader was announced: General Charles Bruce, a genial, energetic bear of a man, known as "Bruiser" to his friends. A former officer in the British army's Gurkha regiment, he used to challenge soldiers from the regiment – tough but diminutive Nepalese men – to wrestle him four or five at a time. At 56, he was as old as many of the previous team, but he seemed a better choice of leader than his predecessor.

Of the 1921 expedition, only George Mallory and another climber named Henry Morshead remained. Other new climbers included Howard Somervell, Arthur Wakefield and Tom Longstaff. They were all doctors, although only Longstaff was brought along as the official team medic. Somervell, especially, was an extraordinary man. As well as being a gifted climber, he was a surgeon, a photographer, an artist and a musician, who would go on to write the score to a film about the early expeditions to Everest.

Another new team member was George Finch, an Australian who had been brought up in Switzerland. He was a notable climber who did much to pioneer modern mountaineering equipment. For example, he invented the down (feather-filled) jacket, which was considerably warmer than the wool and tweed most climbers then wore. Yet he was regarded as something of an upstart by the snootier British members of the expedition, and this undoubtedly prevented some of his good ideas from being accepted.

Also on the team were Edward Norton and Lt. Col. Edward Strutt, both distinguished climbers, and Charles Bruce's young cousin, Geoffrey Bruce. The younger Bruce had never climbed before in his life, but General Bruce thought he was the "right sort of chap" for an adventure like this. And along for the trip was expedition photographer Captain John Noel, who brought both still and movie cameras.

There was intense debate among the team as to whether or not they would use oxygen on the climb.

Recent laboratory experiments, using special chambers to simulate high altitudes, had shown that lack of oxygen in the air caused volunteers to become incapable of "controlled thinking and action" above 7,800m (26,000ft), and to slump into unconsciousness. Everest, it was noted, was at least 900m (3,000ft) higher than this. Finch had taken part in experiments which proved that oxygen would be extremely useful at such altitudes. But many climbers, Mallory especially, seemed to think that oxygen was "unsporting". There was even talk of climbers who used it being "rotters" – a schoolboy term, popular at the time, for cheats or otherwise disagreeable people.

But, despite its obvious advantages, there were two very good reasons not to use oxygen. Firstly, the metal tanks that held it had to be transported from "civilization" (in this case Darjeeling) to Everest. This added considerably to the weight of supplies. Secondly, a climber carrying an oxygen set of four tanks, a metal frame, and breathing apparatus, had an extra 15kg (33lb) to heave up the mountain – a weight equivalent to a heavy suitcase. "When I think of mountaineering with four cylinders of oxygen on one's back and a mask over one's face," said Mallory, "well, it loses its charm." In the end, a compromise was reached. Oxygen would be taken on the trip, but a climber could choose whether or not to use it.

There was another issue too, which was much discussed at the time, especially in the newspapers –

the possible existence on the mountain of a strange, ape-like creature called the Yeti. This report from *The Dundee Advertiser* is typical of some of the more overheated speculation about this mythical beast:

> Living among the perpetual snows of Mount Everest is a race of mystery men known in the Tibetan language as 'Abominable Snowmen', on account of their ferocity and the savage deeds they commit when they come into contact with the more or less civilized inhabitants of the region.

Fortunately, to this day, no one has ever been troubled by such a creature, but the newspapers' speculations must have been an added worry to the men about to scale the mountain.

The team departed for the Himalayas at the end of March. The plan was for their expedition to be completed by mid-June, when the Monsoon was expected to start. By the end of April, they had reached the Rongbuk Valley, well on the way to Everest itself, and began to set up a string of camps at increasingly high altitudes. This tactic was known at the time as "the Polar method", because that was how Polar explorers had set about crossing the frozen wastes of the Arctic and Antarctic. Each camp would be a reasonable distance from the other, allowing a climber frequent stopping places on his route to the top. As a mountaineering technique, it worked so well that it is still used today by most expeditions on Everest and other high mountains.

General Bruce's plan of attack was to allow Mallory and Somervell a first attempt at the summit without oxygen. On May 10, they and a support team set off from Camp III for the North Col, the flat section of the mountain at the bottom of the North Ridge. This was a long backbone of rock that led directly to the North East Ridge, which divided the North and East faces of the mountain, and led, eventually, to the summit. The plan was to establish a camp here, as a staging post on the way to the top.

Most mountaineers begin to experience difficulty breathing above 5,790m (19,000ft). The North Col was 1,200m (4,000ft) higher. When they finally struggled up to it, the climbers found themselves utterly exhausted. They managed to put up five small green tents, but were so listless by the time they finished that they had to force themselves to eat. In order to combat loss of appetite, they had made a special effort to make their food as tempting as possible, hauling canned quail and champagne up the mountain. But no one had camped so high before, and the team soon realized high-altitude cooking brought with it special problems. Their loss of appetite was bad enough. But this high up, water boiled at a lower temperature, so the food they did not want to eat took much longer to cook. (Water normally boils at 100°C, but on the North Col it boils at only 80°C, so it takes around 14 times longer than usual to cook food there.)

When Strutt, the expedition second-in-command, reached the Col for the first time, he spluttered: "I wish that ****** cinema was here," (meaning Noel's movie camera). "If I look anything like what I feel, I ought to be immortalized for the British public."

From the North Col, a small group consisting of Mallory, Somervell, Norton and Morshead, together with four Sherpas, began their climb to the top. The plan was to establish another camp higher up, and rest there for the night. Then, the next day, they would head for the summit. They set off up the ridge on the morning of May 20, wearing their pith helmets, woolly jumpers and tweed jackets, with an optional scarf to ward off the cold. Quality clothes they may have been, but they were so preposterously unsuitable for Everest that mountaineers today still marvel at the courage and endurance of these early pioneers. They pressed on through a cruel wind, getting colder and more exhausted with every step. After three and a half hours, they had climbed a mere 600m (2,000ft) up the ridge. Eventually, at around two o'clock that afternoon, they found two ledges close together, which would be suitable spots for a couple of tents. Now they were no longer needed, the Sherpas were sent back to the North Col with instructions to return to Camp III, and the four climbers tried to rest and eat.

They set off again at eight o'clock the next morning, but almost at once Morshead confessed he didn't have the strength to continue. He returned to his tent, while the others carried on up the ridge. On they went, every step a massive effort, moving at less than 120m (400ft) an hour. Eventually, at around half past two that afternoon, they admitted defeat. But they had reached 8,169m (26,800ft) – higher than anyone had ever stood before.

Mallory, Somervell and Norton got back to their camp on the ridge, where Morshead was waiting, around four o'clock. As it was such a precarious spot, and they reasoned they would feel better lower down, they decided to head back to the North Col camp before darkness fell. This was a courageous decision. They were all utterly exhausted, and Morshead, especially, was no better for his rest.

The four men roped themselves together and descended through freshly fallen snow. Passing by the head of a gully, Morshead suddenly slipped, dragging Somervell and Norton down with him, and all three hurtled down the mountain. In an instant Mallory, who was leading the climb and had his back to his companions, heard them fall. He reacted with lightening speed, plunging his ice-axe into the deep snow and slipping the rope around it. Fortunately, the three falling men had not built up too much speed, and Mallory's quick thinking saved them all.

No one had been hurt in the fall, but all four were badly shaken. They moved down with even greater caution. Morshead became more of a problem. He was suffering from extreme exhaustion and frostbite – a particularly horrible condition where the flesh of the hands, toes or other prominent body parts freezes and can be irreparably damaged. He became irrational (a common symptom of high-altitude sickness), and kept on insisting that they slide down the mountain.

The decent slowed to a crawl and darkness overtook them. Then, to add to their alarming predicament, a storm brewed up in the west and lightning flashes lit their path. Eventually they reached the Col, but they were not safe yet. Several crevasses lay between them and their tents. They had only a crude candle lantern to light their way, and that burned out soon enough. Luckily, they stumbled on a rope that had earlier been fixed to a slope away from the Col, and this led them back to their tents.

It was now half past eleven at night, and the freezing climbers were desperate for food and a warm drink. But fate had played another trick on them. Due to a misunderstanding, the Sherpas had taken all the cooking equipment down to the camp below. The shivering men had to make do with an ice cream-like concoction of snow, condensed milk and strawberry jam. It was probably the last thing in the world they wanted to eat, and gave them all terrible stomach cramps throughout the night.

The lower altitude and a night's rest brought their strength back, and the four men were able to struggle back to Camp III the next day. Safe for the moment, all they wanted to do was drink warm tea. Somervell, it was recorded, drank 17 mugfulls. Morshead had recovered a little, but when the expedition returned to India in the summer, he had to have a toe and several fingers amputated. But, even as they returned down the mountain, they passed George Finch, Geoffrey Bruce and a team of Sherpas, heading up to the North Col with a generous supply of oxygen, all set for another attempt at the summit.

Despite the extra weight they carried, Finch, Bruce and their team found climbing with oxygen much easier. Finch had also fashioned his own clothing. His down jacket, made from the kind of tough cloth used for hot-air balloons, had a quilted lining filled with eiderdown, and was much better suited to Everest than the flimsy clothing worn by the others. Armed with such advantages, he felt he had every chance of making the summit. Finch did worry about Bruce, though. This was the lad's first experience of mountaineering after all.

As they settled down for the night, the weather at the North Col grew worse. A terrible gale battered their tents and Finch recalled that the "wild flapping of the canvas made a noise like that of machine-gun fire". The wind was so savage the men had to shout to hear each other speak. But the next day the weather had settled slightly, and Finch and Bruce, now joined by another member of the party, a Gurkha named Tejbir Bura, headed up the mountain to make another camp along the North Ridge at 7,800m (25,500ft). The wind was so bad they feared their tents would be blown away. Here they stayed, gasping and wheezing in the thin air, their limbs growing numb with cold, for the night, the next day, and the next night. All of them could feel their strength ebbing away. But during the second night, Finch had a brilliant idea. He suggested they rig up their oxygen gear so they could breathe it while they rested. It worked like magic. Almost at once the freezing men felt stronger. Breathing oxygen also had the effect of making them feel warmer. All three slept well for the first time in days.

On May 24, at half past six in the morning, they emerged from their tent to begin their trek up to the summit. Tejbir collapsed soon afterwards, telling Finch and Bruce he had no strength to go on. Defeated, he returned to the tent. Then as Finch and Bruce climbed higher, a terrible wind blew up, making progress extremely slow. At 8,320m (27,300ft) disaster struck. Finch, who was leading the climb, suddenly heard Bruce call out in alarm: "I'm getting no oxygen!" Finch turned to see his companion wavering and about to topple off the mountain. He grabbed him, and they sat down together on a nearby ledge. Here Finch examined Bruce's oxygen set, discovered a broken glass tube, and quickly fixed it with a spare he was carrying. It had been a terrifying moment – at the time it was believed that a climber using oxygen at this height would die if his supply was cut off suddenly. This had proved not to be the case, but as Bruce began to breathe easily again, Finch decided the climb was over. Bruce, determined character that he was, wanted to go on, but the more experienced Finch realized that a nasty shock like this would sap his strength and morale. Despite a burning ambition to

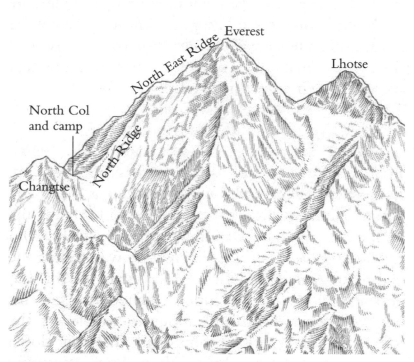

The northern approach to the summit

get to the summit, he decided to turn back before both of them fell to their deaths.

They headed down to Camp III, below the North Col, reaching it in a remarkably speedy 11 hours. Oxygen really did make climbing much easier. Despite their failure to reach the top, both men had climbed higher than anyone before – an especially remarkable achievement for Bruce on his first climb.

With two failed attempts behind them, and most of the climbers suffering from exhaustion or frostbite, the prospects for a third bid for the summit seemed slight. But Mallory was determined to go, and the expedition's backers in London were pressing for a result. It would be one attempt too many. It was now early June. The Monsoon, and the even harsher weather it would bring, would soon fall on the mountain. On June 5, Mallory, Somervell, another climber named Colin Crawford and 14 Sherpas headed up to the North Col. Around 200m (600ft) from the Col they heard a noise like an explosion shake the mountainside, and all were swept away by an avalanche. The British climbers had a lucky escape, but seven of the Sherpas were swept into a gaping crevasse. Everest had claimed its first victims.

The disaster brought the expedition to an abrupt end. Although photographer John Noel noted unkindly that the surviving Sherpas "had completely lost their nerve and were crying and shaking like babies", there were other climbers who were more compassionate. Somervell wrote: "why, oh why could not one of us Britishers have shared their fate? I would gladly at that moment have been lying there dead in the snow, if only to give those fine chaps who had survived the feeling that we shared their loss, as we had indeed shared the risk."

Mallory blamed himself for the accident, despite the fact that the whole team had decided on the route to the Col. It was a sad end to an extraordinary expedition. Yet, despite the dangers and this disaster, success had been almost within their grasp. Another expedition would surely succeed...

"More like war than mountaineering"

The 1924 expedition

There was no expedition in 1923. Funds were low, changes to equipment had to be made and the right people were not available. In 1924, however, a new expedition set off with the usual fanfare of articles in the papers. *The Newcastle Journal* even carried this extraordinary claim:

> Smoking largely contributed to the success of last year's ascent and members declared that Mount Everest would have been completely scaled had not their supplies given out at 27,300ft [8,190m] above sea level.

In our health-conscious age, the thought of wheezing, breathless mountaineers having a cigarette on the giddy slopes near the summit seems unthinkable. But in 1924, it was seriously believed that smoking helped a climber to breathe better and fight fatigue.

"Bruiser" Bruce had proved to be such a good leader on the last trip, he was the obvious choice again, despite his increased age (he was now 58) and shaky health. Edward Norton, another veteran from the 1922 trip, would be his second-in-command. Mallory was asked again too. His renown had landed him a prestigious teaching job in Cambridge and he had only recently moved there with his family, but the Everest Committee wanted him back – he was, after all, their most famous climber. Mallory was beset with doubt. On the previous trip, he had noted "frankly the game (of climbing the mountain) is not good enough… the risks of getting caught are too great… and the margin of strength when men are at such great heights is too small". He was torn between his wife and children, and his ambition to reach the summit of Everest and the duty he felt to his fellow mountaineers. Just before he left England, he told a friend: "This is going to be more like war than mountaineering. I don't expect to come back."

Also along from the previous trip were Howard Somervell, Geoffrey Bruce and John Noel and his cameras. Among the new men (there was no question, in 1924, of women joining the team) was a geologist and experienced climber named Noel Odell, and a young, fair-haired engineering student from Oxford University, named Andrew "Sandy" Irvine. He had little climbing experience, but had shown himself to be a great team player and determined explorer in a recent expedition to the Arctic. On top of this, he was a brilliant mechanic. General Bruce overlooked his lack of experience in the light of all his other obvious qualities. Irvine was a good choice – he was well liked by the team, and adapted quickly to the high-altitude life.

The expedition left Darjeeling on March 25, intending to head up the Rongbuk Glacier and again take the North Col route to the summit. But within two weeks General Bruce had succumbed to malaria, and had to return to Darjeeling. Norton took over. He had been well chosen, and was liked and respected by his team. On the way there, as Everest loomed into view, final plans were made. The climbers were optimistic. Mallory, his doubts now replaced by an iron determination, even wrote to his wife: "It is almost unthinkable... that I shan't get to the top; I can't see myself coming down defeated." He would turn out to be right in some respects – but not in the way he hoped.

The expedition reached Rongbuk on April 28 but, almost immediately, bad weather hampered its progress. Two Sherpas died of frostbite and high-altitude sickness. Then, in the middle of May, heavy snow forced them to abandon the camp they had established on the North Col. During the retreat four Sherpas, too terrified to come down, had been left at the camp. Norton, Mallory and Somervell had to form a rescue party to bring them to safety.

At the end of May the weather improved, but time was rapidly running out. The annual Monsoon would soon bring more snow, so an all-out assault on the summit was quickly mounted. Camps were established again at the North Col, and at two spots up the North Ridge. This final stopping point, known as Camp VI, was only 600m (2,000ft) from the summit. But above it lay some of the most difficult conditions and obstacles of the climb. In the teeth of whatever weather the mountain might throw at them, a climber would have to make his way through a yellow band of slippery, crumbling slabs of rock, which overlapped like roof tiles. After that, they faced a 30m (100ft) wall of rock known as the "First

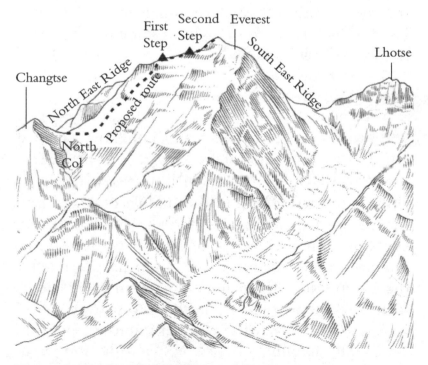

The route via the First and Second Steps

Step". Then, there was a difficult passage up a narrow ridge to another 30m (100ft) wall of rock known as the "Second Step". This was a particularly nasty looking obstacle, which looked like "the sharp bow of a battlecruiser". After that, there was a relatively easy climb up the final peak to the summit. But anyone who struggled up there would have to come down in a state of total exhaustion. It was not going to be easy.

Norton decided that he and Somervell should make the first attempt at the summit and that they would not use oxygen. On June 4, at twenty to seven in the morning, the pair set off from their tent at Camp VI in perfect weather. The high altitude caused immediate problems. Somervell developed a bad sore throat and had difficulty breathing. Norton had forgotten his sunglasses, and soon suffered snow glare so badly he had double vision. Despite this, these two men pressed on through the morning. They planned their route to pass around the two difficult Steps. This would make for a longer climb, but would be safer. Both were making extremely slow progress, and could only move forward 12 or 13 steps before they had to stop to get their breath back.

By midday Somervell could carry on no longer, and sat down to rest on a ledge. Norton pressed on through deep snow for a while, reaching a record height of 8,650m (28,200ft), just below the final stretch. The summit was only about 240m (800 feet) above. But he knew that if he continued, he would never return. Feeling a curious mixture of disappointment and relief, Norton rejoined Somervell, and the two made their way back to Camp VI. Somervell later wrote: "We had been willing always to risk our lives, but we did not believe in throwing them away."

After a brief stop at Camp VI, Norton led off down to the North Col. Then behind him, Somervell had a violent coughing fit, and all of a sudden he couldn't breathe. He couldn't even call out to Norton to help him, and sat down in the snow to die. In a last desperate effort, he pressed hard on his chest and coughed up a huge lump of mucus. Despite being in a great deal of pain, Somervell could breathe again. He felt elated. His narrow escape from death filled him with a fresh energy, and the climbers returned safely to Camp IV. But during the night Norton felt an intense pain in his eyes, and went completely blind for the next 60 hours.

On his return, Norton was convinced that the expedition was over. But as he lay in his tent, draped with sleeping bags to keep out any light, Mallory came to him with plans for a final summit attempt. This time, said Mallory, they would use oxygen. He persuaded Norton, who wrote of him: "I... was full of admiration for the indomitable spirit of the man... in spite of his already excessive exertions, not to admit defeat while any chance remained." There was one point of disagreement, however. Mallory had formed a close friendship with Irvine, and wanted to take him as a climbing partner. Norton felt the more experienced Noel Odell would be a wiser choice. But sick and exhausted as he was, he did not have the strength to argue.

On June 6, Mallory, Irvine and a small team of Sherpas headed up the mountain. The next day the two climbers reached Camp VI, where they slept overnight. Mallory wrote a final message to photographer John Noel, which was carried down to the North Col by the Sherpas, who all returned down the mountain that evening. It said:

Dear Noel,

We'll probably start early tomorrow (8th) in order to have clear weather. It won't be too early to start looking for us either crossing the rock band or going up the skyline at 8:00pm.

Yours ever,
G. Mallory

The "pm" was an obvious mistake, no doubt caused by exhaustion. But the note seemed to indicate that Mallory was intending to go the quickest, most direct route to the summit, through the difficult terrain of the First and Second Steps, rather than trying to bypass these obstacles, as Norton and Somervell had done.

Sure enough, Mallory and Irvine set off for the top of Everest the following morning. For Irvine this was a great adventure, and he was thrilled to be climbing with the legendary Mallory. Perhaps Norton had been wrong to worry about Irvine, for he had proved to be both a fast and capable climber. For Mallory, this attempt was far more serious. He was nearly 38 years old. He had failed to reach the summit on two previous occasions. Supplies were running low, the climbers and Sherpas were exhausted, and the Monsoon was almost upon them. This was surely his last chance, and he was determined to succeed or die.

Also heading up the mountain that morning was the expedition geologist Noel Odell. He had spent the night at Camp V on the North Col and was climbing through a thin mist up to Camp VI, with some supplies Mallory had requested for their return journey.

Odell was delighted to come across some fossils on his way up the mountain. As he pottered, he reached a small ledge around 7,925m (26,000ft). There, at around one o'clock, a mist above him lifted, and he could see right up to the summit. High above, he spotted two tiny specks around the area of the First or Second Step. He was surprised they were so low on their way to the summit, at this point in the day, but noticed they were moving at good speed.

Around two o'clock that afternoon, the weather changed dramatically and a howling wind whipped up a snow storm. Odell, anxious that the returning climbers would lose their way back to the camp, ventured away from the tent and up into the storm, whistling and yodelling as he went, hoping Mallory and Irvine might be listening. But no one was there to hear him.

Mallory had given Odell clear instructions not to stay at Camp VI – there was room for only two climbers in the tent. So when the storm lifted around four o'clock and bright sunshine flooded the mountainside, he retreated to the North Col, after having a final look around for the two men.

Above him, roped together, Mallory and Irvine were struggling. The storm had knocked the strength from their already failing, frozen limbs, and they were fighting for their lives, hoping to return to the shelter of Camp VI before darkness. To add to their troubles, the climb had taken far longer than they planned. Their oxygen had run out, and both had now discarded their heavy breathing apparatus. Having to manage without oxygen at this stage of the climb, when they were desperately in need of all the strength they could summon, was a terrible blow.

As dusk fell, they edged slowly to safety. But they had still not reached the campsite when a moonless night fell upon them. Above Camp VI, perhaps no more than half an hour's climb away, one of them stumbled and fell, dragging his companion behind him. Somewhere on the fall the rope between them snapped. Mallory plunged down the steep North Face, breaking his right leg in two places as he fell. Fighting desperately to save his life, he dug his fingers into the scree, ripping his gloves off in the process. But before he came to a halt he was jerked into the air, and his head hit a sharp rock.

Mallory often thought of his children when he climbed, and perhaps he thought of them then as he lay still, face down on the side of the mountain, crossing his left leg over his broken right in an effort to ease the pain, his fingers digging into the small gravel stones of the slope that would be his final resting place.

Irvine had been injured too, but not as badly as Mallory. He probably dragged himself back up the slope, determined to reach the life-saving oxygen supplies and warmth of his tent. But somewhere in his search for shelter, the second-year Oxford student, who was all of 22, collapsed and died.

Their companions below had no means of knowing what had happened. All through the evening Odell kept an anxious watch on the slopes, but saw nothing either to worry or reassure him. The following morning he took two Sherpas as far as Camp V, but it was too cold to go further.

The next day was June 10. Although the Sherpas refused to go any higher, Odell hauled himself up to Camp VI alone to look for his missing comrades. Ominously, the tent there looked exactly the same as when he had left it two days before. He searched long, hard and heroically, thinking as he did so that "this upper part of Everest must... be the remotest and most inhospitable spot on Earth". Of Mallory and Irvine there was no trace.

There was now little doubt in Odell's mind that they had been killed. His strength ebbing, he returned to the tent and laid the sleeping bags out in the shape of a T – a pre-arranged signal to his companions below that the two climbers were missing. As he gingerly made his way down to the North Col, he glanced over his shoulder at the looming, distant summit. "It seemed to look down with cold indifference on me," he later wrote, "and howl derision in wind-gusts at my petition to yield up its secrets – the mystery of my friends."

Back at the North Col, Odell had yet another signal to relay to Norton and other colleagues at the base of the mountain – six blankets laid out in the shape of a cross. This was a confirmation that Irvine and Mallory were dead. The expedition was over. Before they left the mountain, Somervell and the others built a memorial cairn of stones and slate on a spot overlooking Base Camp. On the slate they recorded the names of the 12 people who had died during the expeditions of 1921, 1922 and 1924. As the century wore on, there would be plenty more names to follow them.

Although their attempts to reach the summit of Everest had ended in tragedy, there was much to admire about these early pioneers. Dressed in tweed jackets and woolly jumpers, they looked, in the words of playwright George Bernard Shaw, "like a picnic in Connemara surprised by a snowstorm". Yet Norton, on the second summit attempt, and maybe Mallory and Irvine after him, had reached a height on Everest that would not be bettered for nearly 30 years.

Norton sent a terse telegram back to London –

```
Mallory and Irvine killed on
last attempt. Rest of party
arrived at Base Camp all
well.
```

Ruth Mallory's telegram from the Everest Committee was a little less brusque –

```
Committee    deeply    regret
received  bad  news  Everest
expedition    today.    Your
husband  and  Irvine  killed
last climb...
```

In the spirit of the times, Ruth Mallory took the news with a controlled dignity. She wrote to a friend: "whether he got to the top of the mountain or did not, whether he lived or died, makes no difference to my admiration for him… (yet) if only it hadn't happened! It so easily might not have." But for months afterwards, it was said, she looked like "a stately lily with its head broken and hanging down".

The news was announced in *The Times* on June 21, 1924. Mallory and Irvine's deaths caused a sensation in the English-speaking world. *The London Sunday Express*, for example, declared the tragedy "a great and heroic story of adventure, courage and fate…" A picture of Irvine in his college blazer appeared in many papers. He looked barely more than a boy. His obituary in *The Alpine Journal* (the Alpine Club's annual review) carried a sentimental poem from a teacher at his old school: "God and the stars alone could see thee die…"

Later that year, a memorial service for the two climbers was held at St Paul's Cathedral in London. Even the Royal family sent representatives.

There was much speculation as to whether or not the two ill-fated climbers had reached the summit. Arguments that they might not have made it were rather overlooked in a tide of sentimentality. Those who were friends of Mallory's, especially, were convinced he had made it to the summit. One of the 1922 team wrote: "… they got there alright… how they must have appreciated the view of half the world; it was worthwhile to them; now they'll never grow old."

No doubt the thought that Mallory and Irvine had succeeded made their friends feel their "sacrifice" had had some purpose. But expedition leader Edward Norton was more level-headed. There was no proof, he said, so no one could say for certain. The Everest Committee agreed with him. As far as they were concerned, Everest had still to be climbed.

Although the names of Mallory and Irvine remain a legend to mountaineers, their fame has faded over the years. Today, Mallory does not even rate a mention in most biographical encyclopedias or dictionaries – yet at the time of his death, he was regarded as one of the greatest heroes of his age. It was Mallory, when asked why he wanted to climb Everest, who gave the famous response, "Because it's there."

"A lifetime of fear and struggle"

The expedition of 1933

It would be nine years before another Everest expedition set out. Tibet's spiritual leader, the Dalai Lama, had been perturbed by all the deaths on the mountain, and British government officials, wanting to keep him as an ally, had forbidden further attempts. Then, in 1929, the world was hit by the Great Depression. As businesses and banks collapsed and unemployment soared, funding climbing trips was not regarded as a high priority.

It was not until 1933 that the Everest Committee was able to clear the way for another expedition – both in terms of raising funds and gaining official permission to climb the mountain. Their determination to continue was prompted partly by other countries badgering the British Government for a try at Everest. The British had used their influence in the region most unfairly to forbid any other nation from climbing the mountain. But the Germans, Swiss and Americans who wanted to try for the summit could not be deterred forever.

Before the British could launch another attempt, they had to recruit a new team. The 1924 climbers had mainly been middle-aged men. Now, nearly a decade on, most would be too old for another trip. A distinguished ex-Indian civil service commissioner, Hugh Ruttledge, was appointed as leader. At 48, he was quite old for mountaineering, and had very little climbing experience. But he had a good knowledge of the Himalayas and the local people there, and was considered to be "the right sort of chap".

The team assembled around him was an extremely strong one. There was Eric Shipton, only 25 and already an experienced and respected mountaineer. Others, such as Percy Wyn Harris, Jack Longland and Lawrence Wager, also had fine reputations. Most well-known and interesting of all was the successful writer and photographer, Frank Smythe. Hardly a likeable character, photographs of Smythe show a frail, irascible-looking man, with sharp, almost feminine features. He could be difficult company, but his prickly exterior hid a personality at war with itself. He was convinced others were stronger and cleverer than him, but was determined to push himself to the limits of his abilities, so no one would ever know. This was just the sort of drive and determination that might get a man to the summit.

Despite its new members, Ruttledge's expedition was little different from the last one. All the climbers came from the same well-to-do social background, their equipment was much the same, and the route they chose to follow was also directly the same as before. But there were two significant differences. Firstly, the Sherpas, with almost 15 years of climbing experience now behind them, had become first-class mountaineers. In the absence of British expeditions, they had climbed other Himalayan peaks with American, German and Swiss teams. Secondly, new equipment was available.

Unlike earlier expeditions, Ruttledge's men brought radio sets with them. Although radio had become an established technology during the First World War, the sets had been too bulky and unreliable to bother carrying up a mountain. But by 1933, radio sets had become much more portable (although by modern standards they were still pretty big, and each needed six large acid batteries to power it). Radio brought obvious advantages. Ruttledge, via relay stations, could send news of their progress to the Everest Committee in London within a day. And by radio, the team could receive advance warning of the arrival of the fearful Monsoon.

In the years since the last expedition, there had also been a major advance in the design of oxygen equipment, and oxygen sets now weighed only 5.75kg (12.75lbs), just over a third of the weight of the old sets. But although the team decided to bring oxygen with them, they were determined not to use it. Opinions on oxygen were still heated, and many people felt its use was "unsporting". One of the climbers on the 1933 trip likened it to using a motor in a yachting race.

The team set up their base camp at Rongbuk Glacier on April 17. Almost at once, appalling weather dogged them. As they assembled for their customary team photographs, Ruttledge must have wondered how many of his men would live to see the summer back home in England.

They sheltered from the storms as best they could, but then illness swept through the party. Flu, upset stomachs, bronchitis, even a gastric ulcer, weakened a team that was facing the most demanding physical challenge of their lives. Eventually, the weather improved. On May 14, almost a month after they had arrived, they set up a camp on the North Col. Like all previous camps on the Col, it was dubbed No. IV.

No sooner had they set up the camp than news came via the radio that that year's Monsoon had already reached Ceylon (now called Sri Lanka). They probably had less than two weeks before worsening weather would make climbing impossible. But even before the Monsoon's arrival, the weather was dreadful. Storms brought the ferrying of supplies up the mountain to a halt for five days between May 16 and May 20. At the camp on the foot of the Col, tents were felled by the wind and men almost froze to death. But there was worse to come.

In the gaps between the storms, the climbers managed to set up a Camp V at 7,620m (25,000ft) up the North Ridge. Then, on May 29, at 8,440m (27,700ft), a single tent made up Camp VI. This would be the final stopping-off spot for two climbers before the summit. It was placed precariously on a ledge so thin that a quarter of the tent hung over the North Face of the mountain. The Monsoon was expected any day. If anyone was going to get to the top, they had very little time left to do it.

Ruttledge had decided the two climbers to make the first attempt at the summit would be Percy Wyn-Harris and Lawrence Wager. They, along with Jack Longland and eight Sherpas, had set up Camp VI. As Wyn-Harris and Wager settled down to rest, Longland returned down the mountain with the Sherpas around one o'clock in the afternoon. The trip up to Camp VI had been exhausting. The climbers, all carrying equipment for the camp, had to stop for three or four breaths between each step. Now, on the way down, they were all dangerously tired, so Longland decided to take them directly down the top of the North Ridge. It was not the quickest route, but it was the safest.

The weather that afternoon was so clear Longland stopped briefly to admire the view. He recalled seeing "peaks that must have been more than 250 miles [400 km] away" – an amazing distance to see, roughly equivalent to the distance between London and Plymouth, or Los Angeles and San Francisco. But then, suddenly, his party was hit by a storm which sprang from nowhere. Snow quickly filled the holds on the rocks and made the scree beneath their feet treacherous. The wind blew so hard, said Longland, that the men could do little but "cling and cower against the rocks".

The North Ridge had been a gamble. It was safer, but Longland did not know it well. As the snow froze on his goggles, obscuring his already limited view, he tore them from his face, only to have his eyelashes and eyelids freeze up instead. Slowly, slowly, they edged down the mountain, stopping every ten minutes to make sure all nine of them were still together. Then, ahead, they saw a tent. Amazingly, they had stumbled upon Mallory and Irvine's Camp VI, unoccupied for the last nine years. Despite their terrible plight, Longland and the Sherpas could not resist a quick look around. In the tent, there was a flashlight which was still in working order.

But this was not a good time to hunt for souvenirs. Besides, when they discovered the tent, Longland began to wonder if they were seriously lost. He thought he knew where Mallory and Irvine's Camp VI was on the mountain, but it was not on the route they were supposed to be taking. Nearby were steep, overhanging ice cliffs, that plunged right down to the East Rongbuk Glacier. In a storm, when visibility was almost zero, this was not a good place to be. Longland kept these thoughts to himself, not wanting the Sherpas to lose their faith in his leadership, but the next half hour was a nightmare. At any second, Longland expected one of his team to slip in the blizzard and plunge down a slippery slope, over the cliff to certain death thousands of feet below.

They pressed on for another half hour. By now, some of the Sherpas were so exhausted that they sat down in the snow. Longland was losing confidence fast, and wondered whether it would be better for everyone just to lie down and die quietly from exposure, rather than be killed in a violent fall after hours of struggle. But he was determined not to give up while there was still hope. Pulling the stragglers to their feet, he urged them all on down the mountain. Eventually, he later recalled, "down through the snow... appeared a little patch of green. I rubbed the ice off my eyelashes and looked again: and it was a tent, three, four tents – the little cluster that meant Camp V and safety, and an end to the tearing anxiety of two hours." Reflecting on his experience, Longland wrote, "I seemed to have crowded a lifetime of fear and struggle and responsibility into that short time." So far, at least, the 1933 expedition had survived without fatalities.

Meanwhile, up at Camp VI, Percy Wyn-Harris and Lawrence Wager sat out the storm that had so nearly claimed the lives of nine of their companions. They rested as best they could at such an exhausting altitude, then set off for the summit the next morning at twenty to six – before the dawn. Their goal lay a mere 490m (1,600ft) above them. Their strategy was to follow Mallory and Irvine's supposed route up the difficult rock faces of the First and Second Steps – the most direct route to the top.

The planned route via the First and Second Steps

An hour into the climb, and shortly after dawn, Wyn-Harris found an ice-axe. It could only be Mallory or Irvine's, for no other men had walked this way. But when Wyn-Harris and Wager approached the First Step, they abandoned their plan. It looked too steep and difficult. Instead, they decided to do

339

what Edward Norton and Howard Somervell had done in 1924, and try to reach Everest's final summit cone by going around the Steps. This route was longer, but it was safer.

They retraced Norton and Somervell's steps in more ways than one. After passing though the yellow band of rock that lies just below the summit cone, they came to a gully full of powdery snow. It was half past twelve and the top of Everest was all of 300m (900ft) above them. But however much they were driven by ambition, Wyn-Harris and Wager had every intention of returning home alive. They reckoned on another four hours of climbing before they reached the top, almost all of it through snow. It would be exhausting and dangerous, but not half as dangerous as the return journey. This late in the day there would be no chance of getting back to Camp VI by nightfall, and they would almost certainly die on the way down. Feeling more relief than disappointment, they turned back. They had reached almost exactly the same height as Edward Norton had done in 1924.

But even as they returned to the precarious haven of Camp VI, another two climbers were heading up the mountain. Frank Smythe and Eric Shipton were both extremely capable and determined men. They knew each other well and had made many difficult climbs together. Perhaps they were the men who would find a way to the summit...

Their summit day did not start well. It was so cold

on the morning of June 1, they could not leave their tent until half past seven – a very late start for the difficult climb ahead. Like their companions before them, they originally intended to climb the First and Second Steps. But as they drew nearer, these steep cliffs seemed too difficult to handle.

There were other problems too. Both men had been high up on the mountain for several days, and Shipton, especially, was feeling the effects of altitude sickness. Just as they reached the First Step he collapsed and decided he could go no further. After a brief consultation they decided that Shipton would return to Camp VI, and Smythe would press on to the summit alone. It was an extraordinarily brave decision, for Smythe was also suffering from the high-altitude sickness that had overwhelmed Shipton.

In a state of near-collapse, he soon began to feel he was accompanied by another climber – a sensation familiar to lone desert and polar explorers in a similar state of exhaustion. Smythe even believed he and his invisible friend were roped together: "If I slipped, 'he' would hold me," he recalled. When Smythe stopped to rest and took out some mint cake (an energy-giving sweet), he even turned around to offer his friend some.

But Smythe's solo attempt was doomed to failure. When he reached 8,600m (28,200ft), only 240m (800ft) up to the summit, he encountered a lethal obstruction. Ahead was a gully which Smythe later

341

recounted with his writer's gift for vivid description: "Snow had accumulated deeply [on the] ledges... soft like flour, loose like granulated sugar and incapable of holding the feet in position. As I probed it with my axe I knew the game was up."

Struggling for breath, his body starved of oxygen, he found he completely lacked the willpower to carry on. Maybe, just maybe, if such gifted climbers had taken the new, lighter oxygen sets, they would have found the energy and determination to reach the summit. As it was, no one would stand higher on the mountain than Smythe had done, that June day in 1933, for almost another 20 years.

The actual route of the 1933 expedition

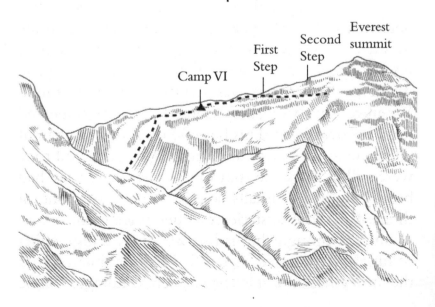

The journey back to Camp VI was a bizarre one. Still accompanied by his invisible friend, Smythe began to pick his way carefully down the mountain. At around 8,200m (27,000ft), when he was 60m (200ft) from the camp, he had the most vivid hallucination. As he later wrote: "chancing to glance in the direction of the North Ridge, I saw two curious-looking objects floating in the sky. They strongly resembled kite-balloons in shape, but one possessed what appeared to be squat, under-developed wings, and the other a protuberance suggestive of a beak. They hovered motionless but seemed slowly to pulsate, a pulsation much slower than my own heart-beats... The two objects were very dark... and were silhouetted sharply against the sky."

Smythe took in this extraordinary vision with a detached curiosity. As well as checking that these mystery objects were pulsating at a different rate than his own pulse, he also noted that they did not move when he moved his eyes swiftly away from them. Whatever they were, they seemed to be disconnected from his own body. This became even more apparent when he looked away and then back again, and they were still in the same spot in the sky where they had been before. Eventually a mist drifted in front of them. When the mist cleared, they were gone.

Smythe thought he had seen "some strange effect of mist and mountain magnified by imagination. On the other hand, it may have been a mirage." Since then, other more fanciful writers have claimed that what Smythe had seen was an Unidentified Flying Object, or UFO. However, it is much more likely that it was an hallucination brought about by lack of oxygen and exhaustion. Whatever the objects really were, Smythe's story – along with stories about the Yeti – contributed further to Everest's air of mystery.

Back at Camp VI Smythe rejoined Shipton, who had recovered from his earlier breakdown. Exhausted, Smythe collapsed and slept until the next day. As the tent was so uncomfortable, Shipton decided to head down the mountain to Camp V before nightfall. Smythe came down the next morning. By chance, both men were caught in sudden storms like the one that had caused Longland and his eight Sherpas such trouble. Flattened against rocks by intense winds, or almost lifted off their feet, they had to cower behind boulders and in crevices, and then dash forward between squalls. This was the year when climbers learned that Everest could have terrible weather in May and early June, even before the Monsoon arrived. But despite the weather, everyone on Hugh Ruttledge's expedition survived.

Looking back on the climb, Smythe wrote tellingly of the hardship he and his comrades had endured: "Toil, discomfort, freezing cold and burning sun, failing appetite, sleeplessness, irritation,

boredom, these are some of the penalties of Everest."
Of the approach to the summit he recalled: "What a
feeble instrument the body is at 28,000ft [8,500m]. A
man who climbs near the top of Everest is a poor dull
creature, barely existing in a grey world devoid of
pleasure... he seems to tread some shadowy line
between consciousness and unconsciousness,
between, indeed, life and death." Yet Smythe also
wrote of "nature at her noblest and most beautiful",
and spoke of the breath-taking sights he had
witnessed near the summit, looking "past the specks
of the Rongbuk Monastery and away over the
golden plains of Tibet, where the wandering clouds
were couched on their own shadows, to the blue
distance where the earth bent over into the fastness
of central Asia".

The reckless Yorkshireman

Maurice Wilson's solo attempt

The papers were full of Everest in the spring of 1933 – not only had Hugh Ruttledge's expedition caught the imagination of the public, but a plane flight over the mountain had also attracted considerable interest. Someone paying very close attention was Maurice Wilson.

Born in Bradford, Yorkshire, in 1898, Wilson had had an unhappy end to his adolescence and this had shaped the rest of his life. Like most British men born in the last decade of the 19th century, he was destined for the carnage of the First World War. Wilson had enlisted as soon as he reached 18, and had found himself, while not yet out of his teens, fighting in the mud of Passchendaele – one of the most hideous battles of the war. His bravery won him the Military Cross, but he was hit by machine gun fire across the chest and left arm. He recovered, but his arm was never the same again.

Many men who survived the intense excitement and terror of the war found the humdrum reality of life back home difficult to take. Wilson was among them. He married, but soon divorced and moved to the United States, and then to New Zealand. Although he had made money and was quite prosperous, he never settled at anything. His 30th birthday came and went, and still he hadn't found a niche in life.

Suffering from depression, he came home. On the boat back to England from New Zealand, he met some Indian holy men who made a great impression on him. He developed a personal philosophy based on both Christianity and Indian meditation. Back in England, he continued to suffer from bouts of depression, and his health deteriorated alarmingly. But after a regime of prayer, and fasting almost to the point of starvation, he managed to make a full recovery. The success of his new philosophy convinced him that people could do anything if they had enough faith and determination. He decided, at the age of 33, that his mission in life was to spread this message to his fellow humans.

He could preach on street corners, and even book town and village halls to spread his teachings, but he recognized that this would almost certainly result in indifference or humiliation. Wilson was canny enough to realize that the best advertisement for his new philosophy would be a feat of daring that would astound the world. What better place to start than a solo climb up the world's highest, and so far unclimbed, mountain? As he said at the time: "When I have accomplished my little work, I shall be somebody. People will listen to me…"

347

His plan of action was remarkably simple. He would fly to India and then to the Himalayas, where he would crash-land a plane as high up the mountain as it would go. (Most planes in 1933 did not have the power to fly over a peak as high as Everest.) Then he would trek on foot to the top.

The fact that he could not fly and had never been up a mountain made his plan both alarmingly stupid and enormously brave. Wilson was the ultimate "can-do" kind of man, much of his confidence stemming from his own imposing frame (he was well over 6ft tall) and physical strength. He enrolled at the London Aero Club for flying lessons, and went hiking in the rugged moorland of the English Lake District, to give himself a grasp of mountaineering. To build up his stamina, he regularly walked from his home in London to his parents' house in Bradford – a distance of some 420km (260 miles).

Following his flying lessons, he bought himself a second-hand Gypsy Moth – a dinky single-seater biplane which he fitted with long-distance fuel tanks and named, punningly, "Ever-Wrest". By the spring of 1933 he was all set to go, and flew up to his parents in Bradford to say goodbye. But crossing over Yorkshire, he crashed the plane into farmland. He survived unscathed, but patching up "Ever-Wrest" added another three weeks to his departure date. By now, Wilson's designs on Everest had made him a familiar face in the British press, who had dubbed him "The Mad Yorkshireman". "He got small photographs in the newspapers, as a man might who announced his intentions of swimming the Atlantic with water-wings", one obituary rather snootily recalled later.

As Wilson prepared to depart from Stag Lane Aerodrome in Edgware, North London, a telegram from the British Air Ministry arrived forbidding him to leave. With a magnificent lack of respect, Wilson tore it up and took to the air. Within a week he was in Cairo, and a week after that he had arrived in India. The mighty wrath of the British government followed him all the way – forbidding him fuel at some stops, and not allowing him to fly over some countries on his route. Yet in 1933, the fact that an inexperienced pilot could make such a journey and survive was a magnificent achievement in itself. His flight gained him a great deal of publicity. Ironically, Wilson had created exactly the kind of impact he had wanted, even before he reached the Himalayas.

Once in India, then part of the British empire, Wilson's plane was impounded and he was refused permission to fly over both Tibet and Nepal. Forced to modify his plans, he decided to sell the Gypsy Moth (which the authorities allowed him to do) and walk to Darjeeling – the Indian city nearest to the Himalayas. All this made it impossible to consider an ascent of Everest that year. By the time Wilson was ready to go, the Monsoon had arrived. So he sat out the rest of the year, living off the proceeds from his Gypsy Moth and training for the ascent on a diet of dates and cereals, coupled with bouts of fasting and deep breathing practice.

It was difficult even for expeditions with the full backing of the prestigious Royal Geographical Society and Alpine Club to get permission to climb Everest. Maurice Wilson had no chance of getting permission at all. But this was not going to deter him. In early 1934, he hired three Sherpas and walked into Tibet disguised as a monk, often moving only at night. By April 1934, he had reached the Rongbuk Glacier, the usual starting point for an ascent up the North Ridge – the only route by which it was thought possible to reach the summit. Here, he met the head monk at the monastery at Rongbuk, who was greatly impressed by this strange Englishman and his spiritual crusade.

On April 16, weighed down with a 20kg (45lb) rucksack, he left his Sherpas behind at his Base Camp and set off alone to conquer Everest. He knew which way to go, as he had studied the accounts of previous expeditions. But he had no real grasp of the extreme difficulties involved in Himalayan climbing, nor did he have any of the necessary equipment for climbing safely in snow and ice. Even when he had the good luck to find a discarded pair of crampons, spiked metal footwear essential for climbing in ice, he didn't bother to attach them to his boots. He kept a detailed journal of his trip, and recorded each day's activity with boyish enthusiasm...

April 20: Still about 2½ miles [4km] to go to Camp III when shall look forward to some hot chocolate.

April 21: 36 today. Many happy returns to myself... hellish cold but alright.

April 22: ... no use going on – eyes horrible and throat dry.

Wilson returned after nine days in a state of utter exhaustion, with a sore throat brought on by altitude sickness, and his war wounds hurting badly. He had been plagued by terrible snow storms, and had not even reached the top of the glacier. He was lucky not to have died of exposure.

After an 18-day rest, he felt strong enough to try again, wisely taking two of his Sherpas with him. They knew the best way through the crevasses and ice blocks of the glacier, and this time they reached the foot of Everest in a mere three days. The three men set up camp beneath the North Col, but were immediately trapped in their tents by fierce blizzards, and suffered terribly from altitude sickness.

In the gaps of better weather, Wilson tried to make his way up the mountain to the North Col. He survived several nasty falls, but was defeated by an imposing 12m (40ft) wall of ice – daunting enough for an experienced climber, and impossible for a man who had previously only walked up a few steep hills.

Once again his diary recorded his triumphs and tribulations, such as when he stumbled across food and other equipment left by the 1933 expedition:

May 17: What do you think I had a couple of days ago? Anchovy paste from FORTNUM & MASON [an exclusive London food store]... There's enough equipment here to start a shop.

May 18: ... nothing of int. except that it snowed and blowed like the D. all day.

May 19: ... am as dirty as they make 'em. Fingernails black and dirt well ground into hands. Shall be glad when the show is over and I can become civilised again.

As the days passed, his handwriting deteriorated with his health and strength, and the dawning realization that he had set himself too great a task. Wilson was admired by his Sherpas – but their patience and faith in him was now exhausted. Deciding they would all be killed if they carried on, the Sherpas tried to persuade him to call off his climb. But having got this far, Wilson was not going to give up. He gave them instructions to wait for him for a fortnight and headed off alone, carrying his tent, some bread and oatmeal, a camera and a silk Union Jack. This had been signed by several female admirers, and he intended to plant it on the summit. The Sherpas called after him: "You go to your death!" But he waved cheerily, and pointed up at the top of the mountain.

On May 31, Wilson prepared for another attempt on the route to the North Col. Before he went, he made an optimistic entry in his journal: "Off again, gorgeous day." They were the last words he ever wrote.

The Sherpas waited, and waited, and then they returned home. Maurice Wilson had vanished. A year passed with no further news. Then, in the spring of 1935, another British expedition arrived to climb the mountain. When the climbers reached the base of the North Col, 6,400m (21,000ft) up the mountain, they were surprised to see a pair of boots and the remains of a tent scattered before them. The scene took on a macabre aspect when one of the climbers, Charles Warren, saw the body of Maurice Wilson lying close by. Warren was soon joined by Eric Shipton, from the previous expedition, and another climber named Edwin Kempson.

The three men made a careful check of the scene, almost as a detective would in a murder investigation, and pieced together Wilson's final days. He had, they supposed, returned from another attempt up to the North Col. How successful he had been nobody knew, but at least he did not kill himself climbing. Instead, he had returned to his tent and died there, exhausted and defeated. During the winter a storm had blown the tent down, leaving both him and his possessions scattered around. His journal, rucksack, stove, even his silk Union Jack, were all found around him, but his sleeping bag had vanished.

All this established, there was only one thing left to do. Warren, Shipton and Kempson wrapped Maurice Wilson in his tent and carried him to a nearby crevasse. Here, they laid his body so it slipped down a steep incline into the deep, forbidding darkness below. Then they built a cairn of stones as a monument on the spot where his body was found. That night, the three climbers sat by the crevasse and read aloud from Wilson's journal. It was a sad, moving document, and each man found something to admire in Wilson's determined and courageous folly.

Strangely, even today, mountaineers pursuing the North Col route still stumble across Wilson's remains. They are occasionally disinterred by the constant motion of the slow-moving glacier, which has also broken up his body and clothing, spreading them over a wide area. His remains were last discovered by the 1999 expedition which set out to find Mallory and Irvine.★

"Occasionally, you find pieces of cloth in the glacier that look like they could have come from the 1930s," said expedition climber Jochen Hemmleb. "The first piece we found was half a femur bone about eight inches long. Not far from it I found one vertebra. Then about 600-900ft [180-270m] down from that was a piece of forearm… Even in death, he shows his determination, refusing to be buried…"

★ See page 420.

The world intervenes

1935-1952

The British mounted three more expeditions to Everest in the 1930s, while other nations were refused permission to climb the mountain. The first of these expeditions, in 1935, marked the arrival of Sherpa Tenzing Norgay, then aged 20, who would go on to play a major role in the history of Everest. But further attempts in 1936 and 1938, all via the North Col route, made no further progress than those of the previous decade.

The Second World War broke out in 1939 and put a stop to Everest expeditions. Even after it ended in 1945, other events intervened to dash any immediate prospect of climbing the world's tallest mountain. India had always been the staging post for Everest expeditions, but in 1947 it gained its independence from the British empire. This brought with it other problems. In the north of the country the nation of Pakistan was created. Many of India's Muslims fled there, and in the process there was much bloodshed. Then Tibet, the country from which all Everest climbs had been made, declared it would temporarily close its borders to foreigners. The upheaval caused by Indian independence had made an expedition inadvisable; this made one impossible. In 1950, China invaded and occupied Tibet, which effectively cut the country off from the rest of the world, ruling out this route to Everest for the foreseeable future. But, as so often happens, what seemed like a bad thing at the time turned out to have unforeseen advantages.

Tibet lies to the north of the Himalayas, but immediately south lies Nepal – in fact, the border between the two countries goes straight up and down the South East and West Ridges of Everest, crossing over the summit. Before the Chinese invasion of Tibet, Nepal had been a mysterious country, which had not allowed foreigners to visit. The invasion changed everything. All of a sudden Nepal needed friends, and Europeans and Americans found themselves welcome.

This was great news for climbers. Nepal, much of which is occupied by the Himalayas, contains some of the highest peaks in the world. For the first time ever, these were now available to climb. Access to Nepal also opened up another possibility with regard to Everest. Howard-Bury's 1922 expedition team had explored all of the territory surrounding Everest. They had sneaked into Nepal to check out the southern face of the mountain and had seen that the path to the lower slopes was blocked by fearsome obstacles. From 4,900m (16,000ft) to 6,100m (20,000ft) lay the Khumbu Glacier – a vast river of slow-moving ice, riddled with crevasses. Halfway down the glacier was a terrifying section of broken blocks called an icefall. Here, the ground beneath the ice dropped sharply, causing the glacier to break into a maze of gaping crevasses and huge chunks the size of tower blocks or cathedrals. Every now and then, one such massive slab would topple over, making a noise like the end of the world and crushing anything that lay beneath. Until the 1950s, that might have been an unwary crow or another one of the few animals that eked out an existence at 5,400m (18,000ft), but now it might be human beings. The icefall was, without doubt, the most dangerous place on the entire mountain.

Yet for anyone brave enough to risk a trip up the Khumbu Glacier, there were clear rewards. The glacier leads to a huge bowl of snow which climbers call the Western Cwm (*cwm* is a Welsh word for a hollow on a hillside). The Western Cwm has three huge peaks towering above it – Nuptse, Lhotse and Everest. From here, the route to the summit is plain to see. There is a steep ascent to the South Col – a flat, windblown plain between the two peaks of Lhotse and Everest. Then a steep seam of rock, called the South East Ridge, leads to the top of the mountain.

This new route was first explored in 1951 by a British expedition led by Eric Shipton. They intended to press up to the South Col, but Shipton was faced with a moral dilemma that no Everest expedition leader had previously had to consider. The

Khumbu icefall was obviously a dangerous route. A mountaineer who climbs for fun, and who has made a conscious decision to risk his life in pursuit of his hobby, can chose whether or not to take that risk. But the Sherpas made their living from helping climbers from other countries explore this mountain. Was it right to put their lives so deliberately at risk too? Shipton decided not. His expedition established that there was a possible route to the South Col, but they themselves did not go that far. The expedition did, however, offer a New Zealand climber named Edmund Hillary his first experience of the mountain. He would return a couple of years later, to try his luck again.

Through "Suicide Passage" with a handful of friends

The 1952 Swiss expedition

In the years after the Second World War, Britain's position in the world was changing. The British empire, which had covered one quarter of the world, was crumbling. Previously Britain had ruled over India and exercised a strong influence on surrounding countries, such as Tibet and Nepal, although they were not official British territories. This had enabled the Everest Committee to ensure that only British climbers got a crack at Everest. Requests from climbers of other nationalities, including Germans and Americans, were persistently denied.

But now, as Britain's influence declined, the Nepalese decided that a group of Swiss mountaineers should be given permission to try to climb the mountain in the spring and autumn of 1952. Switzerland, dominated as it was by the central European Alps, had produced many talented climbers. They had been applying for permission to climb Everest since 1926. Now their time had come. Two Swiss mountaineers, René Dittert and Edouard Wyss-Dunant had been planning this trip since 1949.

They put together what they described as "a handful of friends" – actually the cream of Swiss mountaineers, including Raymond Lambert, a climber of international fame.

British climbers were dismayed that the Swiss group had received permission, afraid that their rivals would succeed in reaching the summit on a first attempt while British groups had mounted seven failed expeditions. So they suggested a joint expedition and the Swiss mountaineers were interested, but the plan failed because no agreement could be reached as to which climbers should be included in the group. Still, despite the rivalry, Eric Shipton went to Switzerland to show the expedition photographs of the new route to the South Col.

There were several clear advantages in an approach through Nepal up to the South Col and beyond, rather than by the traditional North Col route. Very importantly, the most dangerous part of the climb, the Khumbu icefall, was at the start, when climbers were fresh and the altitude was not so crippling. On the North Col route, the two huge obstacles of the First and Second Steps guarded the final route to the summit – daunting hurdles for climbers near to exhaustion. Another advantage of the South Col route was that the way to the summit along the South East Ridge was broader, which meant there were more places to make camp. It also had firmer snow, was less windy, and was in sunshine for most of the day. Altogether, the South Col route now seemed a better, safer way to the top.

By now the Sherpas, who had started their careers as servants to the Europeans who hired them, had become experienced and very capable climbers in their own right. Increasingly, they began to be regarded as equals by the Europeans. Although the Sherpas still addressed European climbers as "Sahib", an Indian word meaning "Boss", times were changing. Recruited for this particular expedition was a 38-year-old Sherpa named Tenzing Norgay. Tenzing had been up Everest three times with British climbers before the war, and had risen to the rank of Sirdar – a Sherpa who hired and managed his own team of Sherpas. He was an excellent climber, and he seemed to share the Europeans' determination to reach the summit.

The Swiss established their Base Camp at Gorak Shep, near the Khumbu Glacier, on April 20, 1952. It took them until the middle of May to set up a series of camps across the glacier and get to the foot of the South Col. It was extremely hard work making their way across the glacier. In all the pinnacles and blocks of shaky ice, a climber could often see no more than a few feet in front of him. Taking the wrong route was exhausting, dispiriting, and happened all too frequently. One section of the icefall was so dangerous to go through, the climbers named it "Suicide Passage". But although there were several near misses, no one was killed or injured by falling ice or snow.

Eventually, the Swiss climbers and their Sherpas became the first people to stand in the Western Cwm, and a camp was set up there on May 6. They now had to figure out how to get up the steep slopes that led to the South Col. Of all possible routes, the most promising was up through a slab of black rock the climbers named the Geneva Spur. This way was not the most direct, but it provided the least chance of being swept away by an avalanche. The climb up was very difficult. At 7,300m (24,000ft), altitude had become a noticeable problem, and the mountaineers had to battle constantly against their own lethargy.

Writing about climbing up to the Col, René Dittert recalled resting halfway up a steep ice cliff while his climbing partner, whom he was roped to, took the lead: "I leaned my forehead on the axe and waited for my heart to calm down... I watched the rope running up between my legs. It rose slowly, by jerks of eight or twelve inches and I dreaded the moment when it would tighten again and I would have to start moving once more."

After a day's climbing, wrote Dittert, "our muscles were as if made of cotton, without elasticity or resilience. At five o'clock, with flabby legs and empty-headed, without feeling, we disappeared into our tents. Ten times I returned to the job of unstrapping my crampons and pulling off my boots."

During this section of the climb, a storm pinned the expedition down in the camp at the base of the Col slopes, causing them to scurry to their flimsy tents like frightened animals. Numbed by fierce cold for days on end, every climber wondered what on earth they were doing in such a dreadful place.

But the storm passed. By May 26, the Swiss were able to set up camp on the South Col and were ready for a summit attempt. Their plan was to make another camp on the South East Ridge above 8,380m (27,500ft). Here, two climbers could shelter overnight, then make a dash for the summit. This camp was set up the next day by four of the team. It was just a single tent, and the two climbers chosen to go for the top were Raymond Lambert and Tenzing Norgay. It was a telling moment in the shift from servants and guides to fellow adventurers when a Sherpa was chosen as one of the mountaineers to make an attempt on the summit.

Over the course of the trip, Lambert and Tenzing had become good friends, and they had developed a great respect for each other's abilities. Marvelling at Tenzing's strength and stamina at high altitude, Lambert had said, "Tenzing, you have got three lungs. The higher you go, the better you get." Tenzing, in turn, had a deep affection for Lambert, calling him, "My companion of the heights, and the closest and dearest of my friends."

They had no cooking equipment or sleeping bags. At that height, Lambert recalled, "Our legs would not obey us and our brains scarcely functioned." When night fell, it was so cold and their bodies became so stiff and numb, it felt as if they had been given an anaesthetic. The heavy-duty canvas duvet jackets the climbers wore offered some warmth when they were moving, but were not as effective while they lay still in their tents. Even without the cold, it was impossible to sleep – the wind roared like a jet plane, and avalanches rumbled in the distance like runaway trains. But this was a blessing. If the two had fallen asleep in such extreme cold, they would almost certainly never have woken up. As they waited for daylight, they had to beat each other's bodies to keep the circulation going and ward off frostbite, then huddle together to gain a little heat. Looking out of the tent and up to the night sky, Lambert recalled the stars were so unnaturally bright they filled him with fear. During the night they both developed a raging thirst, but had nothing to drink. A fragment of ice placed in an empty tin, and melted with a candle flame, was the best they could do.

Eventually the dawn came, and the two climbers emerged from their tent to stinging ice needles hurled by the wind onto their exposed faces. It was cloudy above and foggy below – not a good sign. But both Lambert and Tenzing felt they had come too far to give up. Lambert looked up at the ridge leading to the summit and winked. Tenzing nodded. Both men understood what they were going to do without even speaking.

It didn't take long to get ready. To keep warm during the night they had worn everything they now stood up in, apart from their crampons. After a numb struggle to place these on their boots they were off up to the top of the world.

But there were problems from the start. The high altitude sapped their strength. But worse still, the oxygen equipment they carried worked very poorly at that altitude. The Swiss had no qualms about using oxygen, but their sets repeatedly malfunctioned. Breathing through them required a great deal of effort – so much so that an exhausted climber couldn't climb and breathe at the same time. He had to climb and then stop to breathe oxygen.

Lambert and Tenzing struggled up the ridge, sometimes on all fours, at all times stopping for oxygen after every step. The weather grew worse, but finally the sun came out. As the mist burned away, they could see they were higher than the nearby peak of Lhotse (8,501m, or 27,890ft). But again the bad weather returned, and they were enveloped in fog and frozen snow. Lambert, especially, began to fear for his life. He felt exhausted, but elated – a sure sign of high–altitude sickness. He thought of Mallory and Irvine, and how they had vanished on the North Ridge, wondering if this was how they had felt just before they met with the mishap that ended their lives.

By now they had reached a spot about 200m (600ft) below the South Summit, but the wind was picking up, and the snow was stinging their faces. They had climbed just 200m (600ft) in five hours, and reached a new record height of 8,600m

(28,210ft). The summit lay only about 250m (800ft) above them. But they knew they couldn't possibly reach it. They were totally shattered. Once more, the decision to go back was made without a word. Both men knew they had been defeated by the mountain. It was time to return to the relative safety of the South Col. The Swiss team made another attempt the following day, but were halted by blizzards on the South Col. Still, they had shown just how much could be achieved on the new route.

The first Swiss route (1952)

The Swiss climbers returned, as planned, that autumn, almost certain that this time they would succeed. But their second expedition was less successful. Although they managed to establish a camp on the South Col, the weather was atrocious, climbers were struck by ill health, and a Sherpa was killed by falling shards of ice – the first man to die on Everest since Maurice Wilson in 1934. The Swiss mountaineers had tried their hardest, but the summit remained unconquered. The next year a British-led expedition was due to try the new route. Could they succeed where every other team had failed?

The world beneath
their boots

The 1953 British expedition

The near success of the Swiss team in 1952 had badly
rattled the Himalayan Committee, as the Everest
Committee had recently been renamed. As they
prepared for their own attempt in 1953, the pressure
to succeed was intense. The new South Col route
offered such promising possibilities that the summit
seemed to be there for the taking. Whoever mounted
the next attempt would have, the Committee felt, no
real excuse to fail.

There was another reason, too, for wanting a
British expedition to succeed in reaching the top that
year. Britain's wartime monarch, King George VI, had
died in 1952, and his daughter, Princess Elizabeth,
was due to be crowned in June 1953. The years
immediately after the Second World War had been
dreary ones in Britain, and now there was talk of a
"new Elizabethan era" of prosperity and progress.
What better way to mark the coronation and the start
of this new period of history than by having a British
climbing team conquer the world's most notorious
mountain?

The first thing to decide was who would be the

leader. What the 1953 expedition needed, the Himalayan Committee felt, was a good organizer. And they knew just the man for the job. His name was Colonel John Hunt. He was 43 years old and was an undisputed genius at arranging transportation and supplies. Hunt was also a distinguished climber, though not terribly well known.

Hunt took up his job in October 1952 and, right from the start, there was a strong military style to his leadership. This was nothing new – many of the climbers considered to have "the right stuff" by the Everest and Himalayan Committees were military men. Their jobs, after all, required them to be fit, to be "team players" who could get along with other people in difficult circumstances, and to have personal qualities such as drive, discipline, determination and courage – all the character traits that best suited expedition mountaineers. Also, the armed forces were always happy to allow men leave for such activities, unlike many of the employers of other non-military climbers, who were civil servants, doctors, lecturers and the like. (Perhaps it was the influence of military men on climbing expeditions that led to mountaineering being described in warlike terms. Everest was to be "conquered" by an "assault team", and getting to the top would be a "victory" for Britain, failing would be a "defeat".)

Hunt planned the trip down to the last detail, and was allowed to spare no expense when it came to acquiring the best equipment. In fact, much of the equipment came cheap or free from manufacturers anxious to lend their names to such a potentially prestigious enterprise. There was to be no dithering about oxygen, either. Unsporting or not, its advantages were obvious, and Hunt's climbers were going to use it.

The team he chose, along with the veteran mountaineer Eric Shipton, looked very promising. There were ten experienced and capable climbers, among them Charles Evans, Tom Bourdillon, Alfred Gregory and a couple of New Zealanders, George Lowe and Edmund Hillary, who had been with Shipton on his 1951 expedition. Strictly speaking, of course, the New Zealanders weren't exactly "British", but in those days the ties between Britain and the Commonwealth countries were especially close, and both men had roots that could be traced back to Britain. Hillary's family, for example, came from Yorkshire stock, and he had a brusque "speak-as-I-find" manner that would not have been out of place in the county of his ancestors. He was good-natured, immensely tall, and bristled with restless energy.

Extra team members were kept to a minimum. Physiologist Griff Pugh came to study how the team adapted to high altitudes, and cameraman Tom Stobart and *Times* journalist James Morris came along to cover the story. In exchange for sponsorship, Morris had been given exclusive access to the expedition, although other newspapers also sent journalists out to Nepal to sniff out as much as they could about this fascinating story.

The expedition met in Kathmandu, the capital of Nepal, in early March. Here the climbers met the expedition Sherpas, gathered together by Tenzing Norgay, who had climbed so successfully with Raymond Lambert the previous year. Things got off to a bad start. While the expedition climbers were offered accommodation in the British Embassy, the Sherpas were put up in an Embassy garage, which didn't even have a lavatory. They all protested the next morning by urinating in the street outside the garage, an act which caused outrage among Embassy staff and great interest among Western journalists.

During this era, relations between the Sherpas and the climbers were changing. The Swiss, especially, had treated their Sherpas as equals, although it was still understood that their principal role was to carry equipment. The British, however, had dominated the Indian subcontinent for three centuries, and had not quite shaken off the notion that their Sherpas were servants belonging to an inferior racial group.

The trek to Everest's South side was a more difficult one than the pre-war route through Tibet had been. Tibet was flat enough for pack animals, and a climber and his gear could be transported on the back of a yak or pony. The route through Nepal, however, was too bumpy for animals, so everyone had to walk. This was hard work, but it helped to build fitness and stamina, and ensure a climber was in top condition by the time he arrived at Everest. The route was also very beautiful, especially compared to the dreary, dusty plains of Tibet.

Throughout April, the expedition worked its way up the Khumbu Glacier and through the treacherous icefall. Hunt's team found this route just as unpleasant as the Swiss had done. The names they gave particularly dangerous spots – Hellfire Alley, Hillary's Horror, Atom-bomb Area – show them trying to make light of their anxieties. By early May they had reached the Western Cwm.

It was noticeable right from the start that Hillary and Tenzing hit it off spectacularly well. Both men seemed to like each other and, more importantly, they climbed wonderfully together. Each recognized the ability of the other, and a competitive bond seemed to develop between them – they wanted to surpass each other in daring and perseverance, and also, as a duo, outdo the rest of the team.

Of Hillary, Tenzing said: "he was a wonderful climber... and had great strength and endurance. Like many men of action, and especially the British, he did not talk much, but he was nevertheless a fine cheerful companion; and he was popular with the Sherpas, because in things like food and equipment he always shared whatever he had."

Hillary spoke well of Tenzing, too: "[He] really

looked the part – larger than most Sherpas, he was very strong and active; his flashing smile was irresistible; and he was incredibly patient and obliging…" Hillary also spoke of his transparent, almost ruthless determination, and said of them both: "We wanted for the expedition to succeed – and nobody worked harder to ensure that it did."

On May 7, Hunt called the climbers together to announce his plans for the assault on the summit. There would be compulsory use of oxygen above Camp V, which had been set up on the edge of the Western Cwm. After all, what was the point of a climber wearing himself out on the lower slopes, when he needed all his reserves of energy for the top of the mountain?

There would be a two-pronged assault on the summit. First to go for the top, said Hunt, would be Charles Evans and Tom Bourdillon. They would open up the route to the South Summit, a hump of rock and snow just 100m (300ft) lower than the real summit, then head for the top if they could. Going with them some of the way, Hunt, Gregory and five Sherpas would carry any necessary equipment, such as oxygen, and a tent. The next day Hillary and Tenzing, also accompanied for part of the way by other climbers and Sherpas, would go up the ridge and make a camp around 8,500m (28,000ft). The idea was that they would spend the night there, and then head for the summit on the next day. Hunt's plan was a clever one, because it spread the burden of carrying supplies, saving the strength of the men designated to reach the summit for the final push to the top.

The first step was to reach the South Col, the dip between Lhotse and Everest where the South East Ridge began. While the climbers were trying to reach the Col, the weather turned intensely cold and windy, and it was not until May 22 that Camp VIII was established there. The expedition followed a route which took them up the Lhotse Glacier and then down a few hundred feet on to the Col. Hunt called the Col: "as dreary and desolate place as I ever expect to see… It was a queer sensation to go down like this at the end of our long, hard climb, as though entering a trap; and this feeling was heightened by the scene which we were approaching. For there before us were the skeletons of the Swiss tents… they stood, just the bare metal poles supported still by their frail guy ropes, all but a few shreds of the canvas ripped from them by the wind."

May 26 was designated "summit day". Hunt and two Sherpas set off up the South East Ridge, carrying equipment for Camp IX, and Bourdillon and Evans followed an hour later. They were having problems with their oxygen equipment, but once it was sorted out, they soon overtook the earlier party.

While their equipment was working properly, Bourdillon and Evans made great progress. They reached the foot of the South Summit by one o'clock that afternoon. They were at a record 8,750m (28,700ft) – higher than anyone had ever stood before. But although the summit was within reach, Evans' oxygen gear was causing problems again. He could hardly breathe and was dangerously exhausted. The two climbers had been determined to reach the top of the mountain, but they did not want to lose their lives in the attempt. The climb ahead was still difficult, and the return would be even more perilous. Downcast, they turned back to the South Col, having worn themselves to the point of death.

Hillary, who was up at the South Col camp, watched them return: "They moved silently towards us – a few stiff, jerky paces – then stop. Then a few more paces. They were very near complete exhaustion… From head to foot they were encased with ice. There was ice on their clothing, on their oxygen sets and on their rope. It was hanging from their hair and beards and eyebrows; they must have had the most terrible time in the wind and snow."

Lesser men would have looked at Bourdillon and Evans, and feared to follow in their footsteps. But Hillary was different. Whatever fears he had, he kept them to himself. As a child he had devoured adventure books by Edgar Rice Burroughs, Rider Haggard and John Buchan. His greatest fantasy was to be a hero, and now, as an adult, fate was offering him an unrepeatable opportunity.

Hunt's plan required Hillary and Tenzing to try for the top the following day, but it was too windy. May 28 seemed more promising. So began the expedition's last chance to succeed. According to plan, Lowe and Gregory and a Sherpa named Ang Nyima set off from the South Col first, carrying food supplies and equipment for Hillary and Tenzing, who followed soon after. At 8,500m (28,000ft) Lowe's party dropped off their gear and left Hillary and Tenzing to put up a tent. It was half past two in the afternoon, and both men found the task of finding a suitable spot to put up the tent completely draining. In the end they found a sloping spot that had to be flattened, but this still left one half higher than the other. Tenzing placed his sleeping bag on the lower section, right next to an alarming drop.

Hunt's strategy of spreading the hauling of equipment so the summit teams would have the best possible chance of getting to the top was paying off. After putting up the tent, Hillary and Tenzing still had sufficient energy to spend the rest of the afternoon drinking large quantities of hot lemon, and they even managed a meal. Lowe's team had brought up enough cylinders for them to be able to breathe oxygen during the night, as well as on their trek up the mountain. Bodies starved of oxygen are far more susceptible to cold, so having the gas to breathe in the tent kept them warmer and helped them to sleep.

After the best sleep anyone camping at 8,500m (28,000ft) could possibly hope to have, they fuelled up on more hot lemon and set off up to the summit at half past six on the morning of May 29. Climbing conditions were poor and they needed every ounce of their strength. A crust of thin ice had formed on the snow, and with every step they sank up to their knees. Presently they reached the South Summit, the spot where Evans and Bourdillon had decided it would be fatal to carry on. Bourdillon had considered going around a particularly dangerous-looking snow slope, but Hillary knew their best chance lay in a speedy ascent, even if it meant taking huge risks. For Tenzing, it was the most dangerous place he had ever been on a mountain. The thought of climbing that slope would haunt him for years to come.

Hillary seized the moment, telling himself: "This is Everest and you've got to take a few risks." It was a phrase he repeated often to himself on that day. Edging warily up the slope, his stomach tight with fear, he expected the snow to avalanche at any moment, sweeping both him and Tenzing to their deaths. But the loose snow held in place, and once Hillary had attached a firm rope, Tenzing scurried up after him. By nine o'clock that morning they were at the top of the South Summit, and higher than anyone else had ever been on the mountain. They looked up to the summit itself, still a few hundred feet above them. The path up there was a series of enormous cornices – mounds of snow blown by the wind into solid ledges overhanging the edge of the mountain.

Mountaineers had guessed that the South East Ridge would offer an easier route to the top, but there were still sections where a man could lose his life in an instant. The snow slope had been a terrifying ordeal, but there was worse to come. As they trudged up the ridge they were confronted by a thin, vertical slab of rock and ice about 12m (40ft) high. On one side, the South West Face plunged sharply away, on the other side, the Kangshung Face ran steeply down – both offered a fast and fatal trip down the mountain.

But both men instinctively felt this was their final hurdle. Once up here, the way to the top was theirs. Hillary noticed that there was a small, funnel-like hollow between the rock on one side and ice on the other. He would have to press his back against the ice and lever himself up, with his crampon boots on the ice. The drawback of this particular technique was that if the ice gave way, then he would go flying off down the Kangshung Face to certain death.

Hillary pushed gingerly with a boot against the ice. It held firm. Then, taking his life into his hands, he held onto the rock and braced his back against the ice, digging his boots in under him, so that the whole "chimney" took his full weight. It held. Slowly, he levered himself upwards, expecting at any second the cracking sound of splintering ice that would herald his death. But still the ice held firm. After a half-hour struggle, he wriggled his way to the top and lay there, in his own words, "gasping like a fish". When he had recovered, Tenzing followed him up. For every future Everest mountaineer, this treacherous guardian of the summit would be known as the Hillary Step.

They carried on up the sloping ridge, taking care not to wander too close to the overhanging cornice. Then, at the top of one slope, they noticed the only way further on was down. They had reached the summit! It was half past eleven in the morning and, far below, they could see the East Rongbuk Glacier and the high plateau of Tibet. The view was God-like in its scope and magnificence – Hillary would later write: "I had the world lie beneath my clumsy boots." Both men were grinning wildly. Hillary offered Tenzing a rather formal handshake, but Tenzing returned his gesture with a huge hug. They had achieved the impossible, but their feeling of triumph was tempered by the knowledge that they still faced a very dangerous return journey.

Hillary stared down at the North Ridge and thought of Mallory and Irvine. He looked around him for any clue that they had reached the summit but, if they had, nearly three decades of snowstorms and gales had obliterated the evidence. Then he buried a crucifix John Hunt had given him, and

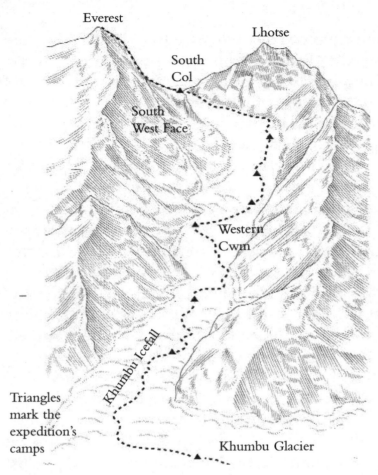

Everest

Lhotse

South
Col

South
West Face

Western
Cwm

Khumbu Icefall

Triangles
mark the
expedition's
camps

Khumbu Glacier

Hillary and Tenzing's route to the top

Tenzing too buried some offerings to his Buddhist gods.

As Tenzing unfurled a series of flags on his ice-axe (they had brought the flags of the United Nations, Great Britain, Nepal and India), Hillary busied himself taking photographs. There were to be no photographs of Hillary – as he later explained rather brusquely, "Tenzing is no photographer, and Everest was no place to begin teaching him."

There was time for a brief snack, so the two men sat together on the summit, higher than anyone else in the world, and shared a slice of Kendal Mint Cake – a piece of mountaineering history and product endorsement that millions of pounds worth of advertising could never hope to buy. (The "cake" isn't really cake at all, but a very sweet, minty fudge, which climbers eat to give themselves an energy boost.) Then it was time to return.

On the way down they passed some half-empty oxygen cylinders, discarded by Evans and Bourdillon, which they still had enough strength to carry down the mountain. Then, eventually, the South Col camp came into view. Hillary's friend, George Lowe, and a Sherpa had been waiting for them. Hillary, in his brisk New Zealand way, and with no appreciation of how the momentous news would be reported in future accounts, announced their triumph by shouting, "Well George, we knocked the b★★★★★★ off!"

They had done it, and they were still alive.

Down at Camp IV, Hunt and the rest of his team waited in a state of high anticipation. The expedition had been equipped with radios. But due to a quirk in

381

the landscape, they worked only intermittently in the Western Cwm. Lowe had been instructed to send a signal down from his camp, but it was too foggy. For Hunt, the strain had been extraordinary. Photographs from the trip show him peering into the camera like a wizened 60 year old, yet he was only in his mid-40s. He had worked tirelessly to ensure the success of this attempt, and now he was about to learn whether his efforts had paid off.

Eventually, the climbers returned from the South Col. At first, those waiting at Camp IV could just see four distant specks. That was good news in itself – at least no one had been killed in the summit attempt. Then, as the climbers got nearer, the men at the camp searched for gestures or any other indication that would suggest a victory or defeat. But cameraman Tom Stobart had planned this moment, and was stage-managing it for his film. He dashed on ahead and asked the four not to give anything away until they were almost back at the camp. Then he returned and began filming their arrival. As Hillary and Tenzing grew nearer, Hunt and his men rushed towards them. Only then did they raise their arms in triumph, and the whole party erupted in celebration – all neatly framed for the film.

James Morris knew he had the hottest news story in the world. He also wanted it to break in time for the Queen's coronation. He talked to Hillary and Tenzing, then despatched a runner to the Indian radio post at Namche Bazar. He carried a coded message which read: "Summit of Everest reached on 29 May by Hillary and Tenzing". From here, it was transmitted to the British Embassy in Kathmandu, and from there to London and *The Times*.

News broke in Britain on June 2, the very morning of the coronation. *The Times*, of course, had the full story, with other papers rewriting what was reported in it. This item from *The News Chronicle* gives a taste of the mixture of national pride and elation brought on by the news:

THE CROWNING GLORY: EVEREST IS CLIMBED

Tremendous news for the Queen
Hillary does it

Glorious Coronation Day news! Everest – Everest the unconquerable – has been conquered... The news came late last night that Edmund Hillary and the Sherpa guide Tenzing, of Colonel Hunt's expedition, had climbed to the summit of Earth's highest peak...

The significance of the event was appreciated world-wide. *The New York Times* declared: "man has completed his conquest of the world", and went on to say, "Hillary... and Tenzing... will take their place with Sir Walter Raleigh and Sir Francis Drake."

One major controversy remained. Who had got there first? Both men refused to answer. "We got there together", or "We got there at almost the same time", they would snap rather peevishly. Eventually, Tenzing spilled the beans in his biography, *Tiger of the Snows*. It was Hillary. But, as Hillary pointed out in his own account: "We shared the work, the risks, and the success – it was a team effort and nothing else is important."

"Someday Everest will be climbed again"

After the 1953 Expedition

When Hillary and Tenzing reached the top, there was a general feeling that Everest had been "done". Now this most difficult of mountains had finally been conquered, many thought that would be the end of the story. John Hunt, leader of the 1953 expedition, noted in his account of the climb (published a mere six months later): "Someday Everest will be climbed again", but he assumed that for the time being at least, climbers would lose interest in this great mountain. But such is the attraction of the highest spot on Earth that, fifty years after men first reached the summit, Everest is still a source of novelty and news. A search for "Mount Everest" on the Internet, for example, reveals more than 116,000 Web sites.

The 1953 triumph was not the end. Hillary and Tenzing might have reached the summit first, but there was still the challenge of taking a different route. Later climbers have done just that. In 1960, a Chinese expedition scaled the North Col and reached the top via the North and North East Ridges, successfully completing what Mallory, Shipton, Smythe and all the other pre-war pioneers had failed to do. In 1963, an American team went up the West Ridge and down the South East Ridge, the first successful traverse of the mountain. In 1975, a British team climbed the South West Face. This was also the year when the first woman, Junko Tabei of Japan, reached the summit. Altogether there are roughly 15 major routes to the top and, as each of these has been climbed, so mountaineers have sought different ways of claiming a "first".

The odd couple

Messner and Habeler's 1978 attempt

As climbers sought new ways to claim a "first" on Everest, it was inevitable that the "oxygen debate", so hotly disputed in the 1920s and 30s, would make a comeback. Hunt's 1953 expedition had settled once and for all the effectiveness of oxygen, and for the next 25 years, it was accepted that to get to the summit, a climber had to use oxygen. But during the mid-1970s a couple of exceptional Alpine climbers decided to champion the cause of "natural" mountaineering, and try for the summit without.

Italian Reinhold Messner and Austrian Peter Habeler were climbing's odd couple. In the words of Everest historian Walt Unsworth, they looked like "every schoolgirl's ideal ski instructor". Lithe, handsome and charming, they had an almost telepathic link, which enabled them to climb together with formidable speed and daring. But for all their brilliance as a team, there was no particular friendship between them. Peter Habeler explained the differences thus: "The applause of the general public is not as important to me. But Reinhold needs recognition. He likes to appear on television; he needs the interviews in the newspapers. His birth sign is Virgo, he likes to shine, where as I am a Cancerian who crawls back into his shell. I don't like any heroic poses."

Both believed passionately that climbing should be as simple as possible. Messner even shunned the common technique of driving metal protection pegs into a rock face to hold a climber if he should fall. The results were an astonishing increase in speed, coupled with a much greater risk of death. Messner's daring was all the more extraordinary considering his brother had been killed on a climb they had made together on the Himalayan mountain of Nanga Parbat.

Messner was "New Age" before the term was invented. One of his books, *The Crystal Horizon*, describes mountaineering as "a symbol of the outermost frontier of the world and the innermost frontier of the ego". With regard to oxygen, he once said, "Mountains are so elemental that humans do not have the right to subdue them with technology."

Having reached the decision to try for the top without oxygen, Messner and Habeler were immediately grounded by bureaucracy. The Nepalese government had a backlog of requests to climb Everest, so the two climbers asked to join an Austrian expedition already cleared for an attempt in the spring of 1978. The leader of this expedition, Wolfgang Nairz, was pleased to have a couple of climbers with such great expertise join his team, and generously made space for them. The aims of his expedition were many – aside from making a first Austrian attempt on the summit, there were plans to try a new route up the South Spur, and even hang-glide down from the South Col. Now they would also include an attempt on the summit without oxygen.

The expedition approached Everest via the Western Cwm, and Base Camp was set up before the Khumbu Glacier in late March. Messner and Habeler were climbing so well, Nairz made their oxygen-free assault his first priority. All set to go for the top by April 23, the pair then hit a major hurdle. Peter Habeler ate a can of sardines which gave him food poisoning. On the way up to the South Col, he became so ill with sickness and stomach cramps he could not continue climbing, and he was forced to return to Base Camp.

Messner, supremely fit and full of confidence, decided to go on alone. He and two Sherpas, named Mingma and Ang Dorje, set up camp on the South Col that night. But they completed their journey to the Col in a terrible storm, and struggled in a fierce gale to set up a tent. The blizzard was so bad, Messner wondered if their tent would be ripped to pieces or if they would be blown off the Col. There was nothing to do but stay under cover and wait for the weather to improve. This was a fine plan for the short term, but the storm continued relentlessly. Sleep in such a cauldron of noise and cold was impossible. Then, as Messner had feared, the tent ripped open. Mingma was so cold and exhausted he could not be roused from his sleeping bag, but Messner and Ang Dorje knew that if they didn't set up another tent, they would die. The two men struggled for an hour in the teeth of the wind and the stinging, icy snow, trying to erect a new tent. Eventually they succeeded, and all three crawled in. Messner was so drained he burst into tears.

The whole of the next day, the storm raged outside. If this tent ripped open too, the three men would certainly die. Mingma and Ang Dorje had quietly decided their lives were over, and accepted their fate quite calmly. Messner, too, was slowly dying of cold and altitude sickness, but he was determined that they were all going to survive. He harangued his listless companions, forcing them to eat and drink.

Fortunately, on the morning of their third day on the Col, the storm lifted, and Messner and the Sherpas returned as quickly as they could to the Western Cwm. From there, Messner returned to Base Camp to rejoin Habeler. On the route back, he nearly died when a ladder taking him over a particularly difficult section of the icefall collapsed beneath him.

The next few days brought perfect weather and the rest of the expedition pressed ahead. Over the next week Wolfgang Nairz and three other climbers reached the summit.

The approach via the South Col

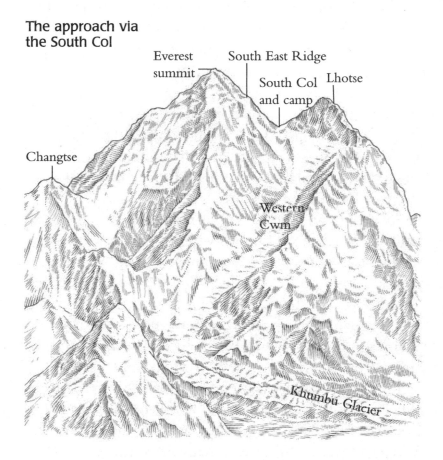

Meanwhile, back at Base Camp, Messner and Habeler were regaining their strength. Habeler had lost confidence in the idea of an assault without oxygen. But after several acrimonious arguments, the pair set out again for the South Col on May 7. With them were an English cameraman, Eric Jones, and three Sherpas. They were determined not to use oxygen, but brought a couple of cylinders with them in case of an emergency.

After a night on the Col, Messner and Habeler set off up the South East Ridge at half past five in the morning. They carried only the lightest of loads. Nairz's team had set up a camp on the ridge, which they could use if they needed. Conditions on the ridge were not good. A storm was raging and there was soft snow underfoot, which took much effort to wade through. Habeler described his state of mind at the time: "I saw only my feet, the next steps and handholds. I was moving automatically... The air became thinner and thinner, and I was near to suffocation. I still remember that a single word went through my mind, matching the rhythm of my steps: 'Forward, Forward, Forward'."

Eventually the two climbers reached the South Summit, pressed on until they were above the storm clouds, and emerged into a clear blue sky. The sunshine gave them extra strength to keep moving up, but Habeler was half-disappointed that the weather was improving. He was so tired he was looking for an excuse to call off the climb.

The Hillary Step loomed before them. Both men made this hair-raising ascent with ice and snow breaking away from their footholds and tumbling down the dizzying drops on either side. They reached the top of the Step, but this dangerous section had done them both in. They lay face down in the snow, gasping for breath in the thin air. Eventually they felt the strength returning to their legs, and pressed on to the summit. The last section up to the top was an easy climb, but Habeler noted: "I was physically finished. I seemed to step outside myself and had the illusion that another person was walking in my place."

They reached the summit at around one o'clock that afternoon. It was an emotional moment. Not given to sharing confidences, or even socializing together, the two men hugged and wept with relief and joy, the tears freezing on their beards. But Habeler, especially worried about high-altitude sickness, was anxious to return down the mountain as soon as possible. Messner, though, remained on the summit to enjoy his triumph. Alone at the top, he unpacked a film cassette for his small movie camera. He was so befuddled he threw the tape away rather than the packaging it was wrapped in. He was, in this most isolated spot, "a single narrow gasping lung, floating over the mists and the summits".

Habeler hurried down the mountain, feeling too tired for words. Once he had achieved his goal, he wanted to get back to safety as quickly as possible. Sometimes he crawled on all fours, sometimes he stumbled one step at a time. Then he began to see double – an especially hazardous condition when one wrong step can mean a fall of thousands of feet.

Somewhere down the ridge, he slipped, sat down
with a jarring bump, and began to slide down the
mountain. Habeler was so tired now, he was hardly
conscious of his own actions. Automatically he
plunged his ice-axe into the ground, and came to an
arm-wrenching halt. He found himself in a sloping
field of fresh snow, which could avalanche at any
second. With great care, he picked his way slowly
back onto firm ground and, eventually, he saw the
South Col camp below.

A final slope lay between him and Eric Jones, three
Sherpas and survival. Elated, Habeler jumped onto
the slope to slide down it, and the snow immediately
began to avalanche. Eric Jones, watching from the
Col, was convinced Habeler was doomed. Caught in
the cascade, he slid down in a mad flurry of white
mist, but eventually slowed to a halt just as he reached
the Col. He had gained a twisted ankle and lost his
ice-axe and snow goggles, but at least he was alive.
Jones ran towards him, to find Habeler mumbling
incoherently, tears streaming down his face. But,
brushes with death notwithstanding, Habeler had
made it from the summit to the South Col in one
extraordinary hour – a speedy descent unimaginable
to previous climbers.

Messner arrived an hour and a half later. He was in
a bad way, suffering from snow blindness. During the

climb he had frequently removed his snow goggles to use his video camera, and now he was suffering the consequences.

The climbers were too exhausted to return to the Western Cwm and had to spend another night in the "death zone". It was a nightmare. On top of their other troubles, another blizzard blew up, and cold gnawed at their burned-out bodies. Messner's eyes were causing him agony, too – but even this was not quite the emergency he had had in mind when the climbers had carried their two oxygen cylinders up to the camp. He refused to take any oxygen, even though it would have warmed him up and helped to ease his pain.

Next day, the storm was still raging. The climbers were in a bad way. Aside from their exhaustion, Messner could barely see, Habeler had a twisted ankle, and Jones was beginning to suffer from frostbite. But they all knew they had to return to the Cwm that morning, or die on the mountain. Their luck held. They met two of Nairz's climbers, who were on their way to another summit assault. One of them was a doctor, and he carried out vital first aid on Messner's eyes. Eventually they reached the Advanced Base Camp on the Cwm. Only then did they know for certain that they had escaped with their lives.

"As heavy as a corpse"

Reinhold Messner's 1980 solo attempt

Being the first to climb to the summit without oxygen was not enough of a challenge for Reinhold Messner. Now he planned a feat of even greater daring: a solo climb. Several climbers had reached the top on their own, but they had been with companions until the very last section, and had been part of large expeditions. Messner wanted to do the whole climb alone and without oxygen – with no back-up, no Sherpas and no additional supplies – just the equipment he carried himself. It was a crazy idea, but if anyone had the courage and guts to carry it off, it was him.

Such is the popularity of Everest, mountaineers have to apply for permission to climb it at least a couple of years in advance of their actual expedition. They go to the Nepalese or Chinese government (depending on which way they want to approach the mountain) and pay a fee, the size of which varies according to the number of climbers in the expedition. Messner realized it would be difficult for him to get permission for a solo climb, not least because it would earn the Nepalese or Chinese government so little money. So he deliberately booked his climb away from the most popular times, in the spring or at the end of the summer, when the weather was at its least dangerous. Instead, he asked if he could go during the Monsoon. The Chinese agreed, and charged him $50,000. They also insisted he took an interpreter, a liaison officer and a doctor. Messner had to put up with the first two of these unwanted companions, but he managed to convince the Chinese authorities to let him take his girlfriend, Nena Holguin, as the team doctor (although her only medical qualification was a first-aid certificate).

The plan was to go up the North Face, via Tibet, taking the same route as Mallory and Irvine from the North Col and up the North Ridge. But when Messner's tiny party arrived at the mountain, they found the snow was too soft and deep for safe climbing. The party retreated and spent a couple of weeks exploring other mountains. Then they returned for another look. This time the snow had hardened, and conditions were just right. There was also a break forecast in the Monsoon. This was exactly the opportunity Messner had hoped for.

On August 16, he and Nena Holguin set up their Base Camp at the foot of the Col. On August 17, Messner shot up the slopes to a crevasse that lay at the edge of the Col. Here, he left a 20kg (44lb) rucksack containing the equipment he thought he would need – no more than a small tent, sleeping bag, plastic mattress, ice-axe and crampons, stove and a small supply of food. Then he went to bed early. On August 18, at five o'clock in the morning, he set off. He was up to the spot where he had left his rucksack in an amazing hour and a half. The dawn was barely breaking as the North Col lay before him. Then, he did something even a novice could usually manage to avoid – he fell into the crevasse.

After falling for what he described as "an eternity in slow motion", Messner came to a bone-jarring halt 8m (25ft) below. He was lucky nothing was broken. Fortunately, he had landed on a snow platform. He didn't know how thin the snow supporting him might be, and was terribly aware that it could give way at any second, leaving him to plunge to the bottom of the crevasse with no hope of rescue. All around him it was pitch black, apart from a small hole above, where he could see a single twinkling star.

The fall had taken away his will to continue climbing. "If I can climb out of here, I'm going straight back down this crevasse-ridden snowfield and we're packing up and heading home," he told himself. He thought of his girlfriend tucked up in her warm sleeping bag, and wondered if she could get a rope to him to save him. But then he realized she had no idea where he was, and there was no hope that anyone else might find him either. If he was to get out of this crevasse alive, it would be up to him.

Messner took stock of his situation. There was nothing else to do but edge up the narrow ledge which led to the top of the crevasse. His luck held, and soon he was out in the open air again. Having escaped with his life, Messner was now taunted by doubts. This, surely, was an omen. He should return to camp, and forget about the whole stupid idea. But on the other hand, if he could survive a fall into a crevasse, then he could cope with anything. He headed out over the North Col and, as he reached the North Ridge, the sun rose. Bit by bit, the mountain was gradually bathed in a magnificent honey-gold glow. It was turning out to be a beautiful day. Messner's optimism returned and he pressed on, establishing a smooth rhythm to his steps, and feeling very much at one with this world of rock and snow.

The whole day he trudged through thick snow, then made camp on a small platform half-way up the Ridge at 7,800m (25,600ft). Here, he was bothered by the feeling that he was no longer alone, but had an invisible companion sitting beside him. This is a common phenomenon on Everest with climbers who are on their own, especially if they are very tired or under great stress. Some people find their invisible partner an irritating presence, but others find it comforting. Messner, who saw climbing as a spiritual experience, decided he would welcome his friend. He was in good spirits as he set up his tent. The sun warmed his body and he felt full of confidence as he munched a meal of dried meat and had some salty Tibetan tea. As the daylight faded, leaving stark, black shadows on the landscape below, the sky turned from blue to orange, and then to red. That night his sleep was disturbed by the occasional rush of wind, but he woke the next morning feeling well prepared for the ordeal to come.

Messner made a later start, setting off after nine o'clock in the morning, when the sun began to shine on the mountain. The climbing conditions were no better than the previous day, with thick snow which was very tiring to wade through. Messner told himself he would never get anywhere this way, and made an astonishingly brave decision. The route he had planned to take had been climbed before, but as it was such hard-going, he would try another route – up across the North Face and on to the Great Couloir, a huge gully that ran up to the summit pyramid. No one had ever been this way before.

The new route was highly dangerous, not least because snow from above could easily cascade down. But as Messner observed this great swathe of rock and snow, he noticed that several avalanches had recently swept across the Face, and he decided that there was unlikely to be another one just yet.

Crossing the North Face was slow, hard work, which filled him with anxiety. Anything – snow, rocks, ice, even a freak gust of wind – could sweep him off his feet and leave him tumbling to his death. As he climbed, his thoughts turned to Mallory and Irvine, the legendary climbers whose courage, daring and mysterious fate still intrigued mountaineers the world over. During a brief rest, Messner even imagined he could hear the long-dead British climbers calling to each other, their final, weary cries forever carried by the wind around the upper reaches of the mountain.

He carried on up, ten paces forward, then a rest to regain his breath. Occasionally Messner found himself fighting back a panicky feeling that he had gone too far to return safely. Mist descended around him, blotting out the warmth of the sun. But Messner was concentrating so hard on climbing and fighting his mounting exhaustion that he didn't really notice how dangerous the weather was becoming.

When the light began to fade and evening came, he was disappointed by how little progress he had managed to make. Most of the day had been spent moving across the mountain, rather than going up it. He had reached 8,200m (26,900ft) – a mere 400m (1,300ft) higher than he had been the day before.

Messner set up camp on a little ridge overlooking a plunging drop. He was within reach of the summit, but the longer he stayed at that altitude, the weaker he would become. That night he had to force himself to eat, drinking down large quantities of luke-warm soup and tea. Then he found it difficult to sleep. He could feel the strength and determination ebbing out of his body, and he wondered how he would find his way back to his tent if the mist grew thicker. The high altitude had dried his throat so much, he felt his windpipe was made of wood.

Daybreak brought bad news. Although the summit above was bathed in a red glow, clouds were already gathering around the mountain and snow was beginning to fall. It was now or never. Besides, Messner realized, tomorrow he could be too weak to try for the top. He left everything he could at his tiny camp, taking only his crampons, ice-axe and camera. He picked his way through the Great Couloir and then onto the rocky North Pillar. Because of the falling snow, he could barely see more than 50m (150ft) in front of him, but he kept heading up.

The higher he got, the more difficult it was to breathe. Now he could go no more than 10 paces at a time before he had to stop to get his breath back. He talked to his ice-axe as if it were an old friend, and again he imagined he could hear voices in the wind. The climb seemed to go on forever, and Messner slowed to a crawl. He could manage only one or two paces before he had to stop, gasping down huge lungfuls of thin air. Acutely aware that a slip here would be fatal, he had to concentrate hard with every step, which wore him out even more. At times, he crept forward on all fours. His heavy boots, he remembered, felt "like anchors in the snow".

Messner carried on like this for another three hours, climbing almost in a trance, continually driving himself on. Even when he stopped to breathe, each breath burned his throat. But just as he felt he could go no further, he saw a cluster of discarded equipment and ribbons above him – it was the summit. The realization that he was nearly at the top brought no extra reserves of energy. He had to crawl up on his hands and knees to get there.

Reaching other mountain tops alone, Messner had felt elated and, in his words, "a witness to the whole of creation". Now, on the summit of Everest, he was too tired to feel anything. It was three o'clock in the afternoon and he had been climbing for six hours.

Messner's solo climb

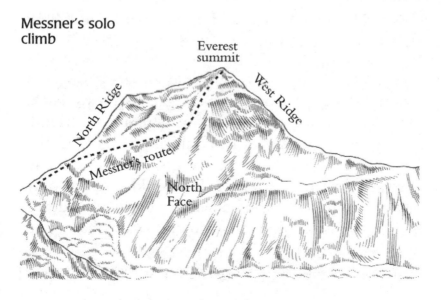

Everest summit

North Ridge

West Ridge

Messner's route

North Face

It was so cloudy, he couldn't see the usual stunning view that greets climbers who make it to the top. Looking back, he wrote: "I was in continual agony; I have never in my whole life been so tired... I am not only as heavy as a corpse, I am incapable of taking anything in."

Despite the danger of staying at the summit and getting caught in bad weather, it was almost an hour before Messner felt strong enough to return. Before he left, he managed to take a photograph of himself by attaching his camera to a special screw on his ice-axe. The journey down was easier, and it took only three and a half hours to get back to his tent. Here he was too tired to eat or drink, or even to sleep, but something in him had changed. The smell of the snow, and the different shades of the rocks, seemed more intense. He was slowly coming back to his senses. He was so tired and lying so still, he felt he could have been dead, but the thought of his success kept his spirit alive.

As he lay awake, Messner began to worry whether he had enough strength to get down the mountain alive. The high altitude was now badly irritating his lungs, and every painful cough made his stomach hurt. But luck was with him, and the dawn brought a beautiful day of bright sunshine and little wind. Leaving everything at the camp apart from his ice-axe and camera, and not even bothering to eat or drink, he edged down the mountain in a robotic trance, remembering almost nothing of the climb back to his Base Camp. But each step brought him nearer to safety. Slowly it began to dawn on him that he was going to live through his extraordinary climb.

Down beneath the North Col, Nena Holguin peered up at the mountain through the telephoto lens of her camera. It was the tenth time that morning she had searched for a sign of Messner, and she was growing concerned. She left the camp site to find water to wash and, as she returned, she caught a glimpse of a tiny figure, moving high on the ridge up by the Col. The figure was moving with some hesitation, exhaustion even. It lurched here and there, as if drunk, but it could only be Messner. Nena burst into tears. At least her boyfriend was still alive. She threw on her mountaineering clothes and rushed up the slopes to meet him.

Only when Messner reached Nena Holguin did he finally allow himself to believe he had succeeded. In his exhaustion he began to hallucinate, feeling both that he was dissolving before her and that he had turned to glass. Then he began to cry. Nena led him back, and looked after him.

The next day Messner did not even have the strength to stand. It took a week before he felt he had recovered. But he had achieved what he set out to do – and his solo climb to the summit is one of the most extraordinary feats of mountaineering ever recorded.

"Not a place for humans"

The commercial expedition disasters of 1996

By the early 90s, Everest had been climbed so many times, and by so many different routes, it had begun to seem less challenging – and less alluring. In the spring of 1993, no less than 40 climbers reached the summit in a single day. On his radio show at the time, Danny Baker even joked that there were plans to build a *MacDonald's* at the top of the mountain. But in due course, Everest would strike back.

In the pre-Monsoon season in April/May 1996, there were 11 teams on Everest intending to climb to the summit via the well-known South Col route. Five of these were made up of top-grade mountaineers, but the other six were so-called "commercial expeditions". These were the ultimate outdoor adventures, where climbers paid up to $65,000 to be taken to the top of Everest by guides. The fact that such expeditions had come into existence was a clear indication of how everyday the climbing of Everest had become. Of course the climbers on these trips (referred to by their guides as "clients") were not novices. They were people with considerable mountaineering experience, and well prepared for their ascent. But they were not the same class as the world-class mountaineers who had climbed Everest in the previous decades.

Despite the obvious risks of amateur climbers trying to reach the summit of one of the world's most dangerous mountains, no one could accuse the commercial expeditions of the 1990s of short-changing their customers. Their equipment was good, they were all supplied with oxygen, and were even issued with a phial of dexamethasone for use in emergencies. This drug combats the effects of high-altitude sickness and gives a climber an energy boost. The guides on the trips all carried radios, and were men and women of great experience and courage.

Rob Hall, for example, the impressively tall expedition leader for the "Adventure Consultants" company, was a New Zealand climber in his mid-30s, who had made the summit of Everest four times prior to 1996. The company's carefully worded brochure told clients: "Skilled in the practicalities of developing dreams into reality, we work with you to reach your goal. We will not drag you up the mountain – you will have to work hard – but we guarantee to maximize the safety and success of your adventure." Hall's record was good too. In five years he had taken 39 climbers to the top of Everest.

Hall's climbers may have been amateurs, but they were deadly serious about their mountaineering. Among them on this trip were three doctors, including the successful American surgeon Beck Weathers, a Japanese woman named Yasuko Namba, and an American journalist, Jon Krakauer. He was an experienced mountaineer, and was coming along to report on commercial expeditions for the climbing magazine *Outside*. Along with Hall they would be climbing with two experienced guides, Andy Harris and Mike Groom, and a party of Sherpas.

Still, serious or not, Krakauer, with his jaundiced reporter's eye, concluded that none of the paying mountaineers in his group would have been good enough to take part in a real expedition, where climbers are chosen on merit. In fact, Krakauer thought they wouldn't stand a chance of scaling Everest without all the help and assistance Hall's company could provide.

Another commercial expedition on Everest that spring was Scott Fischer's "Mountain Madness" group. Fischer was a tall, handsome and charismatic leader. With him were two very capable guides, American Neal Beidleman and Russian Anatoli Boukreev. Boukreev was a mountaineering legend all on his own. He had been up seven 8,000m (26,000ft) peaks, all without oxygen, and had climbed Everest twice. He was tough, and as tall and strong as Scott Fischer, although perhaps not as likeable. He saw his job as ensuring his clients got to the top – after all, that was what they had paid their huge fees to do. But he was not a sympathetic, helpful man. "If client cannot climb Everest without big help from guide," he explained in his grammatically uneven English, "this client should not be on Everest. Otherwise there can be big problems up high."

Fischer's clients were a strong bunch. Among them were Charlotte Fox, an American who had already climbed two of the world's 8,000m peaks, and another notable woman mountaineer, New York socialite and journalist, Sandy Hill Pittman. Tall, glamorous and extremely rich, Pittman had already climbed the tallest mountain on six of the world's seven continents. For her, Everest was the final challenge.

With so many expeditions on the mountain at one time, it was essential that an understanding be reached on when each team would go for the summit. Rob Hall and Scott Fischer knew each other well and had a good relationship, despite their commercial rivalry. They decided they would go up together on May 10. It was a fateful decision.

Their teams encountered no mishaps on the way up to the South Col. After a night in this windswept wilderness, 33 climbers, guides and Sherpas prepared to make their way up the mountain. Hall and Fischer got together and agreed that Hall's team should set off up the South East Ridge half an hour before Fischer's, because Hall's team contained less able climbers. As it was, Fischer's team soon caught up with Hall's, and the two parties mingled together on the way up the Ridge.

The night of May 9 had been a clear, bright one, promising good weather for the day ahead. But the Mountain Madness and Adventure Consultants parties had been let down by mistakes which would cause crucial delays. Any trip to the summit requires speed, as climbers must undertake the dangerous return journey back to their tents before nightfall. On the return, they are exhausted and much more likely to make silly mistakes, while their physical weakness makes them prone to frostbite and hypothermia (abnormally low body temperature).

To speed up the trip to the summit, fixed ropes were supposed to be placed along the South East Ridge but, due to a misunderstanding, this was not done all along the route. Valuable time was lost while the guides set up these ropes for their clients to climb. Then, at the South Summit, there were supposed to be supplies of fresh oxygen. These too were missing, and the two teams wasted more time waiting for Sherpas to bring up the oxygen which should already have been there.

All this added to an already alarming situation. With so many climbers going for the top, lines developed at difficult stages of the mountain, such as the Hillary Step, where ten or so climbers waited in turn, like passengers at an airport check-in desk.

As the day progressed, Jon Krakauer's suspicions about his fellow climbers were borne out. Of his party, only he, an American climber named Doug Hansen and Yasuko Namba would reach the summit.

Fischer's much stronger team had all reached the top. Here, Charlotte Fox felt no great elation – just relief that she had made it. Looking around the extraordinary 100-mile view from the summit, she recalled experiencing "a deep fear that this was not a place meant for humans".

All the climbers knew that they had a "turn around time" – a specific hour when they should turn back if they had not reached the top. But no one could remember whether it was one or two o'clock in the afternoon. Besides, everyone had made this trip to get to the summit – having spent $65,000 and being so close to achieving a lifelong ambition, many were tempted to throw caution to the wind. Then, once on the summit, some of the climbers lingered far longer than they should have done. This was not just recklessness. The combination of high altitude and exhaustion creates a strange, hallucinogenic state of mind, where the passing of time goes unnoticed.

Some climbers from both expeditions were still on top of the mountain at four o'clock. Expedition leader Rob Hall was the last to leave, together with Doug Hansen, who had failed to reach the summit on a previous attempt with Hall the year before. Hall decided he would do everything he could to ensure Hansen succeeded, but in doing so, he delayed their return journey even further.

The hold-ups earlier in the day were now having serious consequences. Getting to the top had drained Hansen of all the strength he had. When his oxygen ran out shortly after he and Hall began to come down the mountain, his life was in very serious danger.

Waiting at the South Summit was Andy Harris, one of the Adventure Consultants guides. He too was suffering from exhaustion and altitude sickness, and was feeling very confused. Hall spoke to him on his radio, and Harris managed to climb up to the summit ridge with two bottles of oxygen. But some time after meeting up with Hall and his struggling client, both Harris and Hansen fell off the mountain. Hall himself had to stop at the South Summit. He could not get the oxygen tank that Andy Harris had brought him to work, and he was too weary to carry on down.

Many climbers were still high on Everest at six o'clock that evening, with darkness only an hour away. Mountain Madness leader Scott Fischer found his strength rapidly fading away. This particular climb had exhausted the normally strong and resilient mountaineer.

With problems rapidly mounting, the weather then stepped in to make things worse. Snow had fallen during the afternoon, making the route back even more slippery and tiring than it had been before. Then, in a final twist of ill luck, a deep, booming sound rolled across the top of the

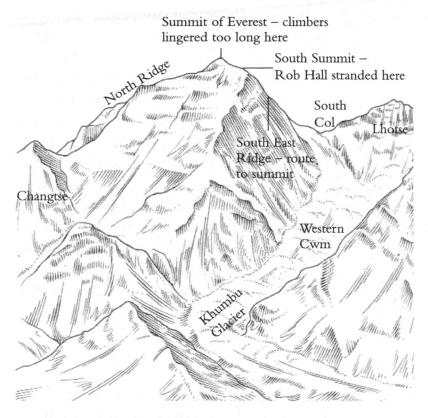

The commercial expedition disasters of 1996

mountain. Some of the climbers thought there had been an avalanche, but this was thunder. Almost immediately, the weary mountaineers were enveloped in a thick blizzard, with thunder and lightning playing around their exhausted heads.

Among the returning climbers was a group from both expeditions, including Charlotte Fox, Sandy Hill Pittman, American climber Tim Madsen, the

413

surgeon Beck Weathers and Yasuko Namba. Together with the guide Neal Beidleman, they had been wandering blindly around the Col, perilously close to the Kangshung Face. They only stopped in the blizzard when they realized they were on the edge of a deep, dark void. Now they had decided their best hope lay in trying to stay where they were, although the wind was blowing at 110kmph (70mph) and the temperature had dropped to -40°C (-40°F). This was a desperate measure, but preferable to the near certainty of falling off the mountain.

The beleaguered party did their best to ward off frostbite by slapping each other to keep their circulation going. But tired, thirsty, hungry, and out of oxygen, they were textbook cases for mountaineering casualties. As they all began to weaken in the face of the storm, they huddled together for warmth. Charlotte Fox recalled: "we just lay together in a heap and waited, I hoped, for that warm fuzzy feeling that comes with hypothermia, and death."

But as they faded away to unconsciousness, the storm blew itself out. Now it was possible to see far enough ahead to make a moonlit search for the tents. Some of the party had strength enough to get to their feet and walk towards the camp, but others were too drained of energy to move. Fortunately, the Mountain Madness guide Anatoli Boukreev had emerged from the shelter of his tent to try to find his fellow climbers. He loomed up before them, and led

Fox, then Pittman, then Madsen, back to their tents. Fox was so cold, she recalled, "I had the weird sensation of my eyes freezing inside my head".

But Namba and Weathers were not so lucky. Boukreev had rescued the climbers from his own expedition, but he did not have the strength to help Hall's clients — and anyway, he thought Hall and his guides would be out to get them. But Hall was high on the mountain, and Harris was dead. Only Mike Groom was left, and he was so frost-bitten and exhausted he couldn't even speak. When others from Hall's party found Namba and Weathers the next morning, they were so badly frost-bitten and close to death it was decided to leave them there, to let nature take its course. This might seem callous, but the decision was made with the best of motives, and with a great deal of heart-searching. There were other injured and frost-bitten climbers who had a much greater chance of survival, and it was best to concentrate on ensuring they got back down the mountain alive, rather than to waste precious time and energy on two climbers who would almost certainly die.

In an even worse predicament was Mountain Madness leader Scott Fischer. He had collapsed on a ledge 350m (1,200ft) above the Col and, like Rob Hall, had spent the night out in the open.

Boukreev didn't realize this had happened until early the next morning. Having slept for barely two hours after his climb to the Summit, he rallied the

Sherpas to make a rescue attempt. But the Sherpas who had been with Fischer the evening before said he was as good as dead. Oxygen had not revived him, and he had not even been able to swallow the hot tea they had given him. Besides, more bad weather was on the way. But Boukreev was having none of this. Scott Fischer was his friend and his employer, and if he was still breathing, he could still be rescued. He spent the day trying to persuade other climbers to help him. Finally, in desperation, he decided to go up the South East Ridge alone.

Shortly after he left the South Col camp, Boukreev saw an extraordinary sight ahead of him. Staggering through the snow was the ghostly figure of a man. He walked with great weariness and held up his hands, which were without gloves, in front of him. Boukreev thought he looked like a surrendering soldier.

As the two men edged towards each other, Boukreev realized this figure was not Scott Fischer; it was Beck Weathers. Beck was incoherent, having spent a night and most of the day left for dead out in the Col. He was rambling wildly about how he was never, never coming back to these mountains. The fact that he was alive was extraordinary, but Weathers' hands were so badly frost-bitten he would eventually lose both of them.

Rather than feeling disappointment that this staggering figure was not Fischer, Boukreev was heartened. After all, if Weathers had survived a night and a day outside, Fischer could too. He pressed on up the mountain, disappearing into the teeth of a blizzard and the fast-falling darkness. It was seven o'clock in the evening when Boukreev came across the frozen body of Scott Fischer. The zipper of his jacket was open, and one hand was without a mitten. There was no pulse and Fischer was not breathing.

Just as Boukreev was coming to terms with the fact that his friend had died, the weather grew even worse. How he got through the dark, the snow, the wind and the cold is a mystery, for he could barely see the route ahead. But Boukreev was a climber of extraordinary skill, strength and heroism. Eventually he found his way back to the South Col, and collapsed in his tent.

Rob Hall had also spent a long, terrible night on the South Summit, tormented by the cold, the wind and the snow. But this tall, wiry, bearded man was immensely strong. By nine o'clock the next morning, he had managed to repair his faulty oxygen gear and was in radio contact with his base camp. But, despite the urging and encouragement of his fellow climbers at the bottom of the mountain, he could not find the strength to stand up and continue the journey down. Two Adventure Consultant Sherpas set out to rescue him. They were 200m (700ft) from the South Summit when the weather, which had remained very cold and windy, forced them back.

Many of those who die on Everest pass their final hours in unimaginable loneliness. Rob Hall spent much of that day talking to friends on the radio. In the early evening he was even able to speak to his wife – patched into his radio via a phone call from New Zealand. Perhaps this was an even more wrenching way to die – talking to a loved one, safe and warm in the family home half a world away, while he slowly had the life frozen out of him at 8,800m (28,700ft).

While they talked, she told him, "I'm looking forward to making you completely better when you come home... I just know you're going to be rescued." But she had been to the top of Everest with Hall three years before, and she knew nothing could be done to save her husband's life. They talked through a crackling, distorted line, then said their final goodbyes.

After that, there was silence. All subsequent attempts to contact Hall on the radio were unsuccessful. Twelve days later, two climbers heading for the summit found his body in an icy hollow, half-buried in the snow.

On those two days in May, five climbers from the two expeditions lost their lives on Everest. The event was widely featured in the media and caused a sensation all around the world. It did, after all, read like the plot from some disaster movie – great courage, selfless heroism, and a cast of glamorous characters dying one by one in the most dramatic location imaginable.

"The wind passeth over it, and it is gone"

The 1999 expedition to find Mallory and Irvine

George Mallory and Sandy Irvine exercise a strong grip on the imagination of the world's mountaineers. When Edmund Hillary first reached the top in 1953, he checked for any sign that the two English climbers had got there before him. Even Reinhold Messner had thought of them as he approached the summit during his epic solo climb in 1980. It was not just the bravery and tenacity of this charismatic pair that caught the imagination, for they left behind a mystery that remains unsolved to this day.

When news of their deaths broke, it was widely and sentimentally imagined they had reached the summit. Although the few climbers who knew Everest, including most of Mallory and Irvine's own colleagues, doubted that this was the case, no one could be entirely sure. Along with their missing bodies, there were two possible clues that lay undiscovered high on the mountain. Firstly, they would have left discarded oxygen bottles somewhere. If a bottle from that era was found, it would give some evidence as to how high they had climbed. Secondly, and most tantalizingly, it was known that one of the climbers had carried a camera. If they had reached the top, there would certainly be photographs.

Everest is such a gargantuan and forbidding mountain, the idea of locating bodies or objects on one of its vast, sprawling faces really is like looking for a needle in a haystack. But in 1975, a Chinese mountaineer named Wang Hongbao stumbled across a dead climber high on the North East Ridge, a short walk away from his camp. Judging by the clothes and equipment, the body was obviously from an earlier age of mountaineering. Four years later, Wang Hongbao was on a Chinese-Japanese expedition up Everest and mentioned this to a Japanese climber, Hasegawa Yoshinori, who knew the story of Mallory and Irvine. Wang gave a rough description of where he had found the body. The next day, Wang was killed in an avalanche. Yoshinori was convinced the body must be one of the missing English climbers, and carried the news back with him. The story broke to world-wide curiosity.

It would take 20 years before anyone thought of following this up. In 1999, a group of American climbers, calling themselves the "Mallory and Irvine Research Expedition", set out to try to establish once and for all whether Hillary and Tenzing really were the first men to stand on top of Everest. More than anything else they hoped to find Irvine and, with a bit of luck, his camera.

The team were well in place on the North East Ridge by April 1999. In early May, the climber Conrad Anker made a startling discovery. While searching the slopes of the North Face he had already come across three other dead climbers. Then, he recalled: "Suddenly I saw a patch of white that wasn't rock and it wasn't snow." There, stretched out face down on the mountain, was a body. Most of the clothes had been blown off, and the remarkably well-preserved exposed flesh was as white as a marble statue.

Anker summoned colleagues on his radio, and was soon joined by other team mates. All of them knew at once they had found something extremely significant. They marvelled at the wool and tweed clothing, the rope made of plant threads, and the hobnail boots they could plainly see. Climber Dave Hahn remembered, "We weren't just looking at a body, we were looking at an era."

Name tags on the clothing quickly revealed that the body was that of George Mallory. The camera and its precious film were nowhere to be seen. However, it was well known that Mallory intended to place a photograph of his wife Ruth on the summit. No photograph was found on the body, leaving yet another riddle to intrigue those who believe Mallory really might have got to the top – although he could, of course, merely have forgotten to bring the photograph with him.

The climbers gathered some of Mallory's possessions, including a boot that had come off his foot, a pocket knife, a compass and his snow goggles, as well as several letters and notes that Mallory had been carrying with him. These were extremely well-preserved, and looked as if they could have been written the day before. Here, in the freezing-dry cold at 8,000m (26,000ft), time had stood still. One of the notes Mallory had carried up the mountain was an unpaid bill from *A. W. Gamages* of Holborn, London – "Motoring, Cycling, Sports and General Outfitters". Mallory had intended to settle his account when he returned. The company had closed decades ago.

Before they set out, the expedition had been in touch with the surviving families of both Irvine and Mallory, to ask what they should do if they found either of their bodies. Now, in accordance with the wishes of Mallory's son, John Mallory, who was then 79 and living in South Africa, they prepared the body for burial. Anker, on John Mallory's direct instructions, took a skin sample for a DNA identification, and then they covered the body with rocks. In the bright, cold sunshine, the climbers huddled together besides Mallory's burial place, and *Psalm 103* was read aloud:

As for man, his days are as grass:
as a flower of the field, so he flourisheth.
For the wind passeth over it, and it is gone;
and the place thereof shall know it no more.

All of the men present were filled with a sense of awe and sadness. They were in the presence of a legend and, for once, the reality had lived up to the myth. Anker recalled how Mallory had "less gear than your average trekker", and how "if that had happened now, it would be like you'd get on the radio and you'd mobilize an army of Sherpas and a guide to haul their ass down. When I got there next to George Mallory, I thought, wow, if he had been here now he would have had a chance."

As to whether Mallory and Irvine had reached the top, one of the 1999 expedition speculated: "This guy obviously didn't let good sense get in the way of his determination. He might have done it. He was just enough of a wild man that he might just have had a good day that day and pulled it off."

None of Mallory's colleagues were alive to hear the news that his body had been found. Edward Norton, commander of the 1924 expedition, died aged 70 in 1954. Climbing partners such as Geoffrey Bruce and Howard Somervell died in the 1970s, old men who had lived to see their children grow up, their nation survive a World War and lose an empire, and men walk on the moon – a feat even more extraordinary, and astronomically more expensive, but less costly in human life than the conquest of Everest.

In all that time Mallory and Irvine's bodies had lain frozen and undiscovered high on the mountain. Irvine is still to be found. Some people might say they, and all the others who have died, wasted their lives. But almost none of the thousands of climbers drawn to this alarmingly dangerous mountain in the eighty years since their deaths would agree…

Glossary

Avalanche A large fall of snow down a mountain.

Blizzard A severe snowstorm.

Chimney A vertical crack on a rock or ice face which is wide enough to climb up.

Col The lowest point between two peaks – often a flat plain.

Cornice An overhanging ridge of wind-blown snow.

Couloir A steep gully that cuts into the side of a mountain.

Crampons A rack of metal spikes that can be attached to climbing boots, to help a mountaineer climb on ice or snow.

Crevasse A deep crack in the ice of a glacier.

Cwm A bowl-shaped valley overlooked by steep rock faces.

Fixed ropes Ropes that have been attached to a mountain for the duration of an expedition.

Frostbite Dangerous medical condition when flesh on fingers, toes or other body parts freezes.

Glacier A slow-moving river of ice which forms high on a mountain.

High-altitude sickness Extreme illness and exhaustion, caused by lack of oxygen while high on a mountain.

Icefall A dangerous section of a glacier where ice is broken into huge blocks.

Monsoon A strong wind which brings extremely bad weather to Asia. Also used to mean the season when the wind arrives.

Overhang A section of a rockface which juts out, so that a climber has to approach it from underneath.

Ridge A narrow line of rock where two rock faces meet.

Scree Small rocks and pebbles.

Sherpa Literally, a member of a group of people who live near to Everest. Sherpas accompany most Everest expeditions as porters, guides and fellow climbers.

Sirdar A head Sherpa, who usually hires other Sherpas for an expedition.

Snowblindness Blindness, usually temporary, caused by the glare of the sun on snow.

South Col A flat plain at 7,860m (26,200ft), between Everest and Lhotse.

Summit The highest point on a mountain.

Traverse To climb sideways across a mountain face. Also sometimes used to mean climbing up and over a mountain, and coming down another side.

Further reading

Many mountaineers are brilliant writers. If you have enjoyed reading this book, you may find the following books are also worth a look:

Blessed Everest
by Brian Blessed
(Salamander, 1995)
A very readable general history and personal account, from the well-known British actor.

Everest – Mountain Without Mercy
by Broughton Coburn
(National Geographic, 1997)
Both a general introduction and a gripping account of the disasters of May 1996, complete with a fantastic selection of breathtaking photographs.

Everest – Eighty Years of Triumph and Tragedy
edited by Peter Gillman
(Little, Brown & Co., 2000)
A fascinating anthology of first-hand accounts, and many wonderful photographs.

Nothing Venture, Nothing Win
by Edmund Hillary
(Hodder & Stoughton, 1975)
An autobiography from the first man to reach the summit.

Into Thin Air
by Jon Krakauer
(Macmillan, 1997)
A rivetting first-hand account of the tragedy of 1996, by a climber who was in the middle of it all.

Everest
by Richard Platt
(Dorling Kindersley, 2000)
A lively look at the history of the mountain.

Climbing Everest
by Audrey Salkeld
(National Geographic, 2003)
A collection of Everest stories from this well-respected mountaineering historian.

Everest – The Mountaineering History
by Walt Unsworth
(The Mountaineers, 2000)
Generally acknowledged to be the most readable and authoritative account of Everest available.

Internet links

There are thousands of websites about Everest. This page describes a couple of the best – you can access these sites via the Usborne Quicklinks Website following the instructions below. National newspaper sites are also a good source of up-to-the-minute news on Everest.

Everest News Website

A fantastic site with links, day-to-day activity, history – in fact, everything you might possibly want to know about the mountain.

National Geographic – Everest Website

This is a comprehensive site from the National Geographic organization.

For links to these two sites, go to theUsborne Quicklinks Website at:

www.usborne-quicklinks.com

and type in the keywords "true stories everest". For safe Web surfing, please follow the safety guidelines given on the Usborne Quicklinks Website.

Acknowledgements

True Polar Adventures

With grateful thanks to Fergus Fleming and Robert Headland, Archivist and Museum Curator, at the Scott Polar Research Institute, Cambridge, for their extremely helpful comments on the manuscript. Thanks also to Shirley Sawtell of the Scott Polar Research Institute Library, and Sir Ranulph Fiennes and Dr. Mike Stroud, who kindly read and commented on their story.

True Desert Adventures

These stories are based on a wide variety of sources and historical documents, but the author is particularly indebted to four writers without whose accounts this version would not have been possible. These are Ralph Barker for Verdict on a Lost Flyer, the story of Bill Lancaster; Charles Gallenkamp for Dragon Hunter, a biography of Roy Chapman Andrews; Annette Kobak for Isabelle, a biography of Isabelle Eberhardt; and Henno Martin for The Sheltering Desert, his own account of life in the Namib Desert.

True Everest Adventures

With grateful thanks to Audrey Salkeld, for reading and commenting on the manuscript; Kate and Keith Lee, The Old Bookshop, Wolverhampton, for generously providing rare and unusual books; and Margaret Ecclestone of the Alpine Club Library.